Fiction, Book 2020

SONS OF GREAT MEN

SONS OF GREAT MEN

Adrian Ross

First published by atwr books, 2026
Contact: atwruk@ntlworld.com
atwr books, c/o The Smith Art Gallery and Museum,
Dumbarton Road, Stirling FK8 2RQ

Text © Adrian T. W. Ross 2026

The moral right of Adrian Ross to be identified as the author
of this work has been asserted by him in accordance with
the Copyright, Designs and Patents Act, 1988.

This book is a work of fiction. Names, characters, places and incidents are products of the writer's imagination or used fictitiously. Any resemblance to actual people, living or dead, events or locales is entirely coincidental.

All rights reserved. No part of this publication may be copied, stored in a retrieval system, distributed, transmitted, reproduced or otherwise made available in whole or in part, in any form or by any means (electronic, digital, optical, mechanical, photocopying, recording or otherwise) without the prior permission in writing of the publisher and copyright owners.

Without limiting the exclusive rights of the author, any contributor or the publisher, any unauthorised use of this publication to train generative artificial intelligence (AI) technologies is expressly prohibited.

A CIP catalogue record for this book is available from the British Library.

ISBN 978-1-9192530-0-8

Cover design by James Brook, www.jamesbrook.net
Pre-publication edit by Jo Ross-Barrett
Typesetting by Laura Kincaid, www.tenthousand.co.uk
Cover photo by Adrian Ross, with thanks to Nairn Museum

Printed and bound in Great Britain by Clays Ltd, Elcograf S.p.A.,
using FSC approved paper.

For my wife, Sarah, who told me I was a writer already.

Content warnings (which include plot spoilers) are available on page 318.

You'll find book group discussion prompts on page 319.

The bonus short story, Lieutenant, begins on page 322.

Time rarely drags its heels…
– Jon Airdrie, from his song *Time Moves On*

If you break someone's heart, that's a great shame, but if you break your own instead, that's pure folly.
– Uncle Xavier, from the play *She Strayed Too Far (Act IV, Sc. III)*

CHAPTER 1

It was the interval of the Saturday matinée. I was kneeling on the carpet tiles in the downstairs bar, picking up broken glass – *yes, how glamorous!* – when the news came. My young Bulgarian colleague, Rad, summoned me to the box office, where an urgent call awaited me.

"She's gone into surgery to have a blood clot removed from her arm," said a kindly nurse's voice. "And you being the next of kin…"

"*Really?*"

I hadn't known that. I'd have expected Mum to give my brother's name. She and William shared a closeness I couldn't fathom. I knew it had something to do with the fourteen blissful years they had together, before I arrived and spoiled everything.

Or so the story goes.

My team of ushers and I herded the hardcore stragglers back into the auditorium for the second half of the play. The lights dimmed. We released the heavy inner doors gently. They gave their usual double sigh as they closed: 'pfff-ubfff'. There was a momentary hush, followed by the restart line.

I raced to the upstairs bar. The plush little den, all mahogany fittings and red velvet upholstery, stood deserted. It was one of the few places in the building where you could get a signal and not be overheard. Theatres run on gossip, and I was determined that my boss should be first to receive this update.

"You must go immediately, Victor," decreed Jim, from the deckchair on his allotment. "You've only got one mother."

I thought that was a strange observation for him to make – and I was briefly filled with horror at the thought of having two.

"Just gimme a mo," he added. I heard the chair clack as he folded it. "I'll come in right now and relieve you."

Jim was true to his word and arrived within minutes, still in his gardening garb. As always, I was impressed by his calmness in a crisis. We raided the costume store. He changed into a suit, then packed a large carrier bag of clothes for me, so I could head straight for the ferry.

"That should see you right for a few days," he said.

Then he made eye contact in a way I find bewildering, because I'm not sure what it means.

"Good luck, sunshine. I hope she's all right."

With that, he actually shook my hand. It felt as if I were going to the gallows. And I was ready for anything, attired in one of my cheap work suits, a navy pinstripe. My mother always emphasised the importance of smartness, even if you were going to your grave. I emerged from the stage door, blinking in the sunlight. Then I tried to remember where, in all of Newport's nooks, I'd left my car. This was in the summer of 2023.

I drove to Cowes faster than usual, but parked out of the way in my secret spot. As a result, I missed the fast catamaran by seconds. I stood cursing at the quayside, watching the approach of the lumbering car ferry on the horizon.

My mind went over and over the scant information I'd been given about Mum. She was seventy-eight and still working, whacking out a weekly column. What if this was it for her? Would I even get there before she died? My racing mind conjured all the worst eventualities that could ensue when I got to London. I tried hard to calm down, telling myself that ageing and illness and death are all part of the cycle of nature. People say they love nature, though I doubt that's strictly true when it catches up with them.

I finally made it on board the ferry. I paced around the deck, watching the island recede from view. I took a photo and – *why not?* – uploaded it. It soon had three likes. The wind was getting up and I caught some seaspray in the face, so I sought refuge indoors. I tried to slouch in a seat that was too upright to be comfortable, my giant bag of costume next to me. I closed my eyes and recalled a story Mum used to tell, about a mysterious Irish woman who lived in her home town in Lancashire.

Old Maggie had a knack of appearing, priest-like, towards the end of people's lives. Tall and thin, she had clouded eyes with tiny bright pupils that shone like paused electrons. Her straggly hair framed a much-lined face that had a searching, mournful aspect. Part of the local folklore was that Maggie was never sent for. She just knew where and when to turn up.

"Who's your angel, my darlin'?" she would ask the stricken patient, who was often fighting the kind of pain that compressed eternity into a minute. "Who can tell you to let go, sweet pumpkin, now the time's come?"

It might take a while, but the poorly person would nominate an angel – essentially the person they were most desperate to see before departing this life – and they would be sent for. Their appearance at the bedside would invariably bring a measure of contentment, followed by blessèd release.

After going through all that drama, the grieving relatives would cross the street to avoid the formidable-looking Maggie. Perhaps that's understandable, but in doing so they were overlooking her essential kindness and compassion. She was no harridan. The old dear lived in loneliness and poverty. She knew bereavement intimately and had cataracts.

Poor soul.

Was she, like me, on the autistic spectrum? I wouldn't bet against it. All the poor woman did was to coach people, whose instinct was to keep fighting for survival, in the difficult sport of giving in; succumbing to the inevitable.

But everyone was spooked by her. My mother, aged eleven, watched Maggie work her magic in a darkened back bedroom, as the grandma I never knew groaned and cried out in pain. The patient had undergone a torturous decline over several months, from a disease that could not be talked about. In Lancashire, in those far-off days of the young queen, the shame of being a witch was nothing compared to the disgrace of harbouring cancer.

At last, a name came from the dying woman's lips – "Alec!" – and her brother was summoned forthwith. There was much surprise at this, as the pair had never got along well, but it worked. Of course it did; he was her angel.

"I love you – and I've always cared for you," she said, her words catching him greatly off-guard. Before Alec could formulate a suitable response, his sister slipped into a state of unconsciousness. She died minutes later.

You don't know what to do with such a story when it's told to you as a child. There's nothing, no experience, to calibrate it with. All the little details are outliers; rocks that sit beyond the shore, poking up between the waves like bobbing seals, asking to be sketched and remembered. And I do remember them, along with several other cheery tales Mum told me when I was too young to discern their meaning. I've hung on to them, in the bleak hope that…

What, exactly?

Well, they might explain something about her; *about us.*

"I don't dislike you," she told me once, as if that cleared everything up.

There were further delays. Two trains to London were cancelled, due to industrial action – or industrial *inaction*, as William would have it. My hurried trip was taking ages. When I clambered out of the taxi at the hospital, the sky seemed to be frowning inky dark blue disapproval of my lateness. We were already in that kissing-gate of pent-up anticipation, between the summer solstice and the start of the holidays.

Main reception was closed, due to lack of staff, so I was redirected to Accident and Emergency. The scene there was hectic, overly bright and cacophonous, like a video directed by Hieronymous Bosch. A man was making a huge fuss about his affliction, which appeared to be a frozen shoulder, while his unsupervised children ran amok. Some people are more theatrical in real life than I am on stage.

"You're here for Mrs De Vries?"

The receptionist on the phone flapped her hand at the young man who'd leaned over her to speak to me. She held her finger aloft until her call was finished. That she recognised my mother's name, in this infernal echo chamber, made me feel a frisson of self-importance. Mum was well-known, or used to be, so I wondered if she were being singled out for special treatment. I hoped so. Then I realised what a selfish thought that was, and felt a bit guilty. The health service is for everyone.

"Please take a seat over there. We need to page the doctor."

I fumbled with my phone and tried once more to reach William. By some miracle, he picked up.

"Sorry the details are so sketchy," I told him. "That's all I know at this point."

He huffed slightly. "Sounds like a heart attack."

He was concerned, in his jaded way, as if Mum's illness were merely one more burden he must bear. I knew he'd been struggling recently, fighting a losing battle to keep people interested in the plight of Ukraine. It being Saturday, he was at his constituency home in the West Midlands. He'd just got back from attending a series of local events.

I knew his rambling mock-Tudor house well. It had two of everything. One branch of the staircase led to a small upper kitchen, where you could prepare snacks or light meals to enjoy in your room. William and the family would be heading to Tuscany soon, he told me, so this was a most unwelcome distraction from those plans.

"I'll come down tomorrow," he said, and that was that.

Time ticked on. I was leaving another voicemail for my daughter, Plum, when a junior doctor appeared. She was clutching a clipboard and calling my name. The medic had captivating grey eyes that shone with missionary zeal. She was tall and sturdy, neat and stylish. Her unnaturally blonde hair was gathered in a full and long ponytail. She sported shoes with slight heels that raised her to about five-ten. I didn't catch her name.

"Oh!"

She did a double-take, as people often do, when I stood up. I've learned to accept that people are ready for you to have red hair, or to be tall, but not both. It's as if I'm breaking some unwritten rule. Actually, my hair's not really red. It's auburn, though it's fading to straw from the temples, as my dad's did. Height-wise, I'm a gangly six-three and a half, though I always tell people I'm six-two.

I come in peace, Earthlings.

"Good evening," I said to the doctor.

"Hi," she replied, giving me a shy smile. "Let's go."

She led me down a long white corridor, into a lift, along another corridor and onto a link bridge. I have no sense of direction, so I was already hopelessly lost. As we quick-marched between a newer building and an older one, I noticed that her shoes clip-clopped, whereas mine squeaked.

We're a cart-horse leading a guinea-pig.

She turned a corner and pulled a door open. A flourescent striplight flickered into life, illuminating a small windowless room that must once have been used for storage. It now housed a tatty cream sofa, a green armchair and a small table on which there was a vase of artificial flowers and an open box of tissues.

Oh, wow! This is where they break the news that someone's dead.

Of course, it was far worse than that – or more complicated, I should say.

'Dr Zeal' perched on the front of the armchair, pressing her clipboard to her chest. She looked down as she delivered her monologue, only glancing at me occasionally.

"We see this a lot, at Christmas and other celebrations," she said.

I tried to pinpoint her accent: Polish or possibly Baltic States, with a twang of canned American. I imagined her grandmother back home, wiping the dust from the graduation photo.

I sat there on the sofa, listening, next to my bag of costume. She referred to a formal luncheon my mother attended: *Women of Achievement*, or something like that. After the meal, Mum complained of excruciating pain in her left arm.

"When old people over-eat very much and quickly, they can overload the entire system," said the doctor. "This causes heart attack or stroke. In case of your mother, is both. Heart attack, then stroke."

She explained how they'd carried out the emergency surgery to remove a blood clot from Mum's arm, but a piece had broken off and found its way to her brain. The bleed was substantial and they were still assessing the damage.

Broken off? Could that have been medical negligence?

Naturally, I avoided blurting this out. I knew complaining wouldn't do much good anyway. We love our health service, but you get what you're given. In any case, the blame for the whole misadventure had already been laid. If my mother had not been so greedy, she would have been just fine. Now, however, she was not fine.

"Good news – condition is stable and she is comfortable," the doctor concluded. "Bad news – there is risk of further stroke. Also, you will notice some changes. Physical issues, short-term memory and awareness."

She seemed to be searching for something to add; anything that offered a soupçon of hope. Then, at last, she found it:

"Long-term memory is very magnificent."

She glanced at me again, half-smiled and asked if I had any questions. I asked about Mum's chances of recovery. The doctor brought her ponytail forward and toyed with it before delivering her verdict.

"Too soon to say for sure, but full recovery? Very difficult."

Having warned me of this, she stood up and pushed the door open with her shoulder and foot. We stood awkwardly outside the Room of Doom for a moment. She seemed to be working up to saying something more.

"If you like to take me to dinner, this is my personal number," she added, holding out a printed card, which I accepted without immediately grasping what she'd just said. She added, rather bitterly: "Is very hard to meet someone when you work here all the time."

I glanced at the card, which gave her first name as Rūta, smiled and tucked it inside my shirt pocket. She looked away, embarrassed. She asked a passing porter to escort me to my mother's ward, then clipped and clopped away.

At a desk in a vestibule, I was handed over to a matronly Scottish nurse. Papers were shuffled and I was asked numerous questions. I felt like a spy in a Cold War movie, negotiating my way through Checkpoint Charlie. According to her identity lanyard, the nurse was called Roslyn.

She muttered my first name several times. I know 'Victor' is old-fashioned, but it happened to be my father's middle name and my great-grandfather's first name, so I've always been quite proud of it. Also, the name itself suggests I might, in some way, prevail.

There were no set times for visiting my mother, nurse Roslyn informed me; I could come and go as I wished. But she asked that visits after 9pm be "exceptional".

"Your daughter's been and gone," she added, not looking up. "She waited a good wee while."

"Oh really? She didn't call me back, though."

I explained about my transport hassles, but my excuse for arriving so late met with a snooty silence. I was led into the ward at last.

"Your mother's been talking, which is a good sign," said Roslyn. "But not making much sense at present. She's lost her swallow and if you ask her to raise her right arm, she raises her left."

I stood stock-still, taking in these details.

"You mean – she's paralysed down one side?"

Roslyn glared at me, as if I'd said something unseemly.

"It's too soon to draw that kind of conclusion, son."

A felled tree of an old woman, with splayed white hair for branches, was lying halfway between recumbent and propped-up positions, eyes closed. She was connected to various pieces of medical equipment.

Roslyn caught me staring at these, and ran through them for me. There was a hydration drip going into the patient's arm, a feeding line going into her neck, wires going from her chest to a heart monitor and there was a pulse oximeter, like a high-tech clothes peg, on the index finger of her non-functioning right hand. I had to peer closely, to find the rounded bit at the end of this person's nose, to appreciate that she was, in fact, my mother.

Here was the very woman who shared with me the wisdom of an old boss she secretly dubbed the Dragon. *Use short paragraphs*, as they're easier to read, and don't try to correct anything. Just 'X' through that line, hit return, and *keep going*. Always keep going. *Be resilient and persevere.*

When you know this relates to the use of a manual typewriter in a busy office, it makes more sense. As a metaphor, I doubt it would have wide appeal, but it works for me.

"Your son's here, dear," said Roslyn, patting Mum's left hand. On the same arm was a bandage from the operation. There was a 'Nil by Mouth' sign hanging on the wall above the bed.

My mum can't swallow any more.

I was shown a dish on the bedside cabinet, containing plastic handles with tiny sponges on the ends. The nurse said Mum could suck water from these, to stop her mouth going completely dry.

Like a monster in a Boris Karloff movie, the patient slowly turned her head towards us. I noticed all the lines that had accumulated on her weathered face. The eyelids cracked open a fraction; just enough to look sinister.

"That's it, dear. Say hello."

The eyes opened and I could see their soft blueness, but the gaze was very diffuse. There was almost no focus at all. Mum's eyes looked like tiny blue violets entombed in a glass paperweight. Despite this, she looked in my direction.

"William!" she gasped. "How lovely!"

Roslyn and I shared an uneasy glance.

"It's Victor, dear. *Victor*."

"Nonsense, woman! D'you think I don't know my own son?"

Outside of stage plays, I can't bear conflict, so I stepped in.

"How are you feeling?" I asked.

"They gave me a medal," she said, ignoring my question. "I want you to see it."

At this, Roslyn opened the door of Mum's bedside cabinet and passed me a large handbag.

"That's the only place it could be," she whispered.

It felt wrong to root around in Mum's personal effects, which were in no particular order. But I managed to pull out a long red ribbon, at the end of which dangled a large gold-coloured medallion. One side was inscribed with Mum's name, *Jayne De Vries*, and the year. The other side read: *Lifetime Achievement Award*. I felt slightly proud, in the way I might have felt gladness for the mother of a friend.

CHAPTER 2

I walked down the steps to Plum's basement flat and pressed a doorbell that hadn't been there on my previous visit. A young woman answered, keeping the door on a chain. She had curly purple hair and a nose-ring.

Her features were distinctive, her pallid colouring offset by hazel eyes and a brooding chin. She had an odd angular beauty that was all her own. I couldn't help picturing her as the most glamorous hag on the heath, in 'the Scottish play'. I explained the situation in a friendly manner, revealing that I had a bottle of wine in my big carrier bag, but to no avail.

"I'm not being difficult, but you could be a con artist for all I know. Plum didn't say anything about you coming to stay. Anyways, it's a two-bed flat. There's nowhere for you to sleep."

The Irish accent made me think of Old Maggie again, and what kind of pep talk she might have given the despairing Macbeth. I pointed out that the sofa folded out into a bed, but this failed to sway the lodger. We tried to call her landlady, who still wasn't picking up.

In desperation, I offered to field any question about Plum she wished to pose. Her eyes narrowed as she scrutinised my features. Then she stood back.

"All right. Why the nickname? Why Plum?"

Ah! An easy one.

I was amazed she didn't know this already. I believe it came from a primary school lesson about healthy eating, but my knowledge is partial as I was away on tour at the time. Actually, I'd already left Plum's mother by then, which makes the event even more remote in my imagination.

"Everyone in the class had to pretend to be a fruit or vegetable," I explained. "Plum's best friend was Peach, and for some reason, both names stuck."

"Oh. I didn't know that – a double act. Peach and Plum."

"Or Plum and Peach," I suggested. "Plum saw her friend as the sidekick."

"Yeah, that would make sense."

I heard the door being taken off the chain and it was finally opened to me.

"Come in, then. I'm Lara. As in Croft. Though my surname's O'Halloran."

Lara laughed at her own joke and I squeezed past her into the hallway. There was now a little shower room and a built-in cupboard on one side, with two small square bedrooms on the other. Ahead was a neat and bright kitchen-diner-lounge. A sun porch led to the cracked concrete patio, with steps up to the communal mess of a garden. Plum had done well with what she had.

The flat now looked bigger than my own terrace bungalow. I was glad to see the lumpy old sofa bed, a cast-off from Mum's house, still dominating the lounge space. Everything else looked new.

Lara was quick to apply corkscrew to bottle and poured two glasses of red.

"I'm about to cook some food," she said. "Nothing fancy, just tuna bolognese. Would you like some?"

I told her that would be great.

I eased onto a barstool and watched as she rounded up the tin, the jar and the packet. It was obvious she was a reluctant cook, and this dish was her one reliable fallback. I started to tell her about my transport problems on the way from the island.

"Sorry," she said. "I can't talk while I'm cooking. I have to concentrate."

We started to live out that strained scenario where you're thrown together with someone, in the absence of the person who connects you. We had a ritualised conversation about Ireland and the Isle of Wight, but our hearts weren't in it. Our hearts were with Plum.

"To absent friends," we said together, clinking our wine glasses.

I wished I was in closer touch with my daughter. Our ups and downs were partly due to historic resentment over my splitting up with her mother, and partly generational tensions. Plum was born in 2000, so that's pretty Millennial, though apparently that makes her part of 'Generation Z'.

Naturally, she blamed me for all her economic problems, though I couldn't help noticing she earned better money than I did. When she invited me to confront my life of enormous privilege, I pointed out that I was only *half* aristocrat, half small-town commoner. My mother was raised in a modest redbrick terrace house. And Plum wasn't short of privilege herself; everyone in the family had spent many a weekend with my dad at The Great House.

"We're all well-spoken," I added, which got my offspring rolling her eyes.

Actually, Plum's voice varied according to the person she was talking to. She could adopt a slight or strong Bristol accent, or a light Estuarial. For her part, Mum spoke mostly in 'received pronunciation'. She'd taken elocution lessons, paid for by my paternal Granny.

"You'll never understand!" shouted Plum, at some point in our conversation, and stormed out of the room.

On another occasion, when she accused me personally of causing the financial crash, I came back with what I thought was a decent alibi. At the time in question, far from handing out sub-prime mortgages, I was busy playing the part of Buttons in *Cinderella*. You'd think that might get me off the hook, but she didn't miss a beat. It was as if I'd only strengthened her argument.

She yelled: "Yeah – and *we* don't go to the fucking *ball*."

Don't get me wrong. I adore my Plummy, even when we have our moments. She's like a little round wren with beady, brown, disapproving eyes, behind designer glasses that make her look fiercely creative. Sitting there in her flat with her lodger, I wished I could do something to make amends – or to help her – but she'd feathered her nest entirely without her parents' interference.

"You said Plum was working late. Is she usually this late on a Saturday?"

"Seven days a week," said Lara, pouring more wine. "They're chasing new contracts. Though, if you ask me, the guy's taking advantage. Big time."

"You mean…?"

"Oh, I'm not privy to *that*. Anyways, my lips are sealed."

She sat back for a moment, in apparent contemplation. Then she leaned forward again, conspiratorially.

"But what does it look like? I mean, he's married. American. Full of bull…"

"You've met him then? Her boss."

"Yeah, we went to the pub one time. And she's all excited because it's a start-up that's trying to get to the next level…"

"She's basically selling software, is that right?"

"Something like that. So yeah. She'd do anything for him. Anything."

We clinked glasses again and exchanged forced smiles.

"So, what were you up to today?" I ventured.

"Work," she said, with a shudder that told me: don't go there.

"What do you do?" I enquired anyway.

I'm such a killjoy.

"Oh, nothing. Bloody retail. It's pants. Literally."

Lara laughed at her own joke again. I smiled.

"What would you *like* to do then?"

"Tonight?" she asked, wilfully misunderstanding. "Watch crappy telly."

"No, I meant – in your career…"

"Huh!"

She took a large swig of wine.

"I'm an actor," she revealed. "All the rest is bullshit."

"I know the feeling," I said, taking a sly sip. "I'm an actor too."

Lara looked puzzled, with strangely kinked frown lines appearing out of nowhere on her smooth young face. I usually have trouble reading faces and remembering them, but Lara's had some fascinating terrain. Her smile revealed high cheekbones.

"Plum said you were a manager."

"Huh!"

That was sort-of true. I'd got to the end of a gruelling panto run at the King Edward. I felt exhausted and washed out. I badly needed a break, so I signed up as a casual usher. The others in the cast found that hugely amusing, but it made sense to me at the time. It was a job and, apart from seasonal panto, touring theatre was in crisis. It had all but dried up.

Since the pandemic, mid-scale venues were barely taking drama any more; they were clogged up with comedy and tribute bands. First-run theatres like the King Eddie staggered on, but offering nothing but the safest, most bankable content, usually with small casts.

I hadn't expected to settle on the island. I just felt a sentimental attachment to the place, from strait-laced holidays there with Granny. Then a few kind words from Jim, and one gig led to another.

"I'm now acting assistant house manager, with no acting required," I quipped, attempting a Lara-style joke.

"That's pretty wild," she said, not noticing. "I don't know too much about theatres. I'm more into telly and film."

I couldn't resist bragging: "I've done a bit of that, too."

A pained look crossed her face, so I added: "Nothing all that epic, though."

Our conversation reached a natural pause and we were no longer anxious to fill the silence. I felt my muscles relax.

"I don't want to do front-of-house forever," I said, voicing this for the first time and wondering if it were true. "Being on stage is still my first love."

Lara laid down her fork, considering my words, then nodded slowly. There's a convention among struggling actors that we try to see past each other's immediate plight, to the great untapped potential that lies beyond. I was wondering if this was still the case with the younger performers. Then she raised her eyes and her glass, and declared, in mock celebration:

"Here's to us, then – both squandering our talents."

In that moment, I knew we could be friends. I started to open up even more. I told her about my twenty patchy years as a jobbing actor; how I always seemed to be sliding down the snake of my career ladder, landing in some unpalatable day-job to stave off destitution.

"Tell me though," she cut in, impatiently. "If you did panto, have you ever played the dame?"

Our eyes met and I gave a half-shrug.

"So many times."

Too many times.

Her eyes narrowed, in that way she had, and she looked at me with newly kindled interest.

"So, you're like a drag queen…"

"I wouldn't say that."

She raised a painted-on eyebrow.

"But you belong to us, right? In the queer community."

Would that I could admit that!

I didn't confirm or deny this proposition, just looked away, feeling a vague sense of regret. I didn't know the answer myself. I couldn't stretch to being the gay friend Lara seemed to desire, and I certainly wasn't ready to explain to Plum that her father was mostly heterosexual, but not entirely.

The silence was growing heavy; I felt the need to elaborate in some way. So I copped out and played it rather straight.

"Actually, I had a girlfriend until a year ago."

"So?"

"I mean – we nearly got together permanently. Her name's Teruko. Mature student on the one-year English course. There's a language school on the island. She worked with me at the theatre. You know – one of my ushers."

Lara looked at me, sceptically. "How mature?"

"She was thirty-five, so…"

"Bit of an age gap," she observed tartly.

Steady on.

All right – I'll admit to being a tad over forty when this

conversation took place. Well, forty-four, to be pedantic about the matter.

"Eight years," I confessed. "She's thirty-six now."

"So what happened?" Lara wanted to know.

"Teruko went home to Japan. I was supposed to go with her, but I chickened out at the last minute. I realised I'd struggle to learn Japanese or find my way around. You know? Such a different culture. I got scared. I believe Japan's one of those places where shouting at people in English doesn't get you very far."

Lara gave me a wry smile and shook her head.

"That, and you're so far into the closet you're practically in Narnia."

The wine was kicking in, and I found myself saying: "Touché."

In no way had my sexuality influenced my decision to stay in the country, but I enjoyed indulging Lara's belief that she'd read me correctly.

"I'm not physically attracted to guys," I declared, which was almost entirely true.

She seemed to be awaiting further explanation, so I continued:

"If there's anything at all, it's more emotional. Quite rare."

"Queer romantic, then?"

"If you say so. I haven't explored that side of me much."

"But you've got dressed up in women's clothes…"

Where's the connection?

"I mean, I've acted in drag," I mumbled, "but I'm not into cross-dressing. I've just worn the right costume for the part. Besides, bras are bloody uncomfortable. Even when they're stuffed with tights instead of socks."

I thought she might have a laugh at this, but she stayed focused and serious.

"You should come shopping with me. I'd find you a comfy one."

"I don't doubt it."

"What make-up do you use?"

"The unsubtle kind."

Lara peered at my face, making plans. It was Teruko who pointed out my symmetrical features, which she said made me handsome. Once she'd told me that, I could see it in my father too. For all the time I've spent in dressing rooms, I'm not a mirror man. I just make sure the look is right – and on I go.

"I'll give you a makeover sometime," said Lara, clearly intending this as an offer and not a threat. It didn't appeal at all, but I didn't want to disappoint her, so I said: "Sure, why not?"

We repaired to the big old ugly couch and settled down to watch reality TV, just as Lara wanted. During an ad break, she turned to me and asked how Mum was doing. I was still processing that whole situation and didn't feel ready to give a sensible answer.

"She's in a really bad way," I said. "But her doctor fancies me."

"What! Male or female?"

Wish I hadn't said anything.

"Female."

"How old?"

"Too young. Late twenties."

"Is she hot?"

"I suppose so. She's very smart."

"Smart clever, or smart looking?"

"Both. Eastern European. Tall. Plump. Gorgeous eyes. Blonde – fake blonde…"

"Feck – you should give her my number!"

Lara giggled at her own joke and I smiled, though it was a rainbow smile, the kind you give people when you feel slightly heartbroken. Talking about the doctor made me think even more intensely about Mum.

Full recovery? Very difficult.

It was sinking in that she might never be truly well again. Would she ever eat or drink normally, or even get out of bed to walk a few steps? The health professionals could gloss it all they liked, but parts of her body and mind were spent. I could see that for myself.

"Mum never loved me," I said.

It sounded as if I were confessing to a crime. To her great credit, Lara didn't jump in and contradict me, as many others might have done. She wasn't shocked. She could tell I was simply reporting some unvarnished truth. She paused the TV.

"Go on."

"She cared for me in material terms," I said, "but not emotionally. She always pushed me away. Though she's been kind enough to Plum."

Lara made it clear that she understood, but said nothing. She reached over and gently pulled my head until it was touching hers. I had the strongest feeling then, that I didn't want Mum to die. At the same time, I felt a pull of resentment that she'd failed to shuffle off cleanly when she had the chance.

With her being in this limbo state, I didn't know what I was supposed to do. Maybe William would suggest something. He always came up with a plan.

"She's still your mammy, so she is," Lara said softly.

"There's a threadbare connection, but yeah."

The TV show we were viewing was a combined cookery and antiques challenge, featuring celebrities I'd never heard of. Contestants had to use historic recipes and serve using crockery bought at auction. Watching two episodes back-to-back made us both feel drowsy. Lara gave me a goodnight hug and sashayed away to her own room.

"Don't tell Plum," I called after her. "What we were talking about earlier."

She turned and gave me the most mischievous smile. "I think she'll know already. But okay – my lips are sealed."

CHAPTER 3

The flat was tranquil. Lara was enjoying a lie-in; I could just make out her faint whistle of a snore. She'd told me that her plan for the day was "to be a lady of leisure and do feck all".

There was distant traffic noise, some shifting of furniture going on upstairs, and rain was drumming on the roof of the sun porch. Having slept across the sofa in my suit, I felt ruffled and manky. I wandered over to the kitchen counter. Plum had left me a door key, a towel and a note:

'Will try to see Nan again on way to office. Love P.'

I ate some granola, had a shower, and poked my head into Plum's room. There was just enough space in there for the double bed and built-in wardrobe. I couldn't tell if she'd slept there overnight, then chided myself for trying to guess, her relationships being none of my business.

I forced myself to call my father. Although Mum and Dad were long divorced, I knew he'd want to know about her illness. We had our usual stilted chat, then he said: "Should I come up and see her?"

Knowing how he disliked London, I replied: "That's up to you, Dad."

"Well," he said, "for now, just keep me up to date with developments."

I rummaged in my carrier bag and found a pair of union

flag underpants from an old Whitehall farce. The fly was sensibly stitched up, to avoid an unwanted guest appearance. I also grabbed some plain socks, a police officer shirt and some pleated grey trousers that were too short and too baggy. I pulled the belt tight and hoped for the best.

At the hospital, I tried to find my own way to the ward but gave up and purloined a porter. I reported to the nurse at the desk, this time a smiling young woman wearing a hijab. Her lanyard gave her first name as Inaya.

"Go straight in, Sergeant De Vries," she said. "Your brother's with her. And your niece."

I wasn't wearing a tie, so I hadn't expected anyone to take my stripes seriously. But *ah!* – that's the wonder of costume. There was a subdued alertness on the sun-streaked ward in this care-worn building. Despite the windows being open, the air smelt of cabbage soup.

Mum's fellow geriatrics fiddled with magazines or cups of tea, or simply watched the staff coming and going. In a far corner, there was one bed in its own glass room – like a coveted corner office – but the occupant looked particularly unwell. He was unconscious and on oxygen.

And there was Mum. It seemed ironic that she'd coped better than many through the pandemic. She pottered about her house in Hampstead, had groceries delivered, did her own gardening, walked on the heath, learned to make video calls. But now this. I noticed a catheter bag, dangling below the bed on her blighted right side. Nurse Roslyn hadn't mentioned incontinence; I guess it's not an especially comfortable talking point.

Mum was propped up and seemed to be awake, albeit her eyes were closed. And there, standing shiftily at the foot of her bed, was William. He'd grown quite paunchy. He was no longer deploying the desperate comb-over he wore on *Newsnight*, when they used to turn to him for backbench comment. True to form, he wore a blue check shirt and mustard knitted tie. If anything, he looked more like a child of the 1950s than Mum did.

I shouldn't be too sniffy about his personal style, though. At least he has one. I'm always trying new looks, without ever settling on anything. I aim to be 'smart casual'. I only wear a tie when required to do so for work.

William's daughter, Henrietta, who worked in his parliamentary office, was occupying the plastic seat by the bed. The middle child and only girl, she was perhaps his best hope of establishing a political dynasty. However, he belonged to the gently odious centre-right of the 'nasty party'; she preferred to associate with more rabidly right wing types.

A broad coalition, in one family.

She stood up and gave me a double air-kiss, masking the ward's cabbage smell with sweet and musky perfume. She was twenty-two; a year younger than Plum, a year older than Lara. This was only possible because I became a dad quite young, while William left it later. In any case, Henrietta was now an ageless Tory woman in a loose-fitting floral dress.

"Plum was just here," she said, "but I expect you two caught up at the flat."

Pah! You know nothing.

I smiled at her blankly.

"Pop gave her a good sales lead," she revealed. "The council leader in the constituency might bite. Though he'll need a little something as a sweetener…"

Now that her unruly hair had been tidied and trimmed to collar length, Henrietta looked grown-up and businesslike. With quite close-set eyes, whenever she expressed any kind of displeasure as a toddler, she looked like a disgruntled barn owl. Now she had a kind of strident elegance; not soft enough for Cordelia, nor harsh enough for Regan, but perfect for Goneril.

'My poor fool is hanged.' The saddest line in all Shakespeare.

"Mother thinks I'm you," said William, whose greetings always implied that we were already in mid-conversation. His endless forehead was creased with self-pity.

"Good to see you," I said, using a well-practised formula. "It's been a while. How's the Ukraine support going?"

He remembered himself, gave me a bleak smile and squeezed my arm.

"So-so," he said. "The recovery conference went well, but you can't recover properly whilst you're still at war. What's all this?"

He gestured to my sergeant stripes and I explained about having to raid the costume store.

"You idiot!" he exclaimed, though with a half-grin. My antics always seemed to take him by surprise. "You total cretin."

Ah, here we go…

The tune was always the same from William, who, incidentally, was tone deaf. "You idiot, you cretin, you moron." This name-calling cycled round and round, droned on and on, and had done all my life. I'm not saying it didn't hurt, but it was so deeply ingrained in our relationship it was almost a benediction. I tried not to take his put-downs to heart. I'd built up my own sense of pride, slowly and painstakingly, over the years. I knew who I was.

I may be a fool, but I'm no idiot.

"Mum thinks I'm you, too," I announced.

I thought my brother had a right to know this. Indeed, he was about to get a demonstration of Mum's skewed notion of her sons' identities.

"Is that you, William?" she asked, turning towards me and opening her eyes.

"Yes, I'm here, Mother," interjected William.

"Not you!" she said. "I want the other one."

Henrietta tried unsuccessfully to stifle a chortle. This felt eerily like living through a mistaken identity scene. Only it was for real, in the unrehearsed throes of everyday life.

"How are you feeling, Mum?" I asked, supposedly as William.

"I want to go home now," she stated, blithely. "Will you take me in the car?"

Henrietta deftly parried this request on my behalf.

"They need to run more tests, Nan."

William turned to me, frowning and shaking his head.

"This is a disaster," he said, sotto voce. "She doesn't even know us."

"I know," hissed Henrietta, behind her hand. "It's really sad."

Hmm…

I spotted Dr Rūta at the far end of the room. She was busy with a patient, but gave me a quick wave. I smiled and waved back.

"I'm not so sure," I whispered. "They say her long-term memory is very good."

William gave a dismissive shrug.

"Well, we've paid our respects," he said, with a note of finality. "She's clearly on her way out. I've never seen a case like this where the person didn't die. It's just a question of when. There's not much more we can do right now."

"Though we'll have to figure out what to do about the house," said Henrietta.

"The house?"

"Absolutely," said William, ignoring my question. "And the

rest of her assets. We need to make sure they don't grab the house to pay for her care."

But it's her house…

I looked round at Mum, unable to divine whether she was listening in to this discussion.

"Can we not talk about this in front of her?"

William was stung to be pulled up like that, and became irritable.

"Then where do you suggest we go?" he snapped.

I swept out of the ward, brother and niece in tow, and paced the white tiles at the double. I had no idea where I was going. The overhead signs were of no use to me. When I'm stressed, letters on signs swim around in a most unhelpful manner. I did recognise the link bridge as I squeaked over it. Soon after that, I found myself at a T-junction and took a random turn. A waiting area appeared, with its own small café opposite.

I knew there'd be something.

I acted as if this had been our destination all along. I became aware that the newer building had air conditioning. Its clinical crispness felt good. While William and Henrietta queued for proper coffee at the counter, I explored the out-of-hours vending machines, as I was low on funds. For 50p you could get one of those flimsy plastic cups of liquid that's too hot to hold. I pressed for 'White Coffee, No Sugar' and received what looked like thin chicken soup concocted from chemicals.

"What the hell is that?" William wanted to know.

I took a sip and scalded my tongue. "Chicken soup," I confirmed.

Henrietta looked flummoxed, in the way that someone highly competitive regards anyone who won't spar. I noticed how her dimples appeared both when she was happy and when she was vexed.

"You could've got *real* soup over there, Uncle Vic."

"I know."

"Bloody idiot," William muttered. He was still in prickly mode.

We sat around one of the tin bistro tables to hold our heated discussion. Now, if there's one thing you should avoid in an argument with a barrister-politician, it's showing your hand too soon. And, of course, I kicked off by saying how disappointed I was that William's priority appeared to be getting his hands on Mum's property, rather than focusing on her care.

"It's only a crummy old hovel, but it's worth a bomb!" said Henrietta; a comment not particularly helpful to either side in this row.

Mum's house was a double-fronted Victorian rectory, set back from the road in its own little grounds. She'd spent fifteen years restoring it. Now the same jobs needed doing, all over again. Shaded by its huge trees, the place was functional and austere – joyously cool in the summer holidays and notoriously cold at Christmas.

Though I'd left some memories there, I could barely call it home. Unlike William, who was a day pupil at a famous London school, I was sent away. From the grand old age of ten, I attended one of the less grand boarding schools in Scotland. It was made clear that this was due to my own bad behaviour.

"Let's consider the evidence, shall we?"

After my opening outburst, William became menacingly easygoing. He fixed me with a pitying, smug smile. Naturally he *wanted the best* for Mother, and he would do all in his power to make sure she got *the finest care*, and that was our agreed priority.

In his well-practised, unctuous manner, he spoke of on-shore accounts, off-shore accounts, asset transfers, trust funds, powers of attorney. Where the dazzling eloquence and bamboozling logic ended, like all conservatives, he just kept saying words until they made no sense at all. The main objective was to assert his own perspective on life, while blocking, disrupting and negating anyone else's.

I may struggle with reading, but I know words. As I grew up, Mum, William and Granny were constantly jumping on my spoken errors. It was only Dad who ever let me be. By the time I started prep school, I had a wide vocabulary and declaimed in grammatically correct sentences. At first, my teacher thought I was a precocious genius, but she soon found me out and lost interest.

"After all," said William, concluding his lengthy oration with a benign smirk, "it's our birthright."

Henrietta looked at me expectantly, willing my agreement.

Hang on a moment. Our birthright!

All right, so Dad was the undistinguished second son of a viscount, which meant he inherited precisely one thousand pounds, plus the miniscule family flat in Great Russell Street. William had more-or-less monopolised that as his London residence.

Whatever assets *Mum* had accrued, on the other hand, were solely the product of her own meritocratic travails as a journalist and author. They had nothing to do with what she was 'born to'. I was secretly furious that my relatives would claim any kind of greatness on the back of her achievements.

"Wait a moment," I said, believing I'd found a hole in William's argument.

As I spoke, his brow became increasingly furrowed.

"If she's as unwell as you're suggesting," I said, my voice wobbling slightly, "then how can she have sufficient *capacity* to sign legal papers?"

A vein appeared above William's temple and seemed to start throbbing. I found myself praying that he didn't explode. I knew he had high blood pressure. The last thing I wanted was for another family member to be hospitalised, so I vowed silently to fall in line with his ridiculous plans.

"Oh, I… expect she'll rally in the short term," he said, vaguely.

And then you can pounce?

"We're only trying to think ahead," added Henrietta, who appeared a little chastened by my opposition.

Desperate not to let William know I was backing down, I shifted my attack.

"Why did you change Mum's next-of-kin details without telling me?"

Now I was being the prickly one. He looked at me blankly, then smiled. For him, this confrontation had barely moved beyond the opening pleasantries. He held his hands wide, palms up, in gentle innocence.

"I didn't," he said. "But as you know, I've been spending more time out of the country. If Mother made such a change, perhaps she realised you'd be easier to get hold of in an emergency."

It was true: William's political career was on the wane, so he'd accepted numerous board memberships and speaking engagements, some in the United States. I'd heard from several sources that he was under pressure to vacate his safe seat and make way for someone younger, more dynamic.

With his prospective elevation to the House of Lords, he was on the brink of attaining – allegedly on merit – membership of the same exclusive, unelected institution our grandfather had attended by accident of birth.

But William didn't want that. Acquiescing to such an arrangement would mean accepting that the flame of his junior ministerial career – which had fluttered for a mere five months – had been snuffed out and would never be rekindled.

The fact that he wasn't removed from office due to incompetence, disloyalty or scandal, but merely by a change of party leader, was something that still rankled with him. I don't know why he was so surprised by this. He'd been quoted during the leadership campaign, saying of its eventual winner: "If that's the mirage, there is no oasis."

I pretended to sympathise with William, while finding his political issues deeply hilarious. Maybe my brother was not so big, nor so great, after all. I towered over him now. But let me tell you how mercilessly *he* used to taunt *me* for being short – which I was – until I had a growth spurt in fourth year. I gained ten inches in eighteen months. My back still hurts to this day, from all that stretching.

Our ad hoc meeting was petering out, William believing he'd won the argument, Henrietta realising he hadn't. I was going to say "let's agree to disagree", but held my sore, chicken soup-afflicted tongue. I wasn't going to stand in his way. William said he had an appointment elsewhere and scuttled off. Henrietta stood up and made eye contact with me.

"Don't take everything to heart," she said, with a sad smile. "This will sort itself out, you know."

Then she rushed away to catch up with her father. I thought that was quite a considerate thing for her to say; it made me wonder about Henrietta. Aside from being a money-grubbing Tory, she wasn't such a bad kid.

I gazed across the corridor to the waiting area, where people were anticipating their appointments in an atmosphere of muted dread. I stole away from there. I had to ask three times for directions before I found my way out of the hospital.

CHAPTER 4

I adore the West End. You can set me down in Trafalgar Square and I can walk in any direction for forty minutes, without getting lost. That's not as good as putting a girdle around the Earth, but it's quite a feat for me. I've performed at a few of the theatres, including Wyndham's and Haymarket – mostly in short runs and regional transfers that didn't quite take off. The successful shows were Pinter, Ayckbourn and a Restoration comedy. Don't get too excited: mine were supporting roles, apart from the Pinter, for which I received glowing notices, but no-one noticed.

The streets were glistening with the morning's rain. Bike wheels made a satisfying swish as they were driven toward their destinations at alarming speed. Vehicles ambled along at a more sedate rate between red lights, belching the fumes their drivers had paid for permission to emit. People were bumping into me as I paused to breathe it all in, feeling an escapee's exaggerated sense of gratitude.

"Here I am, you old queen!"

I met Lara at the corner of Leicester Square, as the Swiss glockenspiel was chiming noon. I'd begged her to come out and do something after all. I eventually lured her from the sofa with a promise of brunchy lunch at the eaterie of her choice. Then we looked at faces in the portrait gallery, one of my favourite haunts. If you're as face-blind as Dad and me, then noticing features and gauging expressions in paintings is a good way to practise. The more you look, the more you get a sense of what's going on in the sitter's life.

Lara said she wouldn't mind seeing more art, so we made for the South Bank, to walk along the riverside to Tate Modern. I stopped half-way across Hungerford Bridge, as I always do, to admire the view towards St Paul's. This is the only place where I feel I still belong to London; I'm not just visiting. Here the width of the river opens up the cityscape, so you can truly see the sky. You can sense the play of natural light and tidal rhythm, while you just stand and stare. I took and uploaded a picture, which immediately got three likes.

The last time I'd stood on this spot, I was with Teruko. She'd been happy and excited about spending time together here. Slight and balletic, she dressed in a simple tomboy style. At work, this often meant black jeans and a branded technician's polo shirt. If she played down her femininity in public, she sometimes revelled in it when we were alone. She was lovely. And I could rest my chin on the top of her head.

She was easy to be with – loveable, funny and serious; respectful and downright blunt. I'd have expected a Japanese person to stand on ceremony to an extent, perhaps displaying a form of awkwardness I would find familiar, but that wasn't Teruko.

"Life is complicated enough," she said. "We shouldn't hide our emotions."

"Why so sad?" asked Lara, giving me a token back-rub that actually soothed the area that always feels stretched. "You're crying."

No way.

I couldn't be crying. I don't cry; almost never. I'm a battler, relentlessly reconciled to my numerous quirks and challenges.

Like Old Maggie, I'm extremely resilient. I keep going. I push and try, and never give up. I brushed the tears off my cheek as if they were raindrops.

"Come here."

Lara gave me an affectionate hug. She was less than half my age, yet had an enigmatic maturity about her that I appreciated. She seemed very grounded and wise.

"Did you know, I was your age when I became Plum's dad?"

She nodded. "I figured that."

We moved on. I felt that Lara was now one of my people. With her, I felt fully acknowledged, fully alive, as I always did with Plum, and William, and Dad, and Jim, and some of my old acting buddies, and Teruko. As for Mum – well, the jury was always out.

On the South Bank, we encountered a middle-aged homeless woman, crashed out on a cardboard mat. She had long black hair and seemed to be groaning in her sleep. We checked she was all right. She declined all offers of help and we moved on. I voiced my dismay at the resumption of rough sleeping after the pandemic, but failed to proffer any kind of solution.

"I've been there," said Lara, without elaborating. She threaded her arm through mine as we walked along.

You've been homeless?

I was taken aback. I wanted to ask about her experience, but knew it may have been very painful. I left the subject hanging in mid-air. I knew I'd circle back to it anyway, because I'm too nosy to let things go. She and I seemed to have that in common.

"I've had to sofa-surf a few times myself," I said, thinking of my brief spell in America.

"Go easy," said Lara, with a giggle. "If you try to surf on our sofa, it'll fall apart."

We walked past the National Theatre. I should feel stronger support for the culture the dated concrete building contains. That's mostly down to envy, I suppose, as I'll probably never get to perform there.

"I'd love the place more, if they'd give me a little run, as a beadle or a page."

"You'll never get your Oscar that way," Lara pointed out, with a yawn.

We got to talking about relationships, including mine with Plum's mum.

"Kelly was... *forthright*," I said, "which was good at first."

Like each woman I've been with, she chose me. It's so much easier to accept an approach, or turn one down as gently as possible, than to do the chasing. Kelly came from an aspirational 'white van' background on the south side of Bristol. She has mixed heritage, as they say.

Kelly's race wasn't something I noticed about her particularly, until she raised it herself in a class discussion of *Othello*. I'm proud that Plum has some Afro-Caribbean ancestry, and I know she is too. But she can be quite touchy about the whole subject, so I leave well alone.

Our living arrangement was exactly what her mother proposed – me being the one acting and going on tour, with Kelly putting her own thespian career on hold before it had even started. I should have been more prepared for the snarling resentment that built up, as I landed the odd part while scratching a living and providing for the three of us.

"You were young," said Lara. "She would be restless, stuck at home."

"That's true."

Of course Kelly would feel frustrated. But her criticism of me built and built, until one day I offered to reverse the whole arrangement. I would stay at home and she could go out to work. Well, she launched a hail of expletives in my direction, accusing me of not meaning what I said. But it was a genuine offer.

"I'll step aside right now," I said. "You can do anything you want."

I picked up the phone – which was still a landline device – and pressed the speed-dial button for my agent, who was less useless in those days. I intended to tell him about my change of circumstances and to get Kelly signed up. Instead, she yanked the phone wire out of the socket and hurled abuse at me.

"You'd only do it so you could be off work for two years!" she screeched.

Without meaning to, I'd called her bluff. I realised then that she didn't want a solution to her career frustrations. She was just using me as an emotional punchbag.

"You can't have it both ways," I told her, and slammed out of the flat.

By the time I got back from my walk, she'd packed a bag for me. I was really shocked, but underneath I felt relieved. Nothing I could have done would ever have been good enough for her. Our parting was inevitable.

"You did the right thing for yourselves," declared Lara. "Though it must have been tough on Plum. Ooh – that reminds me…"

She started working her phone with her thumbs.

"I'm texting you the number of someone we know. Plum said you could hang out with him, as her gran's going to be crocked up for a while, and she hasn't got the time to babysit you…"

"*Babysit* me? I've not even clapped eyes on her yet!"

"Hey!" Lara raised a squiggly brow. "Don't shoot the messenger, dude."

"Oh – sorry. Go on."

She resumed outlining the idea.

"Guy's more your age, I think he's thirty-three, so…"

"So we'll have lots in common?" I asked, sarcastically.

To which she replied, entirely without irony: "Hopefully, yeah. And he's more available in the daytime than either of us. Give him a call. He'll be glad to know you."

The mind boggles.

We fell back in step. I asked about Lara's own parents; they were still together. Her younger sister lived with them, in Navan, which was a nice wee place, but certainly not the queer capital of Ireland. Lara described coming out to her family, a fairly recent event that was both affirming and upsetting.

"I mean, they're not religious," she said. "So I didn't have all that ballocks to contend with. But it still hurt. They don't want to talk about anyone's sexuality, at all, ever. And I could tell they were disappointed."

With Lara already dwelling on a difficult subject, I saw my chance.

"So when were you homeless?"

"A while ago. Not for very long. I slept in the park, back in Dublin. Then I got a place in a refuge. Then I came here."

Poor girl.

Our eyes met. Something or other got exchanged, and we moved on. We drifted around the busy gallery, taking our turn to look at the artworks. I didn't think Lara was enjoying it much, but then she made a vow to do this sort of thing more often. I doubted very much that she was just being polite.

We crossed the Millennium bridge and made our way back, slowly, inexorably, towards the hospital.

"What are you so apprehensive about?" she asked.

I hadn't expressed any such feeling, but she'd picked up my vibe. I'm not fitted with that type of sensitive social radar.

I can't always tell what other individuals are feeling. On the other hand, I *can* tell is what a crowd is ready for: when to ad-lib, when to respond to a heckle, when to bash things to the brink, and when to play it nice and straight.

It's almost too much power to have in your hands. The public love you to hold it, to control it, to make them helpless with laughter. But, truly and honestly, the times I've felt closest to cracking up completely have all been in those upstage moments, when you could do *anything* – you could even fly close to the sun – but you knew you were about to crash through the clouds in a bundle of feathers as soon as the curtain came down.

One time we had a wonderful ovation. The children were buzzing, and the parents and grandparents were delighted. For a moment, I was happy. Then I went backstage, pulled off my wig, slumped into a chair and said out loud to no-one but myself: "This isn't me."

I don't know if I was right, because I was so utterly exhausted, but I believed it at the time. I was a man trapped in a dame's costume, and in her relentless schedule of performances.

"I'm a bit nervous about seeing Mum again," I admitted. "I don't want to let her down. She's convinced I'm my brother, so I'm sort-of representing him. I don't want to let him down either."

Lara looked at me, puzzled. There were those cute frown lines again.

"Does it matter? From the way you talk about him, he sounds like an erse."

Ouch!

I don't mind having a pop at William myself, but I feel strangely protective of him if someone else does it. He may have called me names, but he also indulged me as a kid. When he was home, he invited me into his room and played the odd game with me, or let me sit there and listen while he played his music tapes. For that, I'm truly grateful.

"Deep down, I know he really cares. He just doesn't always know how to show it."

"Then he's an emotionally constipated erse," said Lara, and I couldn't help laughing this time.

"He does have rubbish taste in music," I conceded.

"How bad?"

William was a sucker for novelty records and uncool uncles like Val Doonican and Perry Como.

"That's bad," agreed Lara. "Though we love Val. I grew up with his version of *Paddy McGinty's Goat*."

Oblivious to the apparent contradiction, William liked both German oompah tunes and militaristic music from the classic war films. Whenever I hear a brass band now, it always makes me smile. At the time when Frankie Goes To Hollywood were flying high in the charts, there can't have been too many other adolescents freaking out instead to The Band of the Grenadier Guards.

We walked on until we were nearly at the hospital, and Lara said she would come in with me. She was keen to meet "Plum's gran".

Nurse Roslyn was back on duty when we reported to the desk.

"Your mother's friend is in there, sergeant. The lady who was with her when she was first admitted."

Gosh.

"*Sergeant?* But those stripes – "

I put my finger to my lips to avoid Lara blowing my cover. I was savouring the reverence with which the nurses were treating me, in my unintended impersonation of a police officer.

As Mum didn't have many friends, preferring the occasional

company of work associates, I wondered who the person could possibly be that the nurse had mentioned. We walked into the ward and I glimpsed the visitor, who was hunched forward on the plastic seat, a cape around her shoulders and a designer handbag in her lap.

She was about my mother's age, with piled-up hair that continued to be dyed brown, and lots of poorly applied make-up. I worked out that this had to be Marjorie Buttle-Deary, Mum's literary agent. I hadn't seen her for years, but she recognised me straight away and rose to greet me.

"Oh, Victor, darling," she said, coughing from the rumbling depths of her smoker's lungs, "I can't believe what's happened! Jayne's one of my dearest friends. We must have her back at full strength soon."

That seemed a naïve wish, but Marjorie was serious. Mum had been laid flat and looked serene, eyes closed, as if lying in state. I introduced Lara as my friend and Plum's flatmate.

"I'm really just the lodger," said Lara, correcting me. "But we get along fine."

Marjorie told us about the *Women of Achievement* dinner, how Mum had been on top form, wolfing her food down and giving a wonderful acceptance speech after receiving her award.

"Isn't it cruel how life does this, conflating high and low points?"

Marjorie put on a pained expression that was laughably theatrical, and exaggerated by her deep wrinkles and patchy make-up. Her anguished eyes looked up at me imploringly. She came across as so false, so proud, yet there was something genuinely triste about her as well.

"That's our fate," said Lara, grimly. "Time can be a bitch."

"And none of us is getting younger," said Marjorie, seemingly counting three generations into her lament.

The old woman's haughty manner had dissolved completely. I couldn't help but feel a tug of emotion in her favour.

"You've been friends a long time," I said, with a half-smile.

"We have, we have…"

I realised at that point how little I knew of Mum's 'lifetime achievements', though I'd grown up seeing her smart little volumes of no-nonsense advice in the various bookcases around the house.

I explained to Lara how Mum ran away from home in her teens and got a temping job in Fleet Street, as a copytaker for a national newspaper. Somehow, miraculously, she made the move upstairs into the newsroom. This much mythology I remembered being told as a child.

No, wait!

I knew how she made that spectacular ascent. As a kind of test, she was asked to write an article entitled *Sons of Great Men*. Only she didn't do exactly what they said – and almost as a result of that – she got the career she craved. Something along those lines.

"Jayne's an excellent leader writer," said Marjorie, watching over the pale and inert form of her client. When the agent smiled, I could see that one of her incisors was a gold tooth. "She's a brilliant commentator. Her column's still a must-read…"

"Ah, well," said Lara, soothingly. "It's the end of an era then."

"Ooh, don't say that!" Marjorie looked dumbfounded. "We want to get her well again."

She turned to me once more. "You look like your father," she said, almost accusingly, adding that he was a good man.

"I never understood what Jayne saw in that other chappie. The roving reporter."

She said this as if I knew the story, which I didn't. There had always been a shadow over my parents' relationship, but it was one of those great unspoken subjects, like the jar in the pantry you must never open. They divorced when I was two, but remained on respectful, cordial terms. That's not something Kelly and I managed to achieve. But I'm sure it's far easier when the people in question have never lived, full-time, under the same roof.

"She'll get better, Victor, you'll see," said Marjorie. "Your mother's a fighter. And she's in the best place for now."

The agent got up to leave and said her goodbyes. Suddenly, I didn't want her to go. I asked for her phone number, so we could keep in touch.

"Look here," she said, pointing with her high-heeled shoe. "Her urine's a good colour."

With that, and an imperious wave over her shoulder, she bustled out of the ward. Mum turned her head towards us and opened her eyes.

"Has she gone? That awful woman."

"Mum, that was Marjorie. She's one of your oldest friends."

"She's my agent," she said firmly. "She sees me as a cash cow, William. A *cash cow.*"

CHAPTER 5

I was at Mum's bedside in the early evening; I was back there again in the late morning. I could already feel the days beginning to blur. I was spending so long with her because I felt guilty. I'd been enjoying myself with Lara, while my only mother was stuck here – flat on her back, attached to all these wires.

As well as believing I was my brother, Mum needed to be given news again and again, such was the damage to her short-term memory. If I was lucky, the odd piece of information would eventually get through and land.

After my phantom turn as a police officer, I was welcomed back to the ward as 'Sergeant' De Vries again. I regarded it as an honorary title and continued to enjoy the nurses' boundless admiration. Today the only stripes I was wearing were accompanied by stars, my underpants presumably being the property of an American character in the Whitehall farce. I wore the pleated trousers again, with red socks and a linen grandfather shirt.

Mum gestured in the direction of the water jug, so I wet one of her little sponges, but I didn't give it to her right away.

"Don't drink it all at once now," I told her, and she gave the slightest chuckle.

I was relieved that I could still make her laugh, even in this sad old situation. Some of my earliest memories are of

Mum and William – or Will, as he styled himself then – looking at me expectantly, smirks on their faces, waiting for me to perform. Like a baby seal in a sanctuary, I had to act in certain ways to get my fish. Having arrived years late, or so it seemed, I was expected to catch up quickly. The times I couldn't be sensible or precocious enough, I had to be a clown. People warm to a clown more than to a shy, solemn boy. Comedy is my tragedy, you could say, but I'd rather have that than have nothing.

"Are you still there, William?" asked Mum.

I confirmed that I was. She held up her hand for me to shake.

"Left for rogues," she said, so I shook her left hand with mine. It felt odd, as I'm left-handed, but I knew she wasn't. We'd never done this before. I wondered if it was some kind of in-joke she shared with William. Then the conversation took an even more bizarre turn.

"Wilson was here last night, you know."

It took a few questions to ascertain that Mum was referring to Harold Wilson, the former prime minister. According to her, Wilson had visited her at night, when they'd put the main lights off. He sat on the far side of the bed and they'd had a pleasant chat.

But surely – he's dead…

I knew Wilson had been in office when Mum was young. She'd been a great supporter of his. By contrast, the political figure who inspired William was none other than Margaret Hilda Thatcher. I checked on my phone and discovered that Wilson died in May 1995. I thought better than to mention that inconvenient fact. Mum gabbled on about him for a while longer, then seemed to run out of steam. Her expression changed; she'd thought of something else.

"Have you brought your notebook?" she wanted to know.

"My notebook?"

I had no idea what she was talking about.

"We'll never get this book done if you keep forgetting it," she said. "My memoirs, William – you promised to help."

Your memoirs?

"I'll bring it next time."

She gave me a radiant smile.

"I'm glad the others have gone," she said, though she'd had no other visitors that day. "It's just you and me now. Like it was in the beginning, when I first held you in my arms. It's you and me, William, against the world."

I was baffled by this declaration. It may have been how she felt when my brother was an infant, but she didn't raise him all on her own. Far from it. There had always been a nanny during the week, plus our father and grandmother at weekends, at The Great House. It was the same story for me, before I was sent away.

Mum was in a talkative mood. She launched into a dozen lopsided tales, spoken more to herself than her audience. She opened her eyes and gazed towards the ceiling, sniggering away at the parts she found amusing. I offered to get her propped up, but she declined, rather testily.

"Don't start meddling! I'm perfectly comfortable as I am."

Her stories were dreary anecdotes, some of which sounded faintly familiar. These were evidently what she counted as memoirs, because she would say things like: "Get this down, William. It's important."

She'd already forgotten I was sans notebook. I just nodded along, watching her lips moving, eyes widening, face frowning and smiling. The stroke might have shaken up her mind like a snowglobe, but at least she was showing some zest for life.

"When will they bring me a cup of tea?" she asked, not for the first time.

I handed her another tiny wet sponge instead, which she accepted with good grace. She switched between past and present seamlessly, as you might expect from someone whose long-term memory was judged to be "very magnificent".

Her stories, though, were rambling and inconsequential. They made me feel deflated; I hoped we might take the opportunity to talk seriously. This was surely my last chance to create some kind of emotional bond with her – or have a reconciliation, after past spats.

Yet here she was, probably in a terminal decline, prioritising the dullest possible conversation. It was like watching the mischievous ghost of our relationship dancing around the ward, about to throw itself through one of the open windows and disappear forever.

"Did you hear that Victor's joined the police?" she asked me at one point. "He's got a proper job at last."

Mum had always been less accepting of my choice of profession than Dad. That said, she was one of the few people who saw me in the Pinter play. Afterwards we didn't discuss it; she just described my performance as "chilling". Given the script, I tried to take that as a compliment.

She babbled on. Having drifted away into my own thoughts, I made an effort to listen again. She was recounting a time when a drunken colleague had run his hand up her leg. She'd stamped on his foot, making it swell.

"The boys knew not to mess around with yours truly after that, *and no mistake.*"

In this aside, there was a throwback to her lost Lancashire accent. That was something I always prized. Her original voice always sounded truthful. It came from the girl they called

'Essie' back home, a pet name for Estelle, before she reinvented herself as Jayne.

Those northern notes could evoke that girl – or, perhaps, a scattered piece of soul from one of her elders? She may have been apeing her sainted mother, her wise grandmother, or the auntie who moved in and caused all the trouble.

"Don't mind me, dears," said nurse Roslyn, as she fumbled expertly below the bed and changed the catheter bag. "There you go."

Dr Rūta was notable by her absence on the ward; a young Black medic was doing the rounds instead. When he reached Mum, he flicked through her notes and asked how she was feeling.

"I want to go home," she said, and he laughed, though not unkindly.

"Take it easy," he said. "Your body's had a big shock."

His accent suggested connections to West Africa, though he might have spent time in North America as well. He checked the monitors and made some additional notes.

"Nice and stable," he said to me, before moving on.

No matter how 'stable' Mum was deemed to be, I felt her predicament was still an unfolding crisis. Lara described life as a process of constant change, and I agreed with that. No-one could stay in this kind of state indefinitely.

William's comments were my best pointer to what lay ahead. He'd seen countless people fail. A lot of his 'true blue' activists were elderly, as were his most needy constituents. Whenever he dragged me to his local constitutional club, the union flag was forever at half-mast.

I had to assume, then, that Mum was on borrowed time. I still couldn't guess who her angel might be, if she had one at all. It clearly wasn't any of her visitors so far. Old Maggie might have wheedled the name out of her; I doubted I could.

Mum turned her head towards me once more. Her eyes appeared to fix on something, if only an object in her own imagination.

"Anyway, enough of that," she snapped. "I want to talk about Constance."

At that very moment, her energy lapsed. It was as if someone had forgotten to put a shilling in the meter. Her eyes closed; within seconds she was snoring. I stood up uneasily, having sat on the plastic seat for too long. I wandered off and found my way to the link bridge, then to the little café.

I pressed the button for 'White Coffee, No Sugar' and was awarded either 'Chocomilk' or 'Hot Chocolate', I couldn't tell which. It had no flavour, as all the chocolate was stuck in a huge blob at the bottom of the cup and no amount of stirring was going to disperse it.

A lot was going through my mind. In the absence of anything more useful I could do, I now appeared to have a mission: to avail myself of a notebook and record some of my mother's reminiscences. This was despite my known failings as a scribe, with transposed letters and upside-down words.

Once again, I would be usurping a role that was naturally William's. He'd been a keen calligrapher in his youth. Like the sovereign, he still used a 'stinker' of a fountain pen to sign his name. On the other hand, I possessed more time and patience than he did.

I knew he'd be at his office in the House of Commons, catching up on who-knows-what, while the business in the chamber was powering down towards the summer recess. I sipped my barely-drinkable drink and decided to risk a quick call.

I squeaked back across the link bridge and found myself gazing into an atrium I hadn't noticed properly before. This was part of a new end section bolted onto the old building. It led out to a makeshift courtyard, where some of the staff were sitting at picnic tables, scrolling on their phones or gobbling mistimed meals. From this magisterial vantage point, unlike many parts of the hospital, there was a decent phone signal.

"What's happened?" asked William, sounding alarmed.

I gave him an update on Mum's situation and reported my discomfort at continuing to be his proxy.

"So I need your blessing, to go on being you," I concluded.

"You blazing cretin!" he cried. "I thought she'd kicked the bucket!"

"Sorry."

What am I apologising for? That she didn't die?

"Look, I'll come over," he said. "I'll be there in fifteen."

"There's no need to – "

"I can spare an hour."

"Can you bring me a notebook?" I asked quickly, pushing my luck.

"What am I, a *stationery wallah* now?" he boomed.

"Please. A5, ruled. She thinks we're writing her memoirs."

"Oh, not that old chestnut! She's been on at me for years about that. But it's hopeless – she wanders off at tangents all the time. Well, all right. I'll see what I can rustle up. You have a pen?"

"I have two."

He hung up. I knew his revised plan was to stay in London until his family was due to fly out to Florence. I also knew I was entitled to some compassionate leave, but unlike Mum's illness, it wasn't open-ended.

"You get three days, Victor," said Jim, who sounded as if he was multi-tasking, doing some washing up, with me on speakerphone. "Then Yvonne will want you back. I can do some jiggery-pokery with your annual leave to push that a bit.

Can you be back here for the next Sat mat?"

Bless him.

That sounded as reasonable an offer as I could expect in the circumstances. I wandered back towards Mum's ward.

There were plenty of questions about her life that I wanted answers to. Anything my mother said could be taken down by Sergeant De Vries and used as evidence of the person she'd once been.

Maybe I could help her to put some shape on her stories. I didn't want to listen to her yakking about tête-à-têtes with deceased prime ministers, or about the petty office politics of long ago. I wanted her thoughts to settle, so I could steer her towards more compelling topics.

For instance, I wanted to know how Dad came to be one of the subjects of her test article, *Sons of Great Men*, and how they'd fallen in love so quickly. I wanted to hear her first impressions of The Great House. Surely that must have been a real-life 'Pemberley' moment for her.

Dad's ancestral home was a handsome three-storey Georgian pile. It replaced a Jacobean hunting lodge in Pucklewood Park, an ancient swathe of territory between Bath and Bristol, in what was currently called the West of England. Slightly overpowered by its woodland setting, the house was L-shaped, with a hidden Victorian extension at the back that swallowed up half the kitchen garden.

Draughty and echoey, and sorely underpopulated, The Great House always struck me as a melancholy place. The Westminster chime of the grandfather clock on the landing sang softly to parties of upper-crust people who were long departed. Buckets were deployed in several locations whenever there was driving rain. The glory days were gone. Yet Jayne's presence must have changed the atmosphere of the house, breathing new life into its crannies. And when Dad played jazz on the baby grand piano, he always woke the place up.

William arrived and handed me a notebook, no doubt funded by the taxpayer. But that's okay, I thought: I pay my taxes. Mum did her usual thing and mixed us up again. There was a strange little incident, when William was sitting with her.

"Hold my hand, Victor, won't you?" she asked.

He looked at me, bewildered.

I whispered: "Left for rogues."

He nodded and slipped his hand into hers. For all her customary assertiveness, on some level Mum understood that she was unwell. I was touched that she thought I could provide some comfort, even if it was actually William who did the honours. A beatific smile appeared on her face, which I tried to take as a vicarious compliment.

When William was leaving, he patted me on the arm and said: "Thanks for holding the fort."

"No problem," I said, though by now I was equally keen to escape.

I took it that I had my brother's blessing to go on impersonating him, but I was still troubled by the ethics of Mum's situation. Was it acceptable for me to pump her for information about the deep past, or could that upset her and mar whatever time she had left?

I withdrew to the safety of the atrium and pulled out Dr Rūta's card. I thought it would be good to get a professional opinion, but the call did not go as planned. The doctor made a massive assumption about the purpose of my phoning, and I was too British to point out her error.

"I was not planning for dinner today, but I can make it if we go early," she said, sounding flustered. "There is a nice Thai place near the hospital. I'll meet you there in half an hour."

What? Oh well...

I shrugged inwardly. I wasn't too concerned about the fact of 'going out' with the doctor. Dinner was dinner, nothing more. At least I'd be able to quiz her on a few salient topics. I managed to locate the restaurant by asking for directions a few times. Then I sat inside, to await the arrival of the zealous Dr Rūta Priene.

CHAPTER 6

The junior doctor was in such a rush she seemed quite distracted. Her cheeks had gone red with the effort of getting to the restaurant. She wore outrageously new blue jeans, patterned leather sandals and an immaculate white blouse, with an understated little necklace. She looked all too neat in her casual gear, the way off-duty police officers do. When I rose to greet her, she kissed me on the cheek with freshly glossed lips.

"Hello, honey," she said.

"Nice to see you."

Is this the 'real you', then?

Before she even sat down, Dr Rūta studied her phone and tapped out a quick reply. I half-expected her to be paged, to have to run off and save the world. I got a strong sense of someone who never truly switched off.

It's great to have a vocation, but I've always appreciated being able to wash my face, hang up my costume and walk away, into a different life. I enjoy the peace, after all the sound and fury. I feel relieved by the release from social interaction. I value the anonymity. This is the curious flipside of wanting to be famous as a performer, in the passionate Irene Cara sense. I strive to gain recognition on stage and screen, but not in the street. Celebrity culture isn't my thing at all.

Most of the time, I haven't needed to hide away. But after my stint on *Stories Galories*, the TV series for pre-school children, I was spotted quite regularly for a while. That could be embarrassing, as the show was a triumph of low-budget aesthetics. I didn't pick up on this during filming – I just threw myself into the project with gusto. However, there are only so many times you care to be reminded of miming "the whooshy, whirling wind".

Rūta didn't know I worked in theatre. She thought I was an actual police officer. I'd forgotten all about the previous day's costume, and was perusing the menu, when she asked how long I'd been in the force. I attempted to come clean, in my own droll way, but only confused the issue.

"Since yesterday," I replied, with a goofy grin.

She laughed and clapped her hands.

"You're *funny*," she said, in the way some women have when they're determined to be impressed.

When I explained that I'd been wearing theatrical costume, she assumed I was telling a joke and laughed so much she needed a glass of water. Maybe something got lost in translation. Anyway, she soon composed herself.

"We must talk about the mother," she said; not words I'd normally associate with a date that was going well.

It turned out that William's appointment had been with Rūta's ultimate boss, the head honcho for geriatric medicine. They'd agreed that Mum should have a 'Do Not Resuscitate' order placed on her file, subject to my approval as the designated next of kin. I didn't know what to think about this – apart from how sneaky William had been to arrange it behind my back, and not even mention it to me.

"Are you happy for that, honey?" asked Rūta, looking at me searchingly.

"I don't know," I admitted, feeling quite conflicted. I suspected that, in any circumstances, Mum would prefer to be revived.

"So if she gets worse, we let her go?" I asked, avoiding the forbidden word 'die'.

Rūta reached across the table and took my hand. "Is for the best. If her body starts to fail, this can be an end-of-life event. If we put paddles on her, this is unpleasant and may not work. Think about it."

"I'd rather not."

Nil By Mouth. Do Not Resuscitate. End-of-life event.

I felt my stomach tighten and had no further interest in the menu. It was only quarter past five anyway, and we were the restaurant's first customers of the evening. Thanks to her erratic shift pattern, though, the doctor was hungry. She offered to order for both of us, and I agreed, giving a half-shrug.

Once that business was complete, the cart-horse and the guineapig regarded each other for a long moment. When you take up with someone, there's always this first unclouded view of the person with whom you've formed a tentative attachment. Only I wasn't dating Rūta, was I? Not really. I was here purely as the result of a misunderstanding. Right?

Don't get drawn in.

She tilted her head quizzically, as if trying to solve the puzzle of a tall, shy, red-haired, significantly older guy. For her part, Rūta was as I'd described her to Lara – clever, pretty and gloriously curvy. Unlike her charges, she was in blooming health. It was impossible not to be drawn towards her aura of sweetness and positivity. I gave her a tiny smile and swam in the champagne of her gorgeous eyes.

Rūta was far too young for me, of course: a few years younger than Teruko and – a more chastening thought – perhaps only a few years older than Plum. The thought of my daughter's disapproval was enough to puncture any self-indulgent notion I may have had, of enjoying a fling with this woman.

"Tell me about yourself," I said, flailing, as if this were an interview.

"I come from Riga, Latvia," she responded brightly, and I almost punched the air in triumph and shouted "yes!", for this vindication of my accent-guessing skills.

I'm such a child. (But 'Baltic States' was spot on).

She told me all about her jolly-sounding family. She spoke warmly of her two younger brothers. One had a wife and child already; the other liked motorbikes and looked after the family dog. Her father was an engineer who now taught in a technical institute. Her mother was a school teacher.

Rūta was perfectly charming, but the apparent lack of dysfunctionality in her family forced me to stifle a yawn. I asked about interests outside of work, not expecting her to have much of a hinterland.

"In my spare time, I like to draw," she said. "I make sketches of people."

"Like portraits?"

She nodded and smiled. I was impressed. This woman was an absolute knockout. I wasn't entirely taken in, though. For one term during my training, we had a great Kenyan dramaturg, Wangui, as guest lecturer. She said that inside every person we considered 'normal' or unblemished, there was always a *caveat*. This often took the form of a flaw or a weakness, a distasteful secret or a shadow of remorse. In finding our way into acting roles, she urged us to discover what that caveat was.

"When people seem too good to be true," Wangui declared, "they're hiding things beneath the surface."

To no-one's surprise, and to my amusement, she added that this was especially the case with politicians. I didn't think many people would view William as too good to be true, but despite his dated dress sense and that awful comb-over, in his pomp he could be persuasive.

"Very confident people are usually driven by fear," we were told.

I wished there had been more times in my career when I needed to analyse a role, in the way of Wangui. Many of the parts I played were disappointingly straightforward. Lengthy runs of murder mysteries, in particular, could be quite tedious. If your co-stars liked a laugh and a joke – within reasonable bounds – that made all the difference. I once had a bit part in *Aladdin* and that meant I had to double up as the front end of a camel. The whole enterprise was a hoot, but more for the backstage camaraderie than anything the public got to see.

"I don't actually live in London," I explained to my dinner companion. "I live a long way away, on an island."

As I talked, Rūta was demolishing our 'sharing dish' of chicken satay sticks. I deliberately overstated my love of island life, hoping the distance factor would put my admirer off. Not a bit of it: she expressed a strong desire to visit me, on what she called "the Isles of White", as soon as possible.

"I like the sea," she added. "Will you walk with me on the sand?"

I said I would. I described my meagre one-bedroom terrace dwelling, with its flat roof, in its little cul-de-sac in the hamlet of Crand, just outside Yarmouth. I explained that our enclave was like a 1970s reimagining of Victorian alms houses. It was, in effect, a pensioners' paradise. I thought such details might illustrate my impecunious state.

"I have only a small place too, honey," was her response.

She asked what my father did. I explained that he was now in his eighties, but he still worked part-time for his nephew, in what had once been his mother's brother's piano business in Bath.

"He works pianos?"

They did selling, hiring, moving and tuning, and dealt with electronic pianos and synthesizers, as well as uprights and grands. It was the only job he'd ever had. I told her about The Great House, and how – only in the last couple of years, when his housekeeper retired – Dad finally moved out, into the flat above the shop.

Rūta only wanted to know one thing: "Can he play piano?"

Her question made me chuckle, because Dad was a frustrated classical player who could boogie woogie with the best of them. He'd had lessons as a child, but hated their formality. He could only express himself musically when he let his hair down.

"I used to play flute," said my putative girlfriend. "But I'm not very good."

She ran through her other interests. She didn't like pubs or parties, though she'd occasionally attend a quiz night with colleagues. She liked classes, but couldn't commit to a regular time every week.

"So I do one, where the tutor lets me drop in when I can. Life drawing."

I leaned forward. "You're quite serious about art, then?"

"I like the body," she said. "One time the model was unwell – he was vomiting, actually – so I sent him home. Then everyone was there, with no-one to draw, so I suggested myself…"

"You stripped off?"

She giggled. "Just the one time. It was fun."

I didn't know how to follow that. I cast about for a suitable subject and could only think of dogs. I made the mistake of mentioning Truscott, the yapping little runt that lived next door to me in Crand. I'd foolishly offered to take him for walks, while his owner was between knee replacement operations.

I could understand people giving houseroom to sensible dogs that act as faithful companions. But I struggled to see why anyone would want a creature that yapped at the slightest provocation and skittered across linoleum like a hovercraft trying to fly. His owner called him "a Jack Russell cross", but Truscott was a mutt with his own uniquely annoying attributes.

"He looks like a bathmop."

My description got Rūta laughing again. I couldn't help but keep the entertainment going. Her laugh was beautifully melodic and unconstrained, suggesting an uncomplicated personality. In even thinking that, I knew I was straying from Wangui's path. But the dramaturg's task is to tease out conflict, and in real life I much prefer harmony.

"He weighs less than his own crap," I added. "But he still manages to pull me over."

This happened whenever Truscott felt the impulse to chase a cat or harass a larger dog. So far he'd landed me in a puddle, dumped me onto a muddy path and left me face-down in someone's colourful display of summer bedding plants. Worst of all, Truscott loved me. And now Rūta loved the sound of Truscott.

"I'd like to meet him."

Our main course arrived. We began to mix and match shrimp fried rice and a beef salad. I still didn't have much appetite, so I began by gnawing my way through some lettuce leaves, like a real guineapig. Rūta abandoned her chopsticks and laid into the food with cutlery.

I told her about being an actor, and life in the theatre. She nodded and made appreciative little "mmm" sounds as she ate. I mentioned touring – the issue that brought so much marital strife – and she soaked it up like a sponge.

She appeared to be a woman in a hurry, and this date was going rather too well. I started to panic. Casting about for a deal-breaker, I settled on the obvious one. But asking the lady's age only made things worse.

"This year is the *big* birthday," she confessed, with a beaming smile.

Er, help...

The message could not have been clearer if she'd had the phrase 'The Clock Is Ticking' tattooed on her forehead. At least she wasn't quite as young as I'd feared. And I wasn't entirely against the idea of starting a second family. It's just that I'd thought of doing so with Teruko.

Now I was falling for a different woman, which was not sensible. I tried a more direct line of attack, asking why she liked older men. Briefly, the sparkle left her eyes.

"I don't like older men," she said, gazing at me sadly. "I like *you*."

Oh heck.

Now I felt terrible for putting her on the spot like that. Having discovered a weakness, I felt stupidly protective towards Rūta. She was such a pleasant, sunny person – with or without any caveat.

I changed the subject back to my mother. Believe me, it's coming to something when that's the safe topic of conversation. I explained about the memoirs. I asked the doctor if she had any qualms about my prompting Mum to reflect on the past.

Rūta brightened and quickly reverted to her clinical persona. She said she wasn't a psychologist, but that pushing Mum for memories could unearth a traumatic episode from the past that might reduce her fighting spirit – one of the factors that was keeping her situation stable.

In other words, keeping her alive.

"Just be sensitive. The mother needs a lot of energy to concentrate, then emotional energy on top. All this effort is worth it, if she gets positive benefit from having attention and telling stories."

I told Rūta that my brother had given his blessing for me to go on indulging Mum's mistaken belief that I was William.

"Nothing is ideal in this situation," she said, turning a little gloomy. "We all try our best."

I dispatched a forkful of shrimp and rice, following this with a big gulp of water. I started to hiccup, which got her giggling again. I went on to report what Mum had said about receiving a visit from Harold Wilson. Inevitably, I had to explain who that was.

"Is very strange to us," said Rūta, gently pushing her plate away. "But must make sense to her. Like a dream. Maybe all is unreal to her. Try not to be too disappointed."

I shrugged. "I don't expect much from this. I can listen. I'm here for my mum. It seems important to do what she wants."

Rūta gave me a broad smile and held eye contact with me. She took my hand again.

"You're a good son."

Really? That's a very kind thing to say. Even if it isn't true.

I dispatched the scraps of food that were left. When the waiter returned to offer dessert or coffee, Rūta thanked him profusely, but declined. She leaned towards me and whispered: "You'll come to the apartment, won't you honey? Five minutes from here."

Of course, I nodded. She gave me a heartbreakingly wan smile and insisted on paying the bill.

CHAPTER 7

Rūta lived in a serviced block of flats owned by her employer, one street away from the hospital. Her place was so clean and tidy it barely looked occupied. It was decorated in neutral colours, like a hotel room. The tour didn't take long. She had a studio apartment with a wide view, albeit dulled by net curtains. There was a kingsize bed, kitchen bay, sitting area with coffee table and wall-mounted TV, ensuite bathroom and, curiously, a small guest room with single bed, desk and chair. In here was the nearest thing to any kind of mess: there were two neat stacks of medical books on the desk, with folders in between.

"Are you still studying?" I asked, surprised.

"We always study," she said, with a trilling little laugh.

She reached under the single bed and pulled out a large portfolio bag.

"Here. Have a look at my masterpieces."

The doctor set about making some filter coffee. I turned over sheet after sheet of her artworks, many in pen and ink, others in watercolour, a few in charcoal. The studies were a proper mishmash, on all sizes of paper. Some were strongly anatomical, emphasising bones and muscles, others were more fluid and ethereal.

"These are great," I said, noticing there were more male than female figures.

Why am I feeling jealous?

"You don't seem to have a particular style."

"That's right," she said, gaily. "I have my different moods."

"So what are these?"

I'd picked out a number of portraits on A4 paper, capturing some very expressive faces of older people. I found them fascinating.

"Sometimes I sketch the patient. If they give the permission. I don't often have time, but it's nice to do. If they like them, I keep a copy and give the original."

Fleetingly, I thought of asking her to sketch my mother. Then I realised I didn't want to remember her how she was now, laid up in hospital and in decline. I wanted to remember her as she had been: strong, self-willed, not giving a damn what other people might think. I pictured her in the garden, carrying her trug, having harvested gooseberries to make jam.

Rūta handed me a mug of coffee. We sipped in dubious silence for a moment. She sat close to me on the couch, her hand resting gently on my thigh. This felt quite different from our interaction in the Room of Doom. If I wasn't mistaken, she was hoping for some romance to ensue.

I wasn't sure if I wanted to get too involved straight away, so I initiated a fresh conversation, about the international situation. I told her about William's work on the select committee, helping Ukrainian refugees.

"The brother is a good man," she said, showing some puzzlement.

"But it's not going well," I added. "Innocent people are still being killed."

"It's very bad," she agreed.

The ongoing conflict nagged away at me. Although I'd describe myself as a political progressive, I was finding it hard to believe in the progress of humanity generally, when innocent people were being slaughtered.

"I know," she said. "We had some injured ones at the hospital."

This long struggle was the same as the pandemic: everyone had grown weary of it and wanted to move on. The blue and yellow flags were disappearing. That's why I was proud of William; he could be tenacious when he believed in a cause.

"We are good people and we can do some things," concluded Rūta, in a flat voice.

I turned to the coverage of events, and how people were switching off from reputable reporting, seeking comfort in 'alternative facts'.

"Why do you care about the media?" she asked, rather losing patience.

It was a good question. Mum's influence meant I'd always felt I had a special stake in journalism. From the age of twelve, I forced myself to read as much of her newspaper in the school library as I could manage, between eating lunch and the start of afternoon lessons. I read very slowly, using the magnifying glass I kept in my pocket. It was very hard at first, as I had little knowledge of the social and political context of the news.

People assume that being a poor reader means you can't grasp ideas. But I started to see patterns forming. I discovered that I could anticipate the sorts of things certain politicians might say. I was learning what belonged to left, right and centre.

Mum shared aspects of her work with me occasionally. I knew that she hunted for facts, and weighed them assiduously, before presenting her analyses to the public. She was old-school. She felt a strong sense of duty, and believed the Press bore a heavy responsibility in the service of others. Not a fan of social media, she talked about "separating the wheat of truth from the chaff of chatter".

By this point, Rūta had had enough.

"Do you want some music?" she snapped. "What do you like?"

"Oh – anything is fine…"

She put on some Taylor Swift. She released her hair from its strict ponytail and shook it out. Then she glanced at me, as if I should know what to do next.

I bought a few seconds by imbibing lukewarm coffee. She looked distraught and sat down again. She gazed at her hands, which had fallen loosely onto her lap, one slightly holding the other. Then she turned to me again, with an expression that I read as unbearable sadness and reproach.

I knew I had to decide fast: walk out of there, or get on with it. I'd had breakup sex and makeup sex, and neither was a great idea. I'd never had sex with someone out of sympathy before. At least, that's what I assumed this feeling was. Belatedly, we leaned towards each other and started kissing. It was rather pleasant and slightly horrible at the same time. Rūta stood up and undid the first button of her blouse.

"Do you want to help me with it?"

My hesitation was just long enough to prompt a sharp look of dismay. I popped the next button so inexpertly that she didn't wait for me to do any more. We just began to disrobe, in an atmosphere of guilt and dread.

Then, suddenly, she was laughing her head off again, and pointing at my groin. There can't be many scenarios more disconcerting to the fragile male ego than that.

"So *funny*!" she gasped. "You have flag pants!"

Of course – I'd forgotten I was wearing the costume undies. They might have been an unlikely choice of apparel for sexual seduction, but in the most unexpected manner, the stars and stripes seemed to break the ice between us.

I finally took the warm and lovely Rūta in my arms and gave her a proper kiss. I would accept her approach. There was no going back now, and I felt glad, as well as apprehensive.

What can I tell you about this encounter? Not too much, I'm afraid. It's good to be frank about love-making, but we all have our boundaries. I don't mind admitting that I found Rūta enchanting. She was highly tactile. She was also more adventurous than me, but in a resolutely matter-of-fact way that helped me pretend I was taking it all in my stride.

Growing up, my family had a range of attitudes about relationships. William was furtive; Granny was censorious, equating desire with shame, while Dad seemed to know less about the facts of life than I did. Mum was more forthcoming, and surprisingly laissez-faire, though she made it plain that she discussed 'sexual matters' under sufferance.

Whether in sex or politics, in a vague way, she wanted people to be happy. She could be emotionally generous towards people she didn't know. She imagined a future in which many more of them felt fulfilled. She was very Jeremy Bentham in that respect. William condemned her, not without affection, as a hopeless idealist and a socialist.

That was hardly much of an accusation, considering that she stood in the 1983 general election as a Labour candidate. Those were among the most fraught and unsettling times of my childhood. I was pushed and dragged through innumerable front gardens during the campaign. Mum lost heavily, her stance of professional impartiality blown forever. The whole misadventure did her a lot of damage. She plunged into a self-destructive phase, in which she drank too much and over-relied on a succession of nannies. Though I was young, I remember it vividly.

In the same year, William went up to Cambridge. Mum compensated for this great loss by inviting an unsuitable man-friend to come and live with us for several years, along with his intolerably cutesy daughter, Daisy.

Suddenly, I had an unwanted little step-sister. My only foothold in the family had been as the baby, and even that was being taken away from me. I was horrible to Daisy; she now lives in Belgium. I don't think those two facts are unconnected.

So sorry, Daisy.

Ensconced in Rūta's bed, I thought I could hear the distant chimes of Big Ben, though I couldn't reckon the hour. It turned out to be ten o'clock. We'd whiled away the time in a dreamy zone of our own, another part of the forest entirely.

Now Rūta was stirring, softly reawakening from a little slumber, and we had a lazy cuddle as if we'd been lovers for years. Then she slipped out of bed and started pottering about, slowly gearing up for her nightshift.

"Do you want to stay over, honey?"

Her words punctured the delicate air, and the ambiance turned into an ambulance. I groaned and stretched, my feet appearing beyond the duvet.

"I'd better not stay," I said. "I still haven't seen Plum yet."

Rūta nodded. "Then you must try. She is a good girl. She cares about the grandmother."

While my new girlfriend was in the shower, I sprang out of bed and threw my clothes back on. We parted with a lingering embrace in her doorway. I skipped down the stairwell, feeling loved-up, gladly liberated from all the bleaker aspects of the day.

When I got back to Plum's place, as soon as I clicked the front door behind me, I saw Lara's arm raised in welcome, beyond the high back of the unsightly sofa.

"What kept you so long, you dirty stop-out? Did you get lucky?"

When I neither laughed nor offered a fervent denial, but simply wandered over to the kitchen area, the TV was muted and Lara's head appeared above the parapet.

"Oh my days – you *did* get lucky! With the doctor?"

"I didn't say anything of the kind," I protested, without much conviction, as I leaned against the worktop, swigging apple juice.

"I notice you weren't asked to stay the night. She kicked you out after."

"I had the option of staying," I snapped, taking the bait. "Anyway, whatever you do – don't tell Plum."

As soon as I came out with this, I knew it was precisely the wrong thing to say. There was the slightest of pauses – just long enough for me to experience a sinking feeling, as if I were in a lift that was plunging twenty floors.

"It's a bit late for that, Dad."

Plum's head rose slowly above the back of the sofa. Not surprisingly, she seemed rather peeved. I must have looked aghast, though, because she told me to relax.

"You're a free agent, papa. Go ahead and sow your wild oats with some random doctor if you want to."

Ow! I hate that expression, 'wild oats'.

"You have licence to cavort with whoever you choose."

"And so do you, darling," I said, without thinking.

The phrasing, about cavorting, was a family joke. It derived from a notorious exchange between Mum and William, when he sheepishly asked to bring his first girlfriend home.

Uh-oh.

I watched a shadow of medieval wrath pass across my daughter's face.

"Just *what* did you mean by *that*?"

"What – nothing... I..."

She stomped across the floor, into her room, and slammed the door. There was silence for a moment.

"Wow," said Lara, in a hushed tone. "I've never seen her be so touchy. She must love you a lot."

"*Random doctor*? Did she really say that?"

"I know. I'm sorry. I'm a bit crap at keeping secrets."

"I may have noticed that," I admitted. "But don't worry. I won't tell anyone. My lips are sealed."

Lara gave me an impish smile.

"Touché. I think that's how you said it? Touché."

CHAPTER 8

The next day, I think it was Tuesday or Wednesday, I had an extra snooze after Plum and Lara went to work. Then I rummaged in my costume bag and found a T-shirt, along with a pair of silky boxers to wear under my blue suit trousers. The T-shirt read: 'I'm the big (picture of cheese wedge)'.

Oh well.

Beggars can't be choosers, as Mum might have said. By the time I arrived at her ward, Rūta had already gone off-duty and made the weary trek back to her flat for a few hours of decent kip. We exchanged brief texts that carried the electric charge of a new emotional connection. Mum was fully propped up. Her unseeing eyes were wide open. She looked ready to conquer the world. I had my pen at the ready and reminded her that she wanted to tell me something about Constance.

"Constance? Yes, well…"

Yes, well what?

"D'you know Wilson was here again? He sat right there. Told me how impressed he was by my strength. No, that wasn't it… *fortitude*. That's what he said. My fortitude. Wasn't that nice? And I said: Harold, don't worry so much about the pound. We let it float freely these days, and the sky hasn't fallen in yet."

She chuckled at her non-joke and I sighed, but had little choice but to play along.

"And what did he say to that?"

"Well, he spoke about carefully weighing options, and taking everything into consideration before making a decision. The sort of thing he used to tell LBJ to keep our boys out of Vietnam."

I leaned forward and gave Mum's hand a gentle squeeze. I reminded her that we were supposed to be engaging in the serious business of compiling her memoirs. She turned her head towards me. She seemed keen to focus, but quite unable to do so. I started writing anyway, jotting down what I knew of her childhood and speaking the words as I wrote them.

"How does that sound?" I asked.

"All right, I suppose."

She was grumpy because I'd curtailed her freestyle reverie in favour of something more structured. But she permitted me to continue. When I got something wrong, or she wanted to add some detail, she lifted her arm to get me to pause. She told me things I'd heard a hundred times, but I knew I'd have to be patient with the patient. Despite all the difficulties, we were easing into a kind of working rhythm.

What I can tell you is this. Mum was born Estelle Grace Thornley, on 13 January 1945, in a small town her grandmother said was "not too far from Preston, nor too close to Blackpool". Both parents worked at Lockley's, the local factory, assembling mechanical cash registers and adding machines, under licence to an American company.

Two weeks after watching her mother's earthly remains being lowered into the ground, Essie took and failed her 'eleven plus' – a disaster that gave her a lifelong fear of exams. The result meant she attended the local secondary modern, instead of the grammar school. She recalled how this made her feel, seeing some of her former classmates at the bus stop in their smart uniforms, with satchels full of books.

"I was treated like a failure, but I knew I wasn't one. I was absolutely determined to be a success, whatever I did in life."

I'd heard variations of this declaration since I was very young. I've no doubt it's affected my own attitude to adversity. Mum made an outstanding underdog. She was starting to take charge of her story, placing a strong emphasis on certain facts, but there were few surprises for me as yet. I knew she felt the loss of her mother very keenly, so I asked what she was like.

"She was a practical woman, William. I think she was. Knew how to make a skirt from old curtains. Dad was hopeless. Couldn't cook, clean, or do the laundry."

Her Auntie Mary, Alec's wife, started coming round a lot, supposedly to look after Essie, but actually paying more attention to her father. Once it became clear that her aunt and her dad had fallen in love, Uncle Alec created numerous unedifying scenes.

"He had a punch-up with my dad in the street," she said. "It was terrible."

More than once, the police were called. In the midst of all this turmoil, Mary moved in.

"We were living in a house under moral siege, William. It wasn't fair. We had our windows smashed and nasty things pushed through the letterbox. I had to find somewhere else to be."

Essie's cousins and their friends, whom she'd previously got along with quite well, now shunned her. Surrounded by so much conflict, she eventually found sanctuary at the local library.

"I spent hours there and they were kind to me. They knew exactly what I was going through."

In return, she helped out by shelving returned books. When she got bored, she would sit in a corner and lose herself in a story. She acquired a taste for tales about posh girls at boarding school, and those who owned ponies. This was, of course, a typical tale from that age of social climbing. But the troubled Essie wasn't thinking in such terms yet. She simply felt the need to escape.

"I enveloped my mind in the fog of fiction," said Mum, who rarely bothered with novels as an adult, preferring to read factual books for pleasure.

We hadn't got very far into her life story, but reflecting on an unhappy episode was taking its toll, as Rūta suggested might happen. Mum was becoming tired and tetchy, complaining once more that she was being detained in hospital against her will. She wanted "Sergeant Victor" to straighten things out with the authorities, get her discharged, and drive her home to Hampstead.

"I need to water the plants," she said. "And I want to walk on the heath."

I hadn't the heart to quash such perfectly reasonable wishes, so I side-stepped the situation by suggesting we take a break. I slunk off to my little café. I pressed the button for 'White Coffee No Sugar' and received white coffee *with* sugar – or more accurately, with sweetener. It was a pretty dodgy brew, with a deep layer of froth on top, but a big improvement on the so-called chicken soup and hot chocolate.

I sat down and allowed the intrusion of maudlin thoughts. In Mum's unhappy childhood, I was glimpsing some possible seeds of my own, and even – though it really hurt to acknowledge this – of Plum's. While I was sipping my too-hot drink, I took a call from William. As ever, there was no greeting.

"What have you done about letting the paper know Mother's ill?"

From the echoing footsteps and voices in the background, it sounded as if he were walking briskly down the hollow aisle of a cathedral. It was more likely, of course, that he was sweeping through the lobby of the House of Commons. I confessed I'd done nothing whatever regarding the paper. I assumed Marjorie Buttle-Deary would have informed them.

"But you idiot – she's only Mother's *book* agent! She has nothing to do with the *column*."

Love you too.

"What should I do, then? Ring the newsdesk?"

"Do that and they'll run a story on her. No – best call the features editor personally. I'd do it myself, but I'm stuck for time."

Of course you are. You're 'important'.

I promised to make the call and my erse of a brother rang off without saying goodbye. As the delegated task was something I didn't want to do, my only hope was to search for the number and call it right away. I took the same approach at the theatre, whenever Jim mentioned some unpleasant task Yvonne wanted me to perform. I scurried across the link bridge to the corridor overlooking the atrium.

"Putting you through…"

The features editor was nowhere to be found, but surprisingly, my call was diverted to the editor-in-chief instead. He sounded friendly enough, and sorry to hear about Mum, though there was a sense of lurking menace beneath his tone of voice. Even a great white shark can be on its best behaviour, before demonstrating that you need a bigger boat.

Look out…

He and Mum were old friends and rivals, he said, adding that she was five years his senior. They'd been "newsroom hacks" together in the 1970s. He started to spout accolades, the way Marjorie Buttle-Deary had done, which I found hard to take. I knew Mum had been something of a trailblazer in her time, but now there were hordes of women journalists working at the highest levels, which was only how it should be.

"She could analyse a hamper of bat droppings and make it sound interesting," said the Ed.

There was a momentary pause and I jumped in, asking this veteran Westminster watcher for his opinion of Harold Wilson. He sounded surprised, but I could hear a sharky smile forming.

"Ah, Harold! He was quite a gift to us. Fascinating, formidable. We all had a huge ding-dong about his resignation, as your mother might have told you?"

"Actually, no, I haven't heard that."

"Really? Well, the announcement caught all of us on the hop. Seventy-six. March or April, I think it was. Some wanted to run with it being an establishment stitch-up; others took Wilson at his word – he was getting on a bit and he was tired out. Huh…"

Someone must have entered the emeritus editor's office, because he was now engaged in a wholly different conversation that I couldn't quite make out. Then he just resumed his story, without acknowledging the interruption.

"Your mother thought there was more to it, a different angle. And she was right, to an extent. She went tanking off to the Scilly Isles, didn't she? Took the family as camouflage. D'you remember? Well, it was the Wilsons' sanctuary, wasn't it? Just put it there."

It sounded as if someone had brought him some post, or a cup of coffee. Again, quite unruffled, he continued to tell his tale.

"She picked up the local gossip. Memory issues; his mother's decline. She did well. Those people were so protective of the family. Anyway, with hindsight, perhaps we were wrong to sideline Jayne as we did."

He seemed to drift away, into his recollections of the bitter in-fighting around the conference table.

"She got her own back, though…"

"Oh?"

The smile was long-gone by this point.

"Well, she left us, didn't she? Ran her story in a rival rag."

Even after all this time, I could hear the anger in his voice.

"But she came back to you. As a columnist."

"She did. Thirty years later! Or was it twenty-nine?"

He exhaled loudly and hit a more reflective tone.

"This is a great pity, you know. I've reached that time of life when news like this doesn't shock any more, it's par for the course. You don't think she'll recover enough to write for us again?"

I tensed, my lungs filling right up, as I considered how to reply.

"No, she'll not be coming back," I confirmed, deflating and thinking it best to be clear. "I'm sorry if that leaves you with a headache."

He laughed, rather cynically.

"Oh, don't worry about *us*," he said. "We can always *fill space*."

The way he said it was shockingly final and dismissive.

"She's loved writing for you," I ventured.

My assertion wasn't a known fact, but Mum had met her deadline every single week without fail, since the mid-2000s. Before she went on holiday, she would 'bank' a couple of columns, to avoid anyone having to stand in for her.

"And we've loved having her," he snapped back, with all the feeling of a chat-bot. After speaking so warmly only minutes before, he put the phone down on me.

With those last words ringing in my head, I walked down three flights of stairs and out through the big door, into the courtyard. I needed to breathe, to take a few minutes away from Mum and her story. I'd been caught unawares: I hadn't expected to feel upset about events three years before I was born. She may have discovered one of the reasons for Wilson's resignation, yet they "sidelined" her. That was so unfair!

She took the family as camouflage. Really?

I sat alone at a picnic table, stewing over what I'd learned and becoming aware of the oppressive greenery around me. Everywhere there were large plants in pots, with ivy on the boundary wall. What looked like a pleasant sanctuary from a distance was actually a humid glasshouse.

I returned to the ward, where I found Mum as irascible as ever. She resisted any notion of picking up where we'd left off, plunging me instead into some recollections of a family in the Yorkshire Dales. They lived on a farm and produced gift boxes of fudge and toffee. My notes were becoming an absolute mess.

"When we reached the top, the wind nearly blew our heads off."

This was a saga of walks up and down hills, and family meals around a big kitchen table. Mum made much of the way everyone supported the common cause; father and son running the farm, while mother and daughter operated the sweet factory.

Then she added: "That's where I got the idea of writing an extra piece."

Oh my...

I stopped scribbling for a moment. "Is this about *Sons of Great Men*?"

"Of course it is, William – try to keep up! I clipped the extra essay to my official assignment and called it *Daughter of a Great Woman*. And boy, did they take issue with that! Well, actually – the features editor liked the article so much he spoke up for me, but the editor thought it a great impertinence of me to write it in the first place."

She smiled broadly at the remembrance. This was it: how she'd gained her career in the first place. A lowly copytaker aspiring to become a reporter, she argued back to the boss, insisting that she had, in fact, done what she was told.

"I did everything you asked, sir," said Estelle. "I just exceeded the brief."

Notwithstanding this, were it not for the features editor's intervention, she would have been sent back downstairs forever, under a hail of disapprobation.

"The main piece is acceptable, but this is outstanding," he decreed, holding aloft the paean to maternal greatness. "It has spirit."

Apparently, that was high praise of a young woman in the early 1960s. Accepting his trusted colleague's advice, but not enjoying losing the argument, the editor switched his attack. He launched into a tirade about putting the same amount of effort into every piece of work, which the tearful Estelle promised to do, if only she could be given a chance…

I love this story.

Through gritted teeth, it was agreed that she would join the editorial department. To begin with, she would sit at the right hand of Dolly, and help with the women's page. The editor tried to send Estelle away with a dismissive flick of the wrist, but she wasn't done yet.

"I have some news of my own, sir."

In a final flourish, she revealed that she was about to marry Jeremy De Vries, one of the sons she'd profiled. As well as taking his surname, she would be adopting the first name Jane.

She explained to me that her nickname among the Friday

night crew in the pub was 'Plain Jane', which got shortened to Jane, and she rather liked it. The features editor raised his eyebrows. It might be half an age before this spirited girl would achieve her first byline, but he was nothing if not a detail man.

"How are you spelling that?" he asked. "With a 'y' or without?"

"With a 'y'," said Estelle, making a fanciful, spur-of-the-moment decision.

Thus was born the future women's page assistant, agony aunt and horoscope writer, junior reporter, senior reporter, health correspondent, political reporter, assistant investigations editor, features editor, political editor and leader writer; author, occasional broadcaster and star columnist Jayne De Vries.

Having concluded her tale of triumph, Mum was thoroughly wiped out. She fell asleep with her mouth open, and I was relieved. I'd had enough, for one day, of attempting to compile her memoirs. And I was feeling like a fraud. Her mistaking me for William was like occupying a front row seat at a show I only had balcony tickets for.

I checked my watch. It was edging towards the time I'd arranged to meet Guy, Lara and Plum's thirty-three-year-old acquaintance. After my unfortunate impasse with Plum, I'd asked Lara what I might do to make it up to her, and this was deemed to be my best route to redemption.

I walked briskly along the white tiles of the hospital's long corridors. I followed the only route I could remember, from Mum's ward to the little café, and from there to the main entrance.

I noticed how walking faster, with a sharper sense of mission, made me feel as if I belonged to the hospital. I was in step with the staff – though I wasn't sure that was altogether desirable. The clinical whiteness of the place seemed to be swallowing me up. I was glad to get out.

CHAPTER 9

My cab pulled in at the appointed location: Vimal and Ferhan's indoor market on the King's Road. I'd been to Chelsea before and it was within the bounds of my realm of knowledge, but not somewhere I'd spent a lot of time. The market was a dank, labyrinthine emporium on three levels, with stalls selling art, crafts, vintage clothes, knick-knacks, vinyl records and musty second-hand books well past their prime.

There were more stallholders than customers, and they all looked sad. Some stalls were cluttered with junk but unattended, the proprietors pinning a note of their phone number to the wall, in case anyone should be eccentric enough to want to buy something. A few had abandoned their pitches altogether, leaving only the odd bare cabinet, table and chair.

I nodded hello to a white-haired man with an equally white handlebar moustache, who was presiding over a rail of moth-eaten military uniforms. I asked for Guy and was met with a blank look, so I went in search of him, equipped only with Lara's description of his stall as "bric-a-brac and general shite".

I was touring the whole place for a second time when I noticed an agitated man in a buff raincoat, with long and wavy brown hair. Could he be aged thirty-three? I wasn't sure. He was fully absorbed in a phone call and didn't notice my approach.

"Look, mate – I'll bring it back when you pay me. You owe me two weeks."

The sign behind him proclaimed 'Roddy's Bits'n'Bobs' and gave the number to call when the stall was unattended. Its white wooden shelves and glass cabinet appeared to be populated with house clearance tat.

A cardboard sign read: 'Netsookies £8 each or 3 for £20'. It was tricky to determine the provenance of these items. They were supposedly Japanese treasures, but could have been crude knock-offs manufactured anywhere.

Still, the hunched little figures made me think of Japan, and therefore of Teruko, and for that reason alone I fished in my pocket for some cash. I pointed to a tiny carved tiger. The assistant, continuing his dispute, unlocked the cabinet to retrieve it.

"Ten quid mate," he said, interrupting his call in such a slovenly manner that it almost made me reconsider the entire transaction.

"The sign says eight," I pointed out.

"Oh, does it? This one's ten."

Unwilling to argue further, I parted with the money and watched the spiv slip my banknote straight into his trouser pocket.

"Was there summink else?" he asked, a note of irritation in his voice.

"Well, do you know someone here called Guy? We were going to meet up, but I haven't – "

"Oh – you're *Victor*! Why didn't you say? I wondered when you were gonna show."

He turned his attention back to the phone call. "Look, it's busy now. I'll call you later."

The reputed thirtysomething Guy locked the display case. At least, I presumed it was he, and not Dr Livingstone, as no proper introduction was made. Instead, he inelegantly heaved himself onto the counter, swivelled his legs over it and dropped down on my side.

"C'mon, let's get outta this hole."

"What about the stall?"

"Oh, that's nothing. I just mind it for someone."

Presumably for the retail legend that is Roddy.

Guy breezed down the stairs, his unnecessary coat riding up like a superhero's cape. Once outside, he donned a pair of reflective sunglasses, making himself look like an estate agent trying to be a gangster.

"I thought we could view a property together," he said, with a wary look over his shoulder. He took a puff of vape and enveloped me in a fog of strawberry exhale. I can't stand smoking or vaping, so it seemed that our induced acquaintanceship was doomed from the start.

"I want to broaden my portfolio," he went on. "Or at least, my list of possibles. I want to get into doing up flats and flogging them. There's big money in that, you know."

My heart sank. "Sure," I said, wishing I could teleport to ten minutes earlier in my life and escape.

Then he added, somewhat more relatably: "I can't be a supply teacher forever, Victor. I just can't."

At this point, I'm stopping recording Guy's way of speaking in too much detail. I'm sure you get the gist. His voice suggested white working class, from north-east London. I've already been smoothing over Rūta's delivery a little. You only need a hint of her accent to hear it.

Our temporary dramaturg Wangui impressed upon us that accent is a background element, you see, and not a driver of character – unless you're dealing in stereotypes. There's a big difference between childish imitation, which can soon lead to mockery, and an attempt to embrace a voice.

The front-runners on Guy's list of possible property purchases were located at Laburnum Grove and Flowerday Avenue. He'd secured an appointment to view one of these, south of the river.

As it was tea-time, we grabbed something to eat at a café in Charing Cross, which made me regret parting with my tenner. Any day now, I anticipated receiving a snotty message from my bank algorithm. I felt for the tiger netsuke in my pocket and grasped it. Though unyielding, it worked like a stress ball.

"Let's go," said Guy.

On the train, I was treated to his charmingly trite solutions to the problems of the world. He was about as visionary as a fortune-teller using tea bags. It emerged that he spent part of his free time writing poems and rap songs. I was obliged to listen to a song on his phone. To be fair, it wasn't bad. It was quite brash and cheeky, like the man himself. Thankfully, in the middle of a protest poem, I took a call from Rūta.

"Hi honey, where are you?"

I tried to explain my current, ineluctably strange, mission. She sounded mystified. "Who is this person?"

I looked up at Guy and fake-smiled. "The friend of a friend."

Rūta sounded disappointed that I wasn't spending time with her. I tried to get the idea across that this was just something I had to do, for Plum's sake. That was nigh impossible to express, with Guy sitting across from me.

"Okay, honey," she said, in a weary voice that told me it wasn't really okay.

Guy looked crestfallen, on learning that I'd already found a girlfriend.

"I hoped we'd go clubbing and pull a couple of nice girls," he revealed.

Clubbing! Perish the thought.

Then his own phone bleeped and the message left him looking even more despondent. "Got to work tomorrow. *Dammit*. They're ruthless, Victor. If you turn jobs down, they take you off the list."

This was the supply job. We found some common ground then, trading stories of our least favourite day-jobs. He mentioned stints as a lorry driver, charity fundraiser and call centre operative. Then he described the joys of containing roomfuls of antsy teenagers.

"I used to try and reason with them," he said. "Now I buy them off with cheap chocolate."

As well as property development, Guy espoused other potential get-rich-quick schemes, such as bulk buying mushrooms and selling them at various outdoor markets, as he'd heard they had an amazing profit margin.

"Is it much further?" I asked, noticing that we'd already trundled into the county of Kent.

"The one after Sidcup."

When we arrived at the desired suburb, we set off in search of the property. We walked for a while, along drab quiet streets with permit parking and the occasional tree. I took and uploaded a picture of the suburban scene and got two likes, which slightly bothered me. Had my third follower jumped ship? Perhaps they were indisposed in some way.

Guy kept muttering as he looked for Laburnum Grove on the map on his phone. I got a growing sense that all was not well. At last he stopped, swore a great deal, and explained our situation.

"I've got them two properties mixed up, Victor! Our appointment was for Laburnum Grove, but I've brought you to Flowerday Avenue."

I didn't grasp the scale of this catastrophe immediately. I

suggested we correct our location by hopping back on a train, thinking the journey might be only a few stops.

"But Laburnum Grove's in Chipping Barnet," he said, lowering his voice to signal fake patience. "That's twenty miles away."

Guy sat on someone's garden wall, head in hands, groaning softly and rocking back and forth. I looked up as an ageing gentleman with long grey hair came out of the house and glided down the front steps. He was wearing a cravat and holding a glass of white wine. He reminded me of a director I'd worked with.

"Can we help you?" he asked, almost sarcastically. He clearly believed that Guy's posterior resting on his wall was a territorial infringement that could not be tolerated.

"Hello, Noel," I said, having concluded this was indeed the director I knew. I recognised his voice instantly. "We're slightly lost. We're trying to view a flat in the area."

Having come all this way, I thought we might as well take a look at Guy's second-best prospective property.

"Do I know you?" asked Noel, peering at me and scowling.

"It's been a while," I said. "Victor De Vries."

I should have known that would elicit not one flicker of recognition. He was terrible with names, unless they were in a script.

"Buttons in *Cinderella*. Widow Twankey. And the camel in *Aladdin*."

Noel pursed his lips. "Front or rear?"

"Front."

"Hmm, I don't know. Who played the rear?"

"I think it was Rickie-Lee Stott…"

"Ah!" An almost pleasant look played momentarily across his lived-in face.

"So what are you up to now?" he asked, having already forgotten my name.

"I'm at the King Edward in Newport," I said, somewhat ambiguously, hoping he'd get the impression I was still acting.

"Oh really? I was at the New in Cardiff last year."

"Not *that* Newport," I said, hurriedly. "Newport, Isle of Wight."

He stared off, into the distance, in an effort to remember.

"Is that the one up an alley?"

I nodded. "That's the one."

"Mmm, nice. We did that octopus thing there. Very wet."

Noel straightened up and turned his attentions to Guy.

"So, who's this rather swish young man sitting on my wall?"

It seemed that Guy had an admirer at last, though not perhaps of the age, gender or sexual orientation he might have preferred.

"He's a property developer," I lied. "We've come to see an apartment at Flowerday Avenue."

The front door opened again. Noel's partner, Derek, appeared. He was wearing a tummy-hugging beige cardigan, expandable green slacks and a puzzled look. The ancient scriptwriter gingerly picked his way towards us, also with wineglass in hand.

I knew Derek was substantially older than Noel, if such a thing were possible. He made infrequent appearances during rehearsals, though his name was invoked with some regularity. My favourite among Noel's many forehead-clutching outbursts at the end of a poorly rendered scene was: "Oh God! Derek would be spinning in his grave! – if he wasn't still alive."

Now, here was the revered man of letters himself. He was an outstanding Shakespearean actor and scholar in his day, before he directed West End musicals and began a gradual career decline that took in regional rep and TV drama, before bottoming out at pantomime. He was glaring at me.

"I know you," he said, accusingly. "Weren't you in that advert for some bally cleaning product?"

I smiled reluctantly. This was seventeen years earlier, and it was an ad for sink unblocker; not my proudest moment.

"I was also Buttons in your *Cinderella*. Widow Twankey..."

"And half the camel in *Aladdin*," added Noel.

Derek pursed his lips. "Front or rear?"

"Front," I said. I couldn't bear to wait for the follow-up question, so I added: "Rickie-Lee Stott played the rear."

Derek gave the ghost of a smile, as if this name were the missing link in the anthropological record that distinguished ape from Man, or Man from camel.

We agreed to swap contact details.

"Yours or mine?"

It seemed that Derek carried both of their mobile phones in his cardigan pockets, so they wouldn't get lost; an insight into their domestic life I found rather endearing.

"Oh, yours, definitely," said Noel. "I'll never remember which one he is."

I asked Derek to list me under "V for Victor". He chuckled absently as he poked my details in with his index finger, murmuring the words "Dig for Victory". Noel gave Guy directions to Flowerday Avenue, describing it as "a pot-heads' paradise". Then we said our goodbyes.

In fewer than ten minutes, we were standing outside the right wrong house. A much-freckled student answered the door. He was so jaded by showing people round that he was entirely unperturbed by our lack of an appointment. In the estate agent's absence, he wandered around with us, pointing out all the defects that normally went unremarked.

"The boiler's clapped out," he said. "The shower's knackered."

Then came the clincher: "The dryer's the wrong type and it

doesn't have a vent tube, so the steam goes all over the walls."

Guy nodded studiously as we were shown the resulting mould, growing inside the kitchen cupboards. The whole flat had a musty smell, like putrefying onions, the compound effect of all that condensation. On top of that, the bathroom suite was pink, with some tiles missing. The lounge carpet looked like someone had vomited the 1970s onto it. This flat was a disaster zone.

When we got outside, though, it was as if Guy had viewed a different dwelling entirely. He enthused about its potential and its relative cheapness. I pointed out how much a new kitchen, bathroom and boiler would cost, and described how the kitchen would have to be thoroughly dehumidified before any other work could start. He seemed to take this news hard, as if he'd never focused on the costs and hassle involved in renovating properties, only the potential profits. He puffed out his cheeks and exhaled slowly, removing his sunglasses.

"You see, Victor? It was worth doing the field trip. We've learned a lot there."

I couldn't resist asking: "You think so? What have we learned?"

"Well, for one thing, Flowerday Avenue can come off my list."

What a great lesson for humankind.

We travelled back in a sombre mood, our evening more-or-less in ruins. Guy dropped his previous bravado, which made him a lot more likeable. We got to talking about my reason for being in town. He seemed quite moved by my description of Mum, being attached to all the wires and unable to swallow.

"You know, Victor, if I could bring my old duck back, for one extra day, I would," he said, gazing across the roofs of buildings as the train coasted through the city sprawl. "I'd give anything for that."

We went our separate ways at Leicester Square. Guy called after me, suggesting we get together again soon. He gestured for me to phone him. I smiled and gave him a thumbs-up, mostly out of allegiance to Plum.

I wandered about a bit, but couldn't avoid feeling drawn to the hospital. I meandered there and looked in on Mum. There was no change in her condition; she burbled about Harold Wilson again, then fell asleep. As I sat at her bedside, I watched a few clips from his speeches on my phone, including the one at Downing Street in February 1974, when he's wrested power back from Edward Heath, and he declares: "We've got a job to do".

Rūta was back on duty, so we snatched a hasty conversation. I made her laugh with my description of the bizarre adventure Guy took me on. When Mum fell asleep again, I made my getaway. I bought some prosecco to share with Lara. It occurred to me that I no longer had to ask for directions to the correct stop for the bus to Plum's flat. During the journey, I noticed that my photo of a Kent suburb had received its third like.

CHAPTER 10

As I expected, Plum was at work, or in the arms of her lover, or both. Lara greeted the prosecco with demonic enthusiasm. We quaffed the stuff as she set about me with the mooted makeover.

"I don't see you as a clean girl," she told me, peering at my features. "We need to go glam."

She spread her entire collection of makeup and application tools across the breakfast bar and we sat knee-to-knee on the stools. A strategically repositioned lamp illuminated my face. Lara asked if there was anything I didn't want.

"Well, mostly, I don't want to end up looking like a pantomime dame."

Otherwise, meh.

She nodded. "Anything else?"

"Don't shave my eyebrows off. And you will put moisturiser on first, right?"

She stopped and blinked in disbelief. "Do you think I'm a monster? C'mon, let's do this."

For the first few minutes, I just sat there and took it, brain in neutral. There was no talking now, as Lara was concentrating hard. She slipped off her stool at key moments and bent over me to get the details just right. Then, at last, I broke the silence.

"You're reminding me how great it is to have this done for you, instead of having to slap it on yourself."

She straightened up and smiled. "I know, right?"

More silence. I mused about how slowly the hours were passing, and yet the days were rushing by. So much had happened, and so little. I'd spent some of the bus journey magnifying my notes and trying to decipher them. I was realising something striking about the process of recording a life story: it's very difficult to put events in chronological order. Our memories are distorted by emotion.

Reflecting on Mum's story led to thinking a bit more about my own. If this book were about me, I'd want to tell you immediately how terrible it felt – being sent away to boarding school at a tender age. Then again, aside from the boredom and drudgery of Glenhemfrey, you might be surprised how well I fared there. That's with the notable exception of the final few months.

Chronologically, I couldn't discuss any of this without covering the build-up to Mum's decision to send me away. This is not fun to recall. While I was living through those times, I could never be sure which came first – the chicken of maternal indifference, or the smelly egg of bad behaviour. In truth, it didn't really matter either way, because these actions and reactions perpetuated each other.

I was such a bad kid.

This wasn't a full picture of my childhood, though. All that negativity was balanced, to some extent, by my experiences of visiting Dad and Granny at The Great House. I felt much better about myself when I was there. That distinct feeling is part of my foundation: I could be a good kid after all, if people were nice to me.

The house itself may have been rather sad and formal – the housekeeper still used a dinner gong – but there was some genial fellow feeling in the air. My strong connection with the place, and the need for long train journeys to get there and back, emphasised the distance between my parents. As they were divorced, that made sense. It was only years later that it dawned on me how peculiar their original arrangement had been: a married couple who lived this far apart.

My father was not demonstrative, but he was patient with me, indulgent at times, and even-tempered. Together, in their understated way, Dad and Granny celebrated the fact that I existed; something that didn't happen at home.

Granny even favoured me over William. She had greater access to me, so that was a natural development. Mum had never entrusted her first-born to her mother-in-law's care for a single day, let alone for week-long holidays.

Granny would take me to the Isle of Wight, ostensibly to see her sister, but also to have a measure of fun. My great-aunt lived at Lake, perfectly poised between genteel Shanklin and slightly more vulgar Sandown, both of which I've always loved.

Granny was strict, but I think she forced herself to be as lenient with me as she could bear. Some of her self-discipline rubbed off on me, and some of my silliness rubbed off on her. We rubbed along pretty well together. One time, I was dancing around at the bus stop, showing off, when she said: "For a quiet boy, you're being rather noisy."

Then I knew to rein it in a little. Another time, when I was telling her some boastful story from school, she said: "You don't have to impress me, you know. I'm your grandmother."

Her various pronouncements stayed with me, and have been my guide through all these years.

Lara peered closely at me, then pulled back, satisfied.

"This is working a treat," she said. "You look gorgeous."

She took a break from her intensive operations, but denied me the chance to look in the mirror until her creation was complete. I'd felt brushwork and line work going on. She'd also had a respectful go at my brows.

She sighed. "What am I going to say at my interview tomorrow?"

This was news to me. "What's the job?"

She shrugged. "Art gallery assistant. Rinky-dink commercial place. A skive, with any luck. Did I tell you I have an audition? Not the open one. This is for a mini-series – best friend of the lead. Won't get it, but *ehh*."

"Great to get an audition," I said, feeling a disturbing level of envy. "Good practice, if nothing else."

"Yeah, yeah." She looked at me and winked. "So, what am I going to tell this woman? I know feck all about art."

"You saw a lot of it the other day."

"Yeah, but you were the one reading the labels with a magnifier!"

Thou say'st true.

I got a few famous artworks up on my phone. We began to construct the story of Lara's lifelong fascination with everything from the cave paintings to Tracey Emin's unmade bed.

I could help with this, as art has always been an interest of mine. I couldn't produce anything worthwhile myself, but I appreciated the relaxed anarchy of the art room at Glenhemfrey. In adult life, large galleries became my cathedrals. They give me joy and head space. Over time, I've absorbed a little about the artworks themselves.

I must have expounded about this too much, because Lara yawned and resumed her self-appointed task of making me look beautiful.

"You're so gorgeous now, you could be my flag-bearer at Pride."

The finishing touches were being applied as Plum arrived home. I heard her bolting the front door. I half-expected my daughter to be annoyed by what she caught us doing, but not at all. This was seemingly nothing more bizarre than Lara being Lara, and Dad being Dad.

Plum helped herself to the last of the prosecco.

"How did you get on with Guy?" she asked.

"Yeah, good," I told her, though I couldn't feign too much enthusiasm. "He's a nice guy."

The unintended pun went unremarked, but she looked at me – hands wide, brows raised, expecting more details.

"He took your da on a goose chase," said Lara. "But they bumped into some old friends, so it all worked out fine."

Now Plum was smiling at last. She started making herself some toast.

"I knew you boys would get on. When are you going to meet again?"

"Soon," I said, vaguely. "He is a bit of a fantasist, though, isn't he? Fancies himself as the Mushroom King of Chicago."

Plum gave Lara a glance that seemed to signal mild panic.

"All creative people live a fantasy existence," Lara said, calmly dabbing my nose with a sponge. "Who likes the real world anyways?"

Plum spread mashed avocado on her toast. "Top restaurants just leave you hungry," she muttered.

"So how did you meet Guy in the first place?" I wanted to know.

"Friend of a friend," said Lara, turning the mirror towards me so I could inspect her handiwork at last.

I gasped, because my mask-face actually looked great. She'd gone with a graded crimson theme on my lids, with a single band of shimmer; a touch of blusher on my cheeks, over a light muddy base, with contouring and highlights. The lipstick was a lovely non-glossy dark red. I was impressed. This was how

Ziggy Stardust might have looked when putting the bins out.

"That's amazing," I said, admiring the effect, but knowing it would take a while to wash the mascara off my fair lashes.

I gazed at myself in the mirror and had a strong feeling – almost an epiphany. I knew that I would never, ever, play the pantomime dame again.

"Knew you'd like it," said Lara, taking a photo on my phone. Then Plum took photos on her phone, Lara took several on hers and they posed with me for selfies. We rounded off this flurry of activity with a three-shot on mine.

"Do you mind if I remove it all now?"

"Sure," said Lara, rather sadly. "I've had my fun."

I took a deep breath and uploaded a picture. In no time it had four likes, which slightly bothered me, until I realised that one of my followers may have shared it with a friend.

Almost unnoticed, it had become properly dark outside. There was that tension in the air that foretold of everyone sliding off to bed. I was too energised to let that happen straight away, so I enquired after Plum's work and her boss.

"We're on the right track," she said. "We got quite a lot done today."

I alluded to the corruption that Henrietta was advocating, with her talk of a personal gift to a council leader, in exchange for his awarding a software contract. In view of Plum's high principles, I raised a curated eyebrow at how lightly she shrugged this off as a necessary oiling of commercial cogs.

"There's no problem with that," she told me. "It's all perfectly legal. We just have to ensure there's no paper trail connecting the two things. He wants a load of gravel for his drive, and we deliver it. End of. But we can't go ahead right now, because there's a small matter with the software…"

"A glitch?"

"No, not a *glitch*, Dad." Her brown eyes flashed with annoyance. "It's very tiny, but Franklin's having to work with our existing customers to resolve it. These things happen all the time in our industry. It's not a drama. Really."

My daughter planted a fleeting kiss on my pretty cheek and headed for her own room.

"Night-night, my fabulous darling," said Lara, triumphantly touching her lips to the same cheek. "Is it the surrealists or the cubists I'm supposed not to like?"

"Never mind," I said. "Just tell them you like the Glasgow Boys."

She picked up the empty prosecco bottle and looked at me through it, as if it were a telescope.

I laughed. "Nice prop work, Miss O'Halloran. *Next!*"

She smiled and danced to her door in a sweeping ballet move, acknowledged my applause and disappeared backstage. I pulled the lumpy old sofa out and it metamorphosed into a lumpy old bed. Then I fetched my duvet, got into my makeshift pyjamas, and lay there, tired but unable to fall asleep.

From time to time, I heard a peal of Lara's laughter. Otherwise, there was a blissful hush. It was no good, though: I couldn't sleep. I turned a lamp on and cast about for my notebook.

In her disjointed way, Mum had been painting a picture of the early 1960s quite at odds with what I'd had in my mind's eye. I thought of bleak industrial landscapes with smoke-spewing chimneys, people living dead-end lives in their wake, all presented in a grainy, rainy monochrome, from those 'kitchen sink' melodramas – *A Taste of Honey, Saturday Night and Sunday Morning, This Sporting Life*, and the like.

I first came across these films on Sunday afternoons at Glenhemfrey, when Channel Four ran a season of them, and everyone else in my dorm house was out doing sport, or whatever. Although I couldn't grasp the grown-up themes, I was captivated by the eruptive emotion and driving energy of the cobbled world they presented.

Now Mum was telling me these films were "rubbish". Her world at that time was full of soft furnishings in mauve and lime green; bright red lipstick and London buses; vibrant music with a youthful, carefree beat. It was a new world, pregnant with possibilities. Jobs were plentiful. To reach this promised land, though, like so many adolescent girls of that era, Essie had to run away from home.

She'd been pressured into leaving school aged fifteen, with no qualifications, to earn money for the household. Her aunt didn't work, so that left a hole in the family finances. No regard was given to Essie's intelligence or potential. As she'd failed her eleven-plus, it was assumed she was a dead loss and a burden.

She agreed to leave school, on condition that she was allowed to spend some of her earnings on going to night school in Preston. Her father was baffled by this, but allowed it to happen. So Essie worked in a shop during the day and spent three evenings a week learning the secretarial skills that would become her means of escape.

The problem was, she couldn't bear the thought of taking the final exams. These were due on the last day of February, a few weeks after her seventeenth birthday. So the day before, she and an impressionable classmate, Dottie Woodwald, simply scarpered. They took the bus to Preston and the train to London.

At Euston, a helpful porter bought them a copy of the *Evening Standard* and circled the details of vacant rooms. He commented that some of these, in Knightsbridge, were "not far from Buckingham Palace". They liked the sound of that.

By the evening, they were installed at Mrs French's boarding house at Cromwell Road, and their new life had begun. Or so Essie thought.

Her friend had been quick to find a job in an Oxford Street store, but she was merely playing at life. She must have been homesick, or perhaps she'd always viewed this adventure as a short break from reality. Now she'd seen London, and was ready to go home.

The clue had been there all along, in the girls' choice of luggage. Whereas Essie crammed her possessions into her mother's old shopping trolley, and it took both of them to heave it onto the train, Dottie Woodwald brought only a small cardboard suitcase that could hardly contain anything at all.

After only a few nights away, on the same day the agency sent Essie to Fleet Street for the temporary job as a copytaker, Dottie returned to Mrs French's, where she picked up her little toy suitcase, bustled down the front steps, gave the landlady a quick wave, and was gone.

She didn't even say goodbye or retrieve her deposit. She just left her keys in her room. Essie had magnanimously allowed Dottie to take the large room off the second landing, which had a double bed and a bay window that looked out over the busy, exciting Cromwell Road.

By contrast, Essie took a small room at the top of the house. It was pleasant enough, but with no view to speak of. It was reached by its own narrow staircase – good for privacy, but not for socialising.

Up there in her lonely garret, Essie viewed her naked form for the first time in a full-length mirror; there was one on the wardrobe door. She thought her body resembled two dollops of ice cream from the Italian café back home. She quite liked that. She pulled her feet together, so her legs could be the cone.

Then she spoke her name aloud several times. She decided that now there was no-one around to insist on calling her Essie, she would be Estelle.

"We're at the end of the beginning now, William," Mum told me, with a surprising degree of accuracy, considering how she recounted her memories back-to-front and inside out, leaving me to put them in order.

The last few days of that week were a muddle for me. One of the nurses brought in a copy of Mum's newspaper. It was running a mildly inaccurate paragraph about her illness, along with the sort of photo you might choose for an obituary: a black-and-white shot of Jayne at her typewriter, with piled-up hair and dark eye make-up, wearing a polo-neck jumper. The caption made it clear that she'd 'retired' from writing her column.

It could have been worse, but Marjorie Buttle-Deary phoned me and enjoyed having a good moan about it. I told her about compiling Mum's memoirs; we agreed to meet sometime and discuss them. Marjorie sounded disappointed when I said we weren't aiming for publication.

"Why not?" she asked. "Hers is quite a story. I'm sure she'd be proud to get it out there."

"It's all very scrappy," I told her. "And very personal."

"Like anyone else's memoirs, then," she huffed, and I laughed, but this turned out not to be a joke.

Lara got the gallery job. Then she told her existing supervisor exactly where she could stick her fecking job. William and his family flew out to Florence.

I continued my affair with Rūta, who appeared one time when I was in my little café and asked what I was doing in Neurology. I had no compelling explanation to give her. She laughed and told me she'd done a rota swap with a colleague, whom she also bribed with wine and chocolates, to create a long weekend off for herself.

"So I can come with you, honey," she said. "To the Isles of White."

I almost succeeded in avoiding Guy. He turned up unexpectedly on the ward, to meet my "old duck". He recited some of his poems and raps for her, and cracked a few bad jokes.

"I'm the wizard of viscosity," he said, giving me a wink. "The earl of curl on the river of regret."

He was talking gibberish, but to my astonishment, she lapped it up.

"I like this one," said Mum, smiling. "He's a bounder."

CHAPTER 11

I headed home on the Friday, to be ready for the Saturday matinée. Jim phoned at lunchtime, to check I was on my way. I told him I'd worn nearly everything in the bag of costume, so I'd resorted to a red ruffle shirt that made me look like Austin Powers. I liked it when he laughed. He had the kind of guffaw that shook the seriousness of the world, like a comforting earth tremor.

I was in two minds about saying goodbye to Mum. I didn't want to unsettle her, but thought it would be unfair not to let her know I'd be going away. I had no idea if she'd retain the information, but it made me feel better to impart it.

Don't die now, you old duck.

"I understand, William," she said, going on to tell me I had a busy life that needed my attention.

I hadn't expected Rūta to accompany me on the trip home. But here she was, trailing alongside me to Waterloo, pulling her tiny, noisy cabin bag. She expressed excitement that I understood but couldn't share.

In fact, I felt a bit wobbly about the prospect of showing her around – especially the King Edward, as this was my domain with Teruko. When I used to lock up, we'd often chase each other about the building, or play hide and seek. Teruko's favourite thing was being elevated through the trap door, when she would throw her arms wide and shout "Ta-da!"

It wasn't a strike day, but it was a Friday, so the trains were delayed and balefully slow in screeching their way out of the metropolis. We had seats, but there were grumpy commuters standing over us in the aisle, making us feel guilty. The air being pumped into the carriage was too feeble to cool anything, so the place stank of sausage roll and sweat.

By some chance, though, we caught a fast ferry. Then we retrieved the car from my secret parking place in Cowes. As I pulled up in our little enclave at Crand, Truscott was already going berserk. I was convinced he could tell the sound of one car engine from another.

"Well, this is it," I sighed, as Rūta looked around in wonder.

I was swearing under my breath, and she asked why. I explained there was a certain protocol to parking in our close; I was disappointed to find that my usual spot had been stolen while I was away.

"You're obsessed with the parking," she observed.

I called next door to give my neighbour some relief from Truscott's skittering excitement. I thought the mutt would calm down upon seeing me, but the presence of an additional human was almost too much for his tiny mind to deal with.

He forgot all his lessons in canine etiquette, yapping and jumping up at Rūta in a very ungentlemanly manner, but she was a proper dog person and showed no fear. She tamed him in seconds, whispering to him soothingly in her native tongue.

I was glad to discover that my house was less of a tip than I'd feared. I bundled all the used costume into the washer and discovered, ninety minutes later, that the red ruffle shirt had turned everything else pink.

Rūta was slightly impressed by my modest abode. She liked the bed not being in the sitting room, and the back door opening onto a small patch of grass, though it badly needed cutting.

For a split second, I wished I could have taken her home to The Great House. Then I could have shared with her the delusion we all had about the eminence of our family – even though it had no money or title, apart from Dad being the son of a great man, namely Lord Norman William Harrington Nichol De Vries, DFC and Bar.

Standing here, in my pauper's terrace bungalow, I could feel the weighty graduation gown of Britain's decline upon my shoulders.

"Let's do the love, honey," suggested Rūta, and I was in no mood to argue.

On Saturday morning, we walked Truscott into the village and I pointed out the flat above the bakery that had been my first billet on the island. I used to return there after the carousing that followed the evening performances – we all needed to wind down from the buzz of the show – and the smell of the bread would rip me from sleep at an untimely 5.45am.

Those were (not) the days…

"Is very beautiful here," said Rūta, breathing in the sea air.

I changed into my cheap charcoal work suit and dropped her off at Osborne House, Victoria and Albert's fine residence. The plan was for her to have a good look round, then catch the bus and meet me in Newport for dinner. If I couldn't show her The Great House, at least she could see this.

Afterwards, I'd wangle her a free ticket for the evening performance. That way she would get to see the theatre, but only from a customer's point of view.

The King Eddie has one of those brilliant designs that makes a thousand-seater feel intimate. Its beautiful domed roof gets the acoustics just right, and the curves of the dress and upper circles help to create wonderful sightlines. Only four seats on each level have a partial view, so these are kept for emergencies.

The theatre is a glorious throwback to the age of the actor-managers and their titillating cautionary tales. One of the am-dram companies staged a revival of one of these, *She Strayed Too Far*, and I absolutely loved it. I ended up watching it three times. Some of the performances were over-the-top, but then so was the script.

Lady Petunia has fainted!

Backstage, I was in the habit of ducking below the low doorframes, but every so often one would catch me out and whack my head. There were endless cubbyholes in which to operate equipment and store props; passageways that zigged and zagged; small flights of stairs that failed to join up. The dressing rooms all had sloping ceilings, and there was a Welsh dresser, full of china, in a recess where no catering could possibly take place.

Perhaps the strangest aspect of the building was the frontage, which was quite magnificent, yet stood at right angles to the town's main thoroughfare. It was, as director Noel recalled, "up an alley". There were steps leading to the main doors, now complemented by a ramp. There were small statues, turrets, fake arrow slits and battlements that made the place look like a cross between a town hall and a castle.

Above the entrance and below a magnificent clock that no-one could see, there was a sizeable balcony, also a white elephant, for the same reason. The idea was that visiting stars could appear on the balcony and wave to the crowds below.

But the alleyway was too narrow to enable more than about twenty people to stand in front of the building. They would hardly be able to see anything anyway, as that balcony would be virtually on top of them.

Despite this obvious drawback, the architects and builders pressed ahead. They commissioned a famous artist to paint a vibrant impression of what the frontage would look like, if you could actually stand back and admire it. This large painting, in its ornate gold frame, dominated the foyer.

I trudged round the building, as I'd done a zillion times before, checking the required doors were unlocked, the safety curtain was working and everything was switched on that needed to be. After all the fun and childish joy we shared there, the big space felt empty and tatty without Teruko. It was haunted by her absence, by the uncanny silence that had replaced the sound of her laughter.

When I emerged from backstage, which is notorious for its lack of wi-fi and phone signal, I noticed I'd missed a call from Lara.

"I didn't get the part," she told me, wearily. "But we both knew I wouldn't."

I asked about the new day-job. She told me there was very little to do. Footfall was sparse; her employer only popped in for a few minutes each day.

"Our customers know about money, not art," said Lara. "We're selling 'an experience'. I mean, it's just so *snooty*."

I asked about her audition feedback.

"Yeah, they said they really liked me, and I performed well, but I wasn't right for this particular part."

That's what they say to all the girls.

"Oh, well. You did your best."

"Yeah. And they're gonna keep in touch."

What?

"There's more parts to be cast."

Oh. Okay.

"That's good," I told her. "That's quite unusual."

My colleagues started appearing at noon: a couple of assistants in the box office, the two cleaners and Agnieszka, our stage door receptionist. Then the bar staff arrived and set up. Cast and crew trickled in, and got on with their backstage routines. The cleaners left as the public started arriving. The building was coming to life.

It was a quiet, rather subdued matinée, attended by our ageing band of regulars, some kids from the youth theatre and a scattering of tourist families. In the main, visitors preferred the evening shows, unless it was raining.

On each side of the house, we operated a pairing system. One usher would be on the inside, watching the show, and one on the outside, doing various tasks, but primed to help in an evacuation. I was paired with Pearl, a Chinese girl, who was keen to be on the outside. She'd already seen the show.

I got to sit in and watch. The show was an adaptation of a feelgood British film; the sort of anodyne crowd-pleaser Yvonne was apt to book. It was all right, to a point. Mostly, I prefer fresh scripts – or fresh productions of old scripts. Something arresting, that makes you think.

Over dinner, I asked Rūta how she liked Osborne House.

"I nearly got lost in this palace," she said. "I can never live someplace so big."

It was kind of her to say this, but it did sound a little like "size doesn't matter".

I stood and watched from a box as she took up her free seat at the rear of the stalls. She looked a little overawed, as if she were still stuck in a palace. She glanced around furtively, missing the fact that I was waving to her.

I felt a little pride in the red seats in the boxes and the sculpted gold trim of the balconies, but I knew the whole place needed fresh upholstery and a lick of paint.

Rūta had been worried about what to wear, and I'd said "smart casual", but all she'd heard was "smart". Looking at her now, I had no doubt she would understand the show;

her English was up to it. I was less sure she'd understand the theatre. It was clearly not somewhere she felt at home.

As soon as the house lights dimmed, I scooted downstairs to have a catch-up with Jim. We stood around in the bar, as the staff set up the pre-booked interval drinks. Even through the two sets of double doors, I could tell the performance was sharper, the audience more responsive, than they had been at the matinée. There were warm gales of laughter, in a nice musical rhythm.

My rather negative view of the show started to soften. Some of our afternoon regulars are hard of hearing, so they sit near the front, but they can get too comfortable and nod off. That has repercussions: the cast feel unloved, so they lose energy and pace, then the whole endeavour flags.

"Come with me, Victor," said Jim, leading me out of the building, along the side passage and back in at the stage door. "Let me tell you about the latest management nonsense."

He didn't have an office as such, but we used the old post room behind Agnieszka's cubby for coffee breaks, and Jim ruled the roost in there. The handful of us who worked weekday mornings would gather for what was officially an interdepartmental meeting, but actually a social knees-up.

There was an irreverent party atmosphere, and Jim would sit on his great silver stage throne, swigging tea from his giant mug, allowing chaos to reign for twenty-nine minutes and thirty seconds. He was the best boss ever.

As the kettle was boiling, he told me he'd resisted another move to halve the number of ushers. Jim was careful never to speak against Yvonne, always blaming the nebulous powers above her for penny-pinching and lowering standards. It was rumoured the theatre was barely turning a profit, and would be up for sale again soon. Then came the bombshell.

"They offered me early retirement, Victor. What should I do?"

I just looked at him. It was the first time he'd ever asked for my advice.

"Do you want to retire?"

"Not really. I already retired from the prison service. Though I complain about it all the time, this is a pleasant occupation. It keeps me off the street."

"Then turn them down," I said, firmly.

"I know. But I don't think I'll hear the end of it. I'm at the top of the scale and they want to save money. I figured you might want to step up."

I was proud of my response, though it came as a shock to realise it was true.

"If you leave, I won't want to stay."

CHAPTER 12

The next day, Sunday, was overcast, drizzly and windy. Despite this, I was determined to show Rūta more of the island. We would explore the beach and the pier at Sandown, the botanical gardens at Ventnor, and Shanklin Chine at dusk, its paths beautified by coloured lights. These were all sacred places from my childhood.

Everywhere was busy, as the school holidays had begun. Plenty of people were on Sandown beach, unperturbed by the weather, digging away and building sandcastles, just as I used to do with Granny.

She would direct operations from her deckchair, sending me off at intervals to fetch ice cream or a cup of tea. If the puppet show was there, I'd always watch it. I brought Plum here two or three times when she was the right age, and the island seemed to cast its spell on her in a similar way.

I didn't talk about any of this with Rūta. Perhaps I should have, while I watched her responses to our surroundings. For a while, she removed her scrunchies and allow her hair to blow in every direction. She peeled it away when it flapped across her eyes, but otherwise seemed to be enjoying some rare moments of freedom.

I thought the time was right to open up to her a bit more. I was concerned that our relationship felt too superficial. I started telling her about being sent away to Glenhemfrey Academy. I monologued about Mum accompanying me on the train and bus just once, demonstrating how to manage the journey, and then just dumping me there.

I'm not sure how ready Rūta was to hear this sort of story, so full of childhood angst. She didn't seem to react to it at all. She just gazed at the pleasure craft near the shore, pausing for a moment to put on her sunglasses and look further out, to the container ships on the horizon.

Undaunted, I got the wind in my sails and let it blow us along. I described Glenhemfrey: a cranky old house, in extensive grounds, at the foot of a hill in the Borders. It rained a lot there. The place had a certain familiarity, as it reminded me very slightly of The Great House, but it was teeming with people.

To turn it into a private school, they'd filled the baronial-style manor with desks and chairs, plonked new buildings around it, and rolled out sports pitches and courts anywhere that was reasonably level.

Where the school drive met the main road, there was a tiny, sleepy village with a delicatessen, a newsagent's and a place where you could buy maggots and tackle for fishing by the river.

"Sounds beautiful," said Rūta.

On Saturdays, we had designated time for hobbies, which dragged on forever. I'd get frustrated by failing to draw, or to build anything from the boxes of metal or plastic pieces. Then I'd mooch around the boring village. This was before I even had my own Game Boy.

One time, I got told off for browsing in the delicatessen without buying anything. So I returned to the dorm with a pack of sun-dried bananas. Those black, sweet, chewy sticks were an unexpected hit with my roommates, who instantly became less unfriendly. I'd discovered the phenomenon, mostly known to pet owners, of 'cupboard love'.

On Sundays, I'd go to chapel, even though I wasn't on the list to attend, just to have something to do. You weren't supposed to like the singing, but I did. I noticed I could hold a tune better than most.

In some of our physical education lessons, we did cross-country running. I could do that, too. Being small and clumsy, often having to shift my weight to stay balanced, I found it easy to run on uneven ground. We ran various circular routes repeatedly, so after a while I'd learned them all. I stopped hanging about the village, and went for walks in the countryside instead.

"All that nature to explore," said Rūta, smiling. "You were a lucky boy."

Maybe so. But then again...

It was tough being away from home. I never cried, because this was a test of survival that went beyond a few tears. But after several weeks of living in a state of great apprehension, I realised that nothing terrible had happened to me. In the scheme of things, that was very positive. I didn't have any friends, but I coaxed myself into a routine and started feeling strangely comfortable.

"I don't get it," said Rūta, almost in a shout, as we passed through the noisy amusements arcade on the pier. "Were you happy or unhappy at this school?"

Her binary question reminded me of the way journalists press politicians for 'yes-no' answers, leaving no space for ambivalence or nuance. That was always entertaining to watch, but now I found it less agreeable being on the receiving end, being pushed for a simple answer to a complex question.

"Happy or unhappy?" I repeated, thinking hard. "I'd have to say both."

We were now standing on the peaceful far deck of the pier, from where two stalwart anglers were dangling their lines. Rūta gave me an exaggerated shrug; she couldn't see the point of my story.

I wanted her to understand that being at Glenhemfrey was a desolate state of affairs, and I felt miserable there; of course I did. At the same time, the place was not entirely disagreeable. So, *within the overarching misery*, I felt a measure of day-to-day contentment. Was that so difficult to comprehend?

It was a co-educational school, so there were girls around. You weren't supposed to talk to them, but I did, and made them laugh. We boys followed a quaint convention, of not swearing in front of them. In class, the girls sat on one side of the room and we sat on the other. I often sat on the borderline.

"I would sit next to you," said Rūta, squeezing my hand as we meandered back towards the car.

That was nice. Maybe she was getting some of this. I kept on going, because it felt important to do so. I explained that only a handful of girls were also boarders; they had one house to our three, and it was down in the village. There were a lot of day pupils, both boys and girls, who travelled in by bus.

They got to escape.

My house was West Lodge. We had a houseparent called Mr McNee. He was a weary-looking man who taught History and French. He seemed disappointed by life, but despite this – or perhaps to compensate for it – he liked to gee us up. He praised us for keeping the house tidy and gave us occasional motivational chats, relating the inscrutable nonsense we were taught in class to the scary future world of employment.

When you spoke to him, he always considered what you said more seriously than your classroom teacher was prepared to do. He didn't often have to punish anyone, because seeing him feel wounded was punishment enough.

At the start of each school year, Mr McNee would stand in the sitting room, in the black teacher's robe he wore habitually, and make the same little speech. He explained that he no longer had any family, so he thought of us as his "ain folk", referencing the old Scottish song. He urged us all to get along as best we could.

His parents had died of natural causes, he'd tell us, while his brother had been killed in the Aden Emergency. None of us knew what that was. A boy in my dorm said it was probably part of World War Two. It was ages before I found out the true story.

"Was he gay?" asked Rūta, cutting across my theme.

I was leading her through the rugged Mediterranean section of the botanical gardens. The palm trees had always made me dream of exotic, faraway places.

"I don't know," I said, feeling slightly annoyed, though the same thought had occurred to me. "Nobody knew."

Mr McNee was assisted in the house by two female colleagues; a young morning maid (actually a succession of these) and an older cook, who always made our evening meals. Neither lived in. Our houseparent had a suite of rooms on the top floor, above the junior and senior dorms. He tended to dine alone in his rooms, and no-one was ever to go up there, except in a crisis.

One evening – on the same day we'd all put up and dressed our Christmas tree – I was told by a prefect to report to Mr NcNee's rooms. It was dark and late: I was already in my pyjamas, dressing gown and slippers. This proved to be one of only two occasions when I ever set foot in his study.

I felt nervous on arrival, though Mr McNee was very welcoming and introduced me to his equally smiley guest, a Mr Somerville.

I sat in a big club chair that had a leathery smell, my legs stretching straight out in front of me. I was given a drink of milk and a shortbread finger. I gazed at the tall bookcases and felt quite overwhelmed. The only light was yellowy and issued from a standard lamp.

Mr McNee put a hand on my shoulder and explained I was about to be given a special test. It was like a game, and I wasn't to worry about how well I might do; the important thing was to relax and enjoy it.

Mr Somerville started showing me some printed cards and asking questions. I was invited to read some texts aloud. I had to kneel at a low table and do some writing. I soon felt at ease and soaked up all the attention.

These activities were slightly different from anything I'd done before. They seemed to go on for a long time, and tired me out. Once they were finished, Mr Somerville thanked me and shook my hand. Then Mr McNee told me I'd just been tested for something called "dyslexia".

Though I didn't realise it at the time, my diagnosis was a life-changing event. I thought at first that everyone was taking this test. It took a while for me to understand that I was "different".

Actually, it took years to recognise all aspects of my neurodivergence. As you'll know if you've done the awareness training, dyslexia often comes in a bargain bundle.

In my case, this includes dyspraxia, dysgraphia and what the professionals call an autistic spectrum 'disorder'. I just call it autism, because what seems odd to someone else is only my own normality. It's up to me to make the most of what I've been born with.

"We want to help you succeed, despite your disability," said Mr McNee; words I could comprehend at that age, but could barely process.

Up to then, I'd thought of school as a place of torment. It had never occurred to me that teachers were trying to help us. Now I think back, this may have been the start of my being friendlier towards myself. I internalised the praise and encouragement of the classroom assistants who worked with me in certain lessons.

I stopped seeing myself as someone privileged who was destroying their opportunities, as Mum accused me of being, and started to perceive an alternative script that had me as a disadvantaged person – an underdog – as she had once been.

"I was always top of my class," said Rūta, in a sing-song voice, ending my lengthy rumination.

I clammed up after that and became rather sulky, but she didn't appear to notice. Though she'd listened to me, she didn't seem able to relate to my experiences. I wondered if I'd discovered her 'caveat' – that as someone with a vanilla personality, who led a soft-scoop life, she expected those around her to add the sprinkles.

"You have a lot of baggage, honey," she remarked, as we headed up the chine.

True – but a little harsh?

Up to that point in our relationship, I'd let her project her desires onto me, as if I were a blank cinema screen, or a notebook that hadn't been scribbled in yet.

When we spent time together, I often felt more like 'a boyfriend' than myself. I'm sure a lot of people feel this disquiet, when a partner selects them for their physical presence, instead of their inner being, their personality. Later that day, Rūta told me she'd experienced love at first sight.

"As soon as you stood up in the waiting room, I knew," she said, a little sadly, as if she had no choice but to respond to the fluttering in her tummy.

"I thought you were above my league," I told her. Then I had to explain what that meant, and a potentially romantic moment was gone.

On the Monday morning, Truscott and I walked Rūta down to the Yarmouth ferry. One of the reasons I'd bought a place near Yarmouth was this whimsical idea I had, that I could watch friends arriving and departing via the short ferry crossing.

In reality, prior to Rūta, the only guests I'd had were Plum and her former boyfriend, whom I secretly called 'Passionfruit'. They crashed on my airbed, as free accommodation for a holiday. I didn't mind at all, though I felt quite dejected when they didn't want me to join them for a single outing. Alongside that disappointment, William had never shown any interest in visiting. But then, he didn't have the holiday memories I'd accrued on the island.

It was a perfect summer morning, with bright sunshine, blue skies and cotton wool clouds. There was still some wind, but now it was more of a breeze. We gazed at the boats in the harbour and watched people going in and out of the terminal building.

A woman seemed to be staring at us. Some kids came over and made a fuss of Truscott, which he found gratifying, but he scared them away by getting over-excited. We sauntered part of the way down the long pier, watching the ferry's approach.

"I'll really miss you," I said, which was true. Rūta was good company.

"But you will come back to London, for the mother?"

"Of course."

She gave me a half-smile, but I didn't know what that meant in this context. I wasn't sure if our relationship was beginning or ending. It appeared to be faltering, and I felt sad about that.

"I love you," I said for the first time, with a quiver of desperation.

Rūta nodded and looked away. "I love you too," she whispered into the breeze.

We watched the ramps going down. The first cars and vans rolled onto dry land. As Rūta and I were exchanging sombre kisses, the woman who'd been staring tapped me sharply on the shoulder.

"Aren't you an actor?" she wanted to know, frowning at me.

When I confirmed that I was, she rummaged in her handbag for a pen and paper and demanded my autograph. Then a couple came over and took a selfie with me, without asking.

Rūta took all of this as her cue to walk away, pulling her cabin bag behind her, and disappeared for several minutes as she got on board the ferry. Then she stood on deck, looking down at us. I took a photo and uploaded it. It wasn't my greatest shot, but it got my usual three likes. I watched and waited, fumbling with the tiger netsuke I shouldn't have bought from Guy, until the wretched vessel pulled away from the quay.

Rūta and I waved to each other. I picked Truscott up, and obliged him to wave a paw. She smiled and went inside, and that was it. For all my imaginings of friendly comings and goings, life on an island is just as apt to accentuate your sense of loss. I hugged Truscott to me, and he saw his chance to give me a big, wet, slobbery lick, all over my mouth and nose.

Ugh!

I lowered him carefully to the ground and fussed about with some tissues. I thought of Teruko and our distant dream. Like Lara, she understood that life never stands still. It's changeable and tends to run wild. Maybe you can influence it, but you can never catch hold of it and tame it.

"Life is hard," she told me, when we first met. "But I like it a lot."

She had an unhappy time growing up. She had a strict father and a pushy mother, who wanted to pursue her own ambitions through her daughter. Unlike Rūta, Teruko had to rebel in order to find herself, and discover a path through life that wasn't obvious.

She was tough and tender, and could be brutally funny. She never used sarcasm, unless it was laced with affection. I adored that.

Watching the ferry slip further away, I wondered if Teruko was married yet. I hoped not, though I wanted for her to be happy. For all her unconventionality, she had some mainstream desires.

CHAPTER 13

I got back into my routine quickly. It almost felt as if I hadn't been away. The next show was an am-dram filler, so I helped with their get-in. They were the millionth company doing *The Importance of Being Earnest* for the millionth time, but their backstage crew of three were pleasant enough to invite to our clandestine morning tea break.

The internal politics rumbled on, but there was no substantive update about the theatre being sold, or Jim retiring. Yvonne wafted in for a while, a leggy vision in pastel colours, but she rarely showed signs of doing actual work like the rest of us.

She had a spectacularly patronising way of talking to staff, getting them on side with mumsy confidences, then manipulating them into doing things they didn't want to. She was, she claimed, "a people person".

Yvonne greeted me, as she always did, with a smirk that conveyed mild disdain. She had an attractive, round, pudgy face, with a sweeping fringe and soft eyes that belied the harshness within. She always made it clear she possessed some personal warmth, but was reserving it for others of greater social import. When you've been schooled in assuming superiority over those you meet, it's agony when someone else does it to you.

"How's Mum?" she asked, with a typical touch of over-familiarity. She was already letting out a pseudo-empathetic "*aww…*" as I made my reply.

I didn't usually work a Wednesday matinée. I'd done a swap with Jim, who had to attend a meeting about his village summer pageant. I was on the outside during the performance, compiling a bar order and dealing with a written complaint, when none other than Rad appeared at the door, looking grim-faced.

Not again, surely?

The second coming of my Bulgarian box office amigo felt like a visitation from the Reaper himself. Immediately, I assumed news had come through of Mum's death. But I wondered why the nurses hadn't called me directly, now they had my mobile number.

"You're wanted on the telephone," said the young man. "Personal call."

I scurried into the box office with him and grasped the landline receiver.

"Victor, is that you?"

I dimly recognised the voice, but couldn't place it.

"This is cousin Rennie, in Bath. Your father's had a nasty fall. Went out without his stick. He's at the hospital having X-rays. Thought you ought to know."

I felt completely numb. Of course, it made sense that this could happen. Dad's balance wasn't brilliant, and he was very stubborn about using his stick. But the timing was so terrible, coming so soon after Mum's illness.

"Is he all right?"

Rennie grunted at the stupidity of my question.

"Depends how you mean. He's hurt, obviously, but it isn't life-or-death at this point. If he's broken his hip, well then…"

I made a hard-nosed decision to finish my shift and told Rennie I'd come to Bath the following day. I looked for Yvonne, but she wasn't around, so I phoned Jim and explained the situation. He stepped out of a discussion about giant marrows.

"These things come in threes, Victor," he said, which was not really what I wanted to hear. He sucked air through his teeth, but had no choice but to grant me another round of compassionate leave.

I spent the evening making phone calls, packing, and trying unsuccessfully not to worry. I held off phoning William until I'd assessed the situation for myself. I didn't want to disrupt his holiday needlessly; he needed a proper rest.

After seeing Mum in such a parlous state, I approached Dad's ward the next day with a similar sense of dread. But things were not as bad as I'd imagined.

Dad was up and dressed, sitting in a chair beside his bed. His hair was neatly combed, his right arm was in a sling, there was a plaster on the end of his nose. He looked perky and resolute, but dreadfully thin and frail. He was sporting two days' growth of white stubble.

"Oh, hello, Victor," he said, eagerly. "Have you come to take me home?"

He wasn't showing much surprise at seeing me, considering we hadn't met face to face for four years – since his second wife's funeral, in fact.

It was hard to keep in touch with Dad. He wouldn't use the phone, as he belonged to a generation that thought calls "cost too much". He wasn't especially keen on chatting online either. On the rare occasions he did try, he tended to present me with a live image of the top of his head, still boasting its silvery-white mop.

Out of his earshot, the fake-tanned male nurse explained that Dad was ready to be discharged, subject to suitable arrangements being in place for his day-to-day care. The old man was badly bruised, with hairline fractures of the wrist and elbow. Importantly, though, his hip was intact.

"I can look after him for the first few days," I said, uncertainly. "His nephew keeps an eye on him. They still work together…"

"Sounds like the perfect solution," said the nurse, giving a too-white smile. He told me we'd need to complete some forms. Then we'd have to wait for a doctor to sign Dad off.

Such was the pressure for beds, we were ushered out of the ward straight away. We sat in a waiting room with high-back chairs. The wait took four hours. Dad and I got talking; something we always found difficult, not least because he was practically deaf in one ear.

He asked after Mum, and seemed to blanch when I told him about helping her recount some memories. I knew he wasn't fond of raking over the past. I was conscious of talking at a much higher volume than usual.

"I should have come up to see her," he said, sadly. "I shall do so now, as soon as I'm able."

I asked about his first impressions of Estelle, when she first arrived at The Great House, to interview him as the son of a great man.

"Well, Victor, it's a long time ago," he said, and I thought that might be all he had to offer on the subject. Then he leaned back and sighed.

"She was lovely. Full of life. Very northern, which my mother took exception to. Fearless. Exciting. Impetuous. Everything my life was missing. That *she* showed an interest in *me* – well – it was incredible! Time was going along, and I hardly ever got to meet young ladies…"

"You were twenty-eight; she was nineteen, right? And you proposed on the day you met?"

"No, of course not! Did she tell you that? Not at all. She stayed for the weekend – another thing my mother disapproved of. We spent a lot of time together – walking in the grounds, you know; discussing our lives. It was curious, son. Neither of us was used to talking about ourselves. But it was liberating. *Exhilarating.* She was particularly taken with the Welsh Cobbs, in the field opposite the North Approach…"

I knew all about Mum's love of the horses, so I tried to steer him back to the point. "And the proposal…?"

"I was coming to that!" he snapped. "Now I've lost my thread."

He looked rather put out, and I felt sorry for exasperating him – this man who almost always kept his cool. He took a little while to calm down and muster his thoughts again. Then he leaned towards me.

"It just slipped out in conversation, as I was walking her back to the train halt. I said I didn't suppose she'd consider marrying me, and to my astonishment she said that, actually, she would. She would think about it. She came for another visit a few weeks later, and we got engaged. Then there was a terrible hoo-hah about getting her father's permission, with her being under twenty-one at the time…"

Dad was in full flow, in a way I'd rarely seen before. I was desperate to ask why he and Mum didn't live together, but I knew it was a touchy subject. I was aware he'd travelled to London once, unannounced, in a botched attempt to wrest his bride from her city and her career.

In the event, she'd been so welcoming and loving towards him, and he was so overwhelmed by her smart colleagues, he'd slunk home with his tail between his legs. He never raised the matter again. At least, that was the story as I'd heard it from Mum's point of view. I didn't think I was quite ready to ask for his version.

Time was ticking slowly in this quiet, empty room. It felt as if we were the already dead, in a scene from *In Camera*, and here was our one opportunity to say such things as we'd always left unspoken.

"Why didn't Mum love me?" I asked, simply.

Dad looked startled, but not surprised. Startled, because I'd actually posed the question, but unsurprised by what the question was.

"I'm sure she did love you – *does* love you, Victor," he said. "In her own way."

I'd once asked William the same question and received a similar assurance.

"But…? She's always loved William."

He gave a little shrug, as if I should already know this information. And I did know something. My brother described how Mum wailed inconsolably when she caught sight of my downy, strawberry blonde hair.

"Well, you know, you weren't quite what she was expecting."

"I know. I wasn't a girl."

"That was one thing," said Dad softly.

"What? I… don't understand."

"I can't spell it out for you, Victor. I've said too much already."

Now Dad looked unsettled and unhappy. The doctor noticed straight away, as he swept into the room. He shot me a suspicious look, but said nothing. He gave off an air of forced joviality and talked down to Dad, which I didn't like.

"You must put some meat on your bones," he said, and talked of main meals, snacks, eating little and often, drinking plenty of water.

"At this stage, you can eat anything you like."

He wrote out a prescription for painkillers and handed it to me, but I knew Dad wouldn't take any extra pills on top of his usual medication.

A porter pushed him to the front door in a wheelchair. The old man grabbed hold of my arm and we doddered over to the car, as if we were doing a three-legged race in slow motion. He had a bad back, which meant he always had something of a stoop, but it seemed to have got a lot more pronounced. He eased gingerly into the passenger seat and waved in the direction of the porter, who had already gone.

We struggled up the stairs to the flat. The effort of doing that sent Dad napping in his armchair for a couple of hours. I wandered through the little place, which had hardly changed since I stayed there a couple of times in my late teens. It still had the same textured wallpaper and russet carpet throughout. When I got myself a glass of water, the fitful plumbing howled in pain.

There was a stack of portraits leaning against a wall in the lounge. I recognised the top one as being my grandfather, but didn't know the others. These had come from The Great House and looked hopelessly out of scale here. I examined the foodstuffs in Dad's fridge – butter and an out-of-date frittata – and in his cupboards. There were two tins of soup and a paper bag of Turkish delight that had gone rock hard.

Accordingly, I did a full supermarket run and tried to shop as if I were Dad. I filled the trolley with guesswork and pies. I half-expected my card to be declined at the checkout, but my salary must have landed in my account and saved the day. Even with the sat-nav, I got lost on the way to and from the store.

As he was closing the shop, Rennie popped up to see us. He's my second cousin, once removed, or something like that. Anyway, he's older than me and quite stocky. A former rugby player, he liked to give the impression he could tuck a piano under each arm. He had a musical West Country accent, like all the members of Granny's tribe, apart from her. She'd taken her own elocution lessons in the distant past.

Rennie acted warmly towards Dad, joking about getting him back out on the road, heaving Steinways around, as they'd done together in days gone by. Now Dad just helped out by minding the shop and doing a bit of tuning. He made it clear he was keen to return to work, as he didn't want to be cooped up in the flat for too long.

Rennie motioned for me to follow him into the kitchen, where he adopted a more serious tone.

"Strike one," he said. "But it won't be the last. You can see that, can't you? We do what we can with him, but he's old, Victor. Mentally strong, but physically weak. Time is not on his side."

In the past, I might have pushed back at such a suggestion. Uncle Thomas had established a family tradition of acting as if they were doing Dad a favour by employing him. And I could see it – a bit – from their side: he never learned to drive, so this limited how they could make use of him. It also meant that he and Granny were overly dependent on the housekeeper to drive them anywhere they couldn't reach by public transport.

Dad worked long hours, the firm didn't pay him much, and he was constantly putting his back out while moving pianos. I don't think the heavy manual labour suited his wiry physique. When we went to stay with him, he often had a hot water bottle or a bag of frozen peas strapped to his lower back.

Where Uncle Thomas was exploitative, Rennie was much more caring. This was especially true since Dad's move to the flat. Rennie's French wife, Ginette, was attentive, inviting the oldie to the house every week for Sunday lunch.

"Thanks for all you do for him," I said. "I'll stay until he's settled."

I stood over Dad as he made beans on toast for our tea, with a sausage on the side. Much as he might have enjoyed it, I didn't want to wait on him. But I did want to ensure he could cope.

I insisted that he use his stick, even when he was only moving from room to room, and he mumbled and groaned. They'd put his wrist in a light cast and he was able to slip his arm out of the sling when he needed to use both hands.

"Did you ever hear from that girl?" he asked me, as the beans were starting to stick to the pan. He was referring to the episode at Glenhemfrey that I haven't told you about yet.

"No," I said, as I had done down the years. "I never saw her again."

CHAPTER 14

Helping Dad into bed felt eerily like putting Plum down for the night when she was aged six or seven. As I knelt there, the shifting stopped and a magical stillness was attained. He lay straight, tucked neatly under the covers, looking sleepy.

"I'm very proud of you, Dad."

He looked at me, but his eyes were dull, almost reproachful. "Why?"

I leaned towards him.

"Because you've always done your best. In any situation."

I felt as if I were praising myself.

"And you play *Autumn Leaves* better than anyone I know."

Dad was fond of jazz standards, and I was fond of the mellow sound he produced at the keyboard. He gave a dissenting growl; he couldn't handle compliments. I'd have loved to talk to him about our neurodivergence. I tried to broach the subject once but he made it plain that he preferred not to go there.

No matter: he'd held a job down and been a nice father, both of which were great achievements.

"Good night, son."

"Good night, Dad."

I got into a sleeping bag that was too warm, on a sofa that was too saggy, and let my overactive mind wander. I thought of plucky Estelle Thornley taking the steam train from Bath Spa, along a spur of track destined to be swept away in the Beeching cuts. She would meet The Honorable Jeremy Victor Nichol De Vries; William and I would be the result.

My grandfather, who reputedly succumbed to alcohol addiction in 1960, was not only born great, he achieved greatness – though he never had greatness thrust upon him. A part-time middle-ranking desk job at the Ministry of Defence in Bristol probably felt like scant reward for a twice-decorated hero of World War Two. As a navigator in the RAF, Norman De Vries was shot down after two successive bombing raids over Germany. In one instance, he seized the controls of a damaged Lancaster bomber, limped across the channel and made a crash landing in a field near Hastings.

"Only he and the tail-gunner survived," Dad had told me earlier, as we sat and talked when I'd washed up after tea.

I'd heard that story several times when I was a boy, but this visit was the first time he described his father's struggles with peace. Norman was restless and dissatisfied with life at The Great House; he was often bad-tempered and foul-mouthed.

"When he'd had a drink, he could lash out," added Dad. "But most of the time he turned on himself. He was not a happy man, Victor."

Now Dad's reasons for remaining at the house into adulthood made more sense to me. He was "looking out for" Granny. As we talked about Norman, there was his portrait, lying on its side, perhaps symbolising that he was no longer 'great' in our eyes, and no longer a threat. There were hints of Grandad's dark side all through my childhood. I'd always known that the Lord in our family – the very source of our collective prestige – had been "difficult".

Mum always made it clear that she considered Dad to be a greater man than his father. I'd have to concur: if you treat your own children well and with affection after you've had a rough time growing up yourself, you're a great person.

Norman stayed away much of the time, frequenting the House of Lords and his London club, sojourning at the family flat. The anguish in Dad's voice was the same when he talked of this as when he referred to Mum spending weekdays in town. The penny dropped that, for Jeremy, history had repeated itself. Boy and man, he spent much of his time rattling around The Great House, quietly pining for someone of significance in his life who was largely absent.

At the same time, he was slowly being stifled by a mother who was affirming enough, but who could be fussy and impatient.

"She always thought I should be doing better than I was," said Dad.

Granny was, however, his one constant ally. It was she who organised and paid for his piano lessons. His hesitant renditions of classical tunes were the only actions that won his father's approval.

Dad's elder brother, whom he rarely mentioned, had a different response to the domestic disharmony, clearing off to Australia to seek his fortune as a 'Ten Pound Pom'. Dad told me I'd met him when I was little, but I didn't remember that.

My uncle inherited the title, but didn't give a wombat's wank for tradition. He invested his energy instead in academic pursuits in an invigorating young country. He sold The Great House and its share of Pucklewood Park, pocketing the proceeds, but arranged for Dad and Granny to go on living there, paying a peppercorn rent, on a 99-year lease. In a harsh world, that was decent of him, though he also flogged the fixtures and fittings, including all the family treasures. He was clearly a man who preferred cash to cachet.

The presence of fine furniture, great paintings, antique ceramics and the like, all owned by a landlord, merely added to a sense that the lifestyle being acted out within the walls of the house was a shadow-play, an illusion. Discovering these quaintly humiliating circumstances must have come as a shock to the newly wed, self-styled Jayne De Vries. Although she always stressed that she didn't marry Jeremy for money, she had assumed that *some* wealth still resided with the English wing of the family.

"How wrong I was!" she would admit to me later. "They were poor as church mice, and no mistake."

The wealth had all, literally, gone south; draining away with a swish and a gurgle down the plughole of chance, all the way to the Antipodes. I suppose you'd have to count this revelation as a kind of 'reverse-Pemberley' moment, when appearances are found to be chafingly at odds with legal and financial realities. And yet we've retained some family pride. Many English families believe they're special – and not only special but unique – and not only unique but *exceptional*. We're no different.

In my own small room at The Great House, the artworks were modest: a cheap print of Constable's *The Haywain* and a pair of framed embroidery samplers. These were made by twin girls, Mary and Eliza, in October 1851.

They were my great-great-great aunts and I read their little sentences every time I stayed there. One spoke of the weather, the other of hopes for the future. Both spoke of Godliness and virtue. The samplers always puzzled me, being from an unremarkable point in time, bearing such ephemeral messages and yet having been kept and preserved for so long. I wished that Dad had rescued the pair of them, along with the family portraits.

I got up from the sofa as it was evident that I was not about to fall asleep. I pottered around again, eating toast. It wasn't all that late so I made a courtesy call to Rūta and listened to her news, of which there was not a great deal.

"The mother pulled out the lines again," she said, describing how Mum's sheets and pillowcase had got covered in blood as she ramped up her campaign of civil disobedience against being detained in hospital.

There was part of me, the anarchic side, that wanted to cheer her on, and another part that just felt sad, and guilty for being absent. Thinking about our strained relationship, which had waxed and waned over the years, I'd never stopped trying to please her, though we'd never quite managed to see eye to eye.

"I want to go back to touring," I told Rūta. I wasn't serious – there were no parts – but I wanted to say the most selfish things I could think of. "I'll probably leave the island too."

"You must do what makes you happy," she replied, blandly.

We said good night and I rang off. I badly wanted to call Lara, but then if Plum was around, I didn't want her wondering why I wasn't calling her. I wished I had someone else I could talk to at this rather late hour. I thought hard. I'd had various close friends in different times and places. Some of them had stuck with me, while others drifted, but those loyal and lifelong friends I'd accumulated tended not to live within my regular orbit.

I didn't think I was unusual in that, even out here on my outré social limb. I loved these people dearly and thought about them often, but we were in touch only sporadically. I could send them a Christmas card and might even catch up with them if we made a big effort and if our respective tour schedules allowed. I suppose I'm talking pre-pandemic here, which just underlines the point that I could hardly call any of them now, out of the blue, and seek their support through whatever psychodrama I happened to be living.

Of the friends I'd lost, we might have spent a lot of time together and believed ourselves to be close, only to discover at some turning-point that we were relieved when it was all over.

Thus I lost all but one of my Glenhemfrey friends when I left a year early; I lost my few London friends when I went to drama school in Bristol; I lost most of my Bristol mates when I split up with Plum's mum – Kelly – and drifted away from the rest when I moved to the island. It was quite the life lesson to discover that there are items it's irritating to run out of, such as dental floss or wrapping paper, and that another of these can be 'people'.

I was realising, in this way I have of missing the obvious at first, that without Teruko, my time on the island could have been grievously lonely. But it wasn't; it was wonderful. Even after she'd gone, and I was left high and dry, I didn't feel entirely alone. I can't explain that.

A couple of years into my time at Glenhemfrey, a new day pupil arrived: Jack Busby. His actual name was John, but everyone called him Jack. It was the mildest nickname in our year, probably because Jack was always in a chipper mood and had a winsome, harmless sense of humour.

He attached himself to me on his first day. He stayed loyal, even though I was unpleasant towards him on several occasions. I sensed he was weaker than me. He wasn't; he was just nicer. He was that one person at the school who kept in touch with me after I left.

I should have treated him so much better. One break time, I launched into a merciless mockery of Jack to amuse a group of onlookers. I laid into his mannerisms and refined Scottish brogue. They all laughed but he burst into tears and ran off. He was even late back to class. My gambit may have amused my peers but there's a problem with looking down on others like that: it doesn't make anyone look up to you.

I'm appalled when comedians raise a cheap laugh by putting another celebrity down. In panto I've sometimes fallen back on my old mimicry skills and that's always worked well but it's never made me feel good.

After I lampooned my best friend, I was cornered by a hulking prop forward from the rugby team, who was the nearest thing to a bully in our class.

"Carrot, you've been a complete bastard to Jack," he said.

Although Jack shrugged it off and forgave me, I'd never felt so worthless and reprehensible.

Now my phone rang, making me jump. I couldn't imagine who might be calling, then I guessed: Lara – Plum – the hospital – Rennie…

"Oh, hi Victor," said Guy, in his casual drawl, surprised I'd picked up. "You're a difficult man to track down. I was just wondering how you were."

Uhm?… All right, then. Any port in a storm.

We entered into a lengthy conversation then, more or less mapping out our life histories. I ended up telling him about dyslexia, panto, The Great House, Jack Busby, the lot.

"You've done amazing," said Guy. "Though you are quite classist."

"*Oh?*"

"That's not your fault," he added quickly. "It's just the way you were brung up."

Hmm. Thanks for that.

In return, he told me about his hard-working single mum and high-flying younger sister, who'd become a management consultant in her early twenties. I wondered if her drive and ambition had influenced Guy in a way that understated the importance of due diligence.

"She's always had certainty," he said. "She's very sure of herself in ways."

Pride in his sibling seemed to cloud the irony that she had recently been whisked away on a private jet to advise a client on cutting his carbon emissions. But chatting with Guy made me realise something about him, a rare quality. He was genuinely caring and attentive.

Telephone talk burned off the last of my energy and I fell into a deep dark slumber on top of the sleeping bag. Five or six hours later I had to be shaken awake by Dad, who brought me a fortifying cup of tea.

"Are you all right Victor? You've been dead to the world."

I felt bad that he was looking after me, rather than vice-versa. But then I took heart from that. He was the host; this was a normality of sorts. Most importantly he was up and about, on his feet and coping.

In the afternoon Rennie drove us twenty miles for Dad to do a tuning. He'd quietly insisted on taking Dad to the appointment personally, rather than sending him off in a van with one of the drivers, which would have been the usual routine.

I knew it was unprecedented for Rennie to drive anyone anywhere for the business, especially in his own car. Whether Ginette had put him up to it or not, I appreciated the move. It helped maintain the fiction that Dad still had what he liked to describe, in an awful pun, as "a key role". Despite having only one fully functioning hand and ear, he made a reasonably good job of the tuning.

Rennie's car was very comfortable, with cream leather seats and plenty of leg-room. As we glided through some comely villages of sand-coloured houses with mossy lawns, I mused about Dad's life. This travelling around was how he'd met his second wife, a widow who was the leading light of an amateur operatic society. The company tended to rehearse with their own upright piano, then hire a grand for performances. Dad and Mrs Woods got to know each other over time, when he kept popping up to move instruments and tune them for her.

The precise timing of their intimacy was a matter that existed in a convenient haze of vagueness. There could have been some overlap with the first marriage. In any event, the second bride declined to change her name, as so many people knew her as Mrs Woods. Also unlike Mum, she moved straight into The Great House and lived there full-time. Dad told me that Granny was more welcoming and accepting of her than she had been of Mum.

By then the housekeeper had also become part of the family, joining them for meals and for company in the evenings. The four of them in this ad hoc collective watched an increasing amount of television together. The house never lost its sadness but there was a more relaxed regime now, with plenty of courtesy and good humour. The dinner gong was still used, but as more of an in-joke than a throwback to the grand old ways.

CHAPTER 15

After only one more night on the saggy sofa and one more late-night chat with Guy, I was ready to depart. I said my goodbyes, shaking Rennie's meaty hand and giving Dad a gentle hug, which felt like embracing a scarecrow. I folded the back seat down and loaded the family portraits into the car. They only just fitted. Dad asked me to take them as there wasn't space to hang them in the flat. I'd have the same problem, of course, but I hoped to farm them out to William for safekeeping at his mock-Tudor manor.

I set off without really knowing where I was going. I hadn't used all of my compassionate leave, so I thought of having a sneaky weekend in London. Then I realised I could make it home just in time to cover the 'Sat mat', which would save Jim from doing it. I pulled into a lay-by and called him in hands-free mode.

"No need to hurry back," he said, his affable voice booming from the speakers. "With both your parents unwell, we thought it sensible to make alternative arrangements."

"What do you mean?"

"I'm training Pearl to cover for you."

I might as well have been punched. There was a certain pressure that went with my job, though nothing I couldn't handle, and hearing it fizzle and disperse left me feeling dangerously surplus to requirements.

"But she's a student! She's only on the summer course…"

"Exactly. So you'll be back by the time she leaves," he said, smoothly. "Yvonne said you could use up your holiday allowance first, then take an unpaid leave of absence and return when you're free of distractions."

Oh. They think I'm 'distracted'.

"She thinks I can't function? But I did the Wed mat and it went fine!"

"That's not what we're saying, Victor," he intoned, with that exaggerated form of patience that indicates impatience. "Family comes first – we know that. Do what you have to do. And then we'll see."

I couldn't abide Jim's indifferent tone. He was my main connection to the island; I counted him as a friend. If I were to be cut off from him and this job, I'd be cut off from the island. I'd belong precisely nowhere on terra firma. I'd be in the drink.

I tried not to brood about this as I drove along the M4, but it was difficult. At least I'd been cleared to spend more time in London, which meant I could record some more old duck's tales, for what they were worth, and try to repair my relationship with Rūta. But while I'd gain time, I'd also run out of money. This was a short-term fix that wasn't a solution to anything much.

Damn it!

I made an unashamedly emotional decision there and then. I would drive straight to Mum's house in Hampstead and stay there, instead of sofa-surfing at Plum's or staying over at Rūta's. I still had keys for the house, though I hadn't used them in years. I wanted somewhere more solid as my base; I needed to feel I belonged somewhere.

While using her house, I could go through Mum's contacts book, which she kept next to the landline phone in the hall. I thought it would be a good idea to make some calls and let everyone in her social circle know that she was unwell. At the back of my mind, of course, I wondered whether any of her associates would turn out to be her angel and so bring this whole sorry episode to a conclusion. I longed to get back to normal.

Whatever 'normal' meant now...

Around Swindon, I was startled by the phone's amplified ringtone. I did my usual thing of assuming it was the Call of Doom from the hospital, so I was more than glad to hear Lara's disembodied voice coming through the speakers. She'd been left minding the gallery again.

"This place is dead," she said. "I'm sooooo bored."

I told her about my job being handed to a student with little interest in theatre.

"That's a bummer."

But Lara had a work challenge of her own. She'd been left to organise the private view of an incoming exhibition while her boss was gadding about in New York. The show would only be up for a week, so the preview had to make an impact. She had already enlisted Plum and Guy to help; I felt obliged to join in.

"I mean, she's set me a target of a thousand quid in sales," said Lara. "I've no idea how that's going to happen."

We had a detailed conversation then, about drinks, snacks, canapés. The key themes here were the avoidance of nuts, the need to be culturally sensitive and to keep vegans happy. I knew all about this, as I lived off canapés for two months when I gatecrashed parties, trying to get noticed in Hollywood. This was in the aftermath of splitting up with Kelly.

"She called me a loser, so I wanted to achieve some massive success," I told Lara.

"And how did that go?"

"Terribly badly. But I made a few contacts."

Some of the canapés I tasted in Tinseltown were truly awful. Even the more pleasant ones left you with a feeling of deep hollowness. I hated the things. Because of that, our discussion quickly degenerated into a contest for inventing the worst party food ever.

"Horseradish and apple tartlet," I suggested, garnering a giggle.

Then she countered: "Anyone for Brussels sprout and chocolate fondant cup?"

"That's genius!" I chuckled, wondering if I could trump it. "How about pulled pork and marzipan bite?"

"Almonds," said Lara. "And pork isn't inclusive."

When I got to Hampstead, Mum's ugly little hatchback was on her driveway. It was in its customary position at ten o'clock in the tight turning circle around the rose bush. Its wheels were on full right lock, ready for the next journey. I parked behind it.

I'm obsessed by the parking.

As expected, the porch door was closed but unlocked. The approach to the house was illogical, as you had to go up two steps to enter the large square porch, walk across the beautiful yellow and maroon tiled plinth on which it stood, then go down four steps to the front door. I got into the house easily enough, but then the alarm started beeping and I had no idea what the code was to shut it up.

I expected the siren would soon be howling and I'd have some explaining to do, but the first number I tried, William's birthday, proved to be the right one. It occurred to me that I hadn't heard any more about my brother's dastardly plans to sell the house. Perhaps he'd surmised that Mum was unlikely to be propelled out of hospital and into a nursing home any time soon. Or perhaps he'd taken my misgivings to heart.

And pigs might fly, again.

The house was lovely and cool inside. Very still. With its thick walls and modest headroom, Mum's home looked like a house but felt like a cottage. I could reach up and touch the ceiling and had to duck through two of the doorways. I gathered up the post and flyers from the doormat and shuffled them into a neat pile. I put it on the oval table where Mum always placed her keys, next to the lamp made from a Mateus Rosé wine bottle. I half-expected her to bound in by the side door, as she often did when she returned from the shops or the heath.

The plants!

I rushed into the conservatory and fetched the old measuring jug Mum used for watering the plants. I filled it up and went methodically room to room, giving her drooping triffids a drink. I hadn't appreciated quite how many there were, in pots of all sizes, scattered along the available surfaces, some on the floor. I tried to interest them without making up for lost time. A few had already turned brown but I watered them anyway. You never know.

The house seemed to be waiting for something, for someone.

For Godot? But not for me.

I looked around at all the tidy clutter that reflected my mother's personality. She had more cookbooks than she ever used; there was a shelf of twee china animals; she hoarded some other worthless antiques. The coffee table groaned with books and magazines that had been thumbed through once, then abandoned.

When I went upstairs and edged into my old room, I didn't feel much of an emotional pull. There was no bed in there and it had been turned into a storage space, full of old clothes and defunct electrical appliances. William's room was still intact, though his personal trappings were long gone. I plonked my bag down on the old armchair where he used to sit and listen to his tapes. I would sleep in his room.

I pulled down the loft ladder and climbed into the roof space. This was the obvious place to store the family portraits until William could take them. I'd always felt a boyish sense of adventure going up there, though it was home to yet more useless junk. It was inadequately lit by a bare lightbulb, so I flashed the torch around. There were two large stacks of yellowed copies of Mum's newspaper, perhaps containing contributions she was especially proud of.

I opened an old trunk with a rounded lid, which I used to play with, pretending it was a treasure trove on a pirate galleon. It was full of framed photographs, probably of people from Mum's side of the family, and old hairbrushes, pots of paint and loose snapshots from William's childhood that hadn't made it into albums. There was an old jewellery box, full of all kinds of shiny wonders that I used to wear when I was allowed to dress up.

A shoebox had been added at some point, containing some letters and cards, newspaper cuttings, a brooch, a watch, and a photograph of a man I didn't recognise. He did look slightly familiar, which made me think I might have seen this picture before. But I knew who he was; who he had to be. This was surely the "roving reporter" that Marjorie Buttle-Deary had mentioned, with whom Mum had had an affair.

The photograph was black and white; the man wore a Trilby hat with a jacket and tie. He had a neat moustache, receding hair and gentle eyes that gazed fearfully into the middle distance. I put the lid back on the box and closed the trunk.

"Why didn't you read the letters?" asked Lara, when I grabbed a snack and confessed what I'd found.

"That's hard to say."

I think my reluctance was partly about invading Mum's privacy and partly about not entirely wanting to know the gory details of her affair. Nevertheless, at Lara's urging, I did go back into the attic, and read a small sample of the correspondence.

They were what you might expect: a curious blend of the mundane and the dramatic. Arrangements, fragments of news, protestations of devotion were sent to Mum by this man, sometimes in a quick note from another part of London, otherwise in a standard blue airmail letter from abroad. These missives were decades old, but their contents read with freshness and urgency.

I'd seen enough. I went out to the car and started shifting the portraits. Dad had told me who the sitters were and I'd scribbled down their details. These paintings weren't great works of art but they did represent five generations of our family, including a husband and wife pair I'd always admired. All the time I was shifting the paintings, trying not to mark the walls with them, an assertion by Dad was replaying in my head:

"Technically, these don't belong to us, but morally, they do."

It was strange to think that a holdings company, and later a private equity firm, could simply buy one's family history. It was even odder to think of my father stealing parts of it back. He wasn't reckless about it, though. He left behind all the commercially valuable paintings. These included a view of an East India trading ship at Middelburg that always fascinated me, as Granny said no fine art scholar could determine whether it was arriving or departing.

Another prized artwork was a portrait of our Dutch ancestor. This dubious character was a naval officer who was involved in the successful raid on the English fleet in 1667, who later returned as a spy and then betrayed his country as a double-agent. He revealed military secrets that helped the

English to see off the Dutch as major competitors in trade and empire-building.

We know the disloyal bastard's reward: a viscountcy and a portion of Pucklewood Park, with its disused royal hunting lodge. When you really think about it, our system of deference to pirates and toffs is *not necessarily* the most direct route to equality or social harmony. But that is England.

I stacked the last of the purloined paintings and was about to climb down from the attic when I noticed a rail of old clothes that seemed to belong to me. I pulled out a grey suit that I vaguely remembered. I couldn't resist trying it on, just for the hell of it. The suit had been preserved in a zip cover for decades, and smelt of old books and synthetic lemons. It must have dated from the middle of my growth spurt, because it didn't quite fit; the legs and sleeves were slightly short. But I liked it.

I opened the trunk and the box again and pulled out the photograph of the mystery man. When I tucked it in the inside pocket of my suit jacket, it felt as if it belonged to me even though it didn't. I changed back into my normal clothes, carried the suit down the ladder and hung it on the door of William's wardrobe.

"I'll get my money's worth out of you," I said out loud, half-joking to myself.

Already I was finding it quite troubling being at Mum's house without having her in residence. I knew, with some certainty, that she would never return here. So the whole place felt like a living mausoleum. I shivered. I felt much more alone here, in this dreadful stillness, than I did pottering about my own home on the island. The silence was intolerable. I was listening out for the clipping of secateurs, the growl of the food mixer or the long, careful snip of the fabric scissors.

I walked through to the dining room and just stood there vacantly. As Mum always ate in the kitchen, this space was more of a study and crafting studio for her. From this exact spot, facing towards the bureau – which was rarely opened, as it was crammed full of papers – she'd broadcast some tips to the nation about coping with lockdown.

Now her laptop lay on the polished table, lid down. I sat and laid my head upon my arms, wanting to sob my heart out, but no tears would come. I wasn't only mourning a stunted relationship. I was mourning the ghost of a real person – and one who still lived.

CHAPTER 16

I'd had enough of the empty house. I felt restless and wanted to go to the hospital. But I made myself sit still in the hall, as planned, and leaf through Mum's contacts book. I thought Sunday afternoon was as good a time as any to call people with my bleak update. I sat down on the bench of the telephone table, which made the springs creak loudly in protest. It was an item of furniture like no other, feeling neither entirely comfortable nor uncomfortable. I quite liked it. My house didn't have room for this type of furniture, for only occasional use.

Looking through the entries in Mum's book, using my magnifier, I was surprised to find that half the entries had been crossed through. There was no indication of what that meant. Had these people fallen out of favour, or were they dead? I guessed that a subset of them might be dead people who'd also fallen out of favour while they were still alive.

Before I could start making calls, I received one on my own phone, from Henrietta of all people.

"I wanted to check on you, Uncle Vic," she said. "You seemed really down about Nan."

I could hear splashing in the background and assumed she was calling from the poolside at the family's timeshare villa. It was located in the majestic hills of Tuscany, among the fragrant olive groves. It was a place I'd seen in pictures over the years without ever being invited there.

William and his wife, Susan, would preside. Their eldest, Neville, a BBC producer, would be there with his partner. I imagined the person splashing about in the pool would be Henrietta's little brother Dorian, who was still a young teenager and unfairly regarded within the family as 'an accident'.

I told my niece about being in Hampstead but I didn't mention Dad's fall. She sounded especially pleased that I'd watered Mum's plants.

"It's a nice idea to keep them going, whatever happens to her."

That hadn't been my reasoning; I thought it was just part of looking after the house. But now she mentioned it, there was something life-affirming about caring for Mum's array of potted wonders. We chatted a little more, then Henrietta rang off rather abruptly as she had an incoming call.

I went back to my task. I found Marjorie Buttle-Deary's entry, which was marked with an asterisk. I noticed that she lived in Maida Vale, which I knew to be near Paddington, where Mum and William used to rent the first floor of a house when proximity to the station had been more of a priority.

I gave Marjorie a quick call and we made another vague agreement to meet and catch up. I told her about Lara's gallery opening as I thought she might be the kind of person the owner was aiming to attract.

"I must cut my client list down," Marjorie told me. "I'm always so busy. It's frightful."

There were four entries in Mum's book for Constance Municault, three of them crossed through. The last of these, for an address in Pimlico, included three first names, presumably those of her children – Lucas, Donovan and Meriel.

Even though Mum declined to talk about her, I knew Constance was one of her oldest friends. The name had been mentioned sporadically through my childhood. She'd even been my nanny for a brief period, though I didn't remember that and, apparently, it had been an unhappy episode. I called the Pimlico number.

"Who is this?"

A woman's voice, sounding wary. Perhaps no-one called her on the landline any more. I explained the purpose of my ring-round, but she wasn't familiar with Mum's name.

"Well, Constance was my mother," she said. "But she passed away in 2017."

I must have been speaking to Meriel. I would have liked to chat with her, knowing our mothers had once been friends, but in this situation I could only say thank-you and hang up. It was only later that I thought of referring to Mum as Estelle, rather than Jayne.

There was an entry in the book for Ted Tinmer, which had also been crossed through and three cancelled entries for Judith Tinmer, though on the last of these Mum had written: 'See Howden'. The entry for Judith Howden gave her an address in Ottawa.

I dimly recalled these people, whom Mum referred to as "Uncle Ted" and "Auntie Judith". They were two of her distant friends, who always sent Christmas cards and infrequently, separately, came to stay. I'd never really questioned who they were, because you don't as a kid; you just accept whatever you're told. They were an honorary uncle and an honorary auntie and that's all I needed to know. I had no idea they knew each other.

But now I was looking at Ted's address – a farm in Yorkshire – and putting it together with what Mum had told me about her travels there. She'd talked about "Edward", so it hadn't quite clicked. The aunt and uncle I knew vaguely and separately in real life were, in fact, the brother and sister she'd written about in her assignment, all those years ago. They were the son and daughter of parents both deemed to be 'great'.

I recognised some of the other names as I flicked through the book. I went back to the beginning and started making calls in a systematic way. One person had already heard the news, but the rest hadn't. Several were out, or not answering. I left voicemails. The ones I reached all said: "Thanks for letting us know."

However, even the London-based acquaintances showed little appetite for coming to see Mum. I felt dreadfully sad on her behalf. There didn't seem to be anyone she was particularly close to. I recalled that a few Hampstead denizens used to pop round for coffee, but their details weren't in the book. I was sure that some of them had died.

I toyed with the idea of writing to Auntie Judith in Canada. I wanted her to know about the situation but didn't really want her to travel such a long way, just to see Mum in her current state.

I repaired to the dining room and plucked two sheets of paper from the printer. I sat down and stared at them but wasn't sure I could find the words, or that my writing would be presentable enough for Auntie Judith. I got mad and tore the paper into little pieces. Now I felt even more twitchy – exactly as I used to be when I failed to build things at Glenhemfrey – and heaved myself out of the house instead.

I walked briskly to the tube station. I wished Mum had experienced her medical drama closer to home. That way she would have ended up at a different hospital a five-minute stroll away. She'd spent the odd night there in the past. As it was, I hurtled and rattled and scraped and sighed my way into town on the tube.

The nurse, whom I didn't recognise, was busy with other visitors, so I just breezed into the ward. Straight away I got a shock: there was an old man in the bed where Mum had been. I assumed she'd expired. But then, if and when that happened, I knew someone would call me.

I scanned the ward and it took a few moments to work out that she'd been moved into the glass 'corner office'. Perhaps she'd been promoted, as a particularly deserving case. Or maybe, in view of her public profile, they'd awarded her a discreet little place of her own.

How delightful!

As soon as I got inside, though, I knew differently. There was an overwhelming stench – so much so, you weren't breathing air at all, but vapourised shit. I felt the impulse to retch, but managed to hold it. This place was foul and disgusting, some kind of hell.

I went over and spoke to Mum but I was on her wrong side and she was very drowsy. She was struggling to breathe. She didn't seem to know where she was or what was happening, let alone who I might be. Perhaps she was drugged up. I asked if she wanted to be changed and she said: "Yes please."

I wasn't surprised; she was obviously basking in her own filth. I ran out to the vestibule and gabbled at the nurse, who agreed to change Mum but told me there was little point, as she had diarrhoea.

"As soon as we change her she'll need changing again."

Short of putting her in the shower all day, she added, there was no way of keeping Mum clean. I could see her point but I didn't like her complacency. I noticed she wasn't wearing a lanyard so I had no idea who she was.

"But it's not *liveable* in there!" I raged. "You haven't even opened the window for her."

The nurse gave me a disdainful look – *do you know what pressures we're under?* – but said nothing. She snatched an adult nappy from under the counter and stamped off to change Mum. She didn't even bother to pull the curtain around the bed.

I knew I'd rumbled some awful practice here. The team had shut Mum away in this isolation cubicle and left her for hours at a time, only venturing inside to maintain a minimal semblance of care. They'd let it get so stinky, so contaminated, there could be no other explanation. And Mum was dying in there. They were letting her fade away in the most vile, degrading circumstances. If this was some kind of retribution for pulling her wires out, it was pretty savage.

Perhaps Jim had been entirely right and I needed to give Mum all of my attention now. He knew what happened when no family were there to demand decent treatment. He, as a former prison warder, knew what people got up to when your back was turned.

"I've opened the window," said the nurse, expecting praise.

"It's not enough," I snapped. "We need a fan and some air fresheners. And is she getting dehydrated or something? She seems completely out of it."

"We don't have a fan," said the nurse.

"This is a very big hospital," I said. "Find one."

"If you're going to be aggressive, I'll have to report you."

"And if you don't get my mother out of that glass box within twenty-four hours, I'll make a formal complaint. All I'm asking for is basic care. I'm going to phone Dr Priene in any case."

She half-nodded at that and, over the next two hours, in between performing other tasks for other patients, proceeded wordlessly to provide everything I'd requested. Air fresheners were positioned around the cubicle and a spray was deployed. A fan was set up on a stack of plastic chairs, blowing towards Mum and the open window. A hydration drip was inserted into her arm. Her adult nappy was changed twice more.

I was shocked. If I hadn't taken the initiative, my mother's quality of life would have remained worse than zilch.

Satisfied that the storm had abated, I stumbled off to get something to eat at the Neurology café. I also pushed the button for 'White Coffee, No Sugar' and this time received white tea with sweetener. It tasted of boiled water that a chocolate mouse had died in, which seemed a fair exchange for 50p.

I squeaked across the link bridge, gazed into the atrium and made some calls. I hoped it was late enough to phone Rūta, who was on night shift again. She sounded tired but glad to hear my voice. I asked how long Mum had been cooped up in the glass corner room but didn't get a clear answer. The doctor listened sceptically to the issues I raised, as if she'd heard them many times before.

"This sounds like a nursing issue," she said, robotically. "You should address any complaints to the staff nurse. I deal only with the medicine."

"You're supposed to be a team," I thought, but didn't say. "And dehydration *is* a medical issue."

She invited me over to the flat for actual coffee and I agreed to go there once I'd made a couple more calls. I checked on Dad, who claimed to be eating regular meals. He restated that he would come up to London when he could.

"We were married nineteen years," he added. "We had our good times."

I got hold of Plum as well. She admitted she'd been too busy with work lately to visit her nan. When I asked how it was going, she unexpectedly let loose some anxiety about her affair with Franklin.

"He's losing interest in me," she said, miserably. "We're both spending lots of money at all the best restaurants and clubs, which we never did before. It's like we're trying to regain something we've lost, or win each other back. But it's all a smokescreen, Dad. It's gone wrong and I don't know how to fix it."

I mumbled that I was sure it would work itself out in the end; a knowingly trite assurance that could mean anything. She seemed to be angling for advice, but I was loath to tell her how to perpetuate an arrangement with a married man. I'm not puritanical about such situations, which well-meaning people can easily find themselves in. I'm just not an 'affairs' kind of person.

I've always found it enough of a challenge to maintain a one-to-one relationship, without the complication of extra players. Even this dalliance with Rūta was a mystery to me. After our impasse on the island, I feared we were finished. But then an hour after my call, we were in her bed again. She even went so far as to present me with a very thoughtful gift: a beautifully crafted leather manbag. It wasn't something I'd have chosen for myself but I felt truly touched.

"This is for the notebook, honey," she said, and I knew instantly that the bag and I would become inseparable for years, until it fell apart, and even then I'd probably get it repaired.

"Thank you. I really appreciate this. It's so kind of you."

I walked back to the hospital with Rūta and we both checked on Mum. There was now only a faint smell in the glass room, the sort of mixture of residual scents – poo and nappy cream – that you might encounter in a public baby changing cubicle.

"How are you feeling, Mrs De Vries?" asked Rūta, checking Mum's monitors and adding to the notes on her clipboard.

"Is it lunchtime?" asked Mum, eyelids flickering. "I haven't had them, and it's all of it all…"

"She's fine," said Rūta, moving on. "Just exhausted. Don't stay too long."

I sat on the plastic chair by Mum's good side. I knew she was more than exhausted; she was traumatised. It would take her some time to recover, even to the poor condition I'd previously seen her in. I took her left hand in mine.

"Come on, Mum. *Left for rogues.* Don't fade away now."

"William?" She tried to open her bleary eyes, to no avail.

"Let's do your memoirs," I said. "Why were you unfaithful to Dad?"

I wanted to see if she could focus, so I said the first outrageous thing that came to mind.

"Don't be so *damn daft*!" she retorted, the last in her Lancashire voice.

I was going to leave it there, but she continued: "It wasn't like that at all."

She rolled slowly onto her back, apparently contemplating my question.

"I wanted it to be good between us," she said, with startling clarity, as if she'd just received medication to wake her up, along with some kind of truth drug.

"Not for me – I'm not a sexual person – but I knew it would be important to Jeremy."

"Yes?"

"All I wanted was to try it first. To be able to help, you see. But then…"

"You developed feelings for the other chap? The roving reporter?"

"No need to be sarcastic, William. He was a *foreign correspondent*."

She opened her eyes and stared upwards, both seeing and not seeing.

"When you say you're not a sexual person…"

"No, I was slightly wrong on that. I did find it *intriguing*, in a way. This thing that drives people. And the effect it had, of drawing us together. Me and Jeremy. And me and him."

She frowned and her face muscles tensed, as if she were blocking out pain.

"I'm sorry, William. You don't want to know all this."

CHAPTER 17

The next morning I was woken by my phone, not by its alarm app, which I'd ignored, but by Guy.

"Are you up yet, Victor? I'll be with you in twenty."

I scrambled out of bed and had a shower so hasty I could have been taking part in some curious Olympic sport. I dressed in a new personal best time and rushed downstairs for some breakfast, which I was still dispatching when I heard Guy pulling onto the driveway in Roddy's car.

"We have a deal, see," Guy explained during our late-night chat. "He sometimes lends me his car, rather than paying me."

The would-be Mushroom King had at last taken a punt on the profitability of fungi. So we agreed to set off at the crack of nine and flog the stuff at an outdoor market.

Guy decided his unique selling point would be to offer meal kits for risotto. Alongside the mushrooms we'd sell packets of risotto rice and a recipe he'd found online. He was convinced we'd make a healthy mark-up on the rice as well as the mushrooms.

"This one's a winner, Victor! I can feel it in my water."

I stood in the porch doorway, my new manbag slung from left shoulder to right hip. I looked at the ancient black Volvo estate that was now headlight to headlight with Mum's runabout. Roddy's vehicle looked like nothing so much as a hearse, though the vast space behind the front seats was occupied by boxes of fresh produce rather than a coffin.

"Blimey, this is some gaff!" said Guy, wide-eyed, ambling towards the house.

I knew he'd want a tour before we set off, though this wasn't on our schedule. He cooed at Mum's mismatched furniture and marvelled at her bric-a-brac. No doubt he imagined some of these items on Roddy's stall and longed to add this shabby-chic property to his portfolio of possible purchases.

At my request, he refrained from vaping inside the house and the car. I assumed we'd be selling the mushrooms at the same market, but Guy had other ideas. He was adamant that we needed to split up and sell in two locations at once.

"Otherwise we'll never shift the stock before it goes off."

How appetising.

He revealed that the boxes in the car represented only a fraction of what he'd purchased from the wholesaler at a knock-down price. The rest of the big, flat Portobello mushrooms were languishing in an unrefrigerated lock-up garage in Pinner.

"He says he'll let me buy twice as much next time," said Guy, proudly.

We arrived at the first market, my driver beeping his horn at unwary shoppers as he negotiated the narrow thoroughfare between the stalls. We unloaded all the boxes, cardboard signs with the price on, tape for fixing these in place, a card reader, a jar of change, a large pile of paper bags and a huge bag of recycled carrier bags.

The organiser scowled at us for arriving late and told us off for bringing a horseless carriage into a pedestrian area after the time allotted for setting up. But what was done was done.

"Discount like mad if you have to," said Guy, failing to disclose the minimum profitable price, as, presumably, he hadn't worked it out. "We can't be left with any stock on our hands, or we're dead."

He then attempted to turn the stubbornly lengthy car and backed it into stands selling shoddy sports clothes and knock-off designer handbags, incurring the wrath of all concerned. He gave a smile and a friendly wave and rolled slowly through the less-than-bustling retail outlet before roaring off to collect another load for himself to sell.

With only two products to place, and a stack of recipe sheets, it didn't take me long to set up using the trestle table provided. Then I looked around. It was an overcast morning, the sun struggling to break through. There was a gaggle of uninspired customers and most of the other stallholders were scrolling on their phones. A distant radio tinkled away. I felt quite lost and alone.

I could hear a stallholder at the far end, a proper grocer, shouting traditional market lines – "Come on girls, three for two on your courgettes! All them apples for a quid!" – and knew instinctively this approach was not for me. I felt terribly shy and withdrawn. My only options appeared to be to make a diffident, half-arsed effort and sell next to nothing, or put on a show.

I made a very quick circuit of the stalls and picked up a large bottle of water. Like the true professional I am, I completed some vocal warm-ups – "Ning, ning, ning, ning, *nah*-ah-ah-ah / Ning, ning, ning, ning, nah-ah-ah-*aah*!" – which drew some funny looks. I didn't care; I'd never see these people again.

I decided to adapt the lyrics of numerous well-known songs and make them relate to the meagre fare I had to offer.

My first ditty was one of the most obvious but it brought a smile to those passing by: *Just One Risotto*. I put plenty of ironic feeling into it but kept the volume under control as I didn't want my throat to start feeling hoarse after only a few minutes. I needed to stay the course.

One or two people stood and watched as I performed *Cook Me Tender* and *Twenty-Four Hours From Mushrooms*, but things really picked up when I hit them with *Mushroom Sally* and *Wouldn't It Be Rice*. As I had no backing track, people started clapping the rhythm for me. I threw in some dance moves, bagging mushrooms and holding them out until someone bought them in mid-song. It was all rather camp and they loved it.

A small crowd formed when I started crucifying songs from the shows. *I Don't Know How to Stir It* went down particularly well, as did *The Mushroom of the Night* and, my own particular favourite, *Any 'Shroom Will Do*. With that one, they even joined in, singing the '*uh-o-aahs*'. I couldn't believe it: I still had the touch, I was still the showman. Between numbers, these great people queued patiently to buy their risotto kits. After two hours, I was all sung out and everything was gone. I phoned Guy to let him know.

"Good on you, Victor," he said. "That was quick! I still got loads. I dunno whether I'm chuffed or miffed."

Rather than wait for him, I hid the takings in my bag and found my way, with some difficulty, to the nearest tube station. Then I rode into town to visit Mum.

I was feeling a bit cheap and seedy for extracting a confession from her when she was in a semi-delirious state. I'd only meant to shock her back into moderate consciousness by putting the psychological paddles on her. She'd more or less disclosed that she was asexual, though she didn't use that precise term. She made it clear that she didn't experience sexual attraction but she did have some strongly romantic feelings towards others.

Welcome to the queer community, Mum.

There was a deep irony in her having wanted to make a success of her union with Dad by going off and sleeping with someone else. Whether a mistake or simply a choice, it's one she made at the age of nineteen. And the fact is, teenage Jayne messed up less than I did.

Nurse Roslyn was present on the ward when I arrived.

"Your mother seems brighter today, sergeant."

She informed me that Mum would be leaving the glass room at some point that day. The timing depended upon having enough staff available to move her bed and all the equipment in tandem. I nodded in approval.

I sat on Mum's good side, did 'left for rogues' and got her talking again. She told me some more bits and pieces from various times in her life. It was the same old jumble. Her energy came and went. I scribbled and scrawled as many of the details as I could.

Instead of telling you what she said on that particular Monday afternoon, I can now sketch in the missing sequence of events between the departure of the flighty Dottie Woodwald from Mrs French's boarding house at Cromwell Road and Estelle being set her life-changing test assignment.

This gap had been bothering me. I rather pestered Mum with questions about it during that third week of her illness. As I calculate it, after four days in London, Estelle was sent to Fleet Street by the temping agency. There she had a tricky interaction with the stern middle-aged woman – 'The Dragon' – who was to become her boss.

The youngster reported to main reception and was told to wait in the lobby, with its impossibly tall ceiling and people coming and going. There were couriers delivering photographs, campaigners arriving to be interviewed, reporters dashing out to get their stories – though at that stage she had no idea who these people were or what they did. She just gazed upon this frenetic scene and felt overawed.

She was escorted to the copytakers' office, along a dingy corridor on the ground floor. She had to wait again there. Three young women were typing away, wearing headsets connected to telephones. A fourth was working at a slower pace without a headset, probably typing out some minutes or a memorandum.

The constant clicking of the typewriters and the happy ding that issued from them as lines were completed: these were sounds Estelle was familiar with from her evening classes. They put her at ease.

The Dragon emerged from her office with another candidate, who seemed only too glad to scuttle away to safety. The woman had butterfly spectacles and a bouffant hairdo, the overall effect being terrifying enough, but she had a humourless personality to match. She looked over Estelle's credentials.

"I see you have no experience and no qualifications," she stated.

"That's not right, Miss," Estelle piped up, to the Dragon's fiery displeasure.

Her career turned on this interjection; the copytakers' supervisor had been about to terminate their exchange. Instead she leaned forward.

"Come on, girl – either you have something or you haven't. Which is it?"

"Please, Miss – I've done everything but the exam. I can do typing and shorthand. Let me show you."

"Huh! We haven't got time for that! We'd be here all day."

The Dragon paused though, tempted to dig deeper.

"Can you handle dictation? Have you done audio typing?"

"Ooh, yes, Miss."

Technically Essie hadn't lied, because she had done the

former if not the latter. The Dragon nodded doubtfully then looked up, unsmiling.

"Very well, we'll give you a week's trial. Report to the front desk at 8.30 sharp Monday morning and ask them to buzz copytakers. Never be late, d'you hear? You may go now. Good day t'you."

That the appointment was provisional as well as temporary did not bother Estelle one jot; she was being given a chance. If she could work and earn more money than she spent, she could stay away from her childhood home, possibly forever.

She danced out of the newspaper office and frolicked all the way back to the boarding house. She bought some impossibly expensive sausages in Harrods, to cook using the hotplate in her room and share with Dottie. She didn't suspect that her companion had already departed without a dickey-bird of explanation. As soon as Mrs French informed her of this, there was a further blow.

"You're now responsible for filling the vacancy," declared the landlady, puffing on her cigarette. "Otherwise, I'll charge you for the empty room."

Estelle thought that was completely unfair; she wasn't responsible for what someone else did. Immediately, she opened the front door and saw a young Black woman carrying a hefty suitcase. She had a piece of paper in her free hand. When she paused and set the suitcase down, Estelle called out to her.

"Excuse me, are you looking for a room? We have a vacancy."

Mrs French was horrified. "Haven't you seen my sign?" she hissed, jostling Estelle on the top step. A hand-written note in the window by the door read: '*No blacks. No dogs. No Irish.*'

The girl pointed up the street; she was looking for a different address.

Undaunted, Estelle smiled and waved for her to come up the front steps. Here was an opportunity to wriggle out of the tight spot Mrs French had put her in.

"If you don't give the room to her, when I've found you the girl, then your vacancy is none of my concern," she said, out the corner of her mouth.

The landlady muttered a truculent riposte but now the girl was right in front of them. She was bonny, with a wide smile and neat braided pigtails. She looked tired.

"You have a room?"

"Yes, would you like to see it?" asked Estelle pleasantly, but Mrs French intervened.

"Where are you from, duckie?"

"Bridgetown, Barbados, ma'am."

"I don't normally take blacks," she said, looking the girl up and down, holding her cigarette aloft in a proprietorial manner.

"I'm not a 'black'. I'm a very good girl."

"Very polite too," said Estelle, sensing events moving her way.

Mrs French let out a "*Huh!*"

"It's four pounds, six shillings a week," she added, hoping to put the girl off.

"But the good news is your deposit's already paid," said Estelle, leading them upstairs to the second landing. "Isn't that right, Mrs French? Because you said Dottie never asked for her money back."

The landlady muttered some more. Estelle swung the bedroom door open and the girl entered, looking around uncertainly. Her smile was gone. She hoisted her suitcase onto the bed.

"I'm Estelle. What's your name?"

"Constance."

There was a pause when nobody could think of anything to say, so Estelle added: "Welcome to London." After all, she'd lived here longer than the new arrival.

"Well, how about it – would you like to take the room?" she asked, trying to overcome Mrs French's hostility with her own friendliness. Constance looked from one to the other. Estelle got the feeling she was a proud person, not enjoying being in a vulnerable situation.

"I would like to. If Mrs French agrees? This room is very blessed."

"What work will you do?" snapped the landlady, ever protective of her income.

"I want to be a nurse," said Constance, grimly. "I did some of that back home."

Mrs French rolled her eyes and made a racist and patronising comment about Constance that I'm not going to repeat here. Then she gave a terse recitation of the house rules and handed over the keys. They left the new tenant to unpack and settle in.

CHAPTER 18

So at long last, Mum was telling me about Constance. The myth I'd grown up with centred on how kind my mother had been, standing up for what she called a "coloured" girl at a time when our society was steeped in the most hideous discrimination. In this retelling of the story, I also noticed the usefulness of Constance to Mum. I could imagine that for Estelle, scraping by on savings that had nearly dwindled away, being charged for a second room would have been ruinous.

If she was grateful for Estelle's assistance in finding accommodation, Constance never showed it. In fact, it took three or four times knocking on her door just to be invited in. Then the new girl seemed to tolerate Estelle a little more each time and they became acquaintances. They got along together and did some of the things friends do, but there was always some reserve from Constance. Estelle interpreted this as her housemate having the air of superiority of someone two years her senior; someone who only deigned to walk up to Estelle's room once.

They shared some great moments, though. One night in August of that first year, Constance took Estelle to a small music club near Notting Hill, where a singer from Jamaica was establishing a following. His band, Mack's Hoopers, combined a brass section from the West Indies with what Constance called "English boys" on guitar, bass and drums, all outcasts from previous bands.

The significance of this particular gig was clearly signalled in the banners and flags that festooned the hall. It would prove to be a joyful and exuberant celebration of Jamaica achieving its independence.

The sound was sensational. Estelle had never been to a live gig before and struggled with the loudness but adored the tunes. She hadn't heard anything like them on the radio. They were mostly short up-tempo numbers with instrumental solos, interspersed with soulful rhythm. The band played blues songs and calypso. There was ska, too, a pulsating precursor to reggae.

People stood around the bar or sat at tables, or went to the front for a dance. The style of dancing was ballroom with some adapted jive moves, while ska had its own distinctive rhythmic actions. The odd times I witnessed Mum dancing, she'd either do the twist or perform ska moves, raising her arms alternately. This always set her apart. She eschewed the later freestyle side-to-side jig that others adopted during the 1960s.

On that special night Estelle twirled Constance around for a few numbers, then her partner got talking to some boys and disappeared to the back of the hall for a while. During a break, Estelle approached the horn player to tell him how much she was enjoying the music. He looked at her guardedly but they danced together to a couple of recorded tracks. His name was Danny.

Constance liked to talk about boys. She would giggle and her eyes would shine with excitement. Estelle relished these times. She could feel some warmth coming from her nearly-friend but had little to contribute to the conversation. All the young men she knew were on the end of a telephone line, impatient to dictate their copy.

"We often had a few seconds' chat before they gave me their reports. You know how it goes, William. I was polite but firm with the ones who tried to flirt."

One boy in particular spoke quickly and indistinctly in a strong Nottingham accent and swore at her when she asked him to slow down. In retaliation, she started to substitute words, simplify sentences and make guesses about the reports he was filing.

As she realised later, when she received some training in journalism law, this could have got her sacked. The court reports were supposed to be captured verbatim. However her fiendish habit went unremarked. The Dragon got what she demanded, which was "nice clean copy for the compositors", and everyone was happy.

After three months, the temporary placement became a permanent job. For her part, Constance found work quickly as a hospital cleaner. The girls each worked five days out of seven, on rolling rotas that included weekends.

"Don't mind working my way 'til I meet Prince Handsome!" joked Constance.

After a while the girls pooled their resources and saved up the required eleven guineas to purchase a Dansette record player. There was no question as to where it would reside: in Constance's room. Now Estelle felt like a proper teenager, buying singles and rushing home to play them. She and Constance found they could avoid jogging the playing arm, and thereby scratching the record, by dancing over by the bay window.

One of the first tunes they bought was *Love Me Do*. I know this because I played it myself as a child, along with many other singles in Mum's collection, and the Mack's Hoopers albums. That Caribbean sound, which was so special to

Estelle, has always been a part of my own musical taste. While I was growing up, we had one of those towering 1980s music centres with a record player on the top – it still stood proudly in Mum's conservatory – and I made much use of it when I was bored.

Anyway, back to the story. Just before Christmas, when the girls returned to Mrs French's from a trip to the shops, they found Estelle's father sitting on the bench in the hall. He had a raincoat and an overnight bag. He'd come, he said, to take his daughter home. It appeared that Dottie Woodwald had eventually bowed to pressure and divulged the address.

"Your aunt's been worried sick," her dad grumbled, after a sullen silence.

"She doesn't care about me," said Estelle.

He looked wounded. "Of course she does! We both do. And we want you home, where you belong."

"Why?"

"It's not right, this running away. You're still a child. Anything could've happened to you. And why are you hanging round with someone like *that*?" He jabbed a finger towards Constance. "*They* don't belong here."

Constance folded her arms, stood her ground. "I pay my rent, mister. This is my home, right here."

"Yeah," said Estelle. "If you're going to be nasty to my friend, I'll never talk to you again."

"How dare you! I'm your father. And you'll bloody well do what you're told. You're coming home with me right now!"

Estelle slumped to the floor, refusing to budge. Her dad started trying to drag her from the premises. When Mrs French heard the commotion, she emerged from her ground floor quarters and gave Mr Thornley his marching orders, in a fancy affected voice they'd never heard before.

"You've asked the girl to return with you; she has refused; you have no right to force her," she declared. "If you don't leave, I shall telephone the police station and have you removed."

She opened the front door and held it open. It was obvious that she'd done this before, perhaps many times. Slowly, reluctantly, Estelle's dad picked up his coat and bag. He glowered at Mrs French.

"You haven't heard the last of this!" he bellowed, as he passed through the doorway.

The landlady let the door slam after him, smiled benignly at the girls and disappeared back into her quarters as if nothing of note had occurred. From that point onward, there was a thawing of the frostiness that had existed between Mrs French and the girls. It would be another few months before she took down her hateful handwritten sign, but that did happen.

In the new year, around the time of Estelle's eighteenth birthday, the office junior appeared in the copytakers' room. Several reporters were off with colds and flu; an extra body was desperately needed to cover an event. Estelle's hand shot up but the Dragon was reluctant to let the new girl take on the task. However it was raining heavily outside and the other four girls didn't want to get their hair wet again. Estelle covered the job. In so doing, she entered a whole new world.

First she had to go upstairs and be briefed by the news editor, a tall, suave man with a no-nonsense attitude. Then she had to find her way to the venue, where one of the less prestigious trade exhibitions was being launched. Back at the office, she was obliged to type out her story in the newsroom; a vast, clattering space. Apart from Dolly, the women's page editor, Estelle was the only female present. While this aroused much curiosity, the news editor rebuked the reporters and reminded them about their deadlines.

He rejected Estelle's first attempt, but in a friendly way. He rewrote the 'intro' to make it punchy and handed it back to her as an exemplar. He helped her select the pertinent information from her endless pages of notes, not by doing it for her, but by giving her guidance.

"He asked me a series of questions," Mum told me. "I could see he wasn't trying to catch me out or make me feel daft. He was getting me to think about what I was writing."

She noticed that he asked very *obvious* questions, unlike the obtuse ones they used to ask at school. These built upon a certain notion of natural curiosity and common sense, which she found appealing.

"If *you* find it interesting, the chances are the reader will too," he told her.

She was also summoned to the desk of Causley Symons, a senior sub-editor. He pointed out an error, then enquired how she was enjoying her stint in the newsroom. Causley was a jaded portly man with ruddy cheeks, who reputedly spent lunchtimes eating sandwiches in his car and listening to the cricket on a transistor radio he kept in the glovebox.

"You're a plain little Jane, aren't you?" he observed, a twinkle in his eye.

The following morning, Estelle saw her report in print. It was hidden away on an inside page; it had been cut short and some of the phrasing had been altered, but none of this mattered. Without her reportage the story would not be in the paper. And there it was: 'Latest appliances revealed.'

She was hooked. She'd discovered how much more exciting it was to be a reporter than a typist. As Mum expressed it, as a writer you could learn something about life and then share what you'd found with other people. The fact of publication transformed your solitary activity into a communal experience.

They kept Estelle as a substitute reporter for four days, which was just long enough for her to acclimatise to 'editorial' and its distinctive culture, before she was unceremoniously cast off and sent back below stairs.

But the pit pony had grazed in the field. She was determined to rejoin the writing team permanently, whatever it took.

She started reading the paper thoroughly and spent many of her days off in the public galleries of various courtrooms, as well as the House of Commons.

She was desperate to understand how everything worked – socially, politically, mechanically. She made the Science Museum an annexe of her bedsitting room. Suddenly everything was relevant; her passion for knowledge grew and grew.

Constance didn't appreciate this development. Whenever Estelle tried to share some new interest, the conversation would always arrow back to clothes, music, boys. She was bemused when Constance lent her a disarmingly frank book that discussed dating, love affairs, sex and contraception – including the pill, which had only been around for a couple of years.

She read it from cover to cover, mostly out of curiosity. She returned to the music club near Notting Hill, with and without Constance, where she would have the occasional dance with Danny, the horn player. He seemed to be on the brink of asking her out a couple of times.

"But I only wanted to be friends anyway," Mum told me.

Estelle's professional quest might have proved impossible but for the loophole in the apartheid between journalists and support staff that Causley Symons afforded her. After inviting her to the pub on a Friday, then largely ignoring her there, he told her: "Come again next week, Jane."

So she did. She reminded him of her real name, which he ignored. Thereafter her attendance became a habit. Causley had several acolytes among the reporters – puppies, he called them – all anxious to win his approbation but more likely to receive a sardonic comment, especially if they drank too much, which happened frequently.

Estelle noticed this and made a point of supping only lemonade or orange juice. She began submitting unsolicited news stories and lengthier features in the hope of inveigling her way back into editorial. All of them were spiked – literally, there was a tall metal spike near the news editor's desk on which the unwanted stories accumulated.

"The editor's intrigued by you, Jane," said Causley, in a rare and pithy intervention. "He's not keen on girls. He tries to put them off by giving them special assignments. *Beware.*"

The warning proved to be timely. Estelle was sent a note one day, asking her to report to the editor's office during her lunch break. She sat with the editor's secretary in the outer office for a few uncomfortable minutes, then entered the lion's den.

The editor stood behind his desk, scrutinising some papers in his hand with the aid of a pair of half-glasses. Estelle sat in a small, stiff chair on one side of the door; the news editor was lounging in an armchair on the other.

"Now then, Miss Thornley, I gather you wish to join our pack of newshounds.

We know you're a competent typist and a quick learner, and so forth – so here's what we've decided to do. We want you to write a piece to a specific brief, so we can judge whether your writing is of sufficient quality to move you up here. If not, we'd ask you to desist from sending unwanted stories. Understood?"

"Yes, sir."

"Right then. The article we want you to write will be called, let's see… er, let's call it: '*Sons of Great Men*'. Do you think you can write on that topic?"

"Yes, sir – certainly, sir. Would this be a special assignment?"

Three bags full, sir.

He stopped pacing and peered at her over the top of his half-glasses.

"Well," he said, with an evil smile, "it can be as *special* as you choose to make it."

The news editor added that she would have one month to write the piece and that all the research and interviews would have to be completed in her own time, on her days off. She would not be paid, but reasonable travel and accommodation expenses would be recompensed.

Research? Interviews? Travel?

Estelle's mind was in a whirl. The editor strode over to one of the filing cabinets and opened the top drawer. He lifted out a cash box, which he unlocked. He extracted several notes.

"Here you go. That's thirty-five pounds to get you started. If you need any more, present the receipts to my secretary. That will be all."

Estelle tried very hard to think of ideas around the topic. She knew that time was already ticking away. This was her one chance – and she couldn't even get to grips with the title!

The following lunchtime she went outside and looked for Causley. He was sitting in his parked car in a side street, enjoying a sandwich away from the work mob. When she tapped on the window he waved her away. Undaunted and uninvited, she opened the door and sat in the passenger's seat. Exasperated, Causley turned off his radio and demanded to know what the hell she thought she was doing.

She explained her predicament and he relented.

"Look, it's obviously a trap," he said. "People may be interested in great men, but they don't give a flying fig about their sons. You'll have to find an angle for each one and *make them* interesting."

Estelle understood the approach, as the news editor had already explained the concept of an 'angle'. But she was struggling with the enormity of the challenge ahead.

"All right," said Causley, with an ironic chuckle. "Here's what you'll do. Go to three different parts of the country – say Fife, Yorkshire, the West Country – so your story appeals widely. Cover the different types of greatness. If you don't know what I'm talking about, see Shakespeare – *Twelfth Night*. Look it up. Get local people to point you in the right direction. Keep asking questions until you get what you need. Don't talk to other journalists. Now kindly get out of my car."

CHAPTER 19

Mum was now out of the glass corner room, stationed opposite her original position. A geriatric ward may appear to be static but I was learning that little changes are happening all the time. I glanced around the room at the faces of the old people. Although I'm an unreliable face-reader, I felt sure that only two other patients had been here all the time since Mum was admitted.

By the end of that week of selling mushrooms with Guy and listening to Mum, I'd almost filled a second notebook. I was recording her reminiscences at the front and my own thoughts and deeds at the back.

At the house I worked my way around the garden, filling carrier bags with rhubarb, blackberries and Mum's belovèd gooseberries. I knew she wouldn't want them going to waste, so I gave them to her neighbours.

In terms of Estelle and her assignment, we've almost reached the point in the story where we came in. The only part we've missed is the sensationally unrewarding episode in Scotland.

I can provide a short summary here. Mum's first ever foray north of the border got off to a poor start when a librarian in Edinburgh dismissed the ancient kingdom of Fife as "mostly fields". Despite this, Estelle found an academic at St Andrews, the son of a distinguished archaeologist, who was possibly the most tiresome man she'd ever met. He also wasted a lot of time trying to sweet-talk her into bed, and she was having none of that.

"He put his hands all over me, William. Yuck! I couldn't wait to get away."

The situation was saved when she learned that he had a brother based in London, an architect who was busy pulling down slums and replacing them with high-rise blocks. He was worth interviewing but had a busy schedule. Almost on deadline, Estelle grabbed half an hour with him in Birmingham.

"What one's doing," he said, in a muzzled Scottish accent, "is making a permanent revolution in design that bestows hope and confidence upon the humble."

The news editor had instilled in Estelle the idea that you build a story around the facts; only when you had those could you add any kind of embellishment. This was the only profile, of the four she wrote, that had more embellishment than facts. It was not a masterpiece but it just about fulfilled the brief.

I can say that with certainty because, after searching high and low, I discovered Mum's carbon copy of *Sons of Great Men*. It was in a folder with a lot of unrelated material, in a drawer of the bureau in the dining room. She'd insisted that she had a copy somewhere.

As you can imagine, I was in quite some state when I finally got my hands on that report. I felt like Howard Carter, opening the tomb of Tutankhamun. Well, maybe it wasn't quite *that* epic. But there's no doubt the document was hugely significant: it launched a career and inspired an offbeat marriage. You could even say that, without Estelle tapping on the window of Causley Symons' car, I might never have existed.

Thank you, Causley, for sending her to the West Country.

The sheets of Mum's work were held together by a paper clip that had rusted. When I realised what the piece was, my hands shook and my heart started pounding. I was so worked up that the smudgy blue words swam around on the page. I had to put the report aside, calm down and go back to it later.

Of course I found Estelle's respectful profile of Jeremy immensely touching, even if her language was formal to the point of being clunky. She gave no hint of an emotional bond being forged between them. As for the unsolicited supplement, *Daughter of a Great Woman*, I could see why the news editor had been so struck by it. There's a lightness of tone and an enthusiasm for the family and the rural setting that draws the reader into their world.

After reviewing her words many times that week, I got into a groove of sitting in the conservatory as the sun went down, having a glass of port and listening to the old records until it became too chilly to stay in there. I could have put the heater on, but in the height of summer that seemed rather wasteful.

Mack's voice was astoundingly versatile. I hadn't really given this much consideration before, as it had always been so familiar to me. His vocal range was extensive but it was his ability to handle songs of differing tempos, with their varying densities of lyrics, that impressed me the most. Thus the Hoopers sound could be high, sweet and pure, or it could be earthy and emphatic. The brass section – sax, horn, trombone – felt as if it provided some cushioning from the world, giving off warmth, reassurance and exuberance in troubled times.

The music was saving me from the silence of the house. The stillness had the power to make me feel lonely and restless, so I started inviting people over. I made a batch of mushroom risotto, sharing some of it with Lara and Plum, and putting two portions in the freezer. I guessed we might be glad of these at some later date.

Guy stayed over one night, for quicker access to the lock-up in Pinner while Roddy was making bellicose noises about wanting his car back. I enjoyed Guy's company. It was good to discover that the closeness we'd established in our regular phone chats also worked face to face. As we headed for bed, the Mushroom King pulled three hundred pounds from a wad of banknotes and held them out to me.

"There you go, Victor. I know you're a bit short at the mo."

I felt bad for taking the money until Guy revealed how much he was raking in from our caper at the markets. I had to admit: this was good grubby capitalism.

When we hugged goodnight, neither of us pulled away. We stood there in the passage between our rooms in a loose embrace. I couldn't tell who was comforting whom. When we eased apart, he looked into my eyes and I thought he was going to kiss me. But he didn't.

He just said: "Sleep well, man," and the spell was broken.

Rūta came up and spent her day off with me. We chatted in our empty way and walked on the heath. We ended up making love in Mum's bed, which Guy had just vacated. That was a perfectly practical solution in the circumstances. But it felt just plain weird.

"I want to buy a place," Rūta announced. "But not London – too expensive. So I apply for a new job in Leeds, Glasgow, Liverpool, Manchester…"

As pillow talk goes, this was fairly significant.

"Working in cardio?"

She'd told me how she wanted to move away from geriatric medicine.

"The Newcastle job is cardio. Will you come with me, honey? If you want to leave the Isles of White."

"Sure," I said, giving the preferred answer while I thought about the question.

I could imagine worse scenarios. Rūta enjoyed having me by her side and she was a straightforward person. Even after such a brief romance, I knew how to please her. To make a proper go of it, though, I knew I'd have to pretend to leave my emotional 'baggage' behind. Not being allowed to talk about the past would put a strain on me. Probably more than most people, I lean on past events to guide my present actions.

If I did head north with Rūta, I knew it wouldn't be long before the question of babies would arise. I wasn't sure how I felt about that. It's one thing to take a punt on a relationship that feels a bit of a stretch, quite another to try something that will affect children if it doesn't work out. I'd discovered as much with Kelly and Plum: I'd been so keen to have a child that I didn't take enough care over whom I was having that child with.

There were reasons why I was so desperate to become a young father. They were all bound up with what happened in my last year at Glenhemfrey. You've probably guessed the scenario already but I'll wind the story back to the beginning.

So…

Two girls came up to us at the memorial fountain one break time. I knew them both vaguely from maths class. One was Suzanne, a smart little blonde who did all the talking, the other was Hannah, a brunette with black-rim glasses and a centre parting of untidy wavy hair.

Hannah's uniform was always in disarray. Some girls flouted the rule about skirts and knees, effectively wearing a mini-skirt, whereas hers looked as if it had been hitched up by mistake after a trip to the bogs. As one of the few female boarders, she wore starched-white shirts like my own, but her tie was always a mess. After games, she forgot to roll her socks up.

It took two days to understand what was really going on with these breaktime chats. Jack Busby had to spell it out for me. Suzanne, the blonde, wanted to 'go' with one of our friends and Hannah wanted to 'go' with me.

This was as exciting as it was unexpected. All it meant initially was mooching around together, not having much to say to each other, though I did make her laugh. All the kissing came later. For a day or two we kept hanging around the fountain with the remaining lads, but the dynamic was so altered that I'm sure they were relieved when we took ourselves away, or 'clung off', in the parlance of those times.

Having a friend at the weekends was a hugely positive change for me. I fell in love with exactly those attributes of Hannah that might have been off-putting to someone else: her awkwardness, her awful glasses, unkempt appearance, split ends. She was bookish, too, in a way that I couldn't possibly match. Bookish and Jewish. These days, they'd call her a 'geek'.

I adored her with all my childlike passion and she loved me back with dry humour and dogged loyalty, long after Suzanne and her beau had broken up. At the time we had those little Nokia phones that couldn't do anything apart from making calls and sending texts. We weren't supposed to, but we'd whisper goodnight and fond greetings at inappropriate times, and make our little arrangements to meet.

We lost our virginity to each other. This was surprisingly easy to achieve at Glenhemfrey as there were specialist facilities available at the squash courts. A couple of years beforehand, the head boy had spotted and rescued a double mattress that had been put out for disposal in the village. In a tightly-planned operation, he and his girlfriend installed it in a little-used store room off the viewing gallery.

This room had already been established as a handy place for a tryst. Its upstairs location meant it was too much of a faff to cart sports equipment up and down on a regular basis.

With perfect irony, fifth and sixth-years were permitted to sign out the key to the squash courts, which they did with great regularity. Over time, lamps, blow heaters, an off-cut of carpet and several sets of bedding were added to the unofficial boudoir. Although younger pupils would be allowed to come in and play squash, they knew to keep the widely-known secret of the upstairs room and never to intrude, aware that its use might be a privilege that awaited them in the future.

The great puzzle about this arrangement was that the school authorities never picked up on Glenhemfrey's woefully inadequate performance in senior squash tournaments. As for us, beyond the usual teenage guilt and embarrassment over bodies, hormones, lust and shyness, I didn't have any qualms about what Hannah and I did. We were sixteen; it was loving, lawful and consenting. There was no school rule against any form of sexual activity, so deeply ingrained was the assumption that it wouldn't happen.

We took sensible latex precautions. As far as I knew, everything worked well. Then a few months before we were due to take our highers, Hannah was off sick for a couple of days. We went walking in the hills at the weekend and I remember feeling quietly hopeful about everything, when she told me.

I couldn't believe it. No condom we'd used had split but there was no avoiding the fact that, somehow, one of my swimmers had gone all the way, and fertilised one of her eggs.

After the initial shock, I persuaded myself that everything would be all right. I even adopted an attitude of frenzied happiness. We were going to have a baby. That might not have been our plan, but it would surely be an adventure, right?

Hannah went along with this for a few days; we talked of eternal love, fantastical dreams and baby names. Only she didn't really share my gushing, impractical joy. She seemed uneasy and started making excuses as to why we couldn't meet. About a fortnight later, everything imploded. Hannah disclosed her condition to her favourite teacher.

That's when I received my second and final summons to Mr McNee's rooms. He gave me coffee and an Eccles cake – I remember that distinctly – and we had an agonised discussion about the pregnancy.

"This is the worst thing that can happen to a young man," he told me, in a matter-of-fact way. "It can stall your own development."

He wasn't openly sanctimonious towards me but neither was he fully supportive. I'd clearly crossed a line; there was a cold feeling of implied ostracism. Without this man's support, I sat there alone in my disgrace.

"You've got yourself into this situation," he said. "Only you can make it right."

He didn't elaborate upon how I might be able to do that. McNee seemed to recognise his inability to help beyond this point, because he broke off our discussion and told me he would phone my father and ask him to come to school urgently.

In some ways, this was a bigger shock than the pregnancy itself. There was no reason my houseparent should know of my parents' unusual domestic arrangements: that my mother was the prime mover where the offspring were concerned, that my father was held at arm's length from me by dint of history and geography and circumstance. I didn't intervene, though, as Mum's appearance on the scene would have made matters so much worse. I let events take their course.

Before Dad had time to arrive, I was obliged to suffer a horrible encounter with Hannah's father. McNee facilitated this in an empty classroom in the old house. It was the tired and fidgety mid-afternoon with classes going on around us.

I remember the man was of average height and build, with staring eyes and a birthmark on his cheek. I couldn't take my eyes off it. While McNee sat there impassively, Hannah's father told me how it was all going to be.

"It's been decided," he said – though he failed to mention by whom – "not to go ahead."

There was no mention of the word 'abortion', though I assumed that was the proposed course of action. He and his wife had some sympathy for me, he added, but I "should have known better". To this day, I have no idea what he meant by this. Perhaps it was something about maintaining celibacy, or else using contraception effectively. Even if I agreed with such a suggestion, which I didn't, I lacked the wisdom and foresight that was being imputed to me.

When you're young, you often *don't* know any better, do you? You have to find out. That's the whole painful point about growing up.

He continued: Hannah was being withdrawn from school with immediate effect and would not be returning. There would be no further contact between us. I just looked at him, stunned.

"Is this what Hannah wants?" I asked, my voice sounding low and weak.

I knew it wouldn't be.

"It's what's been agreed," he said, firmly.

"Is she not going to take her exams?"

He looked uncomfortable and McNee answered on his behalf.

"At present, that's not the most important consideration," he said. "Alternative arrangements can always be – "

"I *love* Hannah," I said, in a stronger voice. The two men exchanged a glance.

"We know that, De Vries," said McNee, not unkindly, though sticking to the protocol of not using my first name outside West Lodge. "It just isn't to be."

CHAPTER 20

Dad arrived mid-morning the following day, having taken the sleeper train. I was called out of an incomprehensible economics lesson to meet him in the headteacher's study. He was alone in the room and looking slightly sad and dishevelled, but he brightened when he saw me.

"Don't take it too hard, son," he said.

I never loved him more than at that moment. I was so glad to see him and greatly relieved. I wasn't alone after all.

Dad had never been to the school before. I found myself in the bizarre situation of showing him around, giving him a glimpse of the life I'd had there, which now lay in ruins. He took a keen interest in everything and everyone I introduced him to. I wondered why we'd not done this before.

"You've got bigger grounds than my school had," he said, impressed.

I took him everywhere, though I didn't sign out the keys to the squash courts. I showed him the library where I read Mum's paper and the main hall, where I'd taken part in successive school plays, without suspecting that I might one day become a professional actor.

We gazed at the memorial fountain. We even walked out onto the balcony of the sports pavilion where I'd been required, on occasion, to display the scores of games I didn't play. We paced out the junior cross-country running route. Dad appreciated the views across the rolling hills but the distance was a bit much for his back.

I was feeling twinges of rival emotions – a certain odd pride in Glenhemfrey; an even more alien pride in my father, mixed up with shame, bitterness and despair, all amid the seething politeness that was engulfing me. My friends were all being horrifyingly circumspect, trying their best to support me, but the one friend I was desperate to talk to had been removed from my sphere of influence. Hannah wasn't answering her Nokia; I had to assume its number was null and void.

After the mandatory discussion, with McNee's voice urgently calling me back, I'd slipped away and followed Hannah's father out of the main building. I broke into a trot as he strode towards the car in which Hannah and her mother were waiting. It was a swanky saloon with a voluminous boot that must have swallowed all of the daughter's belongings – everything from her dorm, her locker, her school life. When I ran towards the car, her father wheeled around and held his arm out to restrain me.

"Stay back!" he barked, a look of wild fear in his eyes. "Don't you think you've done enough damage?"

"I just want to say goodbye."

Hannah turned to look through the car's rear window. She wasn't wearing her glasses. I blew her a kiss; her lips formed a quarter-smile in response, but her eyes were heavy with dread. She wiped her face with the back of her hand, then made the gesture that scuba divers use to indicate they're okay.

"That's very precise," I thought, as her dad got into the car. A thumbs-up would have been crass and unhelpful. This sign told me that, within the parameters of not being okay at all, she was okay. I knew so well how that felt and it was a comfort.

The car moved off and drove away, hitting the first speed bump way too fast. It was an automatic and you could hear it struggle to speed up and slow down along the rest of the drive. It was designed to be driven with élan, not impatience. I watched until it disappeared from sight. Then I became aware that McNee was standing next to me.

"Come on, Victor, let's call it a day."

He patted my shoulder but I twisted away from him and stalked off in a sulk. I felt he'd betrayed me and betrayed the black gown I'd always respected him wearing. I couldn't bear to be at Glenhemfrey at that moment. I made a snap decision there and then, based on raging emotion: I would return with Dad to The Great House until, say, the end of the Easter holidays.

When I announced this later at West Lodge, McNee tried to talk me out of it, saying I'd miss too many lessons. I thought of the economics I could no longer understand, and the French I could do standing on my head, and knew that would be no great loss. I assured him I'd take my books with me and try to revise on my own. I was of an age that no longer required me to be at school. This was a fact that weighed on me over the next few weeks. I could exercise some choice here, though none whatsoever regarding the situation I cared about most of all.

We made up a camp bed for Dad in the lounge at West Lodge and he had a cordial dinner with McNee in his rooms. Everything was agreed. My suitcase was retrieved from the store. The next morning, we left after breakfast and arrived at The Great House in the evening.

Granny was waiting for us at the housekeeper's door as our taxi pulled up. She was excited to see me and sympathetic to my plight, despite her puritanical leanings. She spoilt me and listened and left me alone, which was just what I needed.

Most importantly, unlike the folks at school, she wasn't spooked by me; I wasn't some kind of shadow of my former self. I was still her Victor. Dad reverted to his customary understated role, but we'd bonded in a way I'd never thought possible. From that day forward, The Great House became my de facto home base, instead of Hampstead.

After about a week, Mum came over to visit, perhaps out of a trace sense that injury to me was injury to both of us. I appreciated her presence, but her arrival brought an abrupt change of atmosphere. The quiet conviviality of the place seeped away. Everyone was on edge, on their best behaviour. The forced sense of propriety worked its way into the soffits and chandeliers, to suggest a house in mourning.

I walked up the North Approach with Mum so she could look at the Welsh Cobbs in the field across the main road. The farm was still breeding them at that time. She stood by the fence and rummaged in her coat pocket for a lump of sugar.

"Do you want to talk about it?" she asked.

A horse wandered over, not in any hurry, expressing the mildest curiosity.

"Not really," I said, as it licked its treat from her hand.

"All right then," she said, looking relieved, stroking the horse's nose. It gave a slight whinny and withdrew.

When a living part of me, a sparky little satellite existed in the universe, even though it wasn't physically attached to me, I couldn't ignore that or negate it. The reality of a new life was very different from any prior conception I might have had about it. I felt it, in my heart, in my blood, in my bones. That's not to diminish Hannah's rights, which I would always uphold. I just hope that whatever happened in the end was her own choice. I never received confirmation of the outcome, one way or the other.

Having a loving relationship terminated was bad enough. But being pushed out of the conversation about the pregnancy hurt me even more – being treated as a nuisance instead of a father. It isn't only mothers who grieve and brood about what might have been.

What I told Dad was true: I hadn't heard from Hannah since I watched the luxury car being driven so ineptly over the speed bumps. But I had heard about her through Suzanne. Having been made to cut ties with everyone at Glenhemfrey, Hannah got back in touch with her through the old *Friends Reunited* website.

She's on other social media now and seems fine. I'd like to meet up with her one of these days, but doing so might not mean too much. We're either different people in the same world, or the same people in a different world. We can't be the same people in the same world. That's just what time does, and circumstance.

Hannah didn't come to our school reunion and neither did Jack Busby. It was good to see Suzanne, though we struggled to talk about anything beyond our mutual friends. Reunions are uplifting in a downbeat way. People say and do little things that drag you back to earlier times, but only for a moment. You've moved on, no matter how faithful you might have remained to your original character. If Hannah and I had stood there with our flutes of sparkling wine, maybe we'd have felt a fleeting charge of emotion, but no more.

"What are you thinking, honey?" asked Rūta, who had brought a tray of tea and sandwiches up to Mum's room. She was wearing only my T-shirt, which barely covered her bottom.

"Nothing much."

We took the bus into town and Rūta headed for the last of her night shifts in the cycle. She'd had a key cut for me. After seeing Mum, I could let myself into Rūta's flat and crash there.

We staggered our arrival on the ward, though I wasn't sure that served much purpose. Some people must have guessed by now that we were a couple.

Nurse Inaya was on duty and gave me a lovely smile, even though late visits were supposed to be frowned upon. The main lights were turned off and the ward was only lit by lamps. Everything was dusky and peaceful; the few remaining sounds of movement echoed around the room. Mum was slumbering but I slipped my left hand into hers and she whispered my brother's name.

"How are you doing, Mum?" I asked, keeping my voice low.

"I've been thinking about that question you asked."

"What question was that?"

"You asked why Jeremy and I only lived together at weekends."

She remembered! Her short-term memory was working...

"You've got to understand, William, that two opportunities presented themselves to me at the same time. Marriage in one location and a career in another. I wanted both! That was only natural. A lot of men would have done exactly the same as I did. But their choice would never be questioned, would it?"

Can't argue with that.

"I suppose William Shakespeare did much the same thing."

"Huh! Like you care about Shakespeare, William. I practically had to drag you to see *Hamlet*, and you wanted to leave at the interval."

She was getting quite tetchy.

"I hope I'm not annoying you, Mum."

"Of course you annoy me but I'm used to it – my tearaway Tory. You're still my boy, though, aren't you?"

I hesitated.

Go on.

This was easy, surely: it was playing a part. Only it wasn't easy at all. It felt like carrying out a confidence trick.

"Of course I am," I said, the words sticking in my throat. "I'll always be your boy. And so will Victor."

"Victor? Yes, well."

Yes, well, what?

"Mum, why were you so upset when he was born?"

It took a moment for my question to sink in.

"Oh, don't be ridiculous," she said, half-heartedly. "I cried because I was hormonal."

I waited, hoping she might elaborate on that, but she didn't.

"Were you expecting him to be... someone else?"

"Huh!" She turned onto her back again. "Why ask a question when you know the answer? *Of course* I was disappointed. I didn't think she would turn out to be a boy. And it never crossed my mind he might be Jeremy's."

So there it is. At last! Some kind of reason. An explanation...

I was supposed to be another man's child. Perhaps the gent in the Trilby, the foreign correspondent, should have been my dad. Only – if I *had* been his, I wouldn't have been *me*. Someone else would have been someone else. You just can't win with this stuff.

"He was Jeremy's all right," I said, withdrawing my hand.

There were footsteps and a short hunched figure in a cream-coloured jerkin appeared. He perched on the bed at Mum's paralysed right side and she turned her head towards him. I couldn't make out his face. I could barely see more than a silhouette framed by the light spilling from the lamp behind him. I couldn't hear all he was saying; he was softly spoken. But I could detect a slight Yorkshire accent.

It was Harold Wilson. The former prime minister was leaning slightly to his right, as I'd seen him do in clips from several interviews. He spoke from the back of his throat and lifted his chin occasionally as if he'd just remembered something important and wanted to give it an honourable mention.

Despite what Mum had claimed, though, this man in late middle age, with his whorl of greying hair, was talking about medical matters, not politics. I got up and went round to the other side of the bed. He paused and looked up at me. I introduced myself.

"My name is Anand," he replied, without identifying this as his given or family name. "I'm a physician."

Of course he wasn't the late Lord Wilson! How could I have thought that? I didn't believe in ghosts or reincarnation or any of that nonsense. But sometimes we see what we want to see. I'd wanted Mum not to be wrong. And now I understood how she'd confused a living man with a dead one.

I'm too superstitious.

I gripped the tiger netsuke for luck. Dr Anand explained that he had a floating role across the in-patient wards of two hospitals in the trust, looking at complex conditions and multiple afflictions. My mother's case interested him, he said. She was doing so well, considering her scans.

"She always listens to me, which is positive, and she seems to have her own reasons for soldiering on."

"We've been doing a sort of reminiscence project together," I said.

"Is that right, now? How nice. There was a small new bleed a few days ago and we considered whether to operate, but decided against it. We were not confident she would recover from surgery."

"Is that why she's been sleeping more?" I asked.

"Could be," he said. "But you know, she is winding down."

He patted my mother's unfeeling hand and stood to depart.

"Well, Mrs De Vries, you are an example to us all. Take care and I will see you again soon."

Mum's head turned back to the centre of her pillow and her mouth dropped open. She was breathing loudly. I watched her for a few minutes, this one and only mother of mine. She was right in front of me and being fervently alive.

CHAPTER 21

The gallery was up a short flight of steps, in a Victorian terrace. A horribly loud electronic noise rang out when the door was opened; it sounded like E.T. being tasered by the Martians. Lara's workplace was a long, narrow, twee, duck egg green space, in which the owner's partner was still installing the new exhibition.

"*Aw, effing toss-tits!*" was his greeting. "I'm running late, sorry."

He was a puffing overweight man with red-frame glasses, wearing an overshirt to hide his bulging belly. He wielded a cordless screwdriver and a spirit level like a person possessed. We tried to keep out of his way. I was feeling overdressed in my old grey suit but hadn't known what else to wear for a private view.

The partner grabbed a pot of duck egg paint and speed-dabbed at the worst of the marks left by the previous display.

The new exhibition was entitled *Up 'n' Coming: New Urban Responses*, though the information panel didn't explain what exactly was being responded *to*. I watched as the partner expertly screwed a box of 'found objects' to a pillar.

Plum arrived late. She had dark rings under her eyes, her hair was unwashed, her shoulders hunched forward; all sure signs that she was feeling under-par and overwhelmed.

"What's up?" asked Lara.

"Work," said Plum, slumping into a chair. "He's sorted the software but now we're stalling on paying bills. We're in a race against time to save the company."

As everything now appeared to hinge upon winning the contract with the local authority in William's constituency, plans for delivering gravel to the council leader as the required 'sweetener' started to take shape.

"Don't waste money on shipping," said Guy. "I've got my HGV, haven't I? I'll hire a truck and fetch the load myself."

"Can I come?" asked Lara. "I like to ride in a rig. It's a great craic."

"We'll all go," Plum decreed. "But I want to be in the backup car."

I shuddered inwardly. I knew who would be expected to drive such a vehicle and didn't feel too comfortable about doing so. I wasn't the right kind of person to be an accessory to corrupt practices.

"C'mon, people," said the partner, gruffly. "We need to get the drinks out."

He started dragging the sales desk toward the sideboard, to form an L-shape bar. Guy set out the bottles and Plum took the cellophane off a stack of paper plates. I was sent into the cramped little office at the back, to fetch the box of wine glasses and a packet of paper napkins. The caterers arrived with the canapés at just the wrong moment and didn't know where to put anything.

"Jeez, this is a disaster!" cried Lara, though it really wasn't.

Plum and I had to clear catalogues from the tops of occasional tables and to snip the covers off the trays of food to make them look presentable, but everything was coming together reasonably well.

"Is there any red wine?" the partner wanted to know. He came off his stepladder to sample the house white instead.

"Waah!" he exclaimed. "Lighter fuel."

After a good deal more drilling, screwing, dabbing and rearranging, the display was complete and the stepladder was stowed away in the office. Peace descended. While we'd been busy, no-one noticed that we'd crashed the official start time of the opening. Now we sat around waiting and, literally, watching paint dry.

"Plenty of time," said the partner, his mouth full of canapés. "Nobody comes at the start."

One couple arrived and almost backed out of the shop when they heard the siren and realised they were the only attendees. To avoid that happening again, we all began to pose as customers, grazing on the useless finger food and drinking the terrible wine. We'd failed to make any sensible arrangements for our own lunches.

A few more people arrived but the event still didn't feel like a party. Absolutely no-one was talking. I'm probably the worst person in the world to attempt small-talk, but I thought someone ought to take the initiative.

"Have you been here before?" I asked a middle-aged man with long hair, who was scrutinising the price list.

"Of course I have!" he barked. "I'm Penny's brother."

His words hung in the air as I clung off, not having a clue who Penny was. Everyone else looked down at the carpet.

"Well, I'd best be going," said the partner, to no-one in particular.

He picked up his toolbox and was about to depart when the door opened and the siren sounded again. It was Marjorie Buttle-Deary, who bustled in and gave everyone a vague wave. She looked harassed and acted as if she'd parked on double yellow lines, which she quite possibly had.

"Can't stop, can't stop – but I did say I'd look in," she declared, turning forty-five degrees and giving the main wall of artworks a quick perusal.

"How much is that one?" she asked loudly, pointing to a colourful and rather engaging landscape in a repurposed frame. It featured an iridescent sunset above a scene of burnt-out cars and looted shops. The question caught Lara on the hop. She had to look it up on the hand-out.

"That one's two thousand two hundred, I'm afraid."

"Fine – I like to support the rising talent. Can you send it round when it's ready? Victor knows my address. Do you take card payments?"

Lara sprang into action and grabbed the card reader before Marjorie could change her mind. But she couldn't get a signal and was so jittery altogether that Guy had to take over.

"Would you like to add a gratuity, madam?" he asked, smoothly.

Marjorie looked puzzled. "For what?"

"For service," said Guy, brazening it out.

"Fine. Whatever. Take a fiver."

He smiled angelically as he returned her card. Marjorie plucked a glass of orange juice from the bar and sidled over to me.

"You wanted to talk to me, Victor?"

Oh gawd.

I kicked myself that we hadn't yet made a firm arrangement to meet. I was painfully conscious that everyone in the room was earwigging.

"That's right," I said, brightly, then dropped my voice but everyone could still hear every word. "I wanted to ask you about the roving reporter you mentioned. The foreign correspondent. Is this him?"

From the inside pocket of my jacket, I pulled out the photograph of the man in the Trilby hat. She nodded.

"Yes, that's Carlos. He looks quite young there."

She spoke casually, not appreciating that we were talking about my nearly-dad, my almost-father, or however you're supposed to describe such a non-relationship.

"What's he like?" I asked, putting the photo away again.

Everyone was on tenterhooks, awaiting Marjorie's reply.

"Well, he's dead now, of course. He was an obsessive. Off he'd go, to report on all these wars. Then he'd come back traumatised, broken, thoroughly disillusioned by what he'd seen of human nature. He was like a moth to the flame, Victor."

This seemed to accord with the strange, desperate look in the man's eyes.

"So he couldn't get over what he'd seen?"

"Nothing's ever over," said Marjorie, distantly. "Especially not a war."

She sipped some juice. If she was aware that she held the floor, she didn't show it. She leaned towards me, spoke loudly but gently.

"Anyway, his luck ran out in Syria, didn't it? Homs. Crushed under a bombed building. Awful business."

"Really? Did Mum have – "

"Oh, she was *inconsolable*! His wife never understood what he was going through, you see. Your mother was the one to give him comfort."

I looked around at all the raised eyebrows and staring eyes.

"I wonder if we could continue this conversation elsewhere," I said, rather tersely.

"Good idea," she said, pulling out her phone and scrolling through her calendar. "I'd better go anyway or I'll get a ticket. Drat – I've got *so much on*! The only window I can offer you is supper at my place tomorrow night."

"Works for me," I said, not needing to check my calendar.

"Seven all right?"

"Sure."

"Good, good, good."

She turned on her heel and headed for the door, waving over her shoulder in the way I'd never seen anyone else do. The door siren stabbed us through the ears again and she was gone. The partner stuck a red dot on the label by Marjorie's painting, then reached for his toolbox once more.

"That was amazing," he said. "We hardly ever shift the big ones at an opening."

The small group of freeloading arty types shuffled from foot to foot, looking ever more uncomfortable. The partner held the door open for himself and hopped across the doormat, avoiding deafening us with the siren again. The door slammed behind him.

I sat down feeling uncomfortably full, yet hopelessly unfuelled. This reminded me of all those misspent evenings in Los Angeles. The landline phone rang. It was the owner, calling from New York to check how the event was going. Lara gestured frantically for us to make lots of party noise. We all got up and started gabbling away loudly, standing close to her and the phone.

"Yeah," she said. "Pretty busy now."

Guy had the presence of mind to set off the door siren a couple of times, to make it seem as if people were coming and going. They weren't. They were standing still with their hands over their ears. Satisfied, the owner rang off and we all sat down again.

"I thought working here would be ethical," Lara whispered behind her hand. "It's almost as bad as selling one-pound socks and tops sewn together by children."

Of course, getting her old job back was not an avenue she'd kept open. Plum looked up, frowning.

"Does anyone else want to buy something?" she asked, voicing our collective impatience with the dubious clientele.

"That's not something you ask at an opening!" declared Penny's brother.

"Yes it is," said Lara. "Because we're going to start clearing up."

This prompted a general shuffling motion. The party parasites set down their empty wine glasses on the bar and made a wordless procession out of the door. None of them said thank-you or made any comment about the exhibition.

"Tell Penny I'll see her at the Hayward do," said her brother, as he followed the others out.

"Sure," said Lara, with a fake smile.

The door slammed behind him.

"Who's Penny?" I asked. "Is she the owner?"

"Nope," said Lara. "Haven't got a clue."

It didn't take long to wash the glasses, bin the unwanted food and put the furniture back in position. Then we dispersed, with Guy accompanying me to the hospital to see my old duck.

The awful nurse I'd pressured into looking after Mum properly was on duty again and doing her best to ignore me. She still wasn't wearing a lanyard.

Rūta was flitting in and out.

"Is she the one, Victor?" asked Guy, incredulously. "What a cracker!"

He entertained Mum again with his waggish rhymes and banter.

"Which one are you?" she wanted to know.

"They call me the Mushroom King," he said, with a wink to me.

"I thought you were the riverman," she said. "The earl with the curls."

Here was another indication that her short-term memory was working in fits and starts when it chose to do so.

"I have many guises," Guy conceded.

"You're a scoundrel, aren't you?" she said, smiling broadly.

After he left, Mum fell into one of her shallow sleeps. I wandered off to the Neurology café and finally experienced solid food again. I pushed the button for 'White Coffee, No Sugar' and received black coffee without froth or a saccharine additive, which I thought was a reasonable compromise.

This was the fourth Saturday of the crisis and I wondered how much longer it was going to continue. I thought of the King Edward and of Pearl running the Sat mat with just enough English to direct people to their seats.

I checked my phone and saw that William had texted to say he'd touched down at Heathrow. I felt slightly glad about that, and guilty. He decided to return home early when I finally briefed him about Dad's fall. The rest of his family remained at the Tuscan timeshare.

I noticed that I'd also missed a call from Dad. My heart skipped a beat; I hoped this wasn't more bad news. I rushed across the link bridge and called him from my vantage point looking down into the atrium.

Not another fall – please.

"Oh, hello, Victor, how are you?"

Dad sounded surprised to hear my voice, even though he'd called me in the first place. He declared himself fit and ready to come and visit Mum. I found this more than a little surprising, but learned that Rennie was sending him to London on the bench seat of a piano van. If Rennie was involved in this plan, at least I had some assurance that it was reasonably sensible.

Dad said the boys would be making a drop on Monday, to Highworth near Swindon. Then they would continue to London, all the way to the front door of the hospital. I couldn't help wondering if my father would prove to be my mother's angel. Even after all their ups and downs, such a dénouement was possible.

"As long as you're sure," I half-shouted into the phone. "Mum will be delighted."

I didn't want to tell her straight away. I was hoping she might be able to recall some details about her sometime lover, the foreign correspondent called Carlos, who'd failed to be my dad. She wasn't in the mood to reminisce but I wheedled and wormed until she asked to be propped up so she could have "a right good think".

Mum described Carlos as "Anglo-Spanish". He was a freelancer to whom the paper paid a retainer, in exchange for exclusive reports from trouble-spots around the world. He was older than her and married, though he only saw his family sporadically. There was an air of intrigue about this man, Mum told me. When he was in town, he'd tag along to the pub with Causley Symons' crew on Fridays, but would say very little. He'd have a couple of whiskies then disappear.

"He had a certain charisma, you know?" she said. "Everyone treated him with reverence. He had a sort of hallowed space around him that meant we kept our distance. He always looked downcast, I remember that. But if someone spoke to him, he would smile. Like this."

She moved her mouth into a grotesque grin that I didn't believe for a moment.

"You mean he smiled with his mouth, but not with his eyes?"

"Oh, his *eyes* – they were so sad, William. But he was addicted to the raw truth of it all – the excitement, the fear.

And sending the story home, of course."

She paused and appeared to be reflecting, so I passed her a sponge to suck.

"I shouldn't have been so damn *silly*," she concluded, passing it back. "I got it into my head that he was my other choice in life, if anything went wrong between me and Jeremy. Huh!"

"Tell me more," I said.

"There *isn't* any more," she snapped. "We had this row, and suddenly it was all over. Silver Jubilee. I remember that. There were decorations up everywhere, and I'd never felt less like celebrating in my life."

Mum was frowning now, looking downcast herself. I leaned forward and took her hand. I knew I'd pushed her too hard for this information.

"Dad's coming to see you," I said.

She didn't speak, but her face brightened gradually, like the sun chasing reflections of clouds across the floor of a valley. Then it did the same thing five minutes later, when I had to tell her the same news again.

CHAPTER 22

I returned to Hampstead and had a quiet evening on my own, about which Rūta was distinctly more miffed than chuffed. I watered the plants and walked on the heath, just as Mum longed to do. I sometimes find wide open spaces overwhelming; they're too blank. Even this familiar one, with its commanding view of a city that appears touchable and distant at the same time. How do you traverse all of that space and what do you do with it, apart from stand there and feel vulnerable?

Like King Lear.

I much prefer walking by the ponds and through the woods. They give you cover and something to look at. This was where The Kinks made the film for their *Apeman* song, obliging their pianist to dress up in a gorilla costume. That's another of my favourites in Mum's record collection, one of the last singles she bought, along with *Tears of a Clown* by Smokey Robinson and The Miracles. An internet search revealed that these came out in the autumn of 1970, when Mum was twenty-five.

I was humming the *Apeman* tune as I pondered a problem. In the story of Jayne and Carlos, something was not adding up. It was taking me a while to admit that. Maybe it shouldn't have mattered, now that my real father was set to visit my only mother. But it was bugging me nonetheless.

Mum's reference to the Silver Jubilee suggested that her relationship with the foreign correspondent ended in 1977. I checked the year on my phone. Yet I was born in March 1979, a few weeks before Thatcher came to power. Working back, I must have been conceived around June 1978, perhaps a whole year after the end of the affair. Unless they'd got back together briefly for a final fling, which seemed unlikely, given how Mum described their break-up, there was no way Carlos could have been the man whose child I was expected to be.

As far as I knew, that person couldn't have been my temporary sister Daisy's father either. I don't think Mum even met him until the early 1980s. My nearly-dad was probably someone else entirely. There was a missing link in my almost-ancestry and I wanted to know who it was. I hoped Marjorie Buttle-Deary might be able to enlighten me.

When I returned to the house, I put the photograph of Carlos on the dining room table and stood staring at it for a good while. I looked at the hair that was dark where it remained and at the anxious, distracted eyes that were too kind and gentle for what they had witnessed. I had to concede that this man didn't look anything like me. Yet I felt I knew him.

I repaired to the conservatory as the sun was going down, sipped some port and listened to the only album the Hoopers made after Mack died. It's a credible attempt to keep something going but you can almost hear the dissipation of the dream on every track. The beat is still there but it's slightly slowed, as if we're locked in a desolate dance.

There are instrumentals that I treasure; these have a tentative quality and they're beautiful in their own right, but they're patently incomplete without a vocal. Other numbers include nicely harmonised backing vocals but feature a lead singer with a thin reedy voice.

For once, the sadness of being at Mum's house felt like something inspiring and I was glad to be alone to soak that feeling up. Like some kind of pilgrim, I went to bed early and slept for ten hours, waking cleansed and purged of negative and anxious thoughts.

I frittered the next day away, enjoying kicking about Hampstead and watching an old movie from Mum's collection of DVDs. I didn't feel guilty for staying away from the hospital. I exchanged a few texts with Rūta, Lara and Guy, but the rest of the world ignored me. I could tell at the time that this was the ultimate hello-goodbye to Mum's house; a single day when I felt comfortable and contented there.

As the time approached to set off for Marjorie's, I put on my suit and tie again, as I knew that would please her. She had style and standards. I realised my manbag would look awful with a suit, so I left it behind. I held my notebook in my hand as I took the bus to Maida Vale.

Marjorie's three-storey house was the only one in her street that hadn't been converted into flats. It was in a typical Victorian yellow brick terrace, more functional than pretty, but worth an absolute fortune. She'd always aspired to live down the road in Little Venice, she told me, but never had enough savings to bridge the price gap. She liked spending money too much.

There were artworks everywhere. As she could see I was interested, I got the full tour. Marjorie negotiated the stairs barefoot, stiletto heels in hand. She wore a navy sleeveless leopard-print dress with a high neckline. Her left wrist jangled with an articulated silver bracelet. The skin of her arms was dappled, naturally brownish. She might be busy in London but she also spent time with friends in Spain at least four times a year.

"I think this is the wall for it," she said, indicating where she intended to hang her newly bought picture. "But I must have it decorated first. Something neutral would do."

The house was replete with beautiful items. Unlike Mum's place, its contents had been carefully curated. This tour was like walking through the pages of a magazine. A spare living room boasted a Barbara Rae semi-abstract from her Arctic series, while an early Grayson Perry pot had pride of place on a corner shelf.

"My art pieces are my children," said Marjorie.

She seemed to be waiting for me to ask a question.

"Did you want a family, then?"

She sighed and smiled.

"Wasn't in the stars, darling. Oh, I've had *romances*! But for marriage and children, you need two things to align – the right partner and the right time. Well, the man I loved let me down, didn't he? And then I was out of time."

"I'm sorry," I mumbled.

"Oh, don't be! I have a great life. I'm the last person anyone should feel sorry for."

She said that but then looked momentarily lost, unsure whether she was offstage or still putting on a show. She brightened again suddenly and led me back downstairs.

"I'm not really a cook, you know. I just heat things up."

The starter was cold; tangy gazpacho soup with a strip of ryebread and cream cheese. The main course was lobster. I tried, and probably failed, to conceal my dismay. I cracked bits open and chowed down on the rubbery contents, wishing I'd eaten something normal before I arrived.

"Delicious," I lied, dipping some kind of extremity into some kind of sauce.

We talked for some time about Carlos. It occurred to me

that Marjorie was perhaps the only adult in Mum's life who spent time with her both in town and at The Great House.

"We were sisters in arms," said Marjorie, chuckling at the remembrance. "Two ambitious young women who worked together splendidly."

I asked about the books they produced. Marjorie seemed to have a creative hand in them, suggesting themes and titles.

"Jayne has a great way of writing about practical concerns," she said. "When you read her, it all seems obvious because she reasons so well. But the advice is actually very inspired, very considered."

During the pudding course, which was champagne and raspberry posset, I tried to steer the conversation, none too subtly, from the early to the late 1970s, without coming clean and sharing my reasons. Marjorie assumed I wanted to talk about my parents' break-up, which, in a way, I did.

"After all those years of comforting Carlos when he came home, she was finally ready to commit exclusively to Jeremy, and that's when she found out that he was seeing someone else. Can you imagine?"

Before the revelation of his own affair, which Dad played down, Mum had apparently suggested having a second child as a way of refreshing the marriage. After receiving that shock, though, her focus changed.

"She was trying for a baby with someone else, as a way to get back at him," said Marjorie, chuckling at the eccentricity of it all. Her rumbling laugh led to a coughing fit.

"But as we all know," she added, sipping water, "it didn't work out that way."

No, it didn't. Her plan only led to me.

"Who was this *someone else*, Marjorie? Do you know?"

She looked at me, surprised. "Of course I know. It was the Rastafarian."

I shrugged, as I was none the wiser.

"He was in a band that she liked. They'd known each other for years…"

"Danny? The horn player in Mack's Hoopers?"

She smiled widely and I glimpsed her gold tooth. "That was the fellow."

I felt exasperated. I wondered what good it would have done, had Mum's plan worked out and she'd given birth to a little Black girl. Presumably she and Jeremy would have split up sooner. Would she have gone to live with Danny instead?

"I don't think so, Victor," said Marjorie. "He was married at the time. She didn't think it through. It was a turbulent moment, you see. She was acting out of emotion. She ended things with Danny once you were born."

I felt choked up then and couldn't say anything more. I had a strongly ironic feeling that my little Plum had been more like the child Mum once desired. Maybe that's why she'd shown more of an interest in her than in me.

"Oh, I'm sorry, love – "

Marjorie put her hand over mine. "I should have been more sensitive."

I shook my head, took a swig of wine.

"Not at all. You've really helped me. I just wanted the truth."

She nodded but didn't fully comprehend why it mattered. I helped her to load the dishwasher before thanking her and travelling straight to Rūta's flat.

"More baggage," I told her, flopping onto the bed. "I'm a tall white boy and I should have been a little Black girl."

She half-laughed, hoping I was telling a joke.

"That doesn't make sense, honey."

I looked up at her and smiled. "Nope. It doesn't. So, how was your day?"

A contact had divulged that she would be shortlisted for one of the jobs she'd applied for. So life was continuing and plans were progressing. I didn't feel part of it, though. I didn't feel part of anything anymore. Not London, nor the Isle of Wight, nor Bath. It was scary, that feeling of disconnection. I was finally closing the lid on my trunk of childhood malaise and didn't know where to go from there.

Who am I now?

I left with the doctor in the morning and trailed back to Hampstead. I had a long soak in the tub. I pampered myself with bubble bath, which I hadn't done since I was a teenager. I'd forgotten how squeaky it makes your skin feel.

I thought back to that last term at Glenhemfrey and how I'd made a big mistake by returning after Easter, when there were no lessons. There were several weeks before my first exam; they dragged horribly. I spent a lot more time studying than I'd expected to, and that no doubt aided my results. But I couldn't possibly stay on for sixth year now. I made up my mind to leave school the day after my final exam, without telling anyone apart from Jack Busby and McNee. I took no part in the leavers' celebrations.

Returning to The Great House was very liberating. I felt the pressure come off straight away. I had no idea what to do with my life and I didn't care. I found myself applying to a local college and taking some practical courses for a year. One of these happened to be Acting Skills and Fencing, which then spurred me to apply for drama school.

The college course was run by frustrated actors. They attempted to instil a strong work ethic in the group, teaching the rudiments of stage discipline to anyone who could sit still for five minutes and listen. I didn't have any particular friends in that year but I got on all right with the people I needed to collaborate with.

In many ways, that set the template for my acting career. You're mostly surrounded by temporary friends, frenemies, and people you can hardly stand. It can help to keep your distance. Many actors have romantic flings, of course, because of sheer physical proximity to each other and the emotional nature of our trade.

Dad and Granny came to our showcase, in which we gave our final assessed performances. When everyone was splitting into groups and pairs for this exercise, I was left out. So was an overweight girl called Jess, who was known for being sulky and withdrawn at times.

Together we acted a dialogue, suggested by our lecturers, from *Cat on a Hot Tin Roof*. The casting might have been unorthodox – I was rather wiry to be Brick, she was rather large to be Maggie – but it didn't matter. We believed in our roles and didn't just recite the lines. There was a spark of connection between us and we created an enthralling atmosphere for the short time we were on stage.

We were given no external help. Jess looked to me for direction; all she wanted to do was act. As 'director', I thought I should read the whole play, so like a true college kid I watched a VHS videotape of a film version, with Paul Newman and Elizabeth Taylor. Though I didn't fully understand it, I could sense the drama was powerful.

I wanted to know more, so I picked my way through a study guide. Cheating like that only made me desperate to get my hands on a complete copy of the actual play, which I read all the way through, slowly and painstakingly. About halfway I realised that I was picking up on details that I hadn't been prompted to notice. At the time, if you'd mentioned the words 'research' or 'analysis', I'd have curled up into a ball and wished the world would go away. I didn't think I could do these things.

But this one reading began a lifelong habit of deconstructing theatre scripts and a love of Tennessee Williams plays.

I understood that mine needed to be a restrained performance, hinting at hidden depths of character, while I let Jess be the diva. She really shone in a way that never happened before or since in her life. She said it was as if I gave her a wedding. Neither of us had been stars of the course and this late blossoming took everyone by surprise.

We got top marks and gushing feedback on the night. I remember Dad patting me on the back and saying he was proud of me. Granny was more circumspect, probably because of the sexual undertones of the play. After the show, the housekeeper came and picked us up in her old Morris Minor.

I always believed she kept such a car because it suited the old-fashioned style of The Great House. I knew it had been her mother's car, used in her service as a district nurse. I was fond of the whine of its engine and the smell of the leather interior. On the way home, Granny turned round and asked me a question so surprising that I couldn't begin to answer it:

"Victor, how long has that poor girl been in love with you?"

CHAPTER 23

Later that Monday, William, Henrietta, Plum and I stood at the hospital's main entrance with a borrowed wheelchair. We suspected that Dad wouldn't want to use it, but the sheer distance to Mum's ward might be too much for him. Gone were the days when he could just about tramp over hills. As we were waiting, I referred to the impending delivery of gravel to the council leader's home. William looked uneasy.

"You'll have to wait and see how things turn out politically for him first," Henrietta told Plum. "Sir Pieter's got some chancers in his group. Real trouble-makers."

The green van swung into view and pulled into the drop-off lane. I didn't recognise either of Rennie's employees, but they were friendly and didn't seem fazed by the massive detour they'd had to perform. One of them pulled up the handle of Dad's travel case and passed it to Plum. The old man himself was getting down from the cab very slowly. He was as hesitant as Neil Armstrong on the ladder and virtually had to be lifted off the bottom step. When he saw the wheelchair he was only too glad to lower himself into it.

I imagined it would be incumbent upon me to drive Dad home after his three days in the capital, but I didn't mind. Here he was, holding his stick and his bunch of flowers for Mum, being pushed along by my brother, eyes gleaming with what I could only read as gladness and anticipation.

He was the only person who spoke in the lift, cracking a silly joke that put everyone at ease. We rolled across the link bridge and along the corridor next to the atrium. At the vestibule nurse Roslyn was on duty and made a big fuss of Dad. I assumed she would know from Mum's notes that they were divorced, but if so, that detail was conveniently ignored.

"Your wife's very excited about this," she said, taking the flowers, trimming them and jamming them into a vase that was too narrow. "She's been talking about you."

"Nothing bad, I hope," joked Dad, and we rolled on into the ward.

We got him on Mum's good side and, as instructed, he woke her by slipping his left hand into hers.

"Which one is it?" she asked.

"An old admirer," said Dad. "It's *Jeremy*, my dear."

Well, that did it. She rolled onto her side, lifted her head right off the pillow and stared at him, eyes wide, mouth slightly agape. Dad leaned forward and gave her a kiss on the forehead.

"Jeremy. What a treat! Tell me all about it. Are you well?"

"I'm very well, love. Though I'm feeling my age."

She rested her head on the pillow but kept staring.

"William's making me do my memoirs."

Dad turned and nodded at William, who shuffled and looked at his shoes.

"William could write his own memoirs by now, love."

Mum asked politely after Rennie and Ginette. She was given an update on their family news and the general state of the business.

"I keep my hand in," said Dad. "Mainly tuning. When people assume I'm just a pensioner, I tell them no – I'm *semi*-retired. Still on the company payroll. That usually shuts them up."

It was magical to hear Mum's laughter. It didn't seem that Dad was her angel, though. Far from it. Like me, she was getting a boost of energy from his presence.

"You're the same as you always were," she said. "I'm sorry it all went wrong."

"Did it?" said Dad, pretending not to remember. "Oh, yes. But it's mostly been good between us, hasn't it?"

"I still love you," said Mum.

Dad looked around, self-consciously. "Well, I love you too, dear."

It kept up like this for a little while, but soon both parties were physically and emotionally drained. We took Dad for some lunch, which he picked at dutifully. Then William and I took him by taxi to the family flat. He struggled up the two separate flights of stairs, holding onto the handrail for dear life. I unpacked for him while he stretched out on the sofa and had a little snooze.

I was quietly amused that Dad's rare use of his own flat was pushing William out of a space he usually treated as his own. He'd have to spend the next three nights at his club. I did suggest he could join me in Hampstead, which would have cost nothing. He muttered something, but I couldn't tell what he was saying.

Once Dad was settled and comfortable, we left him to it. He said he'd send down for a small pizza later. He could use the entry system to unlock the front door and tell them to walk up with the food. He'd done that many times, he said. He insisted that the people at the takeaway all knew him, which may once have been the case. William told Dad he couldn't live on pizza alone, and invited him to lunch at his club the next day, which he readily agreed to.

"You getting very far with these memoirs?" William asked me, doubtfully, when we reached street level. His eyes were fixed on my manbag, but he didn't make any verbal comment about it.

"I'm joining the dots," I replied. "I know more than I used to."

"Oh well," he said. "Let me know if she tells you anything of significance."

I promised I would, but I didn't know what he would count as 'significant'. That Mum and Dad were both having affairs when I was conceived might have been brushed aside as prurient tittle-tattle. William was well-used to people having affairs. We walked off in opposite directions.

I made a beeline for Lara's gallery, where I told her all I'd gleaned from Marjorie Buttle-Deary. She half-listened, toying with her hair. Lara seemed distracted, sitting there in her purple dungarees. In fact, she'd been out of sorts ever since getting this job.

"I just want them to make a decision," she said. "I've had it with callbacks."

I thought she was referring to some new audition. But no, she said, this was about the mini-series, the one in which she wouldn't be playing the main character's best friend. The process had gone on and on. She'd been in to see them three times.

"I thought they wanted me as an extra," she said. "They did a screen test. It was going on for ages, so I guessed that wasn't it."

Are you kidding me?

"What was the outcome?"

She gave a half-hearted shrug, like an indolent teenager.

"Exactly. There hasn't been one."

I got up and paced around as she sat impassively at the desk.

"What *exactly* did they say the last time?"

I wheeled around and looked at her, like an attorney cross-examining a witness in a black and white American movie of the 1950s. She responded in full colour, a dissatisfied Irish woman of the 2020s.

"Oh, you know – the camera loves me, they're thinking of casting against type, blah blah. Still nothing concrete."

I must admit, my mind did flip at that point. I went over to the desk and leaned on it, trying in an exaggerated way to catch Lara's eye.

"How have they left it? What happens now?"

She squirmed in her seat and looked away.

"They asked me to make another appointment."

Tell me you did.

"Um, so did you do that? Lara?"

She looked up at me, pulled a face.

"No," she said, firmly. "They're messing me around. I mean, they're not even filming 'til next year."

I wandered away from the desk, trying to work out the best way of breaking it to her.

"They're not messing around," I said, softly. "It sounds like they're considering you for the lead role."

She shifted into an upright position, as if getting ready for a bumpy landing.

"But – what – feck! Really?"

"Call them right now," I said. "Right this second. It's paid acting work."

"True," she said, fumbling for her phone. "True enough."

Now she also stood and paced, waiting to be put through. She had to negotiate a lengthy audio menu, then give her name several times as her call was processed.

"Oh really? That's brilliant. Thank you so much! 'Kay, bye."

She turned and looked at me. "Tomorrow."

Then she held her arms out to me and we hugged, but quite soberly. There was so much at stake here. This single part could be the jump leads to the flat battery of Lara's acting career. It could catapult her into the life she craved.

I led her, slowly, delicately, into a foxtrot. To my delight, she followed. Neither of us knew the other could dance. Our reverie was interrupted by the piercing shriek of the door siren, as an ageing art lover entered the gallery. Not knowing a foxtrot from a tango, he whipped off his beret and shouted: "Olé!"

We tried to bring our dance to an elegant conclusion. Lara twirled out of our clasp and bowed gracefully while I lost my balance and toppled over. The nice old man pretended not to notice and applauded.

Back at Mum's house, I felt I was in the wilderness once more. The atmosphere of charm and hopeful sadness that I'd enjoyed for a whole day had disappeared. Now I didn't want to be there on my own.

I reached out to Guy again, who arrived a while later on foot, carrying a little drawstring sports bag containing a change of clothes. We sat and chatted in the conservatory. I chose some different LPs to play, ones Mum had bought in her early thirties: *Silk Degrees* by Boz Scaggs, *Songs in the Key of Life* by Stevie Wonder, *Drastic Plastic* by Be-Bop Deluxe.

"What the hell is this?" Guy asked of the latter.

"They thought this would be the future of pop," I replied, handing him the album cover.

"Some racket!" he said at the end of side one, which made me smile.

We stepped into the garden and had a wander round. I bagged some more fruit. Guy was smoking a cigarette in a wayward attempt to give up vaping.

"I know, I know," he said, when I pointed out these products should work the other way round. He gave me an impish smile and blew some pollution into the air. "I'm a maverick."

He told me he'd set up a business account and the bank had confirmed it would lend him money, but he'd been outbid for the flat at Laburnum Grove.

"We're all on the cusp, Victor, I can feel it. Plum, Lara, you, me. We're on the edge of something great. I lost that flat, but all I need is one bit of luck and I'll be able to kiss teaching goodbye."

I appreciated his optimism, but as ever with Guy, I wasn't sure how much of it was rooted in reality and how much would prove to be delusional. In terms of my own situation, an update came rather suddenly as I took a call from Jim.

He apologised for phoning unusually late; I put him on speakerphone so Guy could listen in.

"I thought you should know that I've parted company with the King Edward," he announced, sounding suitably resigned. "We reached the point of irreconcilable differences, so I had no choice in the end."

Yvonne, he added, was another casualty of a shake-up by the faceless board of directors. She'd been placed on "gardening leave" while they arranged a generous severance package for her. It was rumoured that she already had another job lined up and was only hanging on for the cash. A "bean-counter" from the Salisbury office was set to replace her.

"Does this mean two ushers per level, instead of four?" I asked, thinking of my own position and what it would now entail.

"It does," he confirmed. "The mid-morning meetings are scrapped, obviously. And house management will have to take on more of the cleaning. I'm sorry about that, but I was outnumbered in the discussion. I said my piece, naturally, which is what did for me."

I can imagine.

"Are you getting a payout?"

"Standard redundancy, Victor, because they're axeing my job. So you're it. You're in charge now. But in terms of extra money, don't hold your breath."

There wasn't much else to say then, apart from thanking Jim for his support and wishing him well. We were concluding the call when I remembered to ask how it had worked out with Pearl filling in for me.

"Honestly, Victor? She's not that good, is she? We've been scraping by. I know it's a silly job. It's fun and it's tedious and you can have a laugh, but you need to take it seriously, don't you? Though not *too* seriously. These kids can't grasp that. You had the right attitude from Day One."

A compliment!

"Oh. Thanks," I said, feeling dismayed. "It's been a pleasure, Jim."

You're a true gentleman.

As he was calling from his personal phone, I captured the number. I didn't want to lose touch with him altogether.

"You see?" said Guy. "What did I tell you? You've got a promotion."

I snorted at that and had to explain the workings of our company. The old management had refused even to upgrade my job title to reflect my permanence as assistant house manager, so I had even fewer hopes of getting anything from the new team.

In fact, I was starting to feel profoundly insecure. I imagined losing my temper as Jim had done and walking out on the job or getting fired, then defaulting on my mortgage and having to hand the keys back to the building society.

"I said I'd quit if he did, and I feel that I should," I told Guy. "But another part of me wants to hang in there."

"Then stick with it, Victor. If you don't want to leave."

I knew I wouldn't enjoy the job without my kindly boss being there. I wouldn't like the new cost-cutting arrangements either. But I needed *something* to hold on to. The alternative was to go north with Rūta and become a sort of house-husband. If we had kids, that would be it: that would be my life.

"I'll have to break up with Rūta," I told Guy.

"Why?"

"I've changed my mind. I don't want to leave the island after all."

He nodded but looked concerned. "You seem quite upset."

"I am."

My feeling of dread only deepened as night descended. Guy became so concerned that he ended up inviting me into Mum's bed, much as Rūta had done. I gave him my entire spiel about the slightness of my unexplored leanings and how I didn't see myself as gay.

"Neither am I," he said, after listening carefully. "But you're anxious. And everyone gets lonely."

That's a fair point.

So we snuggled up and talked and didn't have sex, though there was a certain sensuality to our being together. At one point Guy declared "we're brothers", which really confused matters as I could hardly imagine spooning with William.

"I don't ever want to lose you, Victor."

This was a shrivellingly embarrassing sentiment to hear spoken out loud, but I knew that's how he felt. And I'd grown to appreciate Guy, with his untamed imagination and drive to succeed. He was unusual, too, in being naturally kind and thoughtful. We seemed to have in common a sincere wish to belong somewhere.

I don't know if what we did was gay or queer, or on the

gay-queer border. Lara and all the gay people I've known would say it was totally gay. It was certainly queer. I don't think the label really matters. The point is, it was lovely and there was even an innocence about it.

Maybe I should get 'out' more.

It did feel comforting not to be alone. I get the impression that women friends are more ready to report these kinds of informal same-sex experiences than are men friends.

CHAPTER 24

My domestic idyll with Guy proved to be short-lived. We had a lie-in followed by a rather nice brunch. He was smoking in the garden as I loaded the dishwasher and listened to the radio. It was a light news day, it being what Mum always called 'the silly season'. Then William rang through on the landline as I'd left my phone in Mum's room and hadn't heard it. He was at his club and sounded agitated.

"Where's Dad?" he asked. "I'm expecting him for lunch."

I knew this, of course, having seen the arrangement being made. Dad was planning to take a taxi there. It wasn't like him to be late.

"He's not answering his phone," snapped William. "He's not at the hospital. I hoped he'd be with you."

I knew immediately. I could sense it, because all the lightness of the morning evaporated like dew and I was plunged into a feeling of foreboding. I just knew. But I was calm about it.

"Let's not panic," I said. "He was tired. He could be having a lie-in."

That was possible because Dad quite often forgot to switch his phone back on and I thought we'd best handle the situation one step at a time. We agreed to go to the flat straight away and meet outside. At first, William asked me to go there alone; I had to remind him that I'd never possessed keys to the family flat.

I told Guy I had to leave urgently to meet William, though I didn't share my fears about Dad. I didn't want anyone to worry about me. For the moment, I felt fine. Guy seemed happy enough to head out, picking up his little drawstring bag and venturing to the tube station with me, en route to viewing a flat. After doing that, he planned to spend the rest of the afternoon minding Roddy's stall.

"See you, man," he said, patting my back. "Take care. Talk soon, yeah?"

He made his customary telephone gesture. Our relationship had ventured into new realms but he seemed at pains to emphasise that nothing too radical had taken place.

"Sure," I said, smiling and secretly wishing he was coming with me.

The seven stops down the Northern Line seemed to last forever, though I arrived at Great Russell Street a couple of minutes before William.

"We'll still need to order a taxi," he said, in lieu of a greeting. "They stop serving lunch at two-thirty."

We trudged up the two steep staircases, which are separate because of the way the building was divided. Our family used to own the entire house but the rest was gambled away in the 1890s. When we reached the top, William inserted the latchkey and shouted hello. We walked through the hallway and entered the lounge space. Everything looked as it should. We could hear muffled music from the flat below and vacuuming noise from next door. The kitchen tap was dripping an occasional beat, otherwise all was still.

"Damn!" hissed William. "He's not even bloody here."

I drew back the shower curtain; there was no-one behind it. Finally we looked into the tiny bedroom. The lime and orange curtains, which Mum made aeons ago, were still drawn. The sunshine was hammering its way through, revealing the extent of dust in the air. William looked behind the door and I heard him gasp.

Dad was right there, apparently sleeping soundly in his smart blue pyjamas. His aged face was relaxed, his lines fewer but deeper than Mum's and less contradictory. His clothes were folded on the chair, his slippers neatly stowed half-under the bed. On the bedside cube sat his preferred night-time reading: a pulpy old thriller, probably from a charity shop.

William was talking to the old man, trying to rouse him. There was a disconcerting high-pitched squeal as my brother sank to his knees and started wailing.

"He's stone cold!" he howled, tears pooling in his eyes. "*Daddy Jeremy!*"

I knelt next to William and put my arm across his shoulders. He was sobbing uncontrollably. I'd never imagined there was this much emotion in his Tory heart. I wondered what I was feeling and truly couldn't tell. I'd spent so many days preparing for the death of a parent; now one had actually happened, I sensed only a flicker of acknowledgement.

"He looks so peaceful," I muttered.

For me, intellectually at least, this was no tragedy. Dad was long-lived. He'd spent his last day with his own immediate family, the people who loved and valued him the most. He'd been reconciled with his ailing ex-wife. He'd passed away in his sleep, which is the ending many old people hope for. Instead of expiring in the flat above the piano shop, he'd died serenely here – in our little toehold of family and tradition. If he had to die, surely this was a beautiful way to do it: peacefully, without pain, his life's work more-or-less complete.

Bravo, Dad. Bravo.

As my thoughts churned, something magical occurred to me. Dad may not have been Mum's angel but what if *she* had been *his*? Perhaps he'd needed to see her before he could 'let go' in the style that Old Maggie might have advocated. Dad hadn't been ill as such, but as Rennie had pointed out, he was old. I'd seen for myself how he was weakening and wasting away. This had been coming for some time.

William composed himself for the moment and we drifted back into the lounge. I couldn't remember Dad's exact age so I had to work it out.

"He was eighty-seven," I said. "He could have gone any time."

William nodded in a non-committal way and blew his nose forcefully into a cotton handkerchief. Then he started blubbing and wailing again. I decided I couldn't cope with all that drama.

"I'll make some tea," I declared.

"I don't want any bladdy tea!" he howled.

"Yes, you do," I said, filling the kettle and flipping it on. "We're British. Displacement activity is what we do best."

He turned to me, scowling, his voice making sob-like lurches up and down the musical scale.

"Is that – it? Is life just – one – big – *joke* – to you?"

I stood accused but still felt almost nothing. I was disconcerted by my own detachment.

"I'm sorry," I said coldly. "I'm feeling this in a different way. I think I saw it coming."

"Then why the hell didn't you tell me?" William thundered.

Now my own voice started quavering. I didn't like to let my brother down. My words sounded squeaky and feeble.

"I'm sorry. I saw that he was getting thin. Rennie said – Rennie – I didn't want to believe…"

I couldn't speak. I broke down and had a quiet weep of my own. I got into such a state that William sprang into action and finished making the tea. Then we sat and sipped it, in a void of silence.

"I'm sorry Victor," he said, eventually. "You were perfectly right about the tea."

We got on with things then and pulled together. I reminded William to cancel his table at the club. We made practical decisions and phone calls, trying half-heartedly to console each other.

At one point, he turned to me and said gravely: "I'm going to drop this business with Mother's assets."

"Really?"

"Better to let events take their course."

Thank you, brother.

We made more calls. Plum was quite tearful on hearing the news. Dad liked to spend time with her when she was little. He was very patient. He would demonstrate techniques, like the correct way to wind the grandfather clock with the Westminster chime. He would always let her have a go.

"Oh my gosh!" said Rennie. "I thought this would be very gradual."

He sounded genuinely upset about losing Dad, a "cheerful chap" who'd been around forever. While minding the showroom recently, he'd made a couple of impressive sales. Ginette, he said, would be heartbroken. Ever practical, though, his thoughts skipped ahead to the funeral.

"Would you like us to give the eulogy?" he asked, and I said yes please.

As we were speaking, I pictured Dad enjoying Sunday lunch in the bosom of Rennie's family. Then, a surprise: Rennie revealed that he was holding a copy of the old man's Will. This had apparently been handed to him in a sealed envelope when Dad moved into the flat.

"Shall I forward it to you in the mail, Victor?"

This is one of those brutally practical considerations you can be faced with when you're feeling lost in emotion. I thanked him in a rather dazed way, asking for the document to be sent to Mum's address in Hampstead.

More time slipped past. As we waited for the ambulance, William and I took the opportunity to stand by Dad's bed once more. To my surprise, William knelt by his side again and prayed. I had no idea he had any religious proclivities. I was glad he felt comfortable enough to perform this simple rite in front of me.

He looked up and declared: "I don't think I can stay here ever again."

I gave him what I hoped was a sad smile and not a grim one.

"Let's get him out of here before you decide anything at all."

Even though I'd had inklings about Dad's health, he had no particular disease that I knew of, so we couldn't treat the death as 'expected'. William said that, legally, this meant we couldn't ask a doctor to write a certificate; the coroner had to be involved. But it meant that all William had to do was call an ambulance to take Dad to a hospital mortuary.

Given all the long waits people were always reporting, I was surprised by how promptly the paramedics attended. They were the nicest, most sympathetic people. They covered Dad's face, strapped him to a stretcher and expertly guided it down the steep stairs.

Suddenly, we were free to leave the premises. Only we didn't go. We sat there a while longer, drinking more tea, making more phone calls. I rang the King Edward. As Jim and Yvonne had both left, I was happy enough to get through to the box office and explain everything to Rad. I was still on annual or unpaid leave, I wasn't sure which, but I felt the need to keep in touch.

"I feel sadness," said Rad, which I appreciated. He promised to pass the message on to the new boss, the bean counter from Salisbury.

William and I talked and talked about Dad. In his honour, we even sent down for pizza. I opened the windows, aired the bed, put the bedding in a bin bag. I could sense the flat was coming back into William's control and felt glad.

As we ate, he said: "I wish I'd got to know him better."

I replied: "Dad wasn't very knowable."

My brother misheard this as "he wasn't very noble" and we laughed about that. When we did leave the flat, we went together to look in on Mum. We were unsure how and when to break the news to her, but agreed that now was not the right moment. For one thing, she'd raise hell about wanting to go to the funeral.

She mixed us up as usual, asking William how he was finding life in the police force and making rather terse demands to be discharged. He mumbled and shuffled. He was far less comfortable being me than I was being him.

"I know what they're doing to me," Mum said darkly. "They're using my body for science."

William didn't stay too long after that. He escaped to his parliamentary office, saying he wanted to carry out some reorganisation for the coming term. He'd stay the night at his club as planned. I ran into Rūta in the vestibule and told her the news face to face.

"Sorry for your loss," said nurse Inaya, overhearing and looking suitably downcast.

"Have you told the mother?" asked Rūta.

I shook my head. "She won't take it well."

"We can expect a stress reaction."

Yes, but how bad? Will the news kill her?

Rūta seemed to remember herself and snapped out of clinical mode. She rubbed my arm up and down.

"I'm sorry, honey," she whispered. "It's terrible for you."

"Actually, I'm all right," I said, with fake levity.

The finality of all this – that I would never talk to my father again or hear one of his jokes, or his rendition of *Autumn Leaves* – was taking time to comprehend. Yes, I supposed, I would miss him terribly. He'd always been a part of me, despite his absence from chunks of my childhood.

But I knew – I could really feel – that some of his instincts, his attitudes, would live on in me. He'd still be there to guide me, in his quiet, unassuming way. Nature had given us shared looks and nurture had created shared traits.

"Is it all right if I go to yours?" I asked Rūta, forgetting to be discreet.

She glanced around sheepishly. Nurse Iyana pretended to be busy with paperwork.

"Of course, honey," whispered Rūta. "I finish soon."

I walked to her apartment. The last thing I wanted was to be alone that night. I kicked around the little place, feeling annoyingly comfortable. If this was bereavement, it was too easy so far.

Lara called me. "Sorry to hear about your da," she said, sounding genuinely flat.

I said my piece about it not sinking in. Then I remembered about the audition.

"Still messing me around," she said with a heavy sigh. "I don't know how many people I saw today and all of them telling me how well I've done, how *fecking* well. But they're holding out for some American hussy to sign. Some award-winning actor. They won't say who she is. She'll do it with an English accent."

"If she signs."

"She'll sign. She's just being a bitch, wasting everyone's time."

"I'm sorry," I said. "You have done amazingly well, though."

"*Aaarrrhhh!*"

I apologised again.

"What use is any of this, if I'm going to be left with nothing?"

"But it's not nothing," I said, weakly. "You know the camera loves you."

"Hah! If it loved me that much, they'd have cast me."

I couldn't really argue with that assertion.

Rūta arrived home and we spent a quiet evening chatting inconsequentially and watching TV. I cuddled up with her, which felt strange so soon after doing the same with Guy. But I felt lucky, in an oddly general sense, to have some love in my life. It was a gloomy occasion but we wrapped ourselves in each other like shipwrecked waifs hoping to drift ashore.

CHAPTER 25

Lara was still hurting from being the runner-up in her series of auditions. I was keeping her company at the gallery.

"I know I should feel pleased somehow, but this sucks," she said.

"I know," I said, and I really did.

Focusing on her problems was taking my mind off the cloying new reality that I'd just lost my father. I dug deep and tried to console her with my own experience of nearly being recast as the lead in a low-budget movie.

"I had to dye my hair black," I told her and she raised a brow. "I was trying to be a stuntman."

It was the most unlikely gig I ever had, given my questionable balance and co-ordination. I was hired as the stunt double for Stingray Mattisson, a tall white ex-basketball player trying to make it in the movies. I think one of my Hollywood contacts mis-remembered what I did, though he recalled my being tall and got in touch with my agent. He, in turn, talked me into it by claiming the two action pictures we'd be filming back-to-back were "Hollywood productions", despite the location scenes being shot in Crawley.

The West Sussex town was standing in for New Jersey, about as convincingly as I was standing in for Stingray. Everything about the production was poorly organised. The food was worse than my dad's cooking. Some of the scenes we shot were even done without permission.

"It looks more natural that way," claimed the director, who doubled as the cinematographer and walked everywhere with a camera on a tripod tucked under his arm.

There were no retakes, so when Stingray fluffed a line, they told him he could dub it on later. Much of the content was shot in a London studio that was rented by the hour. My work started out well enough. It's fairly comfortable to be thrown through a ground-floor window of fake glass, onto a large crash mat.

It all went horribly wrong, though, when we were shooting a night scene and they asked me to perform wheelies on a motorbike. I could just about manage this at twenty-five miles an hour, which impressed me, but left the crew distinctly underwhelmed. Then, when I tried to do it faster, I fell off and dislocated my shoulder.

That left me taking painkillers for the remainder of the shoot. There was much swearing and hand-wringing at this point. They ended up hiring a stunt double for the stunt double. However, he fell off the bike at a far greater speed and his union ended up suing the company for breaches of health and safety regulations. Meanwhile I was taken aside by the producer, who had flown in for crisis talks.

"We've got a problem," he confessed. "Stingray can't act and you can't do stunts, so we think it's best if you swap over for the second movie."

I was thrilled and flattered by the prospect, but it just didn't happen. Hence the parallel with Lara's situation. The insurers wouldn't cover Stingray to perform stunts. More to the point, the investors threatened to pull out if I was the star. That wasn't a comment on my acting ability, I was assured, but solely because they'd never heard of me.

It wasn't a shock when neither film got cinema distribution and went 'straight to video' as we used to say. One of them – I couldn't distinguish which – turned up as advert-bait on one of the trash channels. I found it hugely entertaining to watch, especially the expressionless lines they'd got Stingray to add in the dubbing suite.

"What happened to him, then?" asked Lara. "Did he make it?"

You're missing the point.

I nodded reluctantly.

"He's had a career of sorts. But not on the scale he was hoping for."

Stingray had a rather grandiose way about him. He spoke of himself in the third person, frequently invoking Arnie, Bruce or Jean-Claude, whom he hoped to emulate and, eventually, to eclipse. When he spoke, he declaimed loudly and gesticulated extravagantly, as if he were broadcasting to the world. I looked around at one point, convinced he was addressing someone else, but we were the only people in the cell (there were some jail scenes).

"Things were not going well for Stingray at that time," he boomed, reflecting on a previous cheap flop.

His publicists added me to his 'holidays' communication list and I always looked forward to receiving those missives. There would be a semi-literate letter that glossed over his latest divorce and a page of pictures. These always included examples of his kids, a Thanksgiving turkey so huge it looked like an inflatable toy and a shot of the great man himself, astride a Harley that I knew he couldn't ride.

"Swedish-American actor and former NBA basketball player, best known for action-comedy roles," Lara read from her phone. "Nominated for best supporting actor by Ackshun

Channel for 2015 heist drama *Serious And Organised*, partly shot in Swansea."

Alas, my anecdote wasn't having the desired effect. It seemed to drive Lara to greater depths of despair. Even Stingray was too successful for her liking.

"I can't go on this way," she said, unwrapping a consignment of prints and shoving them, willy-nilly, into the browsing racks. "I'll just have to give it up, get a real job."

"Don't be defeatist," I countered, trailing after her through the office and out to the bins, where she jettisoned the packaging.

"You've come so far. You can't give up now."

"I'm nowhere," she said, pushing the recycling down so the lid could close. "C'mon, I'm sick of being here. Let's scram."

We walked along the canal towpath, close to where someone had recently been stabbed to death. Numerous bunches of flowers had been left next to a bench in tribute to the victim. The sun was peeking between the shrubs. A family of swans was gliding along, the four offspring now as large as their parents, but their plumage was still grey and ruffled. For some reason, I thought of Rūta. Then I thought of Teruko.

"What can I possibly do with my life?" asked Lara.

"Hold fast and believe in yourself," I said. "You need an agent. Maybe that held you back. Mine's appalling but better than nothing. I could introduce you."

Lara laughed. "That endorsement really makes my heart sing."

She looked on as I took a phone call. I responded with many an 'um' and an 'ah'. I wanted to resist what was being suggested – but I couldn't.

"I'm in London. Can you keep him until I get back?"

I was being emotionally blackmailed.

"Two or three weeks. Right then. Bye."

She looked at me, mystified. "What the holy feck was that about?"

My neighbour on the island might have had new knees, it turned out, but he didn't have a new heart to go with them. A couple of days before my dad, he had passed away too. I found a little space within me to feel sad about that.

I hadn't known him well. He was a lonely old man who wore bland and shapeless clothes. He was desperate enough for company to keep an overly animated pooch by his side. He had a penchant for jelly babies and boiled sweets. Now the dog rescue volunteers were going through his contacts, asking each of them in turn if they were prepared to welcome into their lives the chaotic whirlwind known as Truscott.

Naturally, I said no. Not under any circumstances could I give houseroom to that mutt. My lifestyle was too unpredictable to provide the stability he required. I couldn't afford dog food. I didn't want to be pulled off my feet all the time. I couldn't stand his yapping.

I was thinking all this as they mentioned his age, that the rescue centre was full beyond its capacity. Someone was fostering Truscott in their own home, in the immediate aftermath of his owner's death, but if no-one came forward to adopt him, he might have to be put down. I said no again, asking them to try more contacts. Then they told me I was their last hope, as I was listed under 'V'. Everyone else had declined to help.

"I'm just buying time," I told Lara, "until I can think of a different solution."

There was no way I wanted a perfectly healthy animal to be killed for no reason, even a beast as consummately annoying as Truscott.

"Sounds like the solution is, you've got yourself a dog. That's so sweet!"

"It's not sweet," I said, through gritted teeth. "It's a nightmare."

For some reason, Lara found this hysterically funny. We continued along the scenic route to Plum's flat, in silence for a little while. Then we got to talking about acting and why it meant so much to us. Lara saw it as a potential route to social acceptance, a validation of her looks and her body, about which she was often lacking in confidence.

"But you're gorgeous," I told her. "You don't need public acclaim to know that."

She gave me a grim smile. "I'm a *weirdo*."

In all honesty, I saw myself as much more physically unusual than Lara, but that was something I couldn't change, so I didn't worry about it. If people come in all shapes and sizes, then so do characters.

"In my first year at drama school, I had to play an old man," I told her. "I was eighteen."

I pouted a bit at having such a crap part, but that was the start of discovering the craft. I did that Charles Laughton business of finding the walk.

"Show me," said Lara.

I gave her an exaggerated rendition of my performance, which cracked her up again. A couple walking past raised their eyebrows, but I didn't care. As you'll have gathered by now, I'm not afraid to show off.

"Didn't they make you up like an old guy?"

"Of course they did."

I was expected to apply my own foundation and draw the lines myself. Then the stage manager would spray my hair silver.

"Sounds perfect."

"I never looked back," I said.

Our discussion got quite philosophical. Acting carries the inherent irony that people often want to do it as a form of self-expression, yet they're usually pretending to be someone else.

"There isn't enough in us just to be ourselves," Lara argued. "We need good material."

"I'll write you a monologue," I declared, recklessly. "We can film it as part of your showreel."

She wrinkled her nose, considering my offer.

"I'd rather take the agent," she said. "Then let's go from there."

When we reached the flat, we took cold drinks up into the garden, where we sat and lazed for a couple of hours.

"I could get used to this," said Lara, as she baked in the recovery position, both of us resolutely skulking in the shade.

Plum joined us, but put on suncream and a bucket hat and sat in the sun.

A good while later, I ended up back at Mum's house. I was on my own once more, with plenty to ponder. I enjoyed some late supper and sat in the conservatory with the heater on, sipping a glass of port from a new bottle and listening to Mack's Hoopers, a little louder than usual. Insects of all kinds were hurling themselves at the windows, so I closed the blinds all the way round.

Where was home, and what was my commitment now? It was hard to say. The next move seemed to be to extricate myself from the court of my ailing mother. My task of helping her compose her memoirs had seemingly run its course.

Or had it?

I climbed into the attic once more and shone the torch on the stacks of old newspapers Mum kept up there. I thought they would contain leaders or articles by her that she was especially proud of. They may have done, but the front-page lead stories were all written by Carlos.

I'd asked Mum to tell me more about this man, but my probing was starting to feel intrusive. I'd already established that he had no part to play in my origins, yet I couldn't stop myself from pursuing a slight fascination with him.

"I was sure he was on the brink of asking me to marry him," she'd confessed. "Though we were married to other people at the time."

"Of course. So what happened?"

"What always happens in these situations, William. He got cold feet."

"Would you have left Jeremy for him?"

"I don't know," she said, looking pained. "Carlos was a drifter, a vagabond. Couldn't settle."

I could see he'd filed stories from Biafra, Bangladesh, Vietnam, Ethiopia, Haiti, Yugoslavia, Iraq and more. He travelled the world looking for conflict and misery, and sent it all back to Blighty, gift-wrapped in his erudite reports. I spent a couple of hours poring over his work, then stopped abruptly.

I was familiar enough with this style of reporting. I'm not saying Carlos wasn't a decent exponent of it; his descriptions were vivid and his stories harrowing. It's just that, beyond a certain point, being confronted with truths like these – about hunger, flight, homelessness, fear, loss, disease, injury, death, injustice – is not informative or insightful at all, in the ways it would claim to be.

If it doesn't move you to do something – anything – to make the situation less atrocious, the reporting becomes self-serving, mawkish, voyeuristic. There's no point in hearing it, seeing it, reading it, over and over again, unless there's some way to give active help.

No doubt Carlos thought he was helping by providing facts and using emotive language. But wasn't he really just wallowing in these situations? How could he write so dispassionately about such inhumanity?

His own fascination with what humans will do to each other, or neglect to do, was deeply scarring and damaging to him. Yet he was unable to look away. No wonder he was too jumpy to settle or to make rational choices about a possible future with Mum. All he had the capacity to do was remind himself of the existence of love from time to time, down a couple of whiskies, and keep going.

I pulled another paper from the stack. It was from October 1968. Carlos had written a front-page lead story about Harold Wilson's talks with Rhodesian leader Ian Smith, held aboard HMS Fearless off the coast of Gibraltar. Jayne had contributed a commentary sidebar, but it wasn't clear if they'd both made the trip abroad. I passed my magnifier across the text slowly and read it aloud.

According to these accounts, Wilson was trying to find a route to independence for Rhodesia that would include Black majority rule. Smith and his white minority parliament had made a unilateral declaration of independence instead. The talks, a repeat of a similar attempt the year before, failed to achieve a breakthrough.

I was struck by the downbeat tone of both reports and how critical they were of Wilson. He was depicted as a man who'd lost much of his public support after the devaluation of the pound the previous year. Yet this was the same man whom Mum was always saying she admired.

I added this edition to a small selection of papers and carried them down from the attic, suddenly feeling tired. I stared at the photograph of Carlos on the dining room table once more.

Something started to click. I could now see why he looked both unknown and familiar to me. I just needed to see past the Trilby hat and the moustache and to make an adjustment for the eyes. Instead of this man's uncertain gaze, I imagined confidence and a slight twinkle of arrogance. Then there was no doubt whom I was seeing in my mind's eye. This face belonged to William.

CHAPTER 26

The copy of Dad's Will arrived the next day. The large envelope had been folded in two places to get it through the letterbox. I took the mangled document into the dining room and tried to revive it on the table. I used some of Mum's china animals to hold down the page corners. Then I passed my magnifier across the words. There weren't many surprises, though there was a little more money than I'd imagined.

In echoes of Dad's own inheritance, William and I would get a thousand quid each and the grandchildren would receive five hundred each, as would Rennie and Ginette's kids and the retired housekeeper. The family flat would now pass, officially, into William's custody. The Pucklewood Conservation Trust would get three hundred. The local Liberal Democrats, two hundred. Any residue would go to a local charity for children who were carers.

Of more significance were Dad's wishes regarding the funeral. He'd evidently purchased a plot in the cemetery in Pucklewood Park, on the estate neighbouring that of The Great House. This meant, of course, that we'd have to trundle him all the way back to the West of England. That was fine, but more complicated than William had envisaged. He thought we could get away with holding a brief ceremony at Golders Green Crematorium.

Although he wasn't a church goer, Dad desired a church service. I checked the wording of this section carefully. It didn't stipulate that it had to be Church of England, though I suspected that might have been his preference. I knew that such a send-off wouldn't be available in his home village, as the parish church had long ago become two flats plus the Pucklefoodies Bar and Grill.

I called William and started telling him these details, but he wanted to see the stark legal realities for himself. I was summoned to his club with the Will and he treated me to the kind of sumptuous lunch he'd been planning to share with Dad. The cuisine was meat-based and French and the main course involved a rich sauce, some of which found its way onto the paper under discussion. This caused William, who was already quite animated, to become even more so.

"We can't arrange anything until they release his body," he snapped, stating the obvious. "Then if you sort out the service and burial, I'll organise the reception. I know them at the cricket club. We can use their function suite."

"How many people are you expecting?" I asked, feeling quite unsure about all of this.

"Oh, I don't know," he said, vaguely. "Father was well known in the area, wasn't he? Couple of hundred perhaps."

I said I thought that was rather optimistic. Apart from Rennie's family, perhaps a handful of colleagues and regular customers, Marjorie Buttle-Deary and the retired housekeeper, I couldn't think of anyone else who knew him. A lot of his contemporaries and former classmates had moved away or died.

"All right, let's settle on seventy-five," said William, spearing the chef's choice of seasonal vegetables. "There's always more than you anticipate, unless they don't have any family at all, when there's always fewer."

As he spoke, my eyes followed the contours of his face. Even with my partial face blindness, I was pretty certain that this visage – which was becoming slightly puffy thanks to such fine dining – greatly resembled the one in the photograph that was now back in the inside pocket of my jacket.

I'd had to put on my old suit and tie again, in order to be deemed respectable enough to gain guest admission to the club. I'd never set foot inside it before.

There were blue carpets with gold flourishes; long plush drapes with fussy tie-backs, elaborate chandeliers and large mirrors in heavy frames. The atmosphere was relaxed and muted. You could imagine many a confidence being betrayed within these walls.

I felt that I ought to despise the place, as it represented the worst kind of smug complacency about the social realm. Yet it had a certain creaky charm that reminded me of The Great House, Glenhemfrey and the King Edward.

"This is very tasty," I said, though I thought it was slightly over-salted.

"Yes, they're not bad in the kitchen here," said William. "Always reliable."

I didn't know whether, when or how to broach the subject of Carlos. It already felt indecent to be thinking about this while discussing the funeral of the father we supposedly shared. I knew that if William had been me, I'd have wanted to know the truth: that neither of us was quite the person our mother intended to bring into the world.

Perhaps there had always been a clue in the way William said "Daddy Jeremy", where I would say only "Daddy". These days you might have more than one father but back in the 1960s you'd only use a clarifying name for a grandparent. In Mum's mind was she distinguishing between "Daddy Jeremy" and the unspoken "Daddy Carlos"?

I wondered how William would react upon discovering that, instead of having a blood connection to Anglo-Dutch aristocracy, he was actually descended from rural peasants who'd fled the fascist Franco regime and found political asylum in Britain.

According to Marjorie Buttle-Deary, Carlos's parents had been poverty-stricken opportunists with the drive and passion to create a better life for themselves and their children; exactly the sort of migrants-cum-refugees William wanted to bar from territory he considered his own.

"The tarte Genève is very good here," he said, leaning forward as I perused the menu for a second time.

"Avec quoi?" I queried.

"Avec yoghurt if you like it sweet and tangy, ice cream if you prefer, or custard if you really want to lower the tone."

"What are you going for?"

"I just have it plain, with a dob of whipped cream."

"Custard it is, then," I said, and he mock-winced.

The more I thought about it, the more I realised there wasn't really a polite way to question your brother's paternity. I certainly wasn't going to do so over a plate of tarte Genève.

Hold your tongue.

After dabbing our upper lips and sending our compliments to the chef, we waddled through to the members' lounge where our coffee order was already waiting. We were each handed a copy of the *Daily Telegraph*, and I made a point of asking to swap it for *The Guardian*. I can't abide this kind of insidious presumption about one's political leanings. A fug of Tory tribalism used to hang in the air in the classrooms and corridors of Glenhemfrey. It was too pervasive for me to disperse it, though I made a point of not endorsing any opinionated right wing rants.

"I'll have a look for you, sir," said the tails-wearing flunky with disdain so flagrant he appeared to have pushed English mustard up both his nostrils. Needless to say, he never returned.

To make conversation, I asked William if he recalled going to the Scilly Isles with Mum and Dad, so Mum could get her scoop about Harold Wilson's resignation. My brother would have been in his last year at prep school at the time.

"Oh *that*," he said, still scanning a reheated story about his great leader's wife's tax affairs. "Is that the reason we went there? Worst weekend away ever. Helicopter scared me half to death. It rained all the time and we kept going back to this same little shop again and again."

"I wish she'd got elected," I said, out of nowhere. "She was the right candidate at the wrong time."

William looked up, bewildered. "You really think so?"

"Yes. She'd have done great things. I know she's been able to live that part of her life through you – but you have the wrong instincts, the wrong ideas, the wrong affiliations and the wrong policies."

He cracked a smile at that. "Then I'm in the *wrong family*, Gromit."

I felt a kind of inner shudder. "Oh, don't say that."

"No? Well. You two were always lefties."

"Being to the left of you isn't being a lefty."

He ignored my assertion, taping over it with his own observation.

"And Dad being a secret Lib Dem! Imagine that."

"Incredible," I agreed. "He must have been one of the few who didn't bail after your crappy coalition. It makes him a staunch Remainer, too."

William nodded and sipped his coffee, amused by my political jousting. No blow to his shield would ever knock my brother off his horse.

"Actually," I added swiftly, thinking I might have gone too far, "given the horrendous way things have turned out, I'm rather nostalgic for the coalition."

He smiled, gave one of his open-handed shrugs. "Aren't we all?"

As he went back to reading his propaganda, I glanced around the lounge, its coteries of men associating in a lazy prescribed way. The club was now open to women, but why on earth would they join? This wasn't my world and yet I felt uncomfortably at ease here.

"Are you going back to the flat tonight?" I asked. "I think you should."

He looked up. "Maybe."

"Go on. Take back control."

He gave me a reluctant grin. He could tell that I cared.

"One more night here first, I think. While it all sinks in."

"That's the spirit."

Our postprandial lounging complete, I thanked William for the indulgent lunch and worked off some of it by walking all the way to the hospital. I called in to see Mum, more out of habit than to any great purpose. She was propped up, gazing into the distance. She seemed troubled.

"What's the matter, Mum?"

"Oh nothing. I'm just sad, that's all. Feeling sorry for myself, which I promised I'd never be. You always think your life is building up to something, don't you, and then it just ends." She snapped her fingers. "Like that."

Through all this time, I'd seen Mum being confused and forgetful, or otherwise defiant and purposeful, and I'd seen her utterly drugged up, but the most difficult times were these, when she was lucid.

"I have something to tell you," I said.

When you improvise in drama, you sometimes feel compelled to say a certain line at a particular moment. That's exactly how this felt. I trusted my own judgement and jumped in.

"Dad died, the night he came to see you."

"*No!*"

She turned to face me, her blue eyes searching but unseeing. I calmly described how William and I had found *her Jeremy*, her sometime great love, at peace in the family flat.

"No pain," she whispered. "That's a blessing."

Then something happened that I was completely unprepared for. Mum rested her head on the pillow once more, looked straight ahead.

"Thanks for telling me, Victor," she said. "It's not an easy thing to say."

I squeezed her hand. "You know who I am!"

She gave a soft chuckle. "Of course I do," she said. "I know my boys."

Then she did her classic trick of falling into a deep sleep with her mouth open.

I thought I'd better stick around, in case I needed to impart the same news again when she woke up. It mattered to me that she knew.

I trudged off to the Neurology café and this time paid for a decent flat white, the opulence of the meal at William's club having given me expensive tastes. The extra caffeine, combined with the nice cool air, helped my brain to focus. With Mum having recognised me as Victor, I wondered if this mixing me up with William had been a ploy, some kind of game all along. That seemed pretty sick, but then Mum was pretty unwell. She might have had her reasons.

I exchanged a friendly wave with Dr Anand, who appeared

from one of the consulting rooms and came over to speak to me momentarily before rushing off to another department.

"Isn't your mother amazing?" he asked, pausing at my little tin table.

"Yes, I'm proud of her."

That was true. I felt especially proud that she hadn't gone to pieces when I told her about Dad.

It's always sad to contemplate the end, but slightly easier when you're thinking about someone else's demise. That's not a mark of selfishness or schadenfreude; it's simply that the story of your own life is always unfinished. The departed person's story can be properly rounded off. That's something we can do for them, when we can do so little else.

The more difficult storyline is the open-ended one that just continues, as Mum was continuing – and as we all continue, day after day, edging towards resolutions of this and that situation, but always full of uncertainty. We long to know, as Old Maggie believed – and Bob Marley sang – that everything will be all right.

When someone dies, their story quickly gains a discernible shape and features. It begins to have a life of its own. It starts to float in its own protective sac. The more their story includes the beauty and pain of emotion, the more life it has. The telling brings remembrance, of course, but it also helps us with our ongoing strivings. I knew it would help Mum to know how Dad's story ended.

That's not to say this is easy.

I thought back to a conversation I'd had with Wangui the dramaturg when I was a young student. She'd received some bad news from home. We ended up sitting in the stalls of the theatre, having a passionate discussion after the rest of the class had dispersed.

"All stories are about mortality," she told me, "but not about death. People get confused about that. They're about how to live for a finite term and how worthwhile it is that there is something instead of nothing."

Her eyes, normally sparkling with invention, were dulled by a loss of hope. I was going to ask a question, but she lifted her head high; I'd never seen anyone look so dignified in despair.

"Stories can only do so much, Victor. They can outlast a human lifespan. They can condition and educate us. But they can't actually *save* us."

Wangui didn't go home to Kenya for the funeral as she couldn't afford to. That's something I never forgot. She saw out her contract with us instead.

I wandered back to the ward, nodded hello to nurse Inaya who had come on duty to relieve Roslyn. I slipped my hand into Mum's and she turned her head towards me but didn't open her eyes.

"William. You're back."

"I'm Victor, remember? I just told you the news about Dad."

"Don't be silly," she said. "I know my boys."

I experienced a sinking feeling and a sudden wave of gloom. Mum's use of similar words to recognise me, and then to mistake me for William again, was downright creepy. It didn't seem as if she were playing games with me; more that her period of lucidity was over.

"Do you remember the news, though?" I asked, ready to tell her again.

"Jeremy. He's passed away, poor lamb."

She pulled me a little closer and I thought she was going to say something of enormous importance.

"Tell me," she said, in a hushed tone, "why are women always wearing their glasses on their heads these days?"

"*What?*"

This is very strange.

"I know it's some kind of fad. They think it confers some status on them. But how? Do they think it makes them look learnèd, prepared, *sensible*, what?"

I confessed that I had absolutely no idea. This was a perfect example of the type of conversation we'd have across the kitchen table in Hampstead. I'd always go into these chats hoping they'd hold some meaning, some relevance to *us* as a mother-son unit. And I'd always be disappointed.

"Do you think sending William to a fee-paying school turned him into a Conservative?" she asked me when I was nine.

I knew what a fee was but it wasn't a word I used. I couldn't guess why a school would pay one. I didn't know what a Conservative was but I picked up a strong tone of disapproval. I knew I'd never risk that for myself. I'd never be one of those people.

CHAPTER 27

The next day, Friday, brought further developments. William rang me to say the coroner had completed their report; Dad's body would soon be available for burial. Cause of death had been given as natural causes: cardiomyopathy, leading to cardiac arrest. That didn't sound painless after all, but I hoped he hadn't suffered long. His expression had been so serene.

Dad had been a keen organ donor, but apparently he'd been dead too long to give anyone a new lease of life. That saddened me, though I did wonder how useful an eighty-seven-year-old liver or kidney might have been.

I phoned Rennie for advice about the funeral.

"The nearest church is Highest Praise at Long Marzing," he told me, his voice betraying a note of caution that he didn't elaborate upon.

The pastor at Highest Praise sounded helpful and said he'd be glad to host Dad's service. They could do any afternoon except Saturday, he said, as that's when he and his wife took their kids out for the day.

"Some things are sacrosanct," he joked.

When he asked how many mourners to expect, I told him it would be somewhere between sixteen and seventy-five. He laughed and said that was quite a range. The Hall of Worship was large enough to accommodate all of us; such were the benefits of operating from a converted carpet warehouse.

"We do a good send-off," he added. "You get the rock band for free."

That sounded good. It was only later that I wondered whether it was customary to have a rock band at a funeral. I'd only ever been to three – and two of those had been no-frills cremations. No matter: the deal was done and I felt proud of myself for organising the trickiest item on my to-do list so efficiently.

The day of the funeral would be determined by the next time the council gravediggers would be at large, which turned out to be the following Wednesday, in the fifth week of the overall crisis. I reported this to William, expecting him to get very grumpy and complain that it gave people only five days' notice of the funeral. Not at all; he actually thanked me and got on with arranging the reception. He told me not to worry about costs, as these would be defrayed by Dad's estate.

I found a funeral director in London who was prepared to transport Dad to Long Marzing and thence to Pucklewood Park. I was shown a bewildering array of coffins to choose from, in a folder of laminated pictures. Of the traditional designs I thought Dad would prefer, the choice boiled down to the Milan, the Tivoli or the Palermo.

Actually, the Palermo was too flash, with overly elaborate handles and garish religious imagery. So that was out. The Milan was the safe option but a bit obvious and boring. The Tivoli looked smarter and had bevelled edges but cost a lot more.

"Take your time," said the proprietor's wife as I dithered between the two. She was stout and glamorous with brown skin, dyed black hair and knowing eyes. Her studied patience was putting me off, so I attempted to explain my dilemma.

"This is something you use only once, for a few hours," I said. "But it needs to be symbolic of the person, I feel."

"Absolutely," she said, giving me a fulsome smile.

"But the more I spend on it, the less will go to a really worthwhile charity."

The smile disappeared; she looked almost insulted.

"Well, it's up to you."

Her patience dissipated in a heartbeat. I could only guess what she thought of me – probably not much, as I wasn't rich – and what I ought to do, namely *make my stupid mind up*.

"Fuck it," I mumbled, not meaning to say this out loud.

She started giggling and tried in vain to stop herself. Her husband returned and wanted to know what was so funny. He seemed to think we'd been flirting.

"I have this effect on people," I said, trying to defuse the situation. "I used to be in pantomime."

"Yes, well," said the proprietor. "We try to maintain a mood of respect here."

"Absolutely," I said, giving him a gormless smile.

This set his wife off again and she had to excuse herself. I didn't see what was so funny. I had a serious choice to make, between potentially letting my dad down and letting down his favoured charity.

"We could have a whip-round, I suppose," I said, thinking aloud.

The proprietor just glared at me.

"In the church, I mean. For Dad's charity."

"We can include its information in the notice, sir. In lieu of flowers."

I nodded and wrote down the details in capital letters to make sure they were readable.

"Ahhh dear me," said the wife, returning from her offstage

chortle. "Sorry about that. We haven't had an actor for a while. What parts have you done?"

I told her about Buttons, Widow Twankey, the front half of the camel. She and her husband just looked at me, barely comprehending.

"Is it enjoyable?" she asked.

"Mostly it is. But I'm never going to play the dame again."

This was the first time I'd tried expressing that idea to anyone else.

"Why not?"

I sighed and pondered.

"It takes too much out of you," I said at last. "And doesn't give enough back."

"I know the feeling," she said, with another slight giggle.

Was she flirting after all? Her husband glared at me again and now I couldn't help but corpse as well. We both succumbed and had a damned good laugh. This woman had married for money, then lived to regret it. Even I could discern that, so it must have been blatantly obvious. If she didn't laugh, she would cry.

"Sorry," I said, wiping my eyes. "It's been a tough few weeks."

I picked the Tivoli. Of course I did: you only live once. I told this story to Lara and Guy at Plum's flat, where we were having the tuna pasta with bolognese sauce again. Lara said the woman was totally flirting with me. Guy said I should cancel the limousine because he could borrow Roddy's car instead. Then we'd only need to hire the hearse.

"More money that way, for them kids. The carers."

Given how much the Volvo resembled a hearse anyway, this was a reasonably compelling argument. I made a note to amend my order. I didn't think the funeral director would be amused by my change of heart, but then he seemed to have been born without a funny bone.

"We could give a lift to that old dear," added Guy. "Your mum's friend. Or was she her agent?"

"She's both," I said. "Nice idea."

I'd spoken to Marjorie about the funeral and she'd expressed a wish to attend but also had some doubts about transport. I gave her a quick call and the arrangement was made. I was on a roll with this whole funeral thing. We were still eating our pasta at the table when Plum suddenly arrived home with her American lover-boss.

Franklin nodded hello to everyone: he clearly knew how to work a room. While Plum was moaning about the traffic, he set a bag of takeaway food on the worktop and started unpacking it. Franklin was about Rennie's height and closer to my age than to Guy's. He had a robin redbreast kind of front, his chest curving smoothly into a well-rounded belly. He had an assured manner and laughed gently at something Plum said.

"You were the one who made me detour for Bengali food," he pointed out, without much sting in the accusation. "I was fine with Chinese."

Plum sat at the breakfast bar and allowed herself to be served. It was hard to believe that I'd worried so much about Rūta being too young when Franklin was this old.

"How's business?" I asked.

"We're the second fastest-growing tech start-up in the UK," he replied instantly, not thinking twice about spouting such an audacious untruth.

"What's the fastest?" asked Guy.

"My other company," said Franklin, oozing self-satisfaction.

He was, as Lara had intimated, full of bull.

"That's hardly a start-up *now*," objected Plum.

"And it wouldn't be, my sweet dove, if sales were stronger."

Ooh. Ouch! This fellow's a real bell-end.

The supposed lovebirds perched side by side, consuming their curry in silence. When they put their plates in the dishwasher and sloped off to Plum's room, I knew it was time for me to leave. There's only one thing potentially more yucky than hearing your parents having sex and that's hearing your offspring doing the same, especially with such a hideously unsuitable partner.

I went off in search of my own unsuitable partner and found her at home, studying for her next northern interview. I encouraged her to continue with that while I watched TV with the sound turned down low.

I channel-hopped and found a music documentary. These movies follow a formula but I find them intriguing and uplifting. I like the early part of the story especially, when several youngsters are leading rudderless lives until they start to play or sing in fledgling bands. Initially these are not the band that's turned them into legends. Of course, there's the sex, the drugs, the death, the fall-out, the departure, the replacement, the split, the reunion. But something holds it all together, some kind of shared dream that the fans can join in with.

I remember someone saying that music is our collective memory. I don't know if he was making a profound observation or merely quoting someone else, as he was smoking a joint at the time. That was when I was at drama school. We were all huddled together at a last-night party in someone's unheated house. Classic disco tracks were being pumped out but we were all too shattered to bop.

In fact, that was the night Kelly and I got together. She came over to my patch of carpet, pulled me to my feet, led me upstairs. Prior to that, I had no idea she even entertained thoughts about me. With her almost-Afro hair and sceptical brown eyes, she was quite a catch. If she'd been a tad less prone to picking arguments when we were married, we might still be together now.

Rūta emerged from her little guest room as the final credits were rolling. She looked exhausted. We disrobed and got into bed.

"You are worried," she said. "Is it the mother?"

I shook my head. "I don't think I can come with you when you change jobs."

I explained that I needed to go back to the island and pick up my work again, if only for a while. After the disruption of Mum's illness and Dad's death, I was desperate to return to some kind of routine.

I knew this was faintly absurd because so much had changed at the King Edward in my absence. I'd have to adapt my old routine to the new realities. But I was willing to try. I just couldn't bear being stuck between places and roles. I needed to reclaim my place in the world.

I thought of Wangui, who returned to Kenya once she'd completed her contract, even though she no longer had any work prospects or immediate family there. She simply had to go back in the first instance to regroup.

We kept in touch by email for a few years. She went on to enjoy some success in the performing arts departments of several American colleges and wrote a book that I treasure, though it took me ages to read. The dramaturg made me realise something I'd always thought impossible: that you can learn anything you put your mind to. This was a totally different kind of learning from the dross they peddled at Glenhemfrey.

"It's not about facts," she said. "It's about interest and orientation. You begin with yourself and what interests you and build your knowledge outwards."

Her endless curiosity was applied to all kinds of subjects and they all fed into her writing, directing, and bountiful theatre skills. As she advocated, I started asking obvious questions about the characters I was playing. Soon I was learning bits and pieces of history, psychology, sociology, philosophy.

Having inspired me so much, Wangui married a born-again Christian and appeared to give it all up – everything she knew and felt so passionately about. I wouldn't have imagined that as Route One to making her happy, but you never know. Maybe he was worth it. Perhaps she needed that belief in an afterlife to ward off her depression.

"Life itself is bittersweet," she wrote in her book. "You can focus on the bitter or you can focus on the sweet. I try to live on the border, especially when we're honing a script. That's where you find realism, absurdity, sadness, truth and hope."

I promised myself I'd get round to re-reading her wise words if I ever acted again, however long it took me. Some people do change; this would be a way to resurrect the old Wangui that I knew.

I came back to the here-and-now and realised that Rūta was talking.

"But anyway honey, you are not absurd," she said, half-smiling and patting my thigh. "You must save your job. Live your own agenda. It's fine."

It's not fine, though.

Once again, I'd failed to break through her defences and make any kind of emotional impact.

"What I'm saying is…"

I checked myself. I wanted to be explicit, to tell her that we probably had no future together, but that would have sounded needlessly cruel. I wasn't certain about it either. She seemed to pick up on my mood in any case.

"It's fine," she said again. "We don't own each other. We enjoy, as far as it goes."

She was treating our potential parting like a bump in the road. I was really not expecting that. I thought she might wail and cry or even throw me out. Her pragmatism made me feel even more sure that we weren't right for each other. Then she said something that made me rethink that idea rather rapidly.

"You have grief," she said. "That's hard enough without making big decisions. Take all the time you want, honey."

She was playing down any drama between us, to protect me. How had I not noticed that? I couldn't deny her warmth and affection. We had a real connection, even if it wasn't everything I sought in a relationship. I was starting to feel very confused.

"I do love you, Rūta," I said, and it felt both right and wrong.

The whole truth was that I loved someone else more and I felt viscerally drawn to that person or – I'll admit – to the idea, or the memory, or the *impossible dream* of that person. That was always going to haunt us.

"I know, honey."

She put her hand across her mouth. When she got up and walked around, I knew her tears had come. She felt something for us as a couple: that's what I'd wanted to know. She wasn't taking our relationship entirely for granted; she knew it might or might not work out. I'd got through to her at last.

"When I was young," she told me, wiping her eyes with a tissue, "I believed that if you fell in love with someone, they would love you back. All you had to do was love them with everything you had."

I watched her as she moved around, telling her story.

"And it seemed to work, in those early relationships. I was the one who moved on – I took my love from boy to boy, and they always loved me back. And then, when I was ready to stay with someone, he became the one who moved on. And now maybe you're moving on, too, honey."

I appreciated Rūta opening up like this; I knew she found it difficult. But was it too little, too late? I wasn't sure if I could live in her world, where intimacy was assumed without being nurtured.

"I don't know," I said. "I really don't know."

CHAPTER 28

On the morning of the funeral, I was up early and had the radio on. I was watering Mum's plants when Guy arrived. He accepted my offer of breakfast as he'd got up even earlier and hadn't been ready to eat. He looked smart in a navy jacket, dark grey trousers, light blue shirt and black leather tie. I'd had to go out and buy a black tie, mine being stuck at the back of my wardrobe on the island. I was obliged to wear my old grey suit yet again, with a faded white shirt.

I presented Guy with a sizzling bacon sandwich – his favourite – and threw in a few mushrooms as a joke.

"Roddy sends his condolences," he said, munching away.

I played a voicemail from Lara, urging me not to feel too sad today.

"Your da would want you all to have a decent wake," she said.

She'd missed meeting him, so wasn't coming with us. I regretted that. She could have brought some Irish exuberance to an English funeral. We'd likely be stuck now with the usual diffident misery, alleviated very slightly by the prospect of tea and cake.

It was strange to see the Volvo with its back seat not folded down. We called in to the funeral home's car park, where Dad's Tivoli coffin was already in the hearse. A wreath in the shape of a cross, which I'd ordered on Mum's behalf, was on the lid.

Another, spelling the word 'Dad', was at the rear. Everything looked fine; I felt some relief.

The bearer, a young lad, gave me a meek nod and got into the passenger seat of the hearse. I said good morning to the driver, who was hanging his jacket on a hook in the vehicle.

"Looks like it's going to be a right scorcher today," he said.

The slight chill of early morning had dissipated. The air felt menacingly warm, as if it came from an oven being pre-heated.

"Convoy, sir, or meet at the destination?"

"Meeting there is fine."

The driver smiled. "That's the correct answer, sir."

Our only pick-ups were Rūta and Marjorie, as Plum had arranged a lift with Henrietta. All of William's brood were home now, the rest travelling with him and Susan.

Rūta insisted on coming along and supporting me, even though she hadn't met my dad – she missed him by minutes on the ward. She borrowed a dark jacket from a colleague and wore it with dark grey jeans.

Marjorie was kitted out more formally. She was all in black, with a sleeveless blouse and long skirt, gauntlet gloves and a little hat pinned to her hairstack, a veil flowing from it. She carried a black clutch handbag, her well-powdered face looking rather anxious.

"Jeremy was her great love," she said, twisting around in the front seat to speak to Rūta. "But she was a free spirit. There were Carlos and Danny, then the wearisome man with the little girl, who never knew if he was coming or going."

A rattling noise that had been heard whenever the car accelerated now became a good deal louder.

"What is this sound?" asked Rūta.

"Summink's dodgy," admitted Guy. "But with any luck, nothing too serious."

We were cruising along the motorway, so the only speeding up and slowing down was caused by traffic. The rest of the time the grand old car was making progress in its usual stately manner. We overtook the hearse as we were passing Maidenhead. We continued in silence for a while until we hit roadworks around Swindon. Then the clunking got worse and steam started issuing from beneath the bonnet.

"How old is this car?" asked Rūta, becoming suspicious.

"Quite old," I said, knowing that most of it dated from the mid-1990s. I found myself wishing the bits'n'bobs trade was a lot more lucrative than it appeared to be.

"We'll stop at the next services," said Guy. "We may need to top up the water."

We may need to hire a pony and trap.

On the slip road at Leigh Delamere, there was a loud bang and the engine cut out. The vehicle drifted mutely to a halt in the car park as if nothing untoward had happened. In our stunned state, we took a break for elevenses. We all knew the game was up.

"So near and yet so far," said Guy, nursing a cappuccino. "So unlucky."

Having let the engine cool, he topped up the water but couldn't get the car to restart. I wished I'd never cancelled the limousine.

"Relax, man!" Guy smiled and patted my arm. "We'll get there. Roddy's got breakdown cover."

Then he stood at a respectful distance from us and inhaled some evil fruity concoction. His words were reassuring to some extent, but the wait for a rescuer put our timings out of whack. We'd no longer arrive early and could even be late. I phoned Plum to let her know. She and Henrietta had already arrived. I asked her to inform William of our plight. I couldn't face calling him, and he'd be driving anyway.

The hollow metal cadaver that had recently been a functioning mode of transport was hauled, slowly and mechanically, up a ramp and onto the recovery lorry. I tried my best to be philosophical. I told myself this could have happened if we'd used my car, which was also old, though not this old, and which offered less room and a less comfortable ride.

The cab of the truck had two rows of seats, so Marjorie and Rūta sat alongside the driver, with Guy and myself behind. Marjorie continued telling Rūta confidential information about my parents. I only found this slightly annoying because I was now obsessed with getting to the church on time.

"I'll give it my best shot," said the driver, grinning. "Hold on tight."

He took us for a wild ride, throwing his unwieldy vehicle into corners as if it were a racing car, crashing red lights and thundering along pot-holed back lanes I'd never known before. It was the first time I'd experienced turbulence without being on a plane. After that bumpy ordeal, we zoomed past a passive-aggressive sign that Rūta read out:

"Long Marzing welcomes those who don't speed."

This was followed immediately by a 'Slow Down' message and increasingly severe warnings about speed cameras, all of which were ignored. The driver slammed his brakes on three hundred metres later. We'd arrived.

We were a few minutes late. I gazed down from the cab at the small group of mourners gathered outside Highest Praise Evangelical Church. At the heart of that group stood William, who was shaking his head and muttering. I could make a fairly accurate guess at what he was saying.

The deep growl of the truck's diesel engine, the hiss of its air brakes and the staccato beeping of its horn while reversing into position didn't exactly lend themselves to the most graceful and dignified arrival at a funeral. The carcass of the dead car was laid gently but emphatically upon the main road opposite the church. We thanked the driver, climbed down from his cab and tottered into the church.

I was surprised by the turnout on a midweek afternoon. A lot of church regulars were bolstering the modest ranks of friends and family. This huge place, which must have had the same capacity as the King Edward, was about a quarter full. Dad's coffin was positioned in front of the stage, decorated by the wreaths and flanked by lighted candles in brass stands.

As soon as we were in our reserved seats at the front, the house lights went down and the show began. The pastor bounced into the spotlight and, in an amplified voice, introduced the four-piece rock band. The young men duly performed a lengthy upbeat number about sins being forgiven. Everything was amplified, so the drums sounded like juggling clubs being fired from a circus cannon.

At one point, the lead guitarist embarked on an ill-advised solo. He struggled with his instrument until it almost reached the top notes, but we got howling feedback instead. The singing was better; the lads managed a few nice harmonies.

"We're here to celebrate the life of our departed brother, Jeremy," said the pastor, who ran through some second-hand facts about Dad.

Rennie was invited onto the stage, looking self-conscious in his ill-fitting suit. He stood at the lectern and nervously tapped the microphone before reading out a brief tribute, his amplified monotonous voice booming around the hall.

"He was a true gentleman and I can honestly say that in all the years we worked together we never exchanged a cross word, though we sometimes did share the *crossword*."

There was a collective "*aaah*" at Rennie's joke, which must have pleased him. He got out while he was winning, handing on to his son. I couldn't believe how grown-up Gareth looked. Introverted and slender, he was the opposite of his father. Now a vet in East Anglia, he'd returned specially for the funeral.

Gareth gave apologies for his big sister, who was on an extended holiday in Thailand. He spoke warmly of Uncle Jeremy and how he'd always been a positive presence in his life. I thought that was a nice thing to say. He told us how Dad helped him through some trying times. I'd known nothing of this. It hadn't occurred to me that Dad might be close to Rennie's children.

"He showed more faith in me than I had in myself," said Gareth, becoming emotional. I was feeling quite choked up myself.

Gareth handed on to his mother, Ginette. It struck me that she was even less used to speaking in public than Rennie but she had the awesome knack of talking confidingly, as if we were all ranged around her dining table. She didn't seek to project her voice, just let the microphone do its job. She was her lively, enchanting, still very French self.

Ginette told a tale about Dad turning up one Sunday and handing her a beautiful bunch of flowers, only to spoil the effect by explaining how they'd been intended for a lady-friend but he'd muddled up his dates.

"But this was Jeremy," she said, smiling through tears, "and we loved him. We will miss him terribly."

Plum was crying too. My own emotion was gladness. I was cheered that Dad had been an important force in people's lives besides my own. More than that: I could see that he truly belonged within Rennie's family. These were his people, just as much as we were.

The rock band kicked in again, this time augmented by the available members of a gospel choir. They played what appeared to be the signature tune of the church, as "highest praise" featured strongly in the lyrics. There were also some jarring references to evil and damnation. If you ignored these, then the music was mildly uplifting. My toes were glad enough to tap along.

This whole shebang was not my dad's style at all, but he was gone and we were all here. It was a relief not being obliged to feel maudlin. During the second verse, the rest of the congregation stood up and put their arms in the air, waving them slightly from side to side. We followed suit. I could see William muttering again but he awkwardly joined in, much as he might have felt obliged to do on a constituency visit.

"You complete idiot," he snapped afterwards, as we ambled across the car park. "That was happy-clappy nonsense."

"Oh, don't be so stuffy, William," said Marjorie, lighting cheeky cigarettes for herself and Guy. "That's the most fun I've had at a funeral for a long time."

The four of us now without a car were given lifts to the cemetery at Pucklewood Park. The mood there would have been deflatingly sombre if it hadn't been the brightest, sunniest, hottest day of the year. Everyone was struggling under the sun's relentless rays.

The focus was now on the practical matter of getting the coffin in the ground. William and Gareth were the lead pallbearers, followed by the hearse driver and his lad, with Guy and myself bringing up the rear. It was difficult. I had to stoop to get my shoulder to the right height. But I was determined to do this for Dad, and we didn't have far to stagger.

The pastor said a few words at the graveside, then the coffin was lowered. I found myself marvelling at the sight of the pristine headstone. Dad's name and dates were carved on black granite and painted silver. There wasn't space for his second middle name, so it read 'Jeremy Victor De Vries'.

When I'd ordered it, I hadn't considered that my name would appear as a subset of his. Here was an intimation of my own mortality, I suppose, but I didn't feel morbidly about that. I just felt as proud as ever that he had my name and I had his.

Plum was sobbing again, and so was Henrietta. William stepped forward and was the first to throw a handful of earth into the grave. Then the rest of us did the same. I thought this was a curious tradition, but it felt right. It was strangely loving and well-intentioned.

"God bless you, old friend," said Marjorie as she peeled off a glove and felt the earth in her bare hand for a moment before throwing it in.

I don't know why, but her little gesture affected me more deeply than anyone else's. I didn't cry but came very close. I walked over and put my arm around her. She turned towards me and had a little weep on my chest. I had no idea Dad meant this much to her. Dabbing her eyes with a lace handkerchief, she looked up at me.

"Our lowest points are always our springboard," she said. "You'll see, Victor. Great things will come of this."

As we slowly withdrew, the gravediggers piled in. They shovelled the remains of the displaced earth back into the grave. Here was finality: this was now over. Only I knew it wasn't over – and could *feel* it wouldn't be over – until we'd been through the whole routine again with Mum.

I jogged to catch up with the pastor, to thank him for his kindness and to apologise for our being late. One thing Dad taught me by example was how to go out of your way in the cause of good manners.

CHAPTER 29

People were standing and chatting in the car park. The weather was still hot and becoming slightly blustery. Young Dorian was resisting an instruction to get back in the car. He'd grown a great deal since I'd last seen him, but I knew better than to mention that. He must have been about fourteen now. He was a sweet kid, unsure of himself and full of promise he couldn't perceive.

"Why? What do you want to do instead?" asked his mother, moving to ruffle his gelled hair but he pulled away.

"I want to see the big house," he said. "Get a selfie."

Like a good uncle, I championed his cause. "I'll go with him. We can walk through the grounds to the cricket club."

Plum and Henrietta were keen to come with us. I also persuaded Rūta, while Guy needed no persuasion to catch sight of The Great House, though it was not exactly a property he could add to his portfolio of possible purchases.

To get into the grounds, we'd have to pass through the eastern archway. This comprised a tall central gate and two shorter side gates, each topped with masonry arches. In our times, the tall main gates were always left open and we used to climb the shorter side gates purely for sport. William taught me how to do this, then I taught Plum, who taught Henrietta, and so it went.

Now the main gates were, in fact, locked. So we were obliged to practise the skills of our youth. Dorian was up and over in a flash, landing slightly heavily. I always found it easier to climb down than to jump. Plum and Henrietta followed.

I had to go next, as Rūta wanted me to catch her if she fell. My feet were on the rusted metalwork of the gate, either side of the arch, when my phone rang. Battling against the breeze, I got my balance and answered tentatively.

"Is that you?" said a voice. "Someone's let us down, you see."

"Who is it?" I asked, wobbling slightly and always wary of scammers.

"Anyway," said the voice, ignoring my question, "I said to Noel, how about this *V for Victor* fellow?"

"Derek?"

Why on earth...?

"We're doing an autumn tour, bit of the new year too. Got a grant. Every cow-shed and barn in Wales. *R and J* and *Twelfth Night* back to back. Are you in?"

Yes – absolutely. Say it! Yes!

"What parts?" I asked, leaning down to steady myself. I couldn't believe I was playing hard to get.

"What's the matter?" Plum called out, to which I flapped my arm annoyingly.

"That depends," said Derek. "We're going to workshop it first, see what comes out."

I suddenly felt tired and exasperated and lost all humility.

"Workshop nothing," I told him. "I've had it with all that. I want Mercutio and Malvolio."

I expected Derek to click his teeth at my outrageous demands and give me a verbal pasting for being so undisciplined and unreasonable.

"Okey dokey," he said, not taken aback in the slightest. "Here's what we'll do. Malvolio, yes – I can see that. I'm afraid Mercutio is taken. You'll do fine as Benvolio, double up as Balthasar. Agreed?"

"Yes," I said, meekly. "Thank you."

"Just act surprised when we cast you," added Derek.

I was dumbfounded. This 'open workshop' casting system seemed to be riddled with favours and fixes. In fact, the entire concept was a sham! Why had no-one ever told me this before?

"Shall I send the contract to your agent?"

"If you don't, he'll sue me."

Derek chuckled when I gave the name.

"Not that soused old queen! Thought he'd given up."

"I often think that," I said. Then I had a brainwave. "Have you got anyone for Juliet and Viola?"

"Might have. But go on."

"There's an Irish girl you really ought to see. Just missed out on her own mini-series…"

"They've always missed out on something," Derek muttered.

We concluded our call and I carefully climbed down from the side gate.

"Look out!"

Rūta jumped down and pushed me over backwards, sliding on top of me. I thought I could feel her crying but she was actually laughing. We rolled apart, stood up, brushed the dry earth off ourselves and each other. She laughed some more when she realised that the blob on the end of her nose, which she thought was blood, was only mud.

Finally, Guy climbed part of the way down the gate and jumped the rest. He asked me who the call had been from and I shared with everyone the splendid news that I would be spending the autumn on tour. They seemed quite glad for me, except Rūta, who wrinkled her cleaned-up nose in puzzlement.

"What about theatre on the Isles? I thought that mattered to you, honey."

"Yes, it does," I said. "But this matters *more*. It's acting. Shakespeare."

She shook her head in incomprehension and murmured something, but I didn't catch what it was. We could see the house now, but this was the unimpressive side view with the housekeeper's door on the left-hand side, towards the front of the house. That door now opened and a tweedy old gentleman sauntered towards us, a shotgun over his arm in 'broken' mode.

"Get out!" he yelled. "You're trespassing."

I walked towards him, smiling and holding out my hand.

"Good afternoon. I'm Victor De Vries. We used to live here."

"I don't care!" he shouted wildly. "Clear orf!"

He inserted bullets into the barrels of the gun and snapped it into angry mode.

"All right buddy – we're leaving," said Guy. "You don't need to shoot anyone."

We were now at the front of the house, the old man blocking our way and waving his weapon left and right in our general direction. There was a serious risk that it might go off accidentally. Rūta clung to my arm with both hands.

"Do something Victor! Someone's going to get hurt."

As things stood, this was the most messed-up Pemberley moment any woman in history could have experienced. We bunched together and tried to edge slowly around the old codger, keeping our distance. My fingers felt nervously for the tiger netsuke that I was still carrying around with me. I knew it was only a knock-off reproduction but it seemed to give me courage.

"Can the boy not take a quick photograph?" I whined. "Then we'll go."

"No!" hissed Rūta. "You're putting us in danger."

Yet my ministrations worked. The shotgun was lowered. Dorian walked back from the front door until he had all three storeys of the house in frame. Then he clicked away.

"An old man tried to kill us!" he reported excitedly when we arrived at the cricket club. His story sounded far-fetched enough that his parents were wholly unperturbed.

A pleasant buffet was laid out in the function room. A gaggle of people were ordering drinks at the bar, including members of the rock band. They were in high spirits after their performance. I noticed that several of the circular tables stood empty, a pitcher of orange juice and a circle of glasses stranded in the middle of each. A man in denim dungarees appeared and was soon in earnest discussion with Guy. They left the premises, presumably to prod and poke at Roddy's old wreck.

I eased a sandwich and a slice of cake onto my paper plate, poured myself a cup of tea and sat down at the nearest table. I called out to Rennie and Ginette, who were sitting across from me, to thank them for their eulogies. Rennie gave me a thumbs-up and Ginette blushed.

Rūta pointedly sat away from me at the pastor's table, having taken umbrage at my handling of the incident at The Great House. Marjorie hurried over and sat down next to me.

"That young boy is very nice, but he badly needs to meet someone," she whispered, gazing at Gareth and giving her tea a nonchalant stir. "You can't spend all your time with rabbits and cats. You'd think one of his assistants must be in love with him."

I laughed, which felt good under the circumstances.

"Not everyone is searching for a mate," I told her, though I secretly agreed that the vet probably was.

Marjorie asked when my last funeral had been and I told her it was the one for Mrs Woods, Dad's second wife.

"It's a blessing she never had to deal with Covid," said Marjorie, absently spreading jam on a scone. "That would have finished her."

A few people started coming up to me and offering their condolences. It was nice of them, but I wasn't sure why they were approaching me instead of William. My brother seemed slightly lost, with a faraway look in his eye. He couldn't have resembled Carlos more if he'd tried.

I was realising I'd have to broach the subject of paternity with William at some point. It was a responsibility I couldn't duck. Where and when that might happen, though, was impossible to say. It certainly wasn't going to take place in any kind of proximity to Dad's funeral.

"They're coming to you because yours is the nearest face to the one we've lost," explained Marjorie. "That always happens. It's natural."

I nodded, half-listening. Guy re-entered the room from the balcony, through the French windows, like a character in a Noel Coward play. He only lacked a tennis racquet or perhaps a cricket bat.

"Busted water pump," he announced, slumping into the seat on the other side of me. "All sorted now. I even got Roddy to pay for it."

A little later, I got myself another cup of tea and sat down next to Rennie. I told him about the autumn tour and how I'd be selling up on the island after a few more weeks at the King Edward. Ginette guessed what I was working up to. I needed a small base on the mainland to store my possessions. I also needed a place to go when we got a couple of days off during the tour.

"Of course you can use Jeremy's flat," she said.

"We were going to do it up," added Rennie. "But that can wait."

So much for the easy part. Now came the really tricky request.

"I also need someone to dog-sit for me while I'm on tour."

"I didn't know you had a dog," said Rennie, eyes wide.

"I don't."

He frowned in bewilderment at the nonsense of this. I backpedalled furiously, explaining the whole Truscott saga, playing up the mutt's precarious position. Gareth had joined us by this point and looked concerned.

"They really shouldn't threaten him with being put down."

To be honest, I wasn't sure if the dog was still on death row. I'd been informed that a place had opened up for him at the rescue centre. But whatever his exact situation, I was committed to getting him out of there as soon as possible.

"Of course we'll take him," said Ginette. "It will be no trouble."

"Thanks," I said, though I felt honour-bound to add: "He will be *some* trouble."

This made Gareth laugh; I think he was picturing Truscott with more accuracy than his mother was doing.

I could see that Plum was waving me over to her table, so I thanked the Bath posse once more and took my leave. Across the room, the mood had faded along with the sunshine. My daughter revealed that she was half-expecting Franklin to put the company into administration within days.

"You can't afford to wait and see," said Henrietta. "The only window of opportunity is to strike now, before the council leader quits."

"We should do it tomorrow," said Guy. "Get him to sign and we'll deliver the gravel."

"He can't sign," said Henrietta. "That's what's slowing it down. He has to persuade a senior officer to choose the system."

"Then we'll do the gravel first," said Guy. "Put some pressure on."

"Risky," said Plum. "But I'm running out of options."

After some fruitless further discussion, we all fell into line with Guy's gung-ho approach. He'd get the lorry and the gravel; Henrietta would act as the local guide, ensuring the load went to the right house. I'd drive the so-called backup vehicle, allowing Plum to distance herself from the actual delivery.

It was amazing how much business could be transacted at a funeral. The reception seemed to have gone on for hours, but it ended quite suddenly. It only took the first few people to leave and everyone else followed. Soon we were all standing in the car park saying our goodbyes.

William took me aside. "I'm going to stay home for a while," he revealed. "Can you keep an eye on Mother? I need to get my blood pressure down."

"Absolutely," I said. "You must look after yourself. We're next in line, after all."

He frowned. "For what?"

"Mortality."

"Oh, *that*!" he said, with a dismissive shrug. "I thought you meant something *good*."

I arranged to ride back with Henrietta and Plum on the pretext of allowing Marjorie to lie down on the back seat of Roddy's car, as she had declared herself exhausted. In truth, I wanted to avoid any kind of conflict with Rūta, who was still sulking about my antics at The Great House.

When Henrietta dropped us off at Plum's, we found Lara on the ugly old sofa, looking glum and eating ice cream straight from the tub. Even I know that's not a good sign. The company making the mini-series had offered her a very modest role and she'd turned it down. That's not something you can afford to do as an actor, especially so early in your career. But Lara made a compelling argument, saying that it was just one more instance of them messing her around.

"I mean, they know I'm too good for a bit part. They said it themselves. They don't own me. They don't have any right to humiliate me."

I told her it wasn't something I'd have done, but I was proud of her for standing her ground. I mentioned the Shakespeare tour of Wales and her own possible part in it, but she wasn't too excited.

"I'm not so keen on stage acting," she reminded me. "But thanks. I'll think about it."

She stopped eating ice cream at that point and put the tub back in the freezer. Plum told her about the plan to deliver the gravel. The prospect of riding in the lorry seemed to cheer her up and we settled down to watch crappy telly. When the girls had gone to bed, I found myself lying on the lumpy sofa bed, unable to sleep. It had been a big day and too much had happened to still my racing mind.

After a couple of hours, I decided I'd feel more able to relax on the single bed in William's room at Mum's house. I left a note on the breakfast bar and ordered a taxi. When I arrived, all was quiet. There was almost no traffic on the main road. I let myself in and picked the mail off the mat again. Then I sat down on the bench of the telephone table, which gave out its usual creaky groan.

I sighed heavily and felt weary. But there was something I was determined to do. I'd thought of it ever since I'd come to stay at Mum's, but put it off many times. I lifted the receiver on the landline phone, knowing the old duck would pick up the bill and it would be paid automatically. I called the only number I had, hoping it would still work. My mind was too foggy to calculate what time it was in Japan.

"Moshi moshi," said Teruko.

"Hello? This is Victor."

"*Victor!*"

Everything went quiet for a spell and I thought I'd lost the connection. Then she spoke again:

"I have been waiting. What took you so long?"

CHAPTER 30

Plum was always on driving duty when we rode in my car, to get some practice. She was a competent driver and slightly overcautious, which made this trip up the motorway reassuringly uneventful.

"What will you do when the tour ends?" she asked me.

Good question.

"I won't go back to the island," I said, with more vehemence than I expected. "I love the place, but it's not getting me anywhere. It's been like living in a cul-de-sac."

She was puzzled. "You *do* live in a cul-de-sac, Dad."

"I know," I snapped. "But I was meaning it as a simile."

"Oh! So your life's a cul-de-sac, instead of what – being a road?"

"That was the idea," I admitted, making a mental note never to speak figuratively again.

We then had a conversation about what she would do if this last-ditch bribery didn't work and Franklin's company went under. Plum seemed moderately hopeful. She had enough money in the bank to weather a few months of unemployment. As usual, that was more of a financial cushion than I possessed.

"I've got so much more experience now than when I started."

"That's fantastic," I said. "Maybe you've outgrown this job anyway."

That seemed to be exactly the wrong thing to say; she looked grumpy. We travelled in sullen silence for a while.

"You have a lot of clout in a start-up," she explained eventually, having reflected on the situation. "I won't be queen bee anymore."

The walkie-talkie crackled into life. "This here's the fab cab. How you doing back there?" asked Lara.

"We're fine," I replied into the handset. "Bonding like never before."

This brought a slight chuckle from Plum, so I knew we were good.

I started telling her about my call to Japan. Because of the time difference, I'd almost lived through two Saturday mornings. My catch-up with Teruko had been a lengthy one. Then I'd grabbed a few hours of sleep, before heading off on this adventure – or misadventure – or whatever it would turn out to be.

I described how Teruko was struggling to make ends meet in Tokyo, but was resisting any thoughts of returning to her home city.

"Cut to the chase, Dad. Are you going to get back with her or not? And what about this fling you're having?"

"It's a complex situation," I admitted. "Would you come and visit us in Japan?"

"You asked me that before and I said I would."

"You wouldn't feel abandoned?"

"What – more than when you walked out on me and Mum?"

Ow. Ouch. Ugh.

We both felt glum and gloomy then and another silence reigned.

Then she piped up again: "Sorry, Dad. That was cheap."

"I'm sorry I did the walking out. Really, really sorry…"

"Yes, *all right*, Dad."

There was another long pause. Then I asked: "Can you ever forgive me?"

She reached for my hand, her left finding my right, and gave it a quick squeeze.

"Look, I know you had a difficult time. I just need you to know it had an impact. Of course I fucking *forgive* you. And by the way, I totally know you're bi."

Am I?

"And you wouldn't mind if I were?"

"Frankly, Dad, I'd be more annoyed if you didn't own that."

Lara warned us when our exit was coming up and we eased onto the A-road and into William and Henrietta's little chunk of almost-Birmingham. It felt reasonably familiar. I'd navigated my way there before, with a bit of trial and error.

We found the lane by the golf club, where Sir Pieter's doubtless well-appointed abode was located. We were at the gates of his leafy drive when Guy pulled over. Plum tucked in behind him. Through the walkie-talkie, Lara relayed the news that the council leader had finally bowed to pressure and stepped down. Henrietta had hoped he might last until a vote of confidence during the next week, but you can resign anytime. He just happened to choose the sixth Saturday of this crisis.

We all got out of our respective vehicles and stood in the middle of the lane, debating what to do next. Guy was all for making the drop as planned, believing that Sir Pieter would still have a lot of influence in the ruling group. Not for the first time, I got the impression that the Curly Earl didn't have a very sound grasp of how party politics worked. Henrietta thought the stock should be returned to the yard, albeit at a loss. Lara wondered if the new council leader might have an equal interest in receiving a free load of gravel, but this was thought to be unlikely.

"Then let's go for Plan B," said Plum, the only person present who knew we had one. "We turn around and head for Hertfordshire. I want to pay a visit to Franklin's house."

"What about the gravel?" asked Guy.

"We'll see," said Plum. "I might give it to him instead. As a present from the company."

She told Guy the postcode of the address and he poked it into the sat-nav. She seemed surprisingly unworried by the new situation, which almost certainly meant she'd be out of a job within days. It left her with much to ponder, though, so she asked me to take over the driving.

"It's okay," she said, as we headed off again. "I'm not sure we were doing the right thing anyway."

Amen to that.

Our conversation was minimal as we headed down a different motorway and listened to music. I followed the truck mindlessly. At long last it turned off, rumbled some more, then we arrived. Franklin's rural retreat was in one of those new villages plonked in a field, some of whose residents would devote the prime of their lives to campaigning obsessively against any additional homes being plonked in a neighbouring field.

"I think it's the next house on the right," said Plum into the walkie-talkie. "Yes, it is – I can see his car."

She turned to me. "Pull in here."

I parked within view of a large modern 'executive-style' home. There was an open-top sports car at the head of a tastefully paved driveway, in front of a deluxe integral double garage. Incongruously, the flash car had L-plates on it.

"I've always wanted to get a look at the competition," said Plum, watching intently as Guy knocked on the front door of the house.

He was evidently giving some charming spiel of the type he specialised in, but appeared to be running out of steam. He glanced towards us and shrugged, which got Plum flapping her hand at him.

"Get on with it!" she urged, under her breath. "Oh my god – she looks so *young*!"

A long-haired girl had reluctantly followed Guy outside and he was gesturing towards the drive. In a nicely ironic move, he got her to sign for the delivery. Then he climbed into the cab and his voice came through on the walkie-talkie.

"Are you sure you want me to make the drop here? They really don't need any gravel."

"I think so," said Plum. "Was that really his wife?"

"Of course not – they're both in London. That's the au pair."

Plum looked stunned. "He never said they were getting a fucking *au pair*," she whispered to me. "So *that's* why he's gone cold on me."

She seemed to be seeing Franklin for what he was – a shyster – for the very first time.

"He's giving her driving lessons as well. Isn't that lovely? So he's giving me up for some gap year floozy, not even for his wife."

"Sorry to push you," said Guy's voice, "but what do you want me to do? I've got to get this rig back to base."

Plum scrunched her face up, as she had done when she was five years old, to look as mean as possible. She depressed the button on the walkie-talkie.

"Make the delivery," she commanded.

"Is that wise?" I asked.

"Of course it's not fucking *wise*, Dad!"

We watched as Guy backed the lorry down the drive. He stopped, rather too close to the sports car. He jumped down, went to the rear of the vehicle and opened the tailgate. Stones started pouring onto the drive. Then he got back in the cab. The hydraulic arms lifted the bed of the truck and the gravel started to pour off the end in huge volume.

"No – wait!" I shouted into the walkie-talkie as the sports car's interior was rapidly filled with thousands of stones. As the lorry pulled away, the bonnet was also engulfed. The au pair looked on helplessly.

Plum was giggling as she witnessed her own act of light vandalism.

"He'll know it was you," I warned.

"I want him to," she said, defiantly. "He won't do anything 'cos then he'd get found out."

"He'll have some explaining to do as it is."

"That's his problem. If I'm going to quit, I might as well do it in style."

A smile appeared on her face. The trail of gravel Guy's truck was leaving, like a slug depositing slime, was over two feet high. Sir Pieter's had been a long drive and this was a short one.

"I don't think he'll be giving her another driving lesson for a while," I said, as we observed the au pair going inside and closing the door. Her phone was already pressed to her ear.

I fretted about possible repercussions. I was surprised that Henrietta had neglected to intervene in these proceedings, on the side of law and order. Then again, perhaps this was a Colston moment – when the mob loses patience and pulls the statue down. It was legally wrong but morally right. Plum had, after all, placed her faith in a man who rewarded her with lies and betrayal.

"I feel free," she declared. "I can live my own life again."

"Good," I said, trying to suppress my doubts. "I'm glad."

We headed home quietly. Back in London, we performed an awkward procedure at a set of traffic lights. Lara and Henrietta rushed to join us in the car while Plum handed the walkie-talkie back to Guy. Then he veered off to take the lorry back to the yard.

The mood among the youngsters was ebullient; they seemed to believe that a worthwhile mission had been accomplished. They were even ready to party. I dropped them at Plum's flat before heading back to Hampstead. I was tired and not in the right frame of mind for a Pyrrhic celebration.

I called Teruko again. I told her I wanted to go back to our original plan and join her in Japan. She became very emotional. I was all for jumping on a plane and going to see her straight away, but she didn't want that. She knew I'd be going on tour and thought our having to part again would break her.

"Just get your ass over here as soon as possible," she said. "For always."

The next day, I visited Mum again and took Guy with me. She was still telling her tales, but with less energy – and I'd heard them all by now. I seemed to have pumped as much information from her as I could use for my own selfish purposes. We had little left to say to each other. When Mum tired, Guy stepped in. He gave his usual performance, recounting rhymes, telling little stories, cracking jokes and boasting about deeds he had yet to achieve.

She was lapping it all up, so I left them to it for a while. I sloped off to the Neurology café, where I pushed the button for 'White Coffee, No Sugar' and received… white coffee without sugar. It was a bit frothy and far too hot but here it was at last: the correct drink.

Something's happened.

I knew instantly there was a development on the ward. If you're superstitious, you think of this as a form of intuition. It's not, of course. It's *coincidence* and I knew that, but I couldn't help myself.

I fought the impulse to run back to Mum at full speed. I forced myself to sit there at one of the little tin tables and consume my modest beverage. I focused on my breathing and enjoyed a moment of peace and air conditioning. No-one had phoned to summon me; I didn't have to rush anywhere. But I still felt alarmed.

Once I'd finished my drink, easily the least awful of those I'd sampled, I set off at a brisk pace, breaking into a trot on the link bridge. When I reached the vestibule, Roslyn had been replaced by the neglectful relief nurse, who ignored me. I wasn't having any of that.

"Good afternoon," I said, as I breezed past.

When I reached Mum, she was asleep. Guy looked up at me, puzzled by my haste and the aura of tension I was giving off.

"What happened?" I asked.

"Nothing," he said. "She's fine. Just got tired."

"Are you sure? What were you two talking about?"

He squirmed in his plastic seat and answered me as he might have done a police officer.

"She was just saying, about you and William," he said. "Her boys. How proud she was of you."

"You're not making this up, are you?"

"Why would I? That's all she said. She was proud of you and you're sons of great men."

No way.

I felt every bodily alert possible – a sinking feeling, hairs standing up on the back of my neck, my mind snapping into sharp focus.

Those actual words?

I looked at Guy so hard it freaked him out.

"*What?*"

I clutched his arms. "This is really important. Did she really say that – sons of great *men*? Not sons of a great man?"

His eyes shifted to the side as he thought about the matter carefully.

"No. She definitely said 'men'."

I sat down on a second plastic chair we'd stolen and exhaled heavily.

"That confirms it then. My brother and I have different dads."

Guy still looked perplexed. "Does that matter?"

Yes, mate.

"It matters, because William has a right to know."

Guy shrugged.

"Me and my sister have different dads. Doesn't make any difference. We're still family."

I understood what he was saying and, yes, we were still family. It wasn't that I believed there was any stigma around William's true identity – just that I knew what it was, and he didn't.

To thine own self, be true. But how?

Given how much it meant to me to discover the *nearly* identity I was supposed to have, I imagined William would want to know the truth about his own origins. At the same time, he wasn't me. He might prefer *not* to know, to live in blissful ignorance for the rest of his life. If I told him, he might choose to live in equally delicious denial. To tell, or not to tell?

"It might just upset him," said Guy.

"I know. But I must try. What if he found out later that I'd withheld this?"

"So, what are you gonna do?"

I couldn't possibly know the right thing to do unless I broached the subject in a gentle roundabout way. Using all the verve in my flawed social skills, I'd have to be ready to open up the conversation or shut it down.

"I'll try to lay out the facts," I said. "Allow him to draw his own conclusion. He's been a barrister. He likes to work that way."

These facts would now include Mum's utterance that we were "*sons of great men*", albeit this had been revealed at one remove, through the not-always-reliable narrator that was Guy.

CHAPTER 31

I had a series of missed calls from Rūta, and finally did the honourable thing and rang her back.

"Where are you, honey? I thought you might come here."

I told her I was at Mum's. I confessed that I'd soon be returning to the island and going back to work. She expressed a strong desire to come with me, but I told her I was taking Guy this time. That was something I'd had in mind for a while; at the hospital it became an actual plan. Rūta was sounding rather desperate, so I offered her the chance of sharing my last afternoon with me, once I'd packed and cleared the fridge.

We had a pleasant, wretched time. We walked aimlessly on the heath, which had never felt more like a vast sweep of no-man's land. Rūta told me about her interviews and I half-listened, as you might do with a friend whose passion you don't share. I couldn't bring myself to talk about my own plans, as they no longer included her. I didn't know why I felt so awful about that, as we would both be relocating, but I suspected that being in love with another woman played its part.

"Let's stay friends," I said, as we arrived back at Mum's house. "That would mean a lot to me."

She scowled and astonished me with the strength of her response.

"No way! Boyfriend or nothing."

We hesitated in the warmth of the porch, with me looking at my shoes and at the beautiful tiles I'd so often taken for granted. Then she walked away, without another word, down the drive. I let myself into the house, feeling blissfully relieved.

Thank goodness for passive aggression.

I don't agree that there are fifty pat ways to end a relationship. There are horrible, painful ways and those that are slightly less so. I envied the flippancy of Lee in the song, having no greater moral or practical obligation than to return his key. Which reminded me: I still had a key to Rūta's apartment.

A few minutes later the doorbell sounded and I froze. Thankfully it was only Guy. I put our bags in the car then came inside again to heat up some dinner before we set off.

The doorbell rang again and I just knew it had to be Rūta. She'd come back on the pretext of having left something in the house. We ended up with a second round of twitchy awkwardness. She tried to apologise for being angry and I tried to tell her it was understandable; she tried to get me to hold her and I tried not to.

I prized the latchkey from my bunch and held it out to her: an unmistakeable act of closure. She snatched it out of my hand, said goodbye politely to Guy and attempted to storm off, only you can't do that from Mum's, as you can't get any speed up. You have to negotiate the glazed door and the steps up, then traverse the porch and go down the outside steps. Once she'd done all that she turned and waved – she knew we were watching – then used her hands to make the shape of a heart. I waved back and – what the hell – blew her a kiss.

"Nice girl," said Guy, clearly puzzled by this turn of events.

"Very nice," I said, feeling a truckload of gravelly guilt. "Just not the right one for me."

We made good time en route to the island, the flow of traffic on a Sunday night always being in the opposite direction, returning rats to the race.

I drove beyond Southampton on the mainland, to get the joy of the shorter crossing and the tiniest hop home from Yarmouth. I parked in front of my neighbour's house, which was eerily quiet in his and Truscott's absence.

Guy lost no time in sizing up my little place. It didn't need rewiring or replastering, as I'd had that done before I moved in. He didn't think there was much mileage in adding a second bedroom at the back, as people who wanted two bedrooms wouldn't bother themselves with somewhere as "pokey" as this.

Don't hold back now. Give me your honest opinion.

"It just wants a kitchen, a bathroom and a lick of paint, Victor," he told me, with all the assurance of someone who'd never flipped a property in his life.

But he was right. The little garden at the back was worth preserving and he planned some judicious planting and low-maintenance zones of bark and chippings, literally sketching something on the back of an envelope. He had, at least, watched some relevant daytime telly.

Our scheme was taking shape. We'd get three valuations and he'd pay me the median amount with money borrowed from the bank, then oversee the work while living on the premises.

My bungalow would be a snip relative to London prices. It was the perfect way for him to achieve a quick win, prove his credit-worthiness and make some seed money. In return, I'd get an instant sale and save an estate agent's fee. When the time was right, I'd withdraw to my base camp at Bath, ready for the tour of Wales.

Guy and I shared a bed again, but only because I couldn't be bothered getting the airbed out. We lay there and talked. I noticed how everything sounded more hopeful now, even if some of that was down to Guy's silly bravado. Then he lowered his voice and expressed some anxieties about his social life.

"People palm me off on their friends, Victor, and nothing seems to stick."

"I noticed that," I said, turning towards him. "But we'll stick. Will you come and see us in Japan?"

"If I have the money, I will. Though I don't like sushi."

I laughed. "I don't think it's compulsory. They do good noodles too."

In the morning, we walked along the beach at Freshwater, then it wasn't long before I was waving Guy off on the ferry. I had a lump in my throat as it pulled away, even though I knew I'd be seeing him again in a few weeks' time.

I headed in to work and met the new manager. As well as being a bean-counter, he was young and abrasive with no interpersonal skills at all. He barely looked up at me, just read details out of my file.

"Compassionate leave, annual leave, leave of absence, bereavement leave," he recited. "I thought you might just want to... *leave*?"

I do! But I need to make some money first.

He cackled at his unwitty remark and wasn't prepared for me to answer back.

"It's just the way things turned out," I said, wearily. "People have a right to live their actual lives, you know, as well as performing economically active roles. My attendance was exemplary before my mother's illness."

"Well, quite," he said, casting about in my file to verify my claim.

When he couldn't find any relevant records, he looked up and gave an insincere smile. "Glad to have you back, Vincent."

"Victor."

"Well, quite."

I was put to work under the new worse arrangements and it was mildly unpleasant, though not unbearable. I'd half-expected to quit in dramatic style that very morning, perhaps not with the same panache as Plum, or with the alacrity Lara would exhibit when she finally deserted her post at the gallery.

Instead, I was hanging in there. I knew it was only for a short while. Having to scrape by without enough staff and to clean the toilets more often didn't hold too much horror. It was good to see the few surviving colleagues I knew. Rad had got his diploma from the language school and, like me, was in his last few weeks at the theatre.

Some of the same old hirers appeared that day too, as if nothing had fundamentally changed. I was glad to help them with their get-in. This last stretch at the theatre was going to be precious. It would round off this episode and make me feel ready to move on.

It's never easy to leave a beautiful island. If I had one regret, it was that William had never visited me there. I wanted to share something of the place with him, to show why it was so dear to me.

When the manager left the building to attend a meeting, I downed tools for a while. I sat in my favourite seat in the dress circle, watching the crew erect their elaborate and highly conventional drawing room set. They belonged to the same am-dram company that put on the old melodrama I'd been so impressed by, *She Strayed Too Far*.

My recollections of that production mingled with thoughts of Rūta and whether I might have done a less bad job of letting her down. I recalled a haunting line from Uncle Xavier, a minor character in the play. The actor who performed the role had reached a point in his life when he didn't give a damn what other people thought of him. His wife had just died and everything else seemed pointless and worthless. He only stuck with the production because it's what she would have wanted him to do.

I discovered this because I hung out with him in the staff room after the Sat mat, drinking tea and dunking biscuits. He was lonely, and I'd heard him crying in his dressing room after the show. His performance on stage had been electric. What might have been a bit part in other hands became something fresh and new, truly talismanic.

Xavier, the ageing relative, sidelined and ignored by most of his family, offers sage advice to the few who will listen. The hero's brother wants to break his engagement to an heiress but feels bound to go through with the wedding.

Then Xavier tells him: "If you break someone's heart, that's a great shame, but if you break your own instead, that's pure folly."

The sadness, the weight in that line, the humble experience of Xavier, were all conveyed perfectly by this actor. His own life journey had brought him to an unloved old armchair in an alcove on the set. Ironically, by no longer caring and not presenting his lines within quotation marks, as many amateurs tend to do, this actor – I think his surname was Humphreys – inhabited his role absolutely. He became Uncle Xavier, and Uncle Xavier became him.

The searing modesty of the role, with its precarious blend of hope and defiance, were characteristics not lost on our regulars. They turned up their hearing aids and sat bolt upright to enjoy one of the finest performances any of us will ever witness.

When the curtain call came around, they gave him cheers and a standing ovation. And I mean they gave him *personally* a standing ovation; he was the second-last to take a bow. I never saw that crowd heap such acclaim upon any other actor. That's why he'd cried: he would have loved his wife to see this triumph. Perhaps he didn't realise that if he hadn't lost her, he wouldn't have been able to craft such a relaxed yet affecting performance.

I took out my phone and called William. Keeping my voice down, I tried to persuade him to come for a visit. He hadn't had as much time to rest in Tuscany as he'd been expecting, I argued, and the pace on the island was nice and slow.

"Sounds good," he said. "I'll certainly think about it."

Not quite persuaded?

I continued to press the case: he needed to take a proper break now, while political life was in abeyance. Otherwise, how would he feel when the Commons resumed? I could almost picture him nodding. I'd be the host, though; that was bound to make him vacillate. I'd always stayed at his place, so there would be an element of role-reversal to this arrangement.

"Why are you so keen on this?" he asked.

I told him about my plans to leave the island, go on tour, then move to Japan. This would be our last chance. Plus, I added as casually as I could, there was something I wanted to talk to him about. It wasn't urgent, but it was personal and not something you could go into on the phone.

"No need to be so bloody mysterious!" he barked. "But *all right*. I'll put it to the family and see who wants to come with me."

I wandered down to the stage and made myself useful, fetching and carrying, being an extra pair of hands, making tea. I didn't do this for everyone, but I liked these people. It felt good to be part of a show again, however removed from the performance itself. I got some flecks of paint on my suit trousers and didn't give a hoot.

At home time, I made a point of catching up with Jim at his allotment. He unfolded an extra deckchair for me and we knocked back some lukewarm dandelion and burdock from the plastic cups of old broken flasks. I relayed what little gossip I'd picked up from work, talked about my plans, listened to an irreverent account of Jim's village fayre.

Then we strayed onto the subject of parenting – or in his case, grandparenting. I said I thought I'd become closer to Plum since the crisis of my mother's illness.

"I can still put my foot in it, though," I told him. "I say exactly the wrong things at the wrong times."

He laughed and patted me on the shoulder.

"We can all do that, Victor," he said, smiling. "I've got six grandkids and they give me such a runaround. I don't know if I'm any good as a grandad – it's always so hectic. To be honest, I only come up here to escape from them. But don't quote me on that."

CHAPTER 32

After several days of being back at work, I felt settled once more. The theatre was my only obligation, as Plum, Guy, Lara and Henrietta were all doing their bit to look in on Mum and check she was being looked after properly. They were reporting a deterioration I'd already noticed, that she was sleeping a lot more now and having more interludes of confusion. Henrietta texted me to let me know she'd been up to Hampstead and watered Mum's plants.

William arrived on the Friday for a long weekend, with Susan and Dorian. In a typical move, I was summoned to have dinner at their hotel, Wellesley Hall in Shanklin, so that I became the guest instead of the host. I thought I'd better look reasonably smart, so I donned the jacket of my pinstripe suit. I didn't think the paint-enhanced trousers would add much to my swagger, so I went with a contrasting pair.

The Wellesley was a four-star Victorian château with a small outdoor pool in its front garden. This trip was the first time Dorian's parents had booked a separate room for him, a development he was keen to tell me about.

"My bath's got feet on it," he said. "And my TV's huge."

Above the mantelpiece in the dining room, there was a framed print of Winterhalter's portrait of Queen Victoria surrounded by her young family.

"This is a pleasant little place," said William, tucking into his truffles. I didn't know if he meant the hotel or the island.

"Newport's one big roundabout," added Susan. "I never thought we'd get out of there alive."

Afterwards, we took a stroll in the hotel grounds. These included an ornate side garden with pretty paths leading to a wishing well. Dorian got his mum to time him walking round the outer path, in waddling Olympic style, while William and I sat on a bench under a pergola. He was wearing a cream linen jacket and an open-neck shirt, with a straw Trilby to protect his bald pate from the evening sun. This was about as informal as he ever got.

"So, what did you want to talk to me about?"

I hadn't expected to broach the subject quite so soon. I began my preamble, explaining how I'd learned more about Mum's life while she believed I was William. I told him about discovering I had a horn-playing nearly-dad, which he found intriguing. Then I went on to explain how Mum was probably asexual but not aromantic. He tried to understand, but got a bit lost in the terminology.

"We're going in now," said Dorian, having twice broken the walking record he'd only just set. "Do you want to see my room? There's this dead thing in a glass case outside my door. It's really disgusting."

William leaned towards me, as though interpreting. "A stuffed stoat."

I promised I would inspect it shortly, then continued with my explanation.

I told my brother how our mother had tried sex with Carlos before consummating her marriage with Jeremy. I gave him a potted history of Carlos's career and of the rocky thirteen-year affair between him and Mum.

"This is all very colourful," said William, "but I'm not sure why you think it's so important."

I got in a tangle then, reaching for things to say that would cushion the blow of my main revelation. That just made him jumpy and I was commanded to come to the point. I pulled the photo of Carlos from my jacket pocket and handed it to him.

"*Oh*," he said straight away. "I see."

One man in a Trilby was looking at another, who had the same appearance in all respects apart from the eyes. William went quiet and very pale. As far as I knew, he didn't struggle with face blindness to any degree and didn't need to *look and look and look*, in order to read and assimilate a stranger's features.

Having said that, he studied the image for an age. Then he sat back and exhaled deeply. He emitted a curious little laugh.

"You think he's my father."

I nodded, dreading his response.

Silence.

"If I'm right," I said, "neither of us is who we were supposed to be."

More silence.

"Well, now. Is this chap still alive?"

I shook my head.

I wanted to tell him how Carlos died, as it was a highly relevant pointer to the man's personality, but this wasn't the right moment. I'd known the information for weeks, but I still couldn't work out whether his death was heroic or futile.

Carlos laid down his life in the service of a dwindling tribe of readers of a printed broadsheet newspaper. He continued to put himself in harm's way, quite needlessly, when he was older and less agile than he used to be.

In theory, he could have stepped away and had years of placid contemplation. Yet, from all I knew of Carlos, that would have been even more of a nightmare than staying on the front line. He lived for the story: he was thoroughly locked into his risky lifestyle. The manner of his passing was regrettable, but perhaps inevitable.

"He led a fascinating life," I said. "Though he was haunted by what he saw."

William raised his eyebrows, nodded. He was taking me seriously.

"You could be right about this," he said. "I never had any idea that…"

His voice trailed off.

"I thought you would prefer to know the truth," I said.

He looked up, his expression grave. "Yes, of course."

I'd half-expected my big brother to contest my findings, to sink deeply into denial. I wasn't prepared for something akin to acquiescence. I rarely saw William show uncertainty about anything, let alone his core identity, so this was an instructive moment. I could tell he was becoming more convinced by the second.

"It wouldn't change things *legally*," he declared, as though trying to reassure me, instead of himself. "Jeremy's on my birth certificate, so I still inherit."

He took his hat off and fanned himself with it, though it was getting quite cool, the sun having dodged behind the clouds. Everything went quiet once more. He was thinking hard, trying to filter his entire understanding of the universe through the funnel of this new information.

"Do I think my whole life has been a lie?" he asked himself. "Of course not. I've lived the life I've lived and nothing can change that. Although…"

He gazed straight ahead, towards the wishing well. He laid his hat down on the arm of the bench.

"Mother nearly told me something once, which was most peculiar."

I waited for him to elaborate, but he was lost in his own thoughts. He was floundering slightly, revealing human fallibility, in that way people who push themselves forward always hate to do.

"We'll not be half-brothers," I said, feeling a surge of emotion. "You've always been my brother and always will be."

He scowled at that but his expression morphed into a tiny, wry smile. He grasped that I was trying to give him something, not take it away.

"That's nice of you. Well said. But you know, this will set me free."

I told him about the examples of Carlos's front-page lead articles that I had in my car, but he held his hand up. He'd heard quite enough.

"All in good time, Victor. All in good time."

The sun was descending. From our hilly position we could see pink shafts of light between the clouds and their reflections in the English Channel. It was strange to think that on the other side of this body of water, some people would be climbing into a flimsy inflatable boat, ready to risk drowning to reach their kin. Or to reach an Anglophone country, if that was their dream. Or, if they had no family or language on these islands, perhaps to chase a better life than they believed to be available on the continent.

"I'll not go to the Lords now," said William, revealing this option to me officially for the first time. "I've always felt that was wrong for me. I only entertained it because it seemed the obvious next step."

I admitted that I'd heard a rumour that he might be elevated soon.

"The party wanted it. I thought it was my *destiny*. Now I don't have a bladdy destiny, do I? Family honour – that's all rot," he said, showing a first flash of anger. "I'm not following in the footsteps of *anyone*, apart from two journalists. I can do what the hell I like!"

In no time at all, William was turning some news that might have been depressing, or at least deflating, into the spur that would drive the next phase of his life. That was impressive, but he wasn't allowing himself any time to process my bombshell. He was thinking on his feet, as political people tend to do. He tucked Carlos's photo away, in the inside pocket of his own jacket.

"I'll stand down at the next election," he declared. "Everyone thinks we're going to lose anyway, so what's the point? Backbench opposition is the pits."

An angry silence prevailed.

"What will you do instead?" I asked, tentatively.

"Something different, Victor. Something *exciting*. Not just directorships and speeches. Something I really believe in. You'll see – they'll *all* see. I'm not finished yet. I've got all this experience; I intend to use it. Bloody *Lords*. They can stuff it."

I was intrigued. "Will you do something non-profit?"

"I don't know about *that*, Victor. A man's got to live. But who knows?"

He got up and stomped off. I followed in his wake, carrying his hat. Dorian showed me various displays of taxidermy in glass cases, along the main upstairs corridor of the hotel. As well as his own stoat, there was an inquisitive-looking weasel standing outside William and Susan's room.

I hadn't appreciated how much William and I had both been in a rut. I was rather pleased for him, that he was heading off-road after following the tram tracks of a legal and political career. At the same time, I was sorry that he was losing a sense of belonging to a great family. That had always meant a lot to him.

I hoped his anger would motivate him to find a new vocation, instead of raising his blood pressure even more. I was probably worrying too much; William was very resilient. He was well-used to setbacks. At every election, he would prepare for the prospect of becoming suddenly unemployed if the vote didn't go his way.

"We all have to pick our way down the hill at some point," he said, ruefully. "Things achieved or half-completed. There's never enough time. Well, I'm going to *take* some time. Not like lockdown, though – God, *no*."

He was rambling a bit, but I saw that as a healthy sign. I knew he would come up with a plan eventually. I was sure he'd find his own kind of contentment.

Perhaps even a new kind of bliss?

The next day, we took Dorian to the theme park and had the unusual luxury of just sitting around and watching him go on the rides. We chatted about *something and nothing*, as Mum would say. This was the visit I'd always longed to have on the island and eventually it felt glorious to wave my relatives off, on the ferry from Cowes. It wasn't that I was glad they were leaving; I was happy that they'd come at all.

After this experience, I knew William would never again call me a moron or an idiot or a cretin. I'd finally proved myself a worthwhile peer, capable of wielding serious influence that might make a positive difference to another person's life. I had arrived. Now it was up to me to maintain standards.

In that vein, I kept my word regarding Truscott. On my first full day off after William's visit, I drove down to Chale Green to collect him. This was on the seventh Sunday and I'd already equipped myself with food, bowls, chews, a bed and a stretchy new lead, so the little git couldn't pull me over too easily.

The staff were young and caring, enthusiastic about their canine charges. The place smelt doggy but clean. We completed the paperwork and there was a round of infectious barking as we walked along the corridor to Truscott's quarters.

"Hey, boy – look who it is!" squealed my host, opening the door.

The mutt lay on a small square mat, not moving except for his eyes. He looked miserable. When he saw me, he got up, yawned and strolled out of his kennel. I had to pick him up and hug him, just to make myself feel better.

Please cheer up.

He allowed the girl to attach the new lead and padded along beside me without so much as a whimper. Now the other dogs went completely berserk. While they were all losing their heads, reaching a crescendo of out-of-control noise, Truscott kept his. I was proud of him, but disconcerted.

"Has he been like this the whole time?" I asked.

The girl beamed. "He's been so good. No trouble at all."

Dear, oh dear.

When we went out to the car, Truscott hopped onto the back seat and curled up without having to be persuaded to settle down. I couldn't tell if he was traumatised or just mourning his late owner. Goodness knows – I'm not a dog psychologist.

When we got home, he trotted inside without any fuss. He tried to take an interest, sniffing around everywhere and checking out his new bed, before lying on it, head on front paws. He was breaking my heart. This was not the dog I knew. I vowed to help him lighten up.

When I went off to work the next day, I left the back door open for him. I thought the fences could hold him – and I didn't care if we got burgled. On my return, he looked distraught. Perhaps he thought I'd left him forever.

I took him to a quiet beach and let him off the lead. He wandered away slowly and had a bit of a paddle, then came back to check I was still there. I threw a rubber ball a short distance; he walked over and fetched it, dropped it at my feet.

"Attaboy, Trussy! You know the moves. C'mon, catch me!"

I ran along, feeling the white sand cascade unevenly under my feet. When I turned around, he was still sitting in the same spot. I called him and slapped my thighs. Slowly, reluctantly, he ambled over to join me.

After a few more days of the same dogged behaviour, I was out of ideas. I thought about driving the poor little tyke over to Bath a few weeks early, to see if Rennie and Ginette could help him get his mojo back. That made me wonder what Gareth would do in this situation, so I phoned him. Not surprisingly, he suggested taking Truscott to the vet.

Blood tests revealed that the dog had an infection; I was given antibiotics for him. I couldn't believe I hadn't thought of that. But the people at the rescue centre had missed it too. I took a day off to administer the medicine and coax my animal back to his fully functional, yappy self.

"It's leave to look after a dog now, is it?" asked the manager, in his usual snide manner.

I knew I'd never convince him of my work ethic now. I invited him to come round and see my poor little pooch for himself, if he didn't believe me. He declined, and I took a second day off for good measure.

CHAPTER 33

I wasn't present when my mother died. None of us were. I had to piece together the story of her death, in much the same way as I'd done the story of her life. It was nurse Inaya who called me. She took great care to be kind and helpful. She told me that Mum's breathing had become fast and shallow. She suggested I might like to come in to see her. As I'd been exposed to a lot of health service euphemisms by then, I grasped that this meant she was dying.

Please, just tell us.

I explained that I was at home on the island, so it would take a few hours to get to the hospital. She said not to worry and called again twenty minutes later to confirm that Mum had passed away.

I guess deaths are either neat or messy. Mum's drawn-out illness was certainly messy, though the timing of her actual passing turned out to be neat. She died in late August, meaning I was able to extract more paid bereavement leave from my employer, shortly before I quit altogether to go on tour.

The timing was also good for William, who was still in recess. He took it upon himself to organise the funeral this time. I knew Mum didn't want to be cremated, because of the environmental impact of that, but it came as a surprise to learn that she had opted for a 'natural burial' in a designated copse in the green belt.

On that day, I wandered along the woodland path, gazing at the trees. Perversely, I wished Mum could have battled on for years, as some people do. Sometimes real events happen too neatly and then you feel as if you're living in a play. That's exactly how it felt when I got those phone calls.

This is all too convenient.

Dr Anand, the physician, explained the technicalities of how Mum died. They sounded rather complicated until I focused on some key points. Essentially, she had a final stroke. A sequence of events led to Mum's organs starting to shut down and then her heart gave out. The medics' main concern up to that point was to ensure she was 'comfortable'. That's the euphemism for administering morphine. Then nature was allowed to take its course.

I was upset that Mum was alone when she died. Only, in a way, she wasn't. According to Inaya, there was a trainee nurse in attendance, whose name was Miriam.

"But your mother called her Constance. Always Constance. Even when we told her the right name."

That Constance could be Mum's angel, even though she'd passed away herself a few years earlier, was not something I'd considered possible.

Perhaps even a proxy, like this trainee nurse, could have given Mum a measure of emotional comfort and release at the end.

After all, I'd stood in for William at the bedside and that seemed to satisfy her. And Dr Anand had been a proxy for good old Mr Wilson. Maybe there are times in life when self-delusion is a useful tool. If Old Maggie had been with us, she might have worked this out sooner. But it happened the way it did, and nothing can change that now.

I allowed myself a little sob at Mum's graveside. In truth, I wasn't mourning her so much as what might have been. I told myself, and keep telling myself, that her attitude towards me was not my fault. I'd been born into an existing scenario that had nothing to do with me. I suppose that's the story of all of us.

There was an undeniably positive mood at Mum's burial. It was overcast and even a bit drizzly, but the setting was inspiring. We'd all sent our telepathic goodbyes to her long before she actually left us. Altogether her illness lasted exactly two months – or sixty-one days – though it felt a lot longer.

Henrietta summed it up, in her businesslike way, when she fell in step with me on the way back to the car park.

"This has been awful, hasn't it? Especially for you. But now it's over."

What a sweet kid.

"Nothing's ever over," I told her, but with a smile.

She and I farmed out the surviving pot plants from Mum's house, encouraging family and friends to tend them in her honour. Marjorie was in quite an emotional state again at the burial, glad to take William's proffered arm. They would go on to mastermind an impressive memorial service at the journalists' church in Fleet Street.

Come the day, the place was packed. It was filled with people who may have known Mum, William or Marjorie, but who mainly knew each other. I thought I spotted two failed prime ministers among our ranks. If so, they were keeping a low profile. Neither was worthy of being spoken of in the same breath as Harold Wilson.

Mum's service rated a mention on Radio Four, but there were no TV crews at the door. When we stepped out into the natural light of a sunny day, I found myself a few feet away from an elderly gentleman with grey dreadlocks, who might well have been Danny, the horn player from Mack's Hoopers. I'll never know; I couldn't reach him before he got into a taxi and sped away. I noticed he was carrying one of the leftover houseplants.

The time came for me to leave the island. I'd been so consumed by practicalities, the significance of the moment almost passed me by. The distance from island to shore is as much a mental gulf as it is a real stretch of water. I doubt that will change if they ever build a bridge. The island is a state of mind, a way of being. I knew I would miss it.

Jim knew that too. As a surprise, he joined Guy in waving me off, along with a few of our former work colleagues. I can't tell you how touched I was that the box office manager, with whom I'd never got on particularly well, was present at the quayside.

It had been drizzling and there was a slight chill in the air. But Yarmouth had never looked more sublime. Gazing down from the bow deck, I spotted Agnieszka, the stage door receptionist, alongside Rad and a couple of newly appointed ushers. They held union flags, and those little windmills that children play with on the beach. One held the flag of Ukraine.

These people, Jim most of all, understood how important it is that someone witnesses your final departure, acknowledging that you've been part of a distinct community – and that both you and the community will now move on, in a spirit of conscious uncoupling.

As the boat started to move, they called out and waved their flags. Guy did his usual thing, motioning for me to phone him. I took a photo and uploaded it, and of course it got three likes. I picked up Truscott and hugged him to me with one hand, waved with the other. He seized the opportunity to give me the most affectionate, the most slobbery, the most disgusting lick ever, from chin to nose, and I almost didn't mind.

* * *

"Wow, that looks scary."

Lara crept out from the wings and across the stage to view the empty auditorium. I was thrilled that our first two nights were going to be in a proper theatre. To my mind, this array of plush blue seats offered us a visual embrace. To her, those same seats represented judgement.

She'd performed live enough times during her training but was unable to shake her nerves, even deep into the tour. I could see how she'd be far more comfortable in front of a camera, knowing that any mistakes could be retaken and edited out. Having to push on, to maintain an unbroken illusion, put quite a strain on her.

"Sorry I'm such a pain," she said as we ran lines together. I told her she'd only be a pain if she didn't persevere.

Our experience of the plays was quite similar. We each had large supporting roles in *Romeo and Juliet* – Noel liked the idea of the Nurse being Irish – so we had a strong obligation to contribute a lot of energy and commitment, despite feeling semi-detached from the story. As the text was on the English curriculum, our words were spoken to school kids. They always chanted the famous line.

"Wherefore are we doing this?" asked Lara, her hair sprayed grey and her face caked with yellowy foundation and marked with heavy black lines. We trailed out of the fire exit of a community hall and into Noel and Derek's motorhome, for our fleeting break in Act Two.

Come on, it's not so bad...

When we got to play *Twelfth Night*, we both sparkled. My antics in our comic scene together almost made her laugh every time. This was why the tour mattered to me: it was a delicious golden time in its own right. You could bite into it and taste it, though you knew it wouldn't do much to enhance your career.

I loved that sensation of being on stage once more, having feared I'd hung up my garters for good. I was acting in Shakespeare, instead of pantomime, and listening to Derek's wistful reflections upon his glory days. I was sharing the whole experience with Lara, even though it bemused her.

I like to think it did her some good in a general way, instilling a sense of professionalism by the end that was lacking at the start. I was shocked that she'd had so little regard for turning up on time or nailing her lines. Her cavalier attitude towards the art gallery job should have warned me that she still had a bit of growing up to do. I found myself in an uneasy mentoring role, trying to protect Lara and the productions from each other.

Over time, she came to appreciate that touring is a disruptive force in itself, and the best way to survive it is to get into a rhythm – perform, sleep, perform, travel, perform, sleep.

"I'm not going into town," she said at one point. "I want to curl up and dream of being elsewhere."

There were the usual simmering personality tensions and petty resentments you get in any company of actors, but we had some good moments as an ensemble. I remember our Juliet singing an impromptu duet with Noel as Derek served up steaming bowls of coq au vin.

Lara came back with me to Bath twice when we got days off. I was a gentleman and gave her the bed, though I knew I couldn't sleep well on the couch. I just pottered around and made my plans.

Before the tour, I'd assumed this would be my swansong as an actor; now I wasn't so sure. I was smitten anew by the smell of the greasepaint and the polite applause of the crowd. It wasn't that I needed approval, as I had done when I was younger. I just enjoyed this way of communicating.

When the jilted fiancée in *She Strayed Too Far* takes centre-stage and declaims her seminal line – "Where is my pride, my hope, my future?" – she does so to no-one in particular and flings herself to the floor, in a blubbering heap. She hasn't noticed that Uncle Xavier is sitting right there in his alcove. When he reaches down and touches her, she tries to recover herself and kneels at his side. He tells her:

"My dear, always have pride that you've *come this far*, no matter the road you've taken. Always have hope that you'll find the answer, however vexing the question. And always look forward to a bright new day, no matter how stale and grey today has been."

For me, Xavier is up there with Polonius. I don't know how or where, but when I'm older I want to play each of those roles. I'd love to be a master of understatement and slightly steal the show. For now, though, the show is over.

There was an amusing moment when I came to retrieve Truscott from Rennie and Ginette. She was concerned the hound might not survive the long flight under sedation or cope well with quarantine. I misinterpreted what she was saying, thinking it was a coded plea to keep him. It wasn't.

I won't forget the look of horror that passed across Rennie's face when I suggested that Truscott could stay with them permanently. In the event, I took advice from Gareth and had Trussy in the best possible shape before we made the trip.

That Teruko and I fell into each other's arms, and committed to each other totally and utterly, is almost beside the point. We knew that would happen, if only I could find the courage to migrate. She was surprised when I presented her with a poorly rendered tiger netsuke, but accepted it as if it were a diamond ring. I loved her so much in that moment that I proposed there and then. She accepted, though we haven't made any wedding plans yet.

We're both glad to be with the right person at last, but we don't inhabit some parallel world of relentless happiness. We just get on with things and bumble along like anyone else, having our triumphs and disasters. We wish we had more time and money, though we'll be able to buy a place when my inheritance comes through.

The whole debacle of our delayed plan has meant we don't take anything for granted. It's shown me that it's wrong to live in fear of what you might not be able to do. None of us knows what we're capable of, and there's joy as well as anguish in finding out.

There's nothing quite like a fresh start in a new place for making some new memories. I would never have chosen Tokyo, however lively, colourful and aromatic it may be, but I'm pleased that Tokyo has chosen me. With my move here, I've stopped worrying about what I'm supposed to do, or how I ought to live. I don't dither so much. I just make my choices and if they aren't the optimal ones, well, who cares?

I may never be a great actor, a great lover, a great father, nor even a great uncle. I certainly won't be a great man. That's not important. All that matters is that I keep trying my best. That's what Teruko tells me anyway.

Plum and Henrietta were our first visitors, arriving when I'd barely settled in myself, which turned out to be ideal. I'd expected to feel out on a limb geographically here, but they reminded me we're only half a day from Heathrow.

They were around when Truscott came out of quarantine and helped to calm him down. He remains an over-excitable nuisance. However, he's done as much as anyone to break the ice for me socially over here. People love him, and that gives me an excuse to speak to them.

I'm doing pretty well with my spoken Japanese, though I barely attempt to read or write the language. I get lots of compliments for my pronunciation. The same ear that made me a first-class mimic is being deployed differently these days. Maybe I've grown up a little myself, but I'll always keep playing, and so will Teruko. We'll never let go of the child inside.

I realise I've dodged the question about how the dog and I get along. Surely it's irrelevant, isn't it, what I think of Trussy? He's part of the family now. And family is important to me.

AUTHOR'S NOTE

Sadly, there is no King Edward Theatre in Newport, Isle of Wight. If you want to get a flavour of its grandly intimate interior, you can visit the New Theatre in Cardiff or the Royal Lyceum in Edinburgh. I imagine the King Edward as smaller than the New and larger than the Lyceum.

CONTENT WARNINGS
(including plot spoilers)

Please note this novel includes discussion of: serious illness, possible medical negligence, medical neglect; mortality, death and bereavement; the Covid pandemic; dubious-consent abortion; emotional neglect; homelessness; separation and divorce; loneliness; cheating and adultery; financial pressures; the financial crash; workplace change and insecurity; war, war reporting and post-traumatic stress; alcohol addiction; domestic violence; mentions of racism, risk of drowning and imperialism.

Positive themes include: personal resilience, overcoming disadvantages, bonding, loyalty, forgiveness, honesty and integrity.

BOOK GROUP DISCUSSION PROMPTS

1. Who is the most compelling underdog in the novel and why?

2. Does Victor's neurodivergence make him easier or more difficult to identify with?

3. How would you sum up the relationship between Victor and Rūta? Do they treat each other well?

4. To what extent are Victor and his father privileged?

5. How well does the novel evoke its various locations?

6. Is the storyline more concerned with the past or the present?

7. Overall, what feelings do you have for Estelle / Jayne?

8. Do you think Guy will succeed as an entrepreneur?

ABOUT THE AUTHOR

Adrian Ross has contributed to the *New Writing Scotland* anthology, *The Reviews Hub* website and the print magazines *Postbox* and *Writers' Forum*. He studied Drama and Film at the University of East Anglia, where he was a founding member of Minotaur Theatre Company. His improvised career has ranged across the arts, media and adult education sectors. He also taught evening classes for Cardiff University, in Creative Writing, Film Studies, Theatre and Arts Management. He lives in his native city of Edinburgh with his wife, Sarah, a fellow writer and poet.

ACKNOWLEDGEMENTS

Thanks to Jo, Laura and James for their expert contributions to this project.

Thanks to my brother, Clive, and sister, Louise, for their interest and encouragement (also for still being able to be surprised by me). Thanks to every reader for your time and attention.

As a reader myself, I'm also deeply grateful to Edinburgh Libraries and the National Library of Scotland for the awesome services they provide. When times are hard and budgets are tight, it's important not to take such wonders for granted.

LIEUTENANT
Bonus Short Story

Cool Katie kept her door ajar, so she could snoop on the comings and goings at the lodge. She had the proprietorial air sidekicks often have. No matter how early Dale set off for work, Katie always got in first, so she could regard everyone loftily from her cramped room at the top of the stairs.

He'd bellow good morning as he shook off his raincoat and hung it up; she'd pretend not to hear. Aside from Welsh rugby, Katie's only interests were plodding away at her boring data sets and being a loyal lieutenant to their charismatic chief executive.

Mina ran the trust and was its social whirlwind; a petite thirtysomething of proud Pakistani heritage. She had bonny brown eyes that signalled purpose and intelligence. Nothing escaped her attention. She would often flick her long hair back, as a form of emphatic punctuation in her body language.

Mina would outline the organisation's precarious financial position at the whiteboard, schmooze potential partners at gatherings of name-badged professionals, slag off the local council at every opportunity. The council may not have been innocent in all matters, but it did house the team here, for a nominal rent, in an ivy-clad Victorian outpost at the exit gates of the crematorium.

"I know I'm a bitch, but I get results," Mina would say, with a cheery laugh.

She used several such words that she wouldn't condone anyone else using. One of these was reserved for moaning about the fact that the trust was funded only for 'delivery'. There was no money to employ an admin person, nor a marketing one, so each member of staff – also known as 'the projects team' – did their bit, with varying degrees of success.

At his induction, Mina told Dale that Katie had more-or-less given up on men. This was sad, because she had an honest face. Of course, her dated glasses didn't help. Perhaps she'd get a dog instead. Unless – well, it was worth asking – did he know any single men?

Sondra was more outgoing, she said; a typical housewife who talked constantly about her kids and dreamed of winning the lottery. She was a whizz on social media, but a terrible clock-watcher, never giving her job any extra 'oomph'. As Sondra worked there full-time, Dale wondered, could she really be called a housewife?

There was one more regular presence in the lodge, and that was the frequently invoked ghost of Dale's saintly predecessor, Laurence. This tall, smooth-talking individual exerted an almost supernatural charm over the rest of the team. He had been the designated printer whisperer, coaxing the malevolent appliance into action when it preferred a life on standby.

Because of Laurence, they'd all wanted a 'replacement bloke' in the office. Of course, the job had to be open to all, laughed Mina – but interview scores could always be tweaked.

In the event, Dale didn't need to have his score adjusted, as he aced his interview. This was because someone – probably Sondra, he thought later – had accidentally stapled a sheet of the interview questions and 'model answers' to the role profile when his invitation letter was sent out.

Thus, Dale was appointed on his excellent interview score, not for his personal qualities, which his colleagues quickly found wanting. He couldn't gossip with Mina, talk rugby with Katie or discuss kids and desirable consumer goods with Sondra, in the easy manner that Laurence possessed.

Actually, it was deemed that Dale lacked the humour, charm and team spirit of his predecessor. This was something Mina declared, in a rant behind the new incumbent's back. But it was faithfully recounted to him by Katie one afternoon, when they were the only people in the building, in the hope that he might try harder to fit in.

"You could be *nicer*," she suggested.

When he asked a clarifying question, she gave a sour smirk of superiority. If he really wanted to know, she said, Mina thought he was too distant, too functional, too focused on his own selfish needs – such as asking for a mourner's parking permit when they'd all had to strive and plead and lie *for months* to obtain theirs.

Plus, he was useless with the printer. Dale would poke and prod, and the machine might eventually click and whirr if he was lucky, but mostly blinked its red lights in dissent. He could find no logic to how it operated. Sondra held that it performed better when you sang to it, but he noticed that she wasn't above kicking it when that didn't work.

One day, Mina announced that she was embarking on a nationwide tour, to drum up new business for the trust. The peace that reigned was glorious at first, but soon turned eerie. She was away for too long. Her control-freaky calls back to base became less frequent and then ceased altogether.

Without their boss driving them towards deadlines and 'agreed' performance targets that she alone determined, Mina's team became fractious and unmotivated.

Katie did her best to deputise for Mina and keep everyone in line. But she lacked the requisite leadership skills and, moreover, the crucial information: when would the chief exec be returning? The fact was, Mina had gone AWOL. In time, even Katie fell behind with her own reports. The team was piddling around, answering endless emails, instead of focusing on its project work. Sondra took to going home early, which irked Katie, but not a word was said.

When the chairperson turned up for a quarterly meeting with Mina, Katie coolly covered for her. The boss had just phoned to cancel, she claimed, due to car trouble.

It was a generous lie, considering that Mina had long ago stopped answering her phone. Sondra glanced at Dale, pointedly raising her brows. She thought Katie's loyalty would be her undoing some day.

After five weeks, the truth finally emerged. Mina returned to the lodge and called everyone down to the kitchen for an unscheduled team meeting. She imparted some news intended as a bombshell – but which was not so surprising, given recent events.

"I'm returning to freelance event planning," she announced, with a beaming smile, flicking her hair back with carefree abandon. "And I'm having a baby."

Katie looked crestfallen.

"What about us? The trust?"

"Oh, you'll get by," laughed Mina. "Fresh leadership always brings a bounce."

Dale wanted to ask about the new business she had supposedly been seeking. For once, though, some intuitive feeling persuaded him not to.

"The board has agreed I can step down with immediate effect," said Mina, expertly spinning what had happened.

"How far along are you?" asked Sondra, in a bored voice.

"Just over the three months," came the reply.

"Are you happy?" asked Dale, more out of curiosity than genuine care.

"Ecstatic!" Mina replied.

"Well, that's the main thing," he concluded, without conviction.

At this point, Katie stormed out. She stomped upstairs and slammed her door. She refused to come out, even when Mina was leaving. The outgoing boss handed her keys, alarm fob and ID card to Sondra. Then she turned to Dale.

"Come with me to the car."

They tramped across the lawns of remembrance to one of the parking bays, where Mina climbed nimbly into the cab of her four-by-four and retrieved something from the dash.

"Here. You've waited long enough for one of these."

She held out a large white-on-black printed card, an official numbered mourner's pass.

"Welcome to parking heaven," she said, and stood on tiptoe to plant a kiss on his cheek.

Then she got into her car, gave the briefest of waves and drove off, in no way respecting the ten-mile-an-hour speed limit. Dale stood and watched as the ungainly vehicle zoomed along the perimeter road on the crematorium's one-way system, swerving around the war memorial and accelerating towards the lodge, before slowing at the gates. Soon it disappeared altogether.

Katie was off sick the next day, an occurrence unknown at the trust. But she came back stronger, having moped around, accepted the new reality and regrouped.

"We just have to get on with it now," she decreed, as much to herself as the others.

Once Sondra had left for the day, Dale hovered in Katie's doorway. He wanted to talk to her, he said.

"What about?" She didn't look up from her screen.

"I wondered if you were going for the chief exec's job."

"Why should I tell you my plans?"

He backtracked, saying that he was thinking of applying. But he didn't want to step on her toes, as she was already second-in-command.

"I won't apply if you're going to," he pledged.

"No," said Katie, still typing, and looking both fierce and miserable. "I'm not going for it. I'm happy as I am."

"Will I have your support? If I apply?"

He knew this was a question too far, but wanted to see how she answered.

She paused, gave her patronising smile, and said: "You're not ready. Obviously. But I can't stand in your way, can I?"

"I'll take that as a yes," he joked, and she ignored him as usual.

Two weeks later, Sondra was filling envelopes when she dropped a folded piece of paper onto Dale's desk. It was a copy of the interview questions and model answers for the chief exec job.

"Better the devil that you know," she intoned, gathering the outgoing mail and heading home early, on the pretext of catching the post.

The only sticky part of Dale's interview was when the chairperson asked him a subsidiary question about finance. He'd had to exaggerate his role in signing a couple of orders in a previous job, while he was last-man-standing in a two-person department.

But it worked. On appointment, he tried to arrange a one-to-one with Katie, but she wasn't having any of it.

"You can talk to me anytime," she said, which wasn't strictly true.

Desperate to set some priorities, he hovered in her doorway once again. He pleaded for some pointers. She stopped working, took off her spectacles and gazed straight ahead.

"I expect you'll find the hidden grant money, if you look hard enough."

As pointers go, that wasn't a bad one to begin with.

He realised, quite abruptly, that this was the essence of Katie: she was the ultimate lieutenant. She liked to be near power, without having to be accountable for it. Her loyalty was to 'the boss', not to Mina personally. This meant she could switch allegiance. In fact, she was already helping him out, was she not?

As soon as he understood that, he relaxed. He walked into Mina's office, which was now his office, sat down in her chair, which was now his chair, and started making plans. He sent Katie an email, informing her that he valued her crucial role in the organisation and was making her deputy chief executive.

She replied immediately. Much to his chagrin, she didn't even thank him. She just pointed out: 'You don't have the authority.' Then she sent a second message. 'Do you mind locking up? I'm off now. And don't forget to replace the printer cartridge.'